NORTH

of the

TENSION LINE

NORTH

of the

TENSION LINE

A Novel

J.F. RIORDAN

Library of Congress Cataloging-in-Publication Data

Riordan, J. F.
  North of the tension line / by J. F. Riordan. – First edition.
     pages cm
  ISBN 978-0-8253-0734-8 (hardcover : alk. paper)
  1. Single women–Fiction. 2. Wilderness survival–Fiction. I. Title.
  PS3618.I565N67 2014
  813'.6–dc23
                           2014009539

For inquiries about volume orders, please contact:
Beaufort Books
27 West 20th Street, Suite 1102
New York, NY 10011
sales@beaufortbooks.com

Published in the United States by Beaufort Books
www.beaufortbooks.com

Distributed by Midpoint Trade Books
www.midpointtrade.com

Printed in the United States of America

Interior design by Jane Perini
Cover Design by Oliver Munday

To CJS, my own Deus Ex Machina
with all my love

ACKNOWLEDGEMENTS

Visitors to foreign lands require guides, and I have been extremely lucky to have had many excellent ones to whom I owe my thanks.

My friends of the Breakfast Club, Lucia and Pete Petrie, Betty and Leon Shellswick, and Chari and Ham Rutledge, who very early on spent time with me reminiscing and telling stories about life on the island.

Captain Bill Jorgenson and his crew who permitted me to spend a day on the ferry with them watching them at work, and sharing their chocolate doughnuts, and later, to Captain Bill for reading my manuscript and pointing out that the trees at School House Beach are cedars.

My gracious and delightful hosts, Susan and George Ulm, who know the precise recipe for leaving me alone while making me feel welcome, and Bosun, who allows usurpers to play in his yard.

LeRoy, Bill, and Kay, who came on a Sunday afternoon to pull my car out of the mud.

The friendly and generous people of Washington Island who wave at me whenever our cars pass on the road even when they have no idea who I am.

Mike Nichols, the only novelist I knew, who read with understanding and gave good advice.

My publisher, Eric Kampmann, who called me the same day I wrote to him.

My editor Megan Trank, who demonstrates her Midwestern roots in her kindness, good cheer, support, and professionalism.

Felicia Minerva, my publicist, for her enthusiasm and good advice, but who, to my disappointment, is not a mermaid.

My dear friend, Mary Beth, who has always told me I was a writer.

My husband, Charlie, for his unfailing love, patience, and encouragement, and for laughing in all the right places.

And finally, my friend Roger Kimball, who, beyond all calls of duty or reason, made it his business to see that my manuscript found its way to a publisher. I am deeply grateful.

– J.F. Riordan

NORTH

of the

TENSION LINE

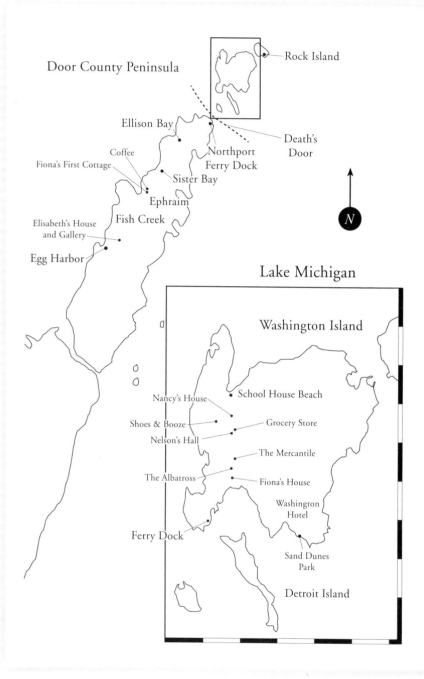

Door County Peninsula

Rock Island

Ellison Bay

Death's
Door

Northport
Ferry Dock

Coffee

Fiona's First Cottage

Sister Bay

Ephraim

Fish Creek

Elisabeth's House
and Gallery

Egg Harbor

Lake Michigan

N

Washington Island

Nancy's House

School House Beach

Shoes & Booze

Grocery Store

Nelson's Hall

The Mercantile

The Albatross

Fiona's House

Washington
Hotel

Ferry Dock

Sand Dunes
Park

Detroit Island

Chapter One ✦

After she had shut the drawer on her finger, spilled the coffee beans, and torn her bathrobe pocket on the stove handle, Fiona decided that it would be better to go out for breakfast. There were still a few beans scattered here and there on the kitchen counter and on the floor when she pulled on a hooded sweatshirt and headed out. It was a short walk from her small cottage on the bluffs down to the village, and the late summer morning was pleasant. She walked slowly, unconsciously timing her steps to a poem about a sloth she had memorized as a child. Irritatingly, she couldn't remember the beginning, only the last two stanzas.

> A most Ex-as-per-at-ing Lug.
> But should you call his manner Smug,
> He'll sigh and give his Branch a Hug;
>
> Then off again to Sleep he goes,
> Still swaying gently by his Toes,
> And you just know he knows he knows.

For some reason, she'd woken up with these lines in her head, and now they were repeating themselves unceasingly. She knew from long experience that the only remedy was to replace the lines with something equally persistent.

Having managed to survive the morning thus far, Fiona was particularly careful to hold the handrail as she walked down the steep steps to the village. It was actually two long stairways from the bluffs down to the water's level, with a street between the two, a nearly vertical drop, and not one Fiona cared to make on her head. Grace had never been her strong suit.

Because, even on good days, Fiona was usually looking down to watch the placement of each foot on the uneven steps, she rarely had the opportunity to appreciate the beauty around her from the stairs. If you were looking up, the view encompassed the whole harbor out to the northern horizon, where Horseshoe Island lay silent and unpopulated. Beyond the Island you could see to the far side of Green Bay, to the bluffs of the state park on the western side. Below, in the village, sailboats were gently drifting at anchor, and on the south side of Eagle Harbor lay a cluster of vintage cottages. The narrow roads of the village snaked up the sides of the bluffs to the modest houses where Fiona's own cottage stood, its owners having been fortunate enough to have obtained an early stakehold in this prime real estate.

Thick shrubs of rugosa roses grew in profusion on either side of the old and precarious cement stairs, poking their branches under the painted metal pipework which formed the railing. Their scent, released by the moisture in the air, rose with the morning mist.

It was a soft, humid morning, and a slight haziness muted the sunlight over the harbor. The tourists were not yet awake, except for the senior citizens who walked determinedly, if a bit aimlessly, around the irregular blocks of the village. Ephraim, lying below and around her, was a picturesque Moravian village which had remained virtually unchanged since the 1850s, when it had been settled in the remote outposts of Door County. The white frame structures of the village: the church steeples, the cottages built into the steep hill, and the nineteenth-century inns for sailors—once ordinary bed and board places, but now decorated with floral quilts and gas fireplaces and whirlpool tubs for two—appealed to the vision of small town life generally held by fashionable Chicago vacationers.

It was an irony, in Fiona's opinion, that the very thing which had preserved Ephraim like a time capsule, preventing the fancy restaurants and chic resorts from taking over, was the village's greatest flaw: Ephraim was dry, and the simple desire for scotch required a drive to the next village.

None of this mattered particularly at the moment, however. It was far too early to think of scotch—even for Fiona—but coffee was a requirement.

Fiona was struck by an intense joy as she looked out over the pristine serenity of the harbor. The sailboats rocked at their moorings, their gleaming white hulls in sharp contrast to the blue of the water, the wooded rocky bluffs rising behind them. The gulls, relentless in their greed, soared over the docks, looking for anything that even remotely qualified as food. Looking out over the scene, Fiona felt the tight places in her heart and mind ease. Even the demons that regularly plagued her sleep, seemed small and foolish.

The smell of coffee drifted around the corner from the shop, and a few tourists were sitting at the outdoor tables reading out-of-town papers. Locals rarely sat outside. They went in where they could talk among themselves, and there was less danger of swallowing a yellow jacket with your coffee.

The establishment was not a trendy coffee bar. In fact, its proprietor was so thoroughly dedicated to utilitarian living that it had no actual name. The word Coffee—in black and gold stick-on letters he had purchased at the hardware store—was pasted rather crookedly across the glass door as its only identifying marker. Locals arranging to meet there simply said "I'll see you at Coffee," or "I'm going down to Coffee," as if it were a proper name.

There were no glazed pottery mugs for sale, no jazz CDs, and no after-coffee mints. There were old-fashioned swiveling counter stools, and a few tables with hard upright chairs. The walls were white, without ornaments, and the interior had the austerity of purpose one might expect in a laboratory. The lighting was harsh and fluorescent. You could have an egg sandwich, or toast, or a doughnut in the morning, and occasionally, in Roger's concession to fashion, a bagel. There were no scones, no biscotti, and just plain, homogenized full-fat milk. In the afternoon, you could have a slice of pie.

Roger Mason, the owner and a retired physicist, claimed that these other things were distractions from the coffee, and besides, just attracted the wrong sort of people. People who asked for froufrou things like skim milk or a latte were frightened into silence by one look from Roger. There were no franchise operations in Door County, just as there were no neon signs. And if you wanted trendy coffee, you were just going to have to go back to Sturgeon Bay, or better yet, Chicago. This was not a choice of style for Roger. It was a personal philosophy.

Roger had left his original line of work for what he described as political reasons, and although he had never told anyone what they were, Fiona suspected that he had irritated someone important. Having known Roger for a year or so, she thought this seemed a likely explanation.

Despite having retired from his first profession, he was a young man, in his thirties, and a distant observer might have called him handsome. But this impression tended to diminish upon acquaintance. He was dressed this morning, as he was every morning, in a white T-shirt, jeans, and boat shoes. His hair stood out at odd angles, and he hadn't shaved. Fiona often studied him, wondering how it was that celebrities could pull off exactly the same hairstyle with a completely different effect. The look on his face was one of simple rage. It was his normal face, not a mood. Fiona had noted that it was intimidating to tourists, but had varying degrees of impact on the locals. She had learned, with some effort, to ignore it.

"Good morning," she said carefully, as the screen door sprang shut behind her. It wouldn't do to be too cheerful around Roger. Peppiness annoyed him, especially in the morning.

"Usual?" Roger didn't bother to turn around or look up.

"Please," Fiona said. Seating herself at the counter on her usual wobbly stool, she picked up the *New York Times* that had been lying nearby. There was a grease stain, and possibly some cherry preserves on the front page, but it looked more or less intact. Fiona enjoyed—mostly—the leisure and the science sections of the *Times*, occasionally the crossword, and especially the Real Estate listings, but avoided everything else. The preening arrogance of that paper had an immediate and measurable effect on her blood pressure, and she was trying to avoid drugs.

Besides alcohol, of course.

The shop was empty at the moment, and Roger never bothered with chitchat. The low hum of the cooler behind the counter was almost soothing in its presence. Occasionally, there was the clatter of cups as Roger went about his work. Fiona felt completely at ease in the familiarity, if not exactly the warmth, of her surroundings.

She had finished her egg sandwich and was drinking her coffee, absorbed in the listings of New Haven Cape Cods for millions of dollars, and pondering the distinction between "newer" and needing to be replaced, when the door of the shop opened, and she felt a hand on her shoulder.

"Elisabeth. When did you get back?"

"I've only just arrived. I couldn't wait to get down here and get back to normal. Besides, there's no milk in the house."

Elizabeth's enormous dog sat patiently, waiting for Fiona to notice him, his tail thumping.

"And Rocco. How are you, Rocco?" Rocco's tail wagged faster, and he dropped one massive paw on Fiona's leg.

Rocco was an enormous, shaggy kind of German Shepherd, with a huge black head, the intellectual capacity of a young child, and the disposition of one of the milder-mannered breeds of cattle. Fiona privately found him to be smarter than most of the children she knew, and an astute judge of human character.

"I ate my egg already, Rocco, but there's a crust. Would you like to lick the plate?" Roger looked darkly at Fiona, but said nothing. She gave him a sunny smile, put the plate on the floor, and kissed Rocco on the muzzle.

"What a good dog," she said softly, smoothing his ears.

Her seat wobbled dangerously as Fiona turned back to Elisabeth, gave her a perfunctory hug, and made room for her at the counter, sliding her plate away. Real estate snooping, as they called it, had become a game for Fiona and Elisabeth, and they spent many hours pouring over real estate listings, visiting open houses, and fantasizing about remodeling them.

"Look at this," she said, pushing the paper through some spilled coffee. "$2.6 million for a beach cottage with two bedrooms, midcentury appliances, and a veranda. What kind of idiot would spend that much for a place like this?"

"Presumably one with $2.6 million. Anyway, as you know, it's all about the beach."

"It's not a lot of beach."

Elizabeth smiled and shrugged, and ordered a cup of coffee. "A fool and his money?" she suggested.

"More money than brains, my father would say."

Fiona acknowledged to herself that this robust sensibility was not in her own nature. Her father wouldn't approve of many of Fiona's own purchases. She looked down admiringly at the Italian sandals she was wearing for the first time. They made her legs look longer.

"And 'midcentury.' When did 1960s kitsch get an upgrade? What possible interest could anyone have in fifty-year-old appliances?"

Elisabeth smiled serenely, her gaze following Roger as he thumped a basket of empty grounds into a bucket. "Maybe I should try selling that refrigerator in the garage," she said. "It's a pink Kelvinator, you know. All the rage."

Roger put a cup on the counter in front of Elisabeth with a

slightly smaller thud than usual. Roger liked Elisabeth, and he looked at her now with eyes which reminded Fiona quite distinctly of Rocco, but still with a Roger-like aura of brusqueness surrounding him.

"How was your trip?" he asked, an uncharacteristic note in his voice, which Fiona could have sworn was sympathy. She noticed that he was fidgeting with his counter rag, an unusual thing for Roger, who normally practiced an admirable economy of effort, Fiona felt.

"Not so bad this time," said Elisabeth, reaching for the cup. "Every time I go back, it hurts a little less, but I will be glad when I have the last of Mom's business taken care of. I've put the house on the market—and that midcentury kitchen should be a big selling point." She smiled again, and pushed a strand of hair from her face.

Elisabeth Wright was a little older than Fiona, and in many ways her opposite. Whereas Fiona was slim, quick, and impatient, Elisabeth was a tall, zaftig woman of about thirty-two. She had brown eyes, wavy auburn hair, creamy smooth skin, and an innate elegance which gave her an almost queenly aura. Fiona thought she was pretty, even beautiful sometimes. But today she looked faded. There was a heaviness around Elisabeth's eyes which showed the strain she'd been under since the long illness and death of her mother last year from cancer.

Elisabeth had a tendency to be outspoken—like Fiona—but in a rough-and-tumble way that came from growing up with five brothers. Her humor tended toward sarcasm, and she laughed a lot. Occasionally, she could be pushy, but that, Fiona believed, came from being the oldest in a large family. Once Elisabeth had an idea, she was convinced that it was the best, and it was difficult to shake it from her. They had been friends in college, but had lost track of each other for many years until just this past year, when they had literally run into each other at a wedding on a Sturgeon Bay dock.

Seeing the fatigue on Elisabeth's face, Fiona sensed the need to change the conversation.

"What's in the plans? Want to go up to the Island? I'm in the mood for a day on the Rocks." This was their name for School House Beach, a shore hidden behind a cedar forest on the north side of Washington Island. The beach had no sand, only hundreds of feet of Lake Michigan shoreline, covered with smooth, lake-contoured stones on the beach and under the water. It was barely known even in Wisconsin, but apparently heavily advertised elsewhere in the world, because you couldn't step anywhere without hearing a different language being spoken there. Walking on it was tricky, lying on it was lumpy, and unlike other Door County beaches, which tended to be shallow enough to wade out very far, the water was cold and deep. But there were rafts to swim out to and dive from, the tiny bay was protected, and best of all, dogs were allowed. Rocco stirred and wagged, recognizing the name of his favorite place. He put his face in his mistress's lap.

"Rocco, off." Elisabeth was rummaging in her bag, looking for something as she spoke. Rocco lay back down and sighed. Roger was lingering, wiping off the counter nearby. Elisabeth stopped rummaging and looked up.

"Listen Fi, I've been thinking. What do you want to do when you grow up?"

Fiona tilted her head and looked quizzically at Elisabeth. Was she being facetious? Fiona was accustomed to her friend's non sequiturs, but this one seemed purposeful. "I guess I thought I was doing it."

"That's assuming you intend to actually grow up, which I don't necessarily recommend." Both women looked up surprised at Roger's contribution to the conversation.

"Well I don't," he said shortly. "Life for adults is too much of the same thing. You think it will be a great adventure, but actually, it's just a routine. It's hard work, and you have responsibilities, and no one gives you amazing Christmas presents anymore."

"What would constitute an amazing Christmas present?" asked Fiona, intrigued. This was the longest speech she had ever heard from Roger.

"A train set." Roger seemed to have reached the limits of his interest in the topic, because he picked up his rag, turned, and walked into the back room.

The door opened, and a tourist couple walked in, followed by Mike and Terry, two regulars. Roger's sigh could be heard from the back room, and there was an ominous clatter of pans before he emerged, his face arranged in his customary look of welcome. He glowered at the beautifully casual young couple before him.

"What would your perfect Christmas present be?" Elisabeth asked Fiona, sidetracked by Roger's comment.

"I don't know. Something wonderful and unexpected, that made you feel if there were magic in the world. A puppy maybe, or an exotic sports car, or maybe a trip somewhere you'd never been."

Oblivious to mood or place, the couple busied themselves with examining the menu on the wall, so Roger turned to his local customers.

"Morning, Roger. You're looking cheery." Terry, a local carpenter, was the only man in town who dared casual chat with Coffee's proprietor. He was a small, wiry man somewhere in his sixties, with blond hair and a weathered face. His hands were battered and his nails rough. He had been a marine in Vietnam, and was one of the few in Fiona's experience who would discuss his experiences at war. He was an easygoing, outwardly cheerful man, and as impervious to other people's emotions as Roger was, only with a gentler nature and a simpler personality. His casual conversation and frequent laughter were underlaid by the kind of intense calm that some men get having faced the worst of life. Fiona always felt that he was the sort of person one could count on in an emergency, as, in fact, he had been, when her roof had sprung a leak last winter.

Mike, on the other hand, was round and quiet, but despite this, or perhaps because of it, Fiona often imagined him as having a secret life, filled with intrigue and lust, like Chaucer's friar. This contrasting image made her smile to herself. Mike was more like a cherub than a salacious monk. A deeply religious man, he was a vestryman for his church, a devoted grandfather, and a member of the county board. Most important, though, he was a gifted painter, whose works were comprised of vivid streaks of color, the boldness and daring of which managed to suggest modern composition, while still being firmly based on an exquisitely skilled representation of nature. No one who met him would ever guess that this mild little man, so charming and unassuming, could contain so much talent or passion. Fiona had heard that his paintings sold in galleries in Santa Fe, San Francisco, and New York for tens of thousands of dollars apiece. Having seen some of them, she believed it. The market for art was capricious, but she found it reassuring that there was room for things other than the piles of dung or the baby dolls placed in garbage bags which so entranced the art critics at the *New York Times* or the judges at the Venice Biennale.

Mike smiled benevolently upon Fiona and Elisabeth, and gently patted Rocco on the head. He was not much of a talker. He had once told Fiona how much lavender one could find in the shadings of the natural world, and this casual remark, unimportant to him and probably forgotten, had changed forever the way she saw the world.

"How are you, Mike?"

His eyes crinkled when he smiled. Rocco had sat up, and was leaning his head contentedly against Mike's knee. Mike stroked his ears, as Rocco leaned harder. "I'm well. And you? And Elisabeth—it's nice to have you back."

This was a long speech for Mike, and Fiona and Elisabeth smiled back, answering him at the same time.

"Fine, thanks."

"Fine, thank you for asking. I'm back for good now."

"Good, good," he nodded, still smiling gently. "Glad to hear it." His plump hand was still resting on Rocco's head when Roger set the egg sandwiches on the counter and turned to the now fidgeting tourists.

Mike seemed relieved to be able to turn from this conversation and to get down to the business of breakfast. He and Terry lapsed into comfortable silence as they ate.

Meanwhile, the young couple who had entered with them were embarking upon their first encounter with the proprietor of Coffee.

"Do you have cappuccino?" the young woman asked.

She was slim, blonde, and impeccably groomed, her perfectly French-manicured nails holding her Hermes bag, and her elegant little toes peeping delicately from her expensive sandals. Fiona thought regretfully of her own calloused heels and long toes. Roger's usual glower changed to stone.

"No," he said.

"Oh. Well, I'll just have a regular coffee, then, with nonfat milk."

"We have regular milk."

"Regular milk?" The woman looked puzzled. "You mean two-percent?"

"I mean regular milk. One hundred percent."

"You mean full-fat?" She looked incredulous. "You only have full-fat milk?"

"That is correct." Roger's economy of expression served him well.

"Oh," she said, studying him as if he were a species she had not previously encountered. "Well, I don't think I can do that." She paused, considering.

"What kind of bagels do you have?"

"Plain."

"Plain? Just…plain?"

"Plain."

"Oh," She said again. She paused for a moment to consider.

"Are you sure you don't have anything nonfat? A flavored cream-er, something like that?"

Anyone who didn't know him might have mistaken Roger's silence for patience. There was a long pause as the woman waited for him to answer, and another when she realized that he wasn't going to. Fiona began to feel a little sorry for her. She seemed like a rather innocent person. It clearly was not her style to bully others in order to get her way. Not getting her way, however, was obviously a new experience for her, and she didn't know how to respond. She looked for some assistance at her husband, who until now had been furtively typing text messages. He looked up. They were probably about the same age, in their early thirties, but there was a boyishness about him that made him seem younger.

"I can't get a signal at all around here. Anywhere. No matter where I try, there's just nothing. It's incredible. You'd think they'd build more towers." "He continued his fruitless typing, shaking his head in disbelief.

Unable to fully accept this odd reality of limited possibilities, his wife turned and looked back up at the menu. Fiona had the impression that she was willing the appearance there of something trendy. Roger's mood was now palpable, the vibrations of his impatience emanating loudly from him. "Perhaps," thought Fiona, "it's like a dog whistle; only regulars can sense it."

"Do you have tea?"

"Coffee," said Roger. "We have coffee."

She seemed not to sense anything wrong, but in the shop a new silence reigned as all chewing, stirring, and drinking stopped. Roger drew a deep breath. Rocco lifted his head.

She looked at Roger, shrugged, and smiled brightly. "Ok. Then I'll have black coffee and a plain bagel. No butter. To go, please. Honey? What do you want?"

"A cappuccino," he said, not looking up.

"Honey, they don't have cappuccino."

"Oh." He looked up, briefly. "What do they have, then?" At the wobbly end of the counter, no one breathed.

"Just regular coffee."

"I'll have that, then," he said, still typing furiously with one finger.

She turned back to Roger, who stood, unmoving, eyes fixed.

"And he'll have a regular coffee. To go, please." She smiled at him and tipped her head to one side, as if to say, "There. I've done it right; haven't I?" She seemed younger now, almost child-like, with a kind of sweet confidence in the benevolence of others.

Strange sounds emanated from under Roger's breath, as he poured their coffee and put her unbuttered bagel in a white paper bag. "How much is it?" The woman asked, still oblivious to the mood of the shop. Fiona had the sense that she knew that she had won some battle. Fiona pondered this.

"$5.25." Roger pushed the Styrofoam cups and the bag across the counter toward the woman, not meeting her eyes.

"Do you take debit cards?"

Before he could reply, she rummaged in her soigné bag and pulled out some cash. "Oh, never mind, I have a ten. Here you go. You can just put the change in your tip jar." She pushed a ten-dollar bill toward him. Roger, who had no tip jar, did not reach out to take the money.

She leaned over the counter toward him and spoke confidentially. "You know, you might want to consider getting an espresso machine. You'd get tons of business. Come on, honey, there's a table outside."

And with this, she smiled a sweet and winning smile, and they left.

There was a long pause after the door closed behind them during which everyone took a breath, and there was the sound of cups being placed on saucers. It was Terry who spoke first.

"I think Roger must either be sick or in love. Maybe both."

He chuckled to himself, and Mike smiled quietly down at his coffee.

Fiona felt that this must be the moment. Surely now the explosion would come. She looked down the counter. Roger was unmoving, a peculiar look on his face. Elisabeth, too, seemed frozen and strangely preoccupied with the contents of her purse.

Behind him, through the window, Fiona could see the couple settled at one of the wooden tables outside, he, still furiously texting. The woman tentatively tasted her coffee, as if testing this unaccustomed flavor. Her lips moved in conversation, the words inaudible. At one point they both looked back at the shop, as if discussing their experience. The first yellow jacket buzzed their heads, and they waved it away.

"Warm-up?" Roger was pouring coffee into their cups, an unaccustomed act of solicitousness.

He disappeared again into the back room, leaving the money on the counter. A new, more comfortable silence wafted into the shop. Rocco put his head down on his paws and sighed.

As normality returned, Fiona continued their earlier conversation.

"What would your perfect Christmas present be?"

Elisabeth was standing up, preparing to leave. "A fur coat," she said without a moment's hesitation. "Full-length, with a hood," and picking up her bag, she led Rocco out of the shop.

Fiona paid her bill, engaged in her usual internal dilemma about whether or not to tip the owner, decided she should, and hurriedly followed them out with a quick smile at Mike and Terry, leaving them to finish their coffee and to get on with their work.

Roger snorted and banged some pots in the back room. It was already eight o'clock, and he still hadn't put his order in for tomorrow's bagels. With luck, there'd be fewer tourists tomorrow.

Outside, Fiona and Elisabeth began to stroll along the waterfront. The sun was on the water, and not one cloud was visible. But the late August air had none of the beginnings of autumn's crispness. Instead, it was moist and languid and lazy. The coming day would be warm.

There was activity along the docks as the non-fishing boats were beginning to go out, with people carrying their coolers and supplies from their cars, checking the sails, and doing whatever it was that people did on boats before they left the security of solid ground. Fiona breathed in the air and felt a kind of calm exhilaration at the scents and the sounds and the prospect of being out in the world. Elisabeth, not immune, but preoccupied, walked thoughtfully with Rocco at her side.

Slightly puzzled by their recent exchange, Fiona looked for a way to jolly Elisabeth along.

"Why don't you go out with Roger?" she asked, teasing. "It's obvious he likes you."

"I've been thinking about it," she said seriously.

Fiona stopped short.

"Really?"

"Well, why not? He's smart and he likes me. What other qualifications are there?"

"For one thing, a willingness to suffer the occasional fool. He's not exactly Mr. Nice Guy. And anyway, I don't think he likes dogs." Fiona looked down at Rocco, who recognized that the word dog usually included him, and looked hopefully at his people.

"Of course he likes dogs. He used to have a German shepherd."

"Really? How did you know that?"

"He told me," said Elisabeth with some irritation. "How do you think?"

Fiona chewed over this new information while scanning the Bay. The prospect of Elisabeth and Roger dating was an odd one, and something she had not actually been prepared for. She dismissed the images that arose to her mind unbidden, and turned her attention to the rest of the day. She had no particular obligations at that point. Her next deadline was three months away, and she had a healthy bank account, relatively speaking, and Italian sandals notwithstanding. The day was hers.

"Well, I think we need an outing. Let's do something. Where shall we go? The Rocks?"

"But I have a million things to do."

Fiona stood her ground, and prepared to wheedle. "It's a perfect day, and there won't be many more this year. Besides, you'll disappoint Rocco."

Rocco was not above wheedling, either, and he pressed himself against his mistress's legs, his big eyes focused intently on her face. He liked the beach, with its cold, deep water, many dogs, and innumerable rocks for retrieval. He liked the trip over to the Island on the ferry, with all the smells of fresh air and dead things, and the attention of the other passengers, at first hesitant, and then enthusiastically, affectionate. He liked the big inn on the Island, where his people might go afterward for dinner while he lay contentedly in the grass, and the other place where dogs could lie under the picnic tables and have their own hamburgers all to themselves, and sometimes their own ice cream. This was the kind of day dogs dream of on winter afternoons, twitching and gently woofing in their sleep.

"Woof," said Rocco, and wagged his tail.

"Woof! Woof!"

He was not imperious, but pleading, his barks sotto voce, his tail low, only the tip of it wagging, like a feather duster.

Elisabeth laughed, and Fiona knew they'd won.

"You just want an Alby burger?" she said, looking down at him, smiling. But Rocco wanted much more than that. And an ice cream.

Chapter Two ❖

S chool House Beach was busy, but not crowded, and
they lay on the shore with rather surprising comfort,
considering the rocks. Washington Island was accessible only by ferry, and the longish drive up the peninsula
to the ferry dock, the wait to board, and then the crossing, had
taken up most of the morning.

It had been a splendid day. Having arrived on the Island,
they went straight to the Albatross Drive-In, their favorite place
for lunch. The name was a misnomer, because finding a place to
park, even this late in the season—and on Washington Island—
was nearly impossible, but they were happy to walk.

Downtown Washington Island was barely three buildings in
each direction, consisting primarily of an intersection with busi-
nesses on three corners. On the fourth was an historic house, dating from around the 1890s, Fiona guessed. It had enormous old
trees, a gabled roof, and a porch which wrapped around two sides
of the house. The house was lived in, and adequately cared for.
Its scale was small, but in perfect proportion to the land around
it, and it gave the impression of being nestled against a small hill,
the embrace of the land protecting it against the elements. Fiona
was frequently distracted from her hamburgers as she contemplated the house and mentally renovated its sagging porch and
slightly overgrown gardens. She fairly itched to see the inside.

As they walked up to the Albatross, Rocco created the usual sensation among the crowd, with people alternately fearful and awed. He was a big animal, nearly a hundred and thirty pounds, but his gentle nature seemed to radiate from him. He seemed to know instinctively that in groups of people he needed to be his calmest self, and although the crowd would part at his appearance, it was in no time at all that people would gather around him, wanting to pet him and offer him their French fries.

Elisabeth had frequently remarked that they were missing an opportunity in not using his wolfish looks to clear the lines, but so far, at least, they had not stooped to this deception.

The Albatross was not a particularly prepossessing place, but its hamburgers were, without question, the best anywhere. Both lines of customers waiting to place their orders were about fifteen people deep, but everyone was filled with cheerful anticipation; so except for the occasional lawyer from Chicago, there was no loss of temper.

Washington Island, the locals said, was "north of the tension line," so no one behind the counter had any particular interest in rushing, and signs warning impatient Illinois tourists that patience was a virtue were prominently displayed. This intersection of philosophy and crowds made for extraordinary waits, sometimes lasting almost half an hour. As a result, a certain amount of strategy was always necessary in placing your order. Should you order your ice cream with your burger, and risk its melting and attracting wasps while you ate your lunch? Or was it better to return to the line and wait another twenty minutes or so for your second order to be completed?

In this case, as Elisabeth had pointed out, it was more a matter of how many calories one should consume before appearing in public in a swimsuit. Fiona noted, wryly, that at this point, it was hard to see that it made much difference. After some consultation, they decided to hold off on the ice cream until later. Throughout the discussion, Rocco watched their faces, his ears perked, his eyes moving from one to the other as they spoke. Calories were of no interest whatsoever to Rocco, nor was he much concerned about his appearance at the beach.

Having made their order—one hamburger for each, only ketchup for Fiona, no onions for Rocco—they stayed as much in the shade as they could, hoping to avoid the ubiquitous yellow jackets, and waited eagerly for their number to be called.

Fiona fidgeted with the straw in her diet soda and contemplated the house across the street. She imagined herself waking on a fall morning and carrying her coffee out to the porch. Not much privacy, really, right there on the main intersection. On the other hand, how much traffic could there be? It would be pleasant to sit in a rocking chair, and look out at the world, feeling sorry for the tourists who would have to leave soon. Fiona sighed, and Rocco, his dog perceptions sharp, shifted his head comfortingly to her foot. Elisabeth was waving away yellow jackets when their number was called over the speaker system.

After they had eaten, they piled back into the car and headed for the beach.

Rocco, whose usual mellow nature was in abeyance, sat up in the back, knowing that they were almost there, and as they turned onto the gravel drive to the beach, he began to cry with excitement.

They had parked, somewhat crookedly, between two cedar

trees, unpacked their things far too slowly for Rocco's taste, and made their way clumsily toward the water. It was impossible to be anything but clumsy on this beach, composed as it was, of rocks the size of slightly flattened tennis balls. At every step the rocks shifted and stirred beneath your feet, and keeping your balance required attention and determination. Only animals ran on this beach. People tottered, exclaimed, and cursed cheerfully.

They spread their towels as Rocco barked madly to encourage their haste. The other dogs—those who were not in the water—came to make their acquaintance, but Rocco, though polite, kept his eye on the prize. He wanted to swim, and he knew he could not without Elisabeth, so nothing could disengage his keen attention on her.

At last they were ready, and Rocco leapt and whirled with delight as he ran with them to the water, an odd trilling sound replacing his usual deep bark. Elisabeth stopped, took aim, and with an expertise developed from long experience, sent the Frisbee spinning out into the gentle waves. Rocco leapt madly after it, until, finally reaching some depth, he began to paddle toward it.

For at least an hour they played and swam, throwing the Frisbee for Rocco, diving with him from the raft, and splashing like children. At last, Fiona was ready for her ritual, and returning to the beach, she retrieved her inner tube, her book, and a bottle of water carefully spiked, and having dragged it all out into the lake, allowed herself to slowly drift in the sun, alternately reading and dozing, and regularly paddling herself away to keep from getting washed back to shore.

At last Fiona had returned to shore, dragging her gear back to where she had started, and carefully arranged herself and her towel among the rocks. The afternoon sunlight was reddening, and the beach was beginning to clear. Elisabeth's eyes were closed behind her big sunglasses, a magazine open across her stomach. Rocco lay with his head on his paws, mostly dozing, except when a particularly piercing cry from the water caused him to open his eyes briefly to investigate.

Fiona, her book abandoned, squinted out at the activity of a group of teenagers on the raft, marveling, not for the first time, at the confidence and audacity of teenage girls in their bikinis. She tried to remember herself at this age, but she could not recall feeling anything like these girls seemed to: utterly unself-conscious, secure, and invulnerable.

Elisabeth spoke from the depths of drowsiness, interrupting Fiona in this rather wistful series of reflections.

"Rocco, you smell like a wet dog." The big dog's head had crept nearer to Elisabeth, hoping to summon either affection or a new activity, wondering if, perhaps, it might be time for another burger.

Fiona snapped back to the present, and she turned to smile at Rocco. She knew what he was up to. Elisabeth brushed a fly away, and patted Rocco's damp flank. Her tone was desultory, but her eyes remained closed.

"I ran into Julia Epstein last week, remember, my roommate from freshman year." It was a statement rather than a question.

"Really? What's she doing?"

Fiona's interest was polite. She was feeling relaxed and easy, and was already planning what she wanted for dinner, and whether she was in the mood for a cabernet, or a white Bordeaux. Beaches, despite the fact that they ought to inspire a regimented diet, always made Fiona hungry.

"Getting married, actually. Again, I mean. She insisted that I come to her wedding in Chicago this weekend 'for old time's sake,' she said, and that means a quick turnaround since I just got back into town." Elisabeth sat up, struck by an idea. "Why don't you come with me? I can bring a guest."

"But Rocco…"

"Oh, don't worry. He's happy as a clam at my neighbor's house. They have children, and he can swim with them all day long. He sleeps in their beds, too, although I don't know what Patty thinks about all that hair on the sheets." Elisabeth looked down at her dog, and ran her hand across his head. "You like that, don't you, baby?" Rocco smiled, and wagged his tail enthusiastically.

Fiona shrugged. "Why not?" And then a memory of a past Wisconsin wedding came to mind. "I have to warn you though; I'm not dancing with you."

Elizabeth laughed. "Never fear. I don't think they'll even have dancing. It's a second wedding, remember." She paused and frowned. "Or possibly third…" She stood up and began packing away her things. "Let's go. I'm getting cold."

Fiona sighed and stood rather unsteadily on the rocks. She shook out her blanket, folded it, stuffed it into her bag, pulled her shorts on over her swimsuit, and wrapped a sweater around her shoulders. The sun was bright, the morning's haziness had cleared, and there was not a cloud in the sky, but she was getting a little chilly. "That's the beauty of this place. At least we don't have sand everywhere *and* a wet dog smell," she said. Let's go get some ice cream before dinner."

Rocco sat up and looked expectant. Ice cream was an important part of his vocabulary.

Fiona was never completely happy with Elisabeth driving. She found Elisabeth's habit of tailgating within inches of the next car's bumper, particularly unnerving, especially when she was looking away from the road as she talked a mile a minute. There was something, too, about driving that loosened Elisabeth's tongue, and since she rarely looked away when she was talking with someone, it made for some rather close calls on the road. Fiona, whose own driving was less than exemplary, often felt that the least she could do as a passenger was to watch the road herself, and her copiloting was all the more angst-ridden for her lack of control. At least in a plane, she told herself, there were dual controls.

Here on the Island, however, the traffic was so limited that Fiona could almost relax, and now, buffered by Elisabeth's uncharacteristic, but contented silence, she loosened her habitual grasp of the armrest and allowed herself to look out of the open window at the passing scenery. The landscape was pleasant, but unremarkable for this part of the world, and if you didn't already know, it would be difficult to tell that Lake Michigan was only just behind the trees. Small farms, wood framed houses, mostly dating from the mid-twentieth century, and aluminum storage sheds were the rule, with a few newly built vacation homes here and there, usually tucked away from the road.

Rocco, too, seemed to have absorbed their mood, and lay dozing in the backseat, taking up a remarkably small space for such a large animal. Even the mention of impending ice cream merited only a brief wag of the tail.

Their route back to the Albatross took them through the center of the Island. Expanses of open land and woods were interrupted by only a few modest houses. The Albatross was considerably quieter at this time of day, and their wait was short. Fiona held Elisabeth's chocolate cone so that Elisabeth could hold Rocco's for him. Rocco, who was only allowed vanilla, had to have his ice cream cone turned for him while he licked neatly around the edges. Despite this apparent delicacy, once he got to the cone it was gone in just three bites and a head toss, leaving only a few small white drops on his whiskers. These he licked appreciatively, and sat back to see if any more were forthcoming. A dog's life is filled with simple pleasures and deep disappointments, however. Talking and eating their ice cream, Fiona and Elisabeth began to stroll along the road, leading further away from the Source of All Ice Cream. Rocco sighed deeply, and followed. It was always possible that they might drop something.

There was still an hour to go before the restaurant opened, and the usual quandary of what to do had arisen. Washington Island had very few options. Despite its dramatic setting, it was too inconvenient to have been truly discovered. Many a disappointed tourist had arrived on the ferry only to discover that the only thing to do was to turn around and go back on the next one.

"Mackinac Island," one native had remarked, "we ain't."

Only the more adventurous—or determined—discovered the hidden town—invisible from the ferry dock—where the Albatross was located, but even this stretched the definition of civilization, and only those with guidebooks or a chatty innkeeper would have any idea of the white sand beach on the south side of the Island, or School House Beach on the north.

Nevertheless, the presence of an extremely good gourmet restaurant and inn made it worthwhile to stay for dinner. Since it only opened at five o'clock, however, if you hadn't had the stamina to stick to the beach long enough, there was always the question of what to do while you waited for the restaurant to open. Fiona and Elisabeth's tradition was usually to go to the bar on the pier across the street from the inn. It was the dock where the private sailors moored their boats, a short way up the Island coast from the commercial pier where the ferry launched. Still, with a long drive ahead after dinner, it didn't do to get started with your drinking too early, or to consume too much. With no one else to drive them home, they were responsible for themselves.

"This place needs a bookstore," Elisabeth complained for the hundredth time. "Anyone who had one, would make a fortune."

Fiona gave her a scornful look. "Oh really? A fortune? Selling to whom?"

"Think of all the tourists who come here looking for something to do. They'd be a captive audience."

Fiona's voice had the tone of someone explaining something to a very small child. "'All the tourists'?" In the first place, there are hardly any tourists here. In the second place, I doubt that any of them come here to read."

Elisabeth was unmoved. "You could sell beach blanket books."

"What would you do the other ten months of the year?"

"Ah. Well, you have me there. But surely the locals read. You never know. They could have a taste for T. S. Eliot and non-Euclidean geometry."

"More likely they'd go for outdoor survival books and self-help psychology. It's not just damned cold up here in January. It's completely cut off from the rest of the world. Not a single fashionable shop; you'd have to wear a parka and snow boots. And there's nothing but ice and snow. I'm not even sure you could get scotch." The way she said it, anyone would have thought that this was Fiona's worst nightmare. Maybe not, she thought to herself, but damned close.

"Of course you could. And anyway, the ferry runs all-year-'round. What do you think the locals do? Some of them even work on the mainland."

"A few crazed hermits do not constitute an argument, much less a clientele." Fiona finished her cone, crumpled her napkin, and looked around fruitlessly for a trash can. "You'd have to be crazy to live up here. We've killed fifteen minutes. What do you want to do? The pier?"

Elisabeth wiped the corners of her mouth with her thumb and forefinger, and tucked her clean napkin into the side of her bag. "The pier," she said, "but I still think a bookstore would be a brilliant addition to the neighborhood."

Together they walked back to the car, Rocco padding silently beside them.

Having dawdled at the supply shop, purchased a T-shirt, and drunk a soda at the pier, Elisabeth and Fiona wandered across the street to the Washington Inn. A white frame building, it had double rows of porches overlooking a long expanse of lawn which ran down to the road, with a vista across the straits. Already guests sat on the porch, chatting and drinking. A medium-size black dog, who belonged to the owner, wandered from group to group, seeking attention, and possibly a snack. The rise and fall of muted voices and laughter traveled across the lawn. Had they been dressed in summer whites and carrying parasols, the picture of a nineteenth-century afternoon would have been complete.

The inn had been built in the nineteenth century by a retired ship's captain for the benefit of other ships' captains, at a time when Washington Island had been a busy port on a well-traveled route. The current owners ran a cooking school there, and specialized in serving only foods grown or raised on the Island. Neither Elisabeth nor Fiona had ever stayed there, but they kept the idea in reserve in case the drive home ever seemed too long to face.

Rocco knew this place, and he knew what was expected. Without being told, he stopped some distance from the porch and lay down on the grass under a chair. The coolness of the grass on his belly, the smells of the earth, and the memory of ice cream, filled him with contentment. He would wait here until his people were ready, and he knew that when they returned, they would bring him something delicious. He sighed a deep doggish sigh, and laid his head on his paws, only the occasional pricking of his ears indicating that he was on duty, not merely resting.

After a five-course dinner of smoked whitefish salad, homemade goat cheese, and roasted lamb, and after Rocco had had his share of the leftovers, they made the long trip back from the

Island to Ephraim. The line of cars waiting for the last ferry was surprisingly long, and they were the second to the last car loaded onboard. Elisabeth felt chilled, and stayed in the car listening to a baseball game, but Fiona stood on the deck with Rocco beside her, watching the sky, and feeling the same sense of sadness she always felt on leaving the Island.

She thought about the conversation they had had about the bookstore. You really would have to be crazy to live there, and yet, there was something about the place which filled her with delight. Fiona could never quite identify what it was. There was nothing particularly distinctive about the landscape; it was very much the same as the rest of Door County. It had few of the kinds of things Fiona normally enjoyed in life: companionship, culture, lovely shops and galleries, and good restaurants; her attraction to it was inexplicable. But there was something about the secretness of the place, of its isolation and solitude which called to her, and of which she felt the loss of as the ferry chugged away in the darkness. It was as if when you were there, the world couldn't touch you, she thought. Removed from the chaos and clatter, you could somehow find the genuine course of your life, connecting to some elemental reality. Every time she was there, Fiona felt as if she had fallen off the edge of the world, and the experience was both comforting and unnerving. As the sky darkened over the waves, and as the shapes of the land became mere silhouettes against the last light, she reached down to touch Rocco's head. He leaned his whole weight heavily against her.

The ride back was quiet, each of them tired and content with their own thoughts. Before separating, they agreed that Fiona would pick up Elisabeth the next day for the drive to Chicago. She said good night to Elisabeth, kissed Rocco on the top of the head, and walked up the uneven rocky path to her cottage. She hoped her blue silk dress didn't need to go to the cleaners, and realized she had better buy a new bathrobe. They could stop along the way. Now, what had she done with the small suitcase?

Chapter Three

The noise and pace of Chicago felt completely familiar, and Fiona and Elisabeth melted into the flow of it without any consciousness of change. It was not until they stepped into the lobby of the hotel, when the city sounds fell away and the lush silence of luxury enveloped them, that they became aware of how different their environment had become.

That evening, Fiona sat in the high-ceilinged hotel lobby, drinking a scotch and reading the *Trib's* real estate section. Really, the prices here were no better than in the East. She scanned the listings for something in her price range. "At this rate, I'd have to commute from Wisconsin," she thought. She was settled comfortably in a large wing chair, happily aware of her splendid, and shockingly expensive, new Italian heels and the soft scent of the lilies in the massive arrangement nearby. The strong winds outside seemed to intensify the luxury of the hotel and its comforts. The pale blue cashmere wrap she had convinced herself that she'd needed that afternoon, was delicately draped across her shoulders, and she was wrapped in a sense of tremendous well-being. Fiona pondered whether it was the circumstances or the scotch. It was awfully good scotch.

Looking up, she watched idly as small familial dramas were being played out around the lobby. The bellmen were busy, carrying luggage in and out, holding doors, and retrieving keys for the valet parking. There were the usual businessmen, bemused, distracted, probably tired, and ready to go home. They wore their power casually, but their shirts were crisply starched and their expensive-looking ties were in fashionable colors. At a hotel like this, it was unlikely they were salesmen, but Fiona was hard-pressed to imagine what their business would be. They had the air of boardroom politics and international mergers.

There was a young couple checking in, very chic, and un-smiling. "There is a lot of pressure on the chic," Fiona mused to herself. "So tricky, always to be wearing the right thing and making the right impression. It must be exhausting."

A mother and father with two small children juggled luggage and paraphernalia as they waited for the clerk to find their reservation. Judging from her clothing, manicure, and luggage, she was a comfortable stay-at-home mom, and he was in upper management, or more likely, a doctor, Fiona guessed. The children's chocolate-covered faces led Fiona to fear for the yellow damask on the upholstered chairs in the seating area near the desk, and she drew her breath in sharply as the little girl tripped and barely missed cracking her head on the corner of a marble pillar. Her cries, echoing throughout the quiet of the hotel, carried with astonishing resonance, Fiona thought.

People tried not to notice, but their reactions, though furtive, were thinly veiled. "Why would you bring children to a place like this," she wondered. "Weren't there hotels with indoor water parks and things?" The thought of such places made her shudder a lit-tle. She had heard about them, but she had never been to one. She sank into her chair, took a deep drink of scotch, and felt grateful.

"Have you started without me?"

Elisabeth, a picture of serenity, sat down in the adjacent wing chair, and scanned the drinks menu. Here was a woman who belonged on yellow damask. She wore an excruciatingly well-cut navy silk suit—"Armani?" Fiona wondered—something lacy underneath, and rather enormous and brilliantly clear diamond earrings. Fiona guessed they must each be at least a carat.

"Sorry. I couldn't resist. They have a terrific selection—much better than anything we get at home. Lots of single malts."

"I'll have the cabernet." Elisabeth smiled at the waiter and put the menu back in its holder. "I don't know how you can stand that stuff. It smells like old socks."

"It's peat, I think, but I don't know, really. I got accustomed to it when I worked at the paper. Everyone drank it, and it seemed the thing to do. Now I like it." She smiled, filled with scotch-induced benevolence. "So tell me about this wedding. Do we know anyone who's going to be there?"

"All I know are Julia and her parents and one of her brothers. The other brother's in Shanghai, or someplace like that, and couldn't get away. There may be other college people there. Hard to say." Elisabeth began idly munching the cocktail snacks from the bowl on the table.

Fiona eyed them with distaste. "That stuff has probably been handled by every disease-ridden person within miles, including that nasty child over there I just saw picking his nose."

Elisabeth rolled her eyes. "Builds immunity," she said, and accepted her glass from the waiter.

But Fiona noticed that she started to reach for another handful, and stopped.

"And who is she marrying this time?" she asked, dimly aware of the slightly evil tone of the question, although she hadn't intended it that way. Fiona had finished her drink, and was distracted by her attempts to flag down the waiter, who had turned away before she'd had a chance to order.

"She told me, but it didn't register. Someone she met at a picnic, she said, although Julia is the last person in the world I can imagine at a picnic. She's more the cocktail party on a yacht, type. Apparently he's an actor."

"Really? An actor? And she likes yachts?" Fiona fidgeted with the ice in her empty glass, allowing the sound to resonate, and tried futilely to catch the waiter's eye. His professional radar, allowing him to sense and elude customer signals, was finely tuned.

"Well, it will be perfect for him. She certainly doesn't need any more money. Her family is positively loaded. Her father owns one of those big agriculture corporations. You know, the kind that advertise on Sunday morning news programs. Farming for subsidies, clearly. What is going on with that child?" Elizabeth leaned around her chair to see what was happening behind her.

Fiona, who had been watching as the mother tried ineffectually to calm the now hysterical toddler, held up her glass to the waiter, who had finally looked over, and raised her eyebrows at him. Having achieved her goal, she sat back and rearranged her wrap. "Doctor's children," she said. "Spoiled rotten. Let's have one more drink, and then we'll go."

The private club where the wedding was being held was one of the oldest in Chicago. The four-story, nineteenth-century building was nestled smugly between skyscrapers, its wood, marble, and brocade interiors providing its monied members with a most luxurious sanctuary from the ugliness of the world. The staff were hopelessly discreet, charming, and well-educated. They would never dream of responding in the negative to any request, no matter how unusual, and although most of the thrills they had came from the proximity of their celebrity members and guests, they were accustomed, every now and then, to bizarre behavior of nearly every kind. Their faces revealed only a slightly warm professional courtesy.

The wedding party clustered in the library after the ceremony. As the evening came on, the lamps were lit. An arrangement of white and pink lilies filled the massive stone fireplace. Original masterpieces graced the walls. Fiona mused on the preponderance of French Impressionists in Chicago's private collections. It must, she thought, have to do with the era in which the old families had acquired their wealth. The air was filled with the scent of flowers, and a musician in a tuxedo played Noel Coward on the baby grand piano. The doors were opened to a private terrace surrounded by a wall of trees. The sounds of the city and the wildness of the wind seemed far away. It was all, simply by contrast, a reminder of one's present comfort. Julia, a fragile blonde, in pale aqua silk. The groom, smiling and affable beside her, looked, in his bespoke suit, much like a character in a television commercial, in a role he'd clearly played before.

The Dom Perignon was served liberally by the staff, and hors d'oeuvres of the exquisitely melting kind were passed among the guests. Fiona resisted the first two attempts, but finally succumbed. It was, as she had imagined, delectable. Tiny shrimps, marinated in something sweet, chargrilled, and served with herbs; bite-size cheese puffs, still warm from the oven, but not so hot that you burned your mouth; pea pod-wrapped bits of sea bass with the perquisite mango salsa ("Why mango?" Fiona always wondered); and tiny bites of rare filet mignon, with just a drop of hollandaise. For Fiona, the scotch had worked its magic, and the world, as F. Scott Fitzgerald observed, had changed "into something significant, elemental, and profound." It would be churlish, anyway—or some deeper form of asceticism—she thought, not to feel deep pleasure and gratitude in such a setting.

Elisabeth, too, glass in hand, looked completely at ease as she chatted happily with a group she had known in college. Fiona noted that her eyes were looking brighter, and wondered whether it had more to do with the champagne or the reception. Fiona herself didn't particularly care for champagne, which she told herself was just as well, given that she had already consumed two rather substantial glasses of scotch. She was debating the wisdom of a fifth cheese puff when she felt, rather than heard, a male voice in her ear.

"Don't you think Noel Coward is a bit cynical for a wedding?"

Fiona turned her head and regarded the man who had spoken. His face was very close to hers, but she found that she didn't mind at all. He was somewhere in his late thirties probably, with a sprinkling of gray in his dark hair. He had blue eyes which twinkled with intelligence, a vague tan, and a general air of prosperity and good sense about him. Fiona decided instantly that she liked the look of him. He wasn't handsome, exactly, but he had an air of relaxed confidence which she found most appealing. "Only for a first wedding," she said, "but after that I think it contributes an air of reality."

"I think the wind is the only reality in Chicago."

"O Wild West Wind, thy breath of Autumn's being," Fiona said, rather absently, and almost to herself.

"Thou from whose unseen presence the leaves dead
Are driven like ghosts from an enchanter fleeing."

Fiona looked at him in surprise. "You know Shelley?"

"My mother was a poet. It was a requirement of family life."

He grinned at her. She grinned back. The pianist had switched to "I Went to a Marvelous Party."

They stood gazing at one another.

"Anyway, I don't actually know many people here," he continued. "But I gather that it's not a first wedding."

"No, of course not," Fiona said. "The bride is wearing a suit, the guest list is small, and the usual trappings of bridesmaids and groomsmen are missing."

"But perhaps they prefer small weddings."

"Ha!" said Fiona, cheerily. "No woman who can afford it wants a small wedding. Not a first one anyway, and besides, if you don't know—"

"—What am I doing here?" He shrugged and smiled vaguely.

Fiona raised one eyebrow.

"How do you do that?" he asked. "I've always wanted to be able to."

"I practiced in front of the mirror all through sixth grade. Now I do it without even realizing it. You're changing the subject."

"Sometimes it works."

"True. But anyway, if you don't want to tell me, I won't insist."

"I prefer to maintain my air of mystery," he said soberly. "But I could change my mind if persuaded." He was looking as if persuasion were an interesting topic when Fiona saw him catch the glance of one of the family who was waving him over. "And now, if you'll excuse me, my presence seems to have been discovered. Perhaps I'll see you at dinner."

He turned and walked over to the man who had gestured to him, tripped, bumped into an elderly lady in a mauve organza dress, and spilled her champagne on the bride. A flurry of activity began as the bridal silk was blotted. Apologies flew merrily.

The pianist broke into a lively rendition of "Why Do the Wrong People Travel." Fiona sighed and took a glass of champagne from the tray of a passing waiter. Perhaps it was too cynical.

Coffee stopped serving at four o'clock, and Roger usually locked up the shop by five. There was generally not a lot to do by then, since the customers tended to come in waves and recede again, leaving him plenty of time to do the routine things necessary to keep the place running. Roger was a one-man shop. He didn't like teenagers with tattoos and piercings, and the idea of a senior citizen waiting on people bothered him. Besides, he preferred to do things his own way.

It was Labor Day weekend. The tourist season was winding

down, and would remain low now until the fall colors began, but today had been busy, and the tourist customers unusually demanding and unreasonable. Things most people might have found stressful simply didn't faze Roger, however, because he tended not to pay much attention to other people's emotions. It wasn't that he didn't care about others. He thought of himself as rather softhearted and sentimental. It was just that people were too difficult to understand. The properties of chemicals, the reasons for the movements of the universe, a nice mathematical formula, these were simple things to grasp. They were predictable. They followed patterns that made sense. But people, well, people weren't reasonable, and Roger found that puzzling.

He liked dogs, although he wouldn't admit it to many of the locals, lest they begin inundating him with badly behaved doggy clientele, but dogs, at least, were simple in their needs and clear in their emotions. A happy dog, a sad dog, an angry dog—they had emotional states that were unequivocal. But women…. Roger turned out the lights and headed for the back. Tonight he would go for a swim and read something challenging. He needed to clear his head. He stopped for a moment and looked back at the darkened shop. He wondered whether he should consider a change.

Elisabeth and Fiona were separated during dinner. Fiona found herself seated next to Julia's brother, Francis, who was a retired ballet dancer turned vice president for a small liberal arts college. He was slim, blond, and very well-dressed. Fiona found that his opinionated approach to everything made him an entertaining companion and suitable distraction. As the first course was served, a tuna carpaccio with cilantro cream, he kept up his monologue. Fiona, who despised both raw fish and cilantro, picked warily at her food and wondered when this herbal fad would move on.

"If you haven't seen their new shop, you simply have to. When I first walked in, I wept. No, really. I wept—You don't know me well enough to realize that I never exaggerate—but a woman with your sense of style—no really—I noticed that cashmere wrap the minute you walked into the room—that color is perfect for you—But it's not to be missed. Do you like antiques? There's a little place right next store that is to die for. No, really."

As her dinner partner chatted, Fiona caught herself watching the table across the room, where Champagne Man, as she now thought of him, seemed to be conducting himself respectably and without a spill. She noted with some regret that he was laughing much too heartily for her taste at the remarks of an attractive woman probably ten years younger.

"Rats," she thought, and picked, rather drearily now, at the remaining edges of her dinner.

She was regretting both the cheese puffs and the scotch, and felt herself expanding into the narrow allowances of her blue silk. Francis, ever the dancer, had not touched his dinner roll or his Potatoes Anna. A still glistening pool of a perfect sauce béarnnaise and half of his entreé had been left on his plate, but he chatted happily as he sipped his lemon water. His charm was waning, Fiona felt.

"Fi?" Elisabeth was behind her, leaning down to whisper in her ear. "Can you come out to the patio for a bit? I need a breath of air. It's stifling in here."

Fiona nearly sprang to put down the fork, the last of her dinner still uneaten. "Will you excuse me?" She smiled at Francis. He was a decent sort, really. "I can hardly fault him because his discipline is stronger than mine," she thought. He leapt gracefully to his feet before she could rise and held her chair, looking as if he might have been about to embark on a series of pirouettes, flinging petals as he went. Feeling lumpish and somewhat ashamed, Fiona followed Elisabeth out the French doors onto the patio. Elisabeth stopped and stood in the midst of the garden, posed like a particularly voluptuous Victorian statue—albeit an Armani-clad one—happily breathing in the night air. Here, with the flowers already spread at their feet, there would be no need for petal flinging. Turning, she took a look at Fiona's face and frowned.

"Something wrong?"

Fiona shrugged and shook her head. "It's nothing—just that I can't stand men whose thighs are smaller than mine." Fiona looked as if Francis's thighs were a personal affront, but even as she said it, she knew that this was not the reason for the tight feeling in her chest.

Elisabeth, blessed with a perfect comfort in herself, was completely unimpressed. "His whole body is smaller than mine. I probably couldn't fit one arm in the leg of his jeans."

"It's worse than that, actually. You should have sat next to him at dinner. I felt as if I were Jabba the Hut and he was Princess Leia."

Fiona sighed and paused, and sighed again.

"You can't help liking him, though. He's a very kind and gentle person."

They were both silent for a moment, breathing in the warm night air. It was remarkably sweet-smelling for the city, perfumed with the roses which grew in elegant profusion around the pathways of the garden.

The sounds of the party floated out from the club. A jazz combo was warming up, and dancing was about to begin. Men's and women's voices carried in a mix of conversation and laughter, the soft buzz of it making individuals mostly indistinguishable, except for one woman with an exceptionally penetrating laugh, who was apparently being entertained with a series of brilliant witticisms. Fiona was reminded, briefly, of an aviary's tropical exhibit.

Elisabeth had reverted to a dreamy state, whether brought on by reminiscences or wine, Fiona had no idea. She was staring blindly into the darkness, absently playing with the clasp of her evening bag, plainly far away.

"Where have you gone off to?"

Elisabeth stopped clasping and unclasping and came sturdily back to earth. "Roger."

"What?" Fiona was newly aware of her one raised eyebrow.

"Roger," said Elisabeth firmly. "I was thinking of Roger."

Fiona spent the rest of the evening trying to arrange an accidental meeting with Champagne Man, only to be continually foiled, first by introductions and happenstance, and then by his seeming popularity. Observing him from across the room she could see that he was continually sought after and introduced eagerly from group to group, little bursts of laughter erupting whenever he joined a conversation. Inwardly she chided herself for being coy. "You're a grown woman, for heaven's sake. You can just walk up to him." But she could think of no graceful way of accomplishing this, and her usual casual approach to conversation seemed to have died within her. He, after all, had excused himself earlier. He, therefore (she reasoned), should approach her this time. On the other hand, she argued with herself, he had first spoken to her. Perhaps it was her turn?

Annoyed with herself, she set out to have an interesting evening. She danced with Francis, who, to Fiona's surprise, made her feel graceful rather than moose-like, chatted with the pianist on his break, and told funny stories to Elisabeth's college friends. When Francis invited her to see a play with him, she was able to hide her astonishment sufficiently to make a gracious refusal. She noticed, in spite of herself, that on several occasions, Champagne Man had begun to move toward her, only to be waylaid in conversation by other guests, his eyes meeting hers as he was drawn into yet another eager circle.

In this way the evening passed, until, finally, Fiona mentally shook herself and decided to take fate into her own hands. Excusing herself from a group of particularly earnest and pedantic golfers, she set out to find him. He had been missing from the room for some time, but she was certain he was still there. And then she saw him.

He was clearly looking for someone as he moved toward the door, when he caught Fiona's eye and stopped. Facing her, he came fully to attention, and with crisp military precision he saluted her. Then he turned on his heel and walked out alone, a flurry of lesser mortals in his wake. Fiona noticed his dinner partner on the other side of the room, flirting aggressively with Francis. A sound like an exotic birdcall filled the room. Despite her disappointment, Fiona felt a small surge of joy.

Chapter Four ✤

Fiona's feelings of post-reception exhilaration did not last. She had awoken depressed and hung over, and after multiple coffees she felt depressed, hung over, and jittered.

The drive home from Chicago the next day had been quiet. Normally full of chatter, Fiona and Elisabeth were tired and hungover to varying degrees, and each was preoccupied with her own thoughts.

Despite the balm of Elisabeth's company, Fiona had spent the drive continuously replaying the events of the night before and cursing her own mind. The last few miles of the route along the peninsula seemed interminable to her, but arriving at last at Elisabeth's, Fiona dropped her off and lost no time in continuing north to Ephraim.

Elisabeth brought her bags in and immediately headed back out to her own car. She looked forward to picking up Rocco at the neighbors' and spending a quiet evening at home.

Fiona walked in the door of her cottage feeling drained and flat. The familiar smell and lovely order of the place failed to work their usual charm upon her. The house felt stale and damp; the flowers in the vase on the kitchen table were dead; an aura of desertion had settled over everything. Dumping her bag in the bedroom closet, she kicked off her shoes and went to the kitchen to rummage in the refrigerator. Finding nothing of interest, she returned to the living room and stood looking out at the water, far below. The weather was gray, and the bay, true to its name, was a murky green.

She found, in a rare circumstance, that she was bored with her own thoughts. In the depths of her mind, she knew the reasons for her restlessness, but refused to acknowledge them. Walking to the bookshelf, she poured herself a glass of sherry from the decanter, and returned to the window, looking down, feeling the weight of her mood descend upon her.

Elisabeth's house and gallery were an old farmstead. She had inherited the place from her grandfather some years before, and having opened the gallery at first in a simple outbuilding, as her success had grown, she had expanded the gallery space to include the barn, the loft, and a gravel-pathed sculpture garden.

The house was simple and comfortable, filled with pieces Elisabeth had found on her travels, and art she hadn't been able to part with at the gallery. Living on the premises, it was easy for her to keep long hours or short ones. It was a life whose freedom and limitations she enjoyed, and she felt no resentment or sense of intrusion on those occasions when strangers appeared on her doorstep asking to see the gallery.

She felt, therefore, no concern when, around six o'clock, she heard the brass bell at her back door ringing. Slipping her shoes on from where they lay on the floor beneath her chair, and putting down her book on Venetian glass, she went to the door, Rocco padding laconically at her side. His bark at the silhouetted figure behind the door's frosted glass was purely a matter of form. He, too, had developed a sense of calm security in this remote, but familiar place.

Elisabeth was vaguely conscious of a dim sense of recognition of the figure waiting there, but when she opened the door, she was nevertheless startled to find Roger. He was standing, his back to the door, hands in pockets, his head lifted toward the sky. At the sound of the door opening, he turned toward her, the look on his face seeming to convey surprise that he should find her here, in this, of all places.

"Why, Roger," she said, not succeeding at all in keeping the astonishment from her voice. "What a surprise." She had almost been about to say, "What are you doing here?" but her manners caught up with her just in time. "Come in. I was just about to pour myself a glass of wine," she lied. "Would you like some?"

Roger hadn't said anything so far, but he nodded and stepped in. Rocco's presence offered a convenient buffer, and whatever he had been unable to say to Elisabeth, Roger felt no such restraint with the big dog, seeming almost effusive, Elisabeth thought.

"Hey there, Rocco," he said.

Rocco wagged his tail and sat to have his head scratched. Roger spent a minute or so with Rocco, and then together they followed Elisabeth into the dining room where she kept a good collection of red wine in a rack on the sideboard.

Elisabeth was a person whose external serenity was a perfect reflection of her inner life. Few things ruffled her, and her gracious optimism came to her naturally and without art. Nevertheless, she felt a bit aflutter as she opened a bottle of red wine from Abruzzo, and poured two very full glasses. She could do with a glass, and a bit of something to help with conversation wouldn't hurt, she felt.

Roger followed her into the living room with his glass, exuding the faint scent of coffee, and sat in one of the deep, soft armchairs Elisabeth loved. A pair of French doors stood open to a stone patio, and the sound of birds came in with warm, soft air. Elisabeth had been known to open these doors in a snowstorm, so even on a gray day like this one, the sweet scent of fresh air was in the room making it a bit damp, but welcoming.

They sat together with their wine glasses, Rocco having settled again on the rug, his chin flat on the floor, his big dark eyes moving from one person to the other, his doggish mind occupied with deciphering the circumstances. Elisabeth's calm, which he could read instinctively, was a signal to him that all was well, and finding nothing here which required his attention, he sighed a deep sigh of contentment and closed his eyes.

There was no strain in the silence that descended on the room. Roger revolved his wine glass, looking at its contents in the light, not out of expertise, but rather out of a simple appreciation of the color. Elisabeth, whose brief nervousness had resolved into happiness, simply smiled at him across the room. Whatever fatigue she had felt from the night before and the long day of driving now fell away. Apart from a brief conversation about the book she was reading, which Roger had asked about, they talked very little. Gradually the bottle emptied, the light outside the doors faded, and the evening came down.

When Roger stood to go, Elisabeth accompanied him to the door. He turned and looked at her for a moment. "Thanks," he said, and disappeared into the night air to his car parked on the other side of the barn.

Returning to the living room, Elisabeth found Rocco immovably asleep by the hearth. She stood for a moment breathing in the night air before she closed the French doors and went to bed, a halo of joy around her heart.

Fiona spent a bad night, her anxiety jumping from finance, to deadlines, to mortality, to memories of the things she should have said, and moments of excruciating embarrassment twenty years old. It was just dawn when she gave up and threw back the covers, returning to the window to look at the harbor.

The weather was the same. Neither rainy nor foggy. Just a steady gray which seemed to reflect her own interior blandness. Fiona knew from experience that if she did not break this mood, she would be in its grip. She needed to be out and with people, even if she was alone among them. Staying at home and indulging herself would only make things worse. She pulled on some jeans and a sweatshirt, put a baseball cap over her hair, and grabbing a jacket, headed down to Coffee. Roger may not be chatty, but at least he was a presence. *I need a dog,* she thought for the millionth time.

The walk down did nothing much to lift her inner fog. She felt herself descending in every way as she walked down the decrepit stairs to the village. Even the smell of the water, and the garrulousness of the gulls did not console her.

There was no one else around; the tourists were gone, the locals safely inside or at work on a Monday morning. Many of the sailboats, too, were gone, safely stored away for winter. After the cheer and bustle of the summer, there was an air of abandonment in the village. It had rained in the night, and the dampness felt as if it were seeping into her bones. The only sign of human activity was the scent of coffee coming from the shop. Fiona had the sense of grasping for a preserver as she reached the door of Coffee and walked in.

Inside, the familiar utilitarian white walls had disappeared. A luminous yellow permeated the shop, trimmed with glossy white moldings. A collection of black- and- white photos, which Fiona recognized as the work of a local artist, identically framed, hung along the inner walls. The gentle sound of jazz emanated from a small, artful stereo on a newly installed shelf. Fiona stood inside the door, stunned confusion on her face. Roger, more disheveled and unshaven than ever, his eyes red with sleeplessness, and exuding his usual charm, looked at her with his normal expression of fury.

"What's wrong with you?"

Fiona looked him in the eye, paused for a moment, and walked over to her seat at the counter. It still wobbled comfortingly. She felt a moment of reassurance. "Not a thing. I'll have the usual."

Roger poured her coffee, and began the preparations for an egg sandwich. Fiona picked up a used copy of the *Green Bay Press Gazette*. Now that summer was over, the *New York Times* would be harder to find left around. Remembering her lack of dinner the night before, she decided she'd better dilute the coffee.

"I guess I'd like some milk, too," she said.

Roger continued his cooking without turning around. "Regular or nonfat?"

Fiona stopped turning the pages of the paper for only the briefest fraction of a second. "Nonfat," she said, casually.

Fiona ate her egg sandwich in bemused silence, but she couldn't help noticing two things: One, that the yolk of her egg and the yellow of the walls were nearly identical, and two, that Roger was lingering unnecessarily, seemingly in need of conversation. This possibility struck Fiona as being highly out of character, but she could think of no other explanation for his behavior. For the second time in two days, Fiona found herself out of her element and uncertain of how to proceed. Never having actually conversed with Roger before, in any actual human sense, she was unable to locate a precedent to act on.

Apparently, neither was Roger, because, although he continued to linger, repeatedly wiping the counter, refilling her cup, and making too many trips to clear her place, he never said a word. He coughed. He cleared his throat. He took a number of deep breaths. But silence reigned, with only the soft jazz playing as background. There seemed to be, Fiona sensed, a surreal quality to the atmosphere. At last, having endured this stalemate to her limit, Fiona took out her money and began her preparations to leave.

It was at this moment that Mike and Terry walked in, carrying with them fresh air and a vigorous indifference to nuance.

"Whew!" said Terry. "Paint fumes are so much you can't

smell the coffee." He planted himself cheerfully at the counter, Mike beside him, his faithful friend.

This was the tonic Fiona required. Even Roger seemed to relax a little. She smiled at them and settled back on her seat. It wobbled comfortingly.

"Hi, Mike," she said. "How have you been?"

Mike's kind eyes crinkled as he smiled back at her, exuding gentle affection. "I'm well, thank you; I'm well." He nodded repeatedly as if continuing to check the veracity of his answer and finding it still correct.

"Looks like you've been busy around here, Roger. Nice work." Terry looked around appreciatively. "I like the photos. They're Tom's, aren't they?" He mentioned their mutual friend whose work was well- known in the county.

"Thanks. Yeah, they are," said Roger. "I've had them for a while, and decided they'd be better here than in my closet."

The cheerful bustle of their arrival stilled for a moment at the unexpectedly lengthy reply, and then resumed, only slightly changed.

"We're gonna do breakfast," said Terry, settling in. "Morning, Fiona," he continued, turning toward her as Roger began to make their egg sandwiches. "Roof hold out the rain last night?"

"It did, actually. And I never cease to be grateful."

"I don't ask for gratitude from my customers, so long as they've paid the bill." Terry said this comfortably as he took his first swallow of coffee.

Fiona had a brief moment of anxiety before she realized that he was not speaking about her particular bill. She remembered quite clearly having written the check.

"So Mike," Terry spoke loudly so that he could be heard above the sizzling of the grill. "I saw your boat was out last night. Catch anything?"

Fiona, now comfortably surrounded by voices and human activity, returned to the real estate listings, their voices receding into a meaningless background. There was little of interest for sale, just the usual 1960s ranches, multimillion-dollar condos, and new construction, and she was about to move on to the crossword puzzle, when she saw it. Buried in the middle of a column with a tiny black-and -white photograph, was the house across the street from the Albatross. "Washington Island Classic," the heading read. She read the text again. *Picturesque traditional home with huge potential, located in the heart of Washington Island*, it said. *Original hardwood floors, big kitchen. 3 bedrooms, 1 bath, outbuildings. Ready to renovate. Property being sold as is.*

Fiona rapidly searched her brain for euphemisms. As is, picturesque, and potential all meant the same thing: The place was a mess. Probably irredeemable.

"Look at this," Fiona turned to show the ad to Mike and Terry, interrupting their conversation comparing Lake Michigan water levels over the years. "Do you know this place?"

Mike looked it over and chuckled. "Sure. It's the old Goeden place." He tapped the ad with his finger as Terry craned his neck a bit to read over his shoulder. "Remember Joe Goeden?" he asked Terry.

"Sure do," said Terry. "Best finish carpenter I ever met. The things he could do with a piece of wood." Terry shook his head slowly and looked into the distance, as if he were watching an old memory. "Yeah. Good guy. Too bad he had such lousy taste in women." Mike nodded. "What was his wife's name, again? Laura? Lana?…"

"Lena," said Mike, frowning a little, whether with concentration or dislike Fiona couldn't tell.

"Lena. That's right. Man, she was a spoiled brat—even if she was a grown woman. Joe'd probably have stayed on at his folks' place if it hadn't been for her."

"Why? What happened?" Fiona was in the mood for conversation. Roger put their plates in front of them and leaned against the counter in the classic pose of a roadside café server, a clean towel over his shoulder, listening to the story. Like Fiona, he was a newcomer, and didn't know the local tales.

"Well," began Terry, "She was one of the summer people. Came from money. And Joe was an Island kid. They met one year and it was like an explosion. Couldn't keep 'em apart. Nobody thought it would work—and nobody liked her, not even the other rich kids who'd known her practically her whole life— but you couldn't tell him anything." Terry shook his head again. "Can't blame him, really. She was a beautiful girl."

Mike turned to Fiona, his gentle voice reflective. "She had gray eyes and straight, blonde hair. The kind that looks as if there's a light always shining on it. Lots of gold and red in it, and some blue undertones," he added. "But the thing that was really remarkable about her was her voice. Remember her voice, Ter?"

"Oh yeah, I remember. It was all low and sweet, as if there were a song in it. That girl's voice was the most seductive thing about her. When she wasn't hollering, at least."

Mike chuckled. "That came later. She didn't start hollering until after they were married."

Terry nodded. "Yeah, but everyone knew what she was like. She pushed him around from the beginning. Always pouting and crying about something. Lot of guys hanging around her, though. Everywhere she went there was a little pack of 'em. Like dogs hangin' around a bitch in heat." He stopped guiltily and looked at Fiona. "Sorry."

Fiona smiled and shrugged. "So what happened?" she asked, even though, by now, the story seemed predictable.

· "They got married within about six months. Her parents weren't too happy about it—and his mom wasn't, either, as I recall. As I say, everyone knew what a bi-." He caught himself. "Pain she was. And she was used to having things. Joe was just an ordinary guy. He didn't stand a chance, really."

Mike nodded in agreement, and Terry lifted his mug toward Roger, who was refilling cups. Fiona asked for more milk, and there was a silence as they all drank their coffee, the jazz playing softly in the background.

Terry put his mug down and sighed a deep contented sigh. He loved telling stories. "Joe's dad had died some years before, and Joe had always taken real good care of his mom," he continued. "He took care of the family place on the Island, and everyone always knew that someday it would be his place. His mom was an independent lady, but he was always there, keeping things running good. He built some mantels and cabinets in that place that were first-class work." Terry nodded in reminiscence. "Yup. Those were some of the nicest pieces of carpentry I ever saw. Remember that banister he did?" he asked Mike, who nodded. "That was really something. Curved railing pieces and hand-turned balusters. It was a real fine piece of work. Took him six months, I bet."

Fiona's interest was piqued. "Really? Is that stuff still in there?"

Terry glanced at Mike and they both shrugged. " I dunno," said Terry. "Prob'ly. Hard to imagine anyone taking them out." He paused. "Unless, I suppose, someone decided to renovate it, and bought some of those cabinets from the Home Depot down in Green Bay."

Fiona grimaced. "Who would rip out hand-built carpentry?" she asked.

Terry grinned. "Happens all the time. People buy these little places because they're full of charm, and then they rip the charm right out of them. Like new things, I guess."

"That was the whole problem with Joe and Lena," said Mike, returning to the story. "He planned to live on the Island on the family place, and take care of his mom. Guess he figured he could have a nice family life up there. But Lena wanted new—new house, new clothes, new car—and there was no way she was going to be happy on that Island. She started complaining about that around the first week."

"Yup," said Terry. "Didn't take long. I'm thinking they lasted there about six months before poor Joe had to take her out of there. Guess they moved down to Illinois or Milwaukee or something. Don't know what happened, really after that. He came back when his mom died, about ten years ago, or so, but we didn't see him. Just heard he'd been here from one of the neighbors up there. Guess he sold the place and went back to wherever."

"Were they still married?" asked Fiona.

Terry slowly shook his head. "Hard to say. Though I'm guessing if he'd been on his own he would've come back. I doubt he was happy, though. He was a small town guy, and didn't have much to do about city things. And he was the kind of guy who always tried to do the right thing. Guess things didn't turn out the way he'd hoped. His mom was a nice lady; raised him right. Probably lonely there at the end, but she never said nothing about it. Kept herself busy, I guess, and had a nice little group of church ladies who looked out for her." He looked into his cup. "Things didn't probably turn out the way she was hoping, either. But life's like that."

"Yeah," said Mike. "House got pretty rundown there at the end without Joe around to take care of it. Too much for a woman alone to handle a place like that."

"So who owns it now?" asked Fiona.

"Somebody from downstate," said Terry, dismissively. "Nobody from around here. Why?" he asked, a gleam in his eye. "You thinking of buying it?"

Fiona laughed and shook her head. "Not likely!"

"It's a rental," said Mike. "Rental places up there aren't all that popular. Too remote for most folks. Probably not in the best shape."

Terry laughed. "Genuine dump, by now, I'd say. Not the kind of place you'd want, Fiona."

Mike smiled at her kindly. "Can't imagine you up there all on your own."

"No," said Fiona, finishing her coffee. "No, neither can I."

Fiona felt better as she left the shop, but she still needed a distraction, something to keep her mind busy. It was unseemly, she felt, at her age, to be pining over a man she'd barely spoken to. Thinking that some intellectual work would keep her busy, she headed up to the big library in Sister Bay to do a little research on an article she'd been contemplating.

Libraries were rapidly becoming as unnecessary as newspapers for many people. But for Fiona, library research was a habit, and the process of looking for things there and developing notes created a kind of mental jumping off point for her. It was what she had always done, and it seemed to signal her brain that it was time to focus on a particular project. It was her beginning ritual, and she saw no point in changing it.

The library was newly built and pleasant, with large windows looking out on perennial beds, big comfortable chairs and a fireplace. Fiona tried to settle into her work, hoping to become engrossed in her reading. But her mind wandered no matter how firmly she tried to redirect it. It had begun to rain again, and the dismal weather suited perfectly Fiona's rather miserable mood.

Exasperated with herself, she went over to one of the computer cubicles, and began an aimless coasting from site to site. She read some political commentary, looked up the rates for airfare to Paris, through the process of association bought herself a boutique Parisian cologne that was difficult to find, and was about to log off when it occurred to her to check out the Goeden house posting.

She found the site easily enough, and then idly clicked through the pictures. The house was pretty. It was difficult to see much, because there weren't many photos, and most of these were of the exterior. The yard was larger than she'd imagined, and there was a small barn or large shed in the back: the out-buildings mentioned in the ad. Probably the interior is too rough to show pictures, she thought. It would make a good project for someone. But she couldn't imagine life up there on Washington Island. It was too remote. Fiona needed civilization.

It was after three o'clock when her stomach finally drove her to pack up her notebooks and drive back to Ephraim. Coffee would probably be closed by the time she got to town, but Elisabeth would be around tonight. Maybe they could go get dinner somewhere.

As they sat together in the atmosphere of a 1960s supper club their conversation was neither serious nor confiding. For reasons she could not completely articulate to herself, Elisabeth did not feel like talking about her visit with Roger. Fiona, for her part, did not know if she should comment too much on Coffee's transformation, and her feelings about Champagne Man and the missed opportunity were too confused and painful to dwell on. The evening was therefore cheerful and unburdened by heavy emotion. Elisabeth met several people she had known since childhood, and chatting effortlessly, introduced Fiona with her usual grace. Happily ensconced in scotch and good food and admiring her friend's charm, Fiona was able to escape herself. By the time coffee was served, they were both relaxed.

Elisabeth had spent the day shopping in Sturgeon Bay, and was describing her purchases. "Oh," she said, reaching for her big leather purse. "I almost forgot. I picked up some real estate flyers. Want to go touring next weekend?"

Fiona reached for one of the newsprint magazines and idly flipped through it. "Did I tell you the house across from the

Albatross is for sale?" she asked as she glanced at the photos. "I saw it this morning at Roger's. It must be in here." She found it on the bottom of a page and folded it back to show Elisabeth.

Elisabeth leaned over to look. "It's a charming little house. Bet it needs a lot of work, though. And besides, I don't know anyone who'd want to live on the Island."

Fiona smiled and shrugged.

"We could always buy it for you," Elisabeth said, laughing. "You'd love being over there without a shoe store."

"And no scotch," said Fiona. "Don't forget the scotch." She smiled indulgently into her glass.

That night Fiona dreamed that she was driving endlessly in circles. Traffic surrounded her; cars appeared from nowhere to cut her off, the road turning and twisting unexpectedly. She found it difficult to reach the pedals, and the windshield was strangely opaque. Landmarks from unrelated places seemed to whiz by the windows, and she was unable to gain a sense of where she was or where she was going. At first she was afraid she would lose control and hit one of the massive trees along the road, but then she found herself all at once in a big city, and the freeways were filled with even more traffic moving at death-defying speeds. Fear filled her, her heart pounded, and she realized suddenly that she was driving at full speed on a high suspension bridge. And just as the idea dawned that this could be even more dangerous, her car left the road, and breaking through the wire cable barriers, she felt and saw herself, in the car, making a long soaring arc through the air, toward the deep water below.

Chapter Five

When she reached Coffee the next morning, Fiona had to remind herself about the changed atmosphere before she entered. She was surprised at how much she was looking forward to being there in its warm yellow ambience. Not, she thought to herself dryly, at all like the ambience of the proprietor.

When she walked in, Elisabeth was already there, and Fiona, alert for signs of a developing romance, noted nothing different in her behavior or Roger's. Fiona, though her mood was tenuous, was wobbling without angst on her stool next to Elisabeth when Terry arrived.

"Morning, all," he said, taking off his jacket and leaving it on the hook by the door. "Still yellow in here, I see. Thought maybe it might have changed again overnight."

Fiona grinned at him, but Elisabeth was rummaging in her bag, and Roger said nothing, his back to them as he made a new pot of coffee. Terry bent to say hello to Rocco, who was curled between Elisabeth and Fiona.

"Morning Terry," said Fiona. "Where's Mike?"

"He's off somewhere catching the light. Probably be in soon." Terry settled onto a stool and accepted the cup of coffee Roger poured for him without asking.

"Good morning for it," said Elisabeth. "Nice and soft." She

had taken out the real estate magazines again and spread them on the counter in front of her. "Want to plan the open house itinerary?" she asked Fiona.

"So you're not going to buy the old Goeden house?" Terry asked in mock surprise. "I can just see you up there in February, Fiona. All dressed in mukluks and down, and dangling from the chandeliers." He chuckled to himself at this image, and Elisabeth smiled at him.

"You never know," said Fiona lightly. "I might look good in mukluks."

Terry smiled down at his coffee and looked up at her again. "People don't really change," he said kindly. "No offense, Fiona, but you're a city girl, born and bred. You'd never survive a winter up there."

On any other day Fiona would have laughed and agreed with him, but today, the hangover from her dreams had made her normally cheerful self inaccessible, and she was struggling mightily not to be offended. She was not a native, it was true, and she was a relative newcomer, but she liked to think of herself as a hearty survivor. She could manage anywhere if she wanted to. It was the wanting to part, she told herself, that was missing in this case. Living on remote Washington Island had appeal for a very limited sector of the population, and she knew she was not one of them. Nevertheless, her mood was dangerous. Fiona was unaccustomed to teasing, and although normally she managed to play along with good grace, today her emotional margins were thin.

"Oh, I don't know," she said as casually as she could, her irritation rising. "I'm pretty tough."

Elisabeth, usually attuned to Fiona's moods, was distracted this morning, and missed the signals. "Sure you are," she teased. "If tough means surviving the shoe sale at Neiman Marcus."

Even Roger laughed at this, and Fiona felt herself getting angry. "You underestimate me. I didn't survive all those years as a reporter by being a wimp."

"There's city tough, and then there's wilderness tough," said Terry, still teasing. "Do you know how often the power goes out up there?"

Elisabeth joined in. "No Italian sandals on W.I. No single malt, either, I'm guessing. How would you manage?"

"First morning the electric coffee maker wasn't working, and she'd be out of there," said Terry, and they all laughed.

"Have to get yourself some Italian snowshoes," said Elisabeth, her wit getting the better of her judgment.

There was more laughter. Fiona felt herself flush, her ability to talk herself down seriously compromised by sleeplessness and nerves and frustration. "Maybe you don't know me as well as you think you do," she said, her defensiveness growing.

The mood of the shop was not finely attuned to the subtleties of emotion. The laughter was a delightful and longed for break in the tension all around. Everyone was having fun except Fiona.

"Oh, I think we know you pretty well," said Elisabeth.

"Well enough to know this much," said Terry, grinning.

"Do you really think I couldn't?" asked Fiona, her eyes focused intently on the menu on the wall in front of her.

"Couldn't and wouldn't," said Terry definitively.

"Never in a million years," added Elisabeth. And then she added, unthinkingly, "I dare you."

The laughter broke around her like a wave as Fiona felt a rush of adrenaline. She slid off the stool and headed for the door.

"Leaving already?" asked Terry, still laughing.

"I accept," she said, affecting an air of lightness. "I accept the dare."

Everyone turned to look at her, but Fiona kept on moving. Elisabeth, suddenly alert to their miscalculation, called out. "Fiona, wait! You don't have to go! Don't be ridiculous."

Fiona raised her hand in acknowledgment without turning around. "I'll be back later," she said over her shoulder, and pushed through the door.

It was Roger's voice which answered. "Yeah. See you."

As the atmosphere of normality settled back over the shop, the men still chuckling, only Elisabeth was aware of what had just happened, and she sat glued to her seat, aghast at her own stupidity. It did not occur to her that Fiona might actually do anything rash, but she felt terrible at having misread her friend's state of mind. "Oh well," she thought to herself. "Let her cool off. Time enough to make amends." The men, utterly tone-deaf, continued their conversation, meandering on to other topics.

As the door closed behind Fiona, Terry's voice floated back to her from his seat at the counter. "Now you got some atmosphere in this place, you ought to think about replacing the lighting."

"It's been a rental for a few years now," the agent was speaking distractedly as she struggled with the front door lock.

"Might be a bit stale-smelling."

Marcy Landemeir was a perpetually youthful blonde whose perfume reminded Fiona of the cards inserted into department store bills. She was in her fifties, Fiona guessed, and wore a great deal of makeup, a red blazer, and a skirt that was just a little too short and a little too tight for anyone older than sixteen. She spoke, however, with the authority of someone who had been around the Island all her life, and gave the impression that her outer image belied a rather tough and intelligent interior.

The day had cleared, and the sunlight sparkled against the windows of the little house. It had a benevolent air about it, as if it were a character in a children's book, Fiona thought, sitting and waiting for the right person to come and make it happy. Fiona inwardly rolled her eyes at herself for this silly line of thought. Still, she couldn't help herself. It did have its own character. There was something, some personality about the little house that appealed to her.

Ablaze with indignation and angst, Fiona had left the coffee shop and headed directly to Northport and the ferry. It hadn't been a long wait; it was early enough in the season that they were still running hourly. The trip over had given her time to cool down, and as they landed, she was already planning her return. But she was hungry, so she decided to head up to the main crossroad. The Albatross might be closed for the season, but she knew several establishments where she could get a sandwich. Inevitably, she passed the little house on her way, and its beautiful proportions and that charming little personality struck Fiona anew. Might as well look at it, she thought to herself. Won't do any harm. But later. After lunch.

She'd had her hamburger and diet soda sitting at the bar, chatting with the proprietress, a native Islander. With more momentum than actual intention, she then headed down to the realtor's office, only a few doors away from the house. She didn't really expect much. She didn't even expect to find the realtor in. But she had been. And after a few moments of waiting while Marcy had made a brief call and closed up the office, the agent drove her SUV to the house, Fiona following behind in her own car.

The door finally let go, and Fiona followed Marcy into the front hall. She drew a breath, and was immediately struck by the smell. Stale did not begin to describe it. The air was thick with something both fishy and sweet, and a bit of sour milk added in. Fiona stopped breathing through her nose and remembered something from high school biology about smell molecules actually touching your brain cells. Eyes slightly wide, she turned to Marcy, who was busily opening a blind in the adjacent room, and seemed blessed with either no sense of smell or a heretofore undiscovered talent for the theater. "What is that smell?" Fiona gasped, almost fearing the reply. Surely the place was empty? No eccentric cat-lady had died unbeknownst?

Marcy continued opening drapes and blinds, sweeping through the room with unconcern. She spoke over her shoulder as she struggled with a stuck window. Despite her distress, Fiona made a mental note of all the sticking things in the house.

"It's probably the refrigerator," Marcy said. "The last renters must have left something in there and it was turned off. I just never thought to check. Tell you what, I'll open up the windows and air things out a bit, and you go on out back and look around the barn and garden. It's a little bit overgrown, but lovely."

Fiona did as she was told, and breathing as little as possible, moved rapidly through the ghost-green kitchen, unbolted the door, and stepped out onto the back porch, but not without noticing that the cabinets were the hand-built originals Terry had described.

"What the hell am I doing here?" she asked herself. "God-forsaken rat hole. Probably a dead body in the cellar somewhere." She took a breath of clean air, and then another. "You are too old to accept dares," she told herself, "as if you were ten. You can't afford a house; especially not a dump like this one."

She stood still, exhaling the stink from her nose and mouth and lungs, gratefully aware of the scent here of late roses and cut grass. Huge ancient hydrangeas encircled the porch, their green and white heads drooping heavily to the ground. There were lilies of the valley spreading unchecked from the beds, their bloom long finished, massive blue hostas, two sturdy apple trees heavy with fruit, and an enormous maple near the small, wood-framed barn at the back. It was a good-sized building, with, it appeared, a second story, and a diamond window overlooking the yard.

Fiona found herself drawn to the barn, and crossing the yard, she tentatively tried the latch on the door. Finding it open, she pushed it back, and looked in. Unlike the house, the shed was immaculately clean. It still held the sweet smell of hay, of animals long gone, and a faint whiff of gasoline, probably from the ancient lawn mower in the corner. Long shafts of sunlight slanted across the floor through the three large windows. There were two stalls, with gates and latches, each sharing a long trough. Simple wooden shelves, skillfully made, lined the rest of the wall, and there were hooks and nails where tools and ropes, and other necessities had once hung. Sunlight pierced the cracks between the planks in the ceiling, and Fiona noted a narrow wooden stair in the far corner.

Testing it first with only part of her weight, she climbed the steep steps—more ladder than stairway—holding the rope banister, and watching her feet. As she reached the top, she peered around, her head just barely above the floor. The loft was darker than below, having only the diamond window and its mate on either end, but at this time of day, the sun's angle was just beginning to appear at the edge of the western one, and a long shaft of light spread across the floor.

Fiona paused on the step, her chin resting on the floor as she took in the space. It felt like a child's hidden fortress. the kind of place you wish for when you are ten. Standing there, she remembered with exquisite clarity the sense of security and freedom of childhood summer nights: security in knowing that home was around the corner, the freedom to come and go, without schedule or expectations, wandering from boredom to adventure through the long lifetime between one school year and another. Fiona felt something within her roll over and click into place. She breathed deeply, and taking one long look around the loft, she slowly backed down the stair.

Feeling slightly dazed, she crossed the sunny yard, its grass nearly ankle high, and sat down on the porch steps. She could hear bumping and Marcy's footsteps on the wooden floors inside, probably cleaning out the refrigerator, poor woman. Fiona put her chin in her hand, and stared at the apple trees. She was startled when, ten minutes later, Marcy opened the door and called out to her.

"I think I got the worst of it taken care of. Would you believe someone left a whole chicken in there? Disgusting! Thank God I carry room freshener in the car."

Fiona noticed a fresh stain on Marcy's red blazer, and the smell of artificial apple and cinnamon in a sort of haze behind her.

"Do you want to come on in and look around now?" Marcy stood blocking the door as if she were expecting Fiona to bolt.

"What is the price, again?" Fiona asked. Marcy named the price in the brochure, and stood as if she were waiting to be struck. There was a pause, as Fiona gathered the momentum of some inner wave.

"Ok," she said finally. "Let's do this thing." And she stood up to shake Marcy's manicured, though slightly damp hand.

Chapter Six ⟡

After Fiona's precipitous departure from the coffee shop, Elisabeth had returned home with a gnawing sense of unease. She had tried to call Fiona several times, but cell signals being what they were on the peninsula, it was not particularly surprising when there was no response. She had left three messages, the first quite long, the second rather long, and the third a simple, "It's me, again." She had done all she felt she should, left it to Fiona to return the call, and went on with what turned out to be a busy day at the gallery, remembering only occasionally what was bothering her when the pace of visitors and phone calls slackened here and there.

It was after six when she finally locked the doors to the gallery and crossed the gravel path to the house. Rocco had run ahead, following a scent trail around the back where there was a field used for extra parking during openings. Elisabeth heard him bark three times, but it was otherwise peaceful, the comforting sounds of locusts, crickets, katydids, and birds all around. She rounded the corner to the porch, thinking again on the misunderstanding with Fiona that morning, and wondering if she should call one more time, when she noticed the figure seated on the porch bench by the door. Rocco was happily seated beside Roger, who was stroking the dog's head. Roger was dressed as usual, in jeans and a clean white T-shirt, his hair wet and combed straight back from his forehead. He was looking straight at Elisabeth, expectant, though not smiling.

Elisabeth ducked her head for a moment, smiled, and approached. "Hi, Roger," she said, her delight sounding in her voice. "Why didn't you come to the gallery?"

"It was quieter here," he said, still stroking Rocco's ears.

"Will you come in?" she asked, unlocking the door to the kitchen.

"I'd rather sit here," he paused. "If you don't mind."

Elisabeth, her heart beating fast, put her keys and things on the kitchen table, and then returned to the porch and sat down on a rather gaudily painted rocking chair. It was not her taste, reminding her unpleasantly of the brightly colored and expensive papier-mâché creatures often displayed at fashionable galleries. Elisabeth had never been sure if they were supposed to be a particular animal, or just some generic artsy species created expressly for socialites who hoped to be admired for their avant-garde insouciance, and, of course, their wealth.

Elisabeth had amused herself one summer by using the opportunity of a children's art class to have her group of first and second graders create their own such animals. The results had been so similar to the expensive gallery versions as to be indistinguishable. The gallery creatures were just another lamentable example of the emperor's new clothes phenomenon so common in art these days, Elisabeth thought, and she always found them—a view Fiona shared rather more contemptuously—a defining indicator of ostentation.

But the chair—noisy, yet still, at least, useful—had been a gift from its painter, and she had been obliged to display it. This was one of the disadvantages of living and working in the same place, she had thought at the time. You can't take something home and have it simply disappear. She consoled herself with the hope that it would wear faster outdoors.

Grateful to sit after a long day, her emotions roiling beneath the surface, Elisabeth rocked gently. Roger and Rocco sat together across from her, Rocco by now leaning his massive head against Roger's leg. They could all have been arranged for a portrait as they remained in this way for some time, each preserving a comforting silence, the sounds of the garden continuing around them, the darkness slowly gathering.

At last Roger stood up.

"Would you like to stay for dinner?" asked Elisabeth.

He shook his head. "I've got some work to do. Got to get back." He turned to the big dog now standing silently beside him and patted his head. "Bye Rocco." He looked at Elisabeth. "See you," he said.

Elisabeth wandered slowly back into the house and poured herself a glass of wine to drink while she fixed herself something to eat. She had always enjoyed the solitude of her house, and the comforting ritual of preparing dinner. But tonight, for the first time, the silence of the house echoed around her. Even Rocco seemed restless and ill at ease.

She wondered, briefly, what Fiona was doing.

Fiona was in a state of mixed shock and euphoria. She had been among the first on the ferry in the waning light of early evening, and had stood at the railing for the entire trip, looking back at the Island, and then at the wake of the boat as it chugged across the strait. She wished she could have moved in that night, and at the same time she wondered when she would begin to regret her hastiness. She was quite certain that she would. For the moment, however, she couldn't imagine it. Despite the smell, the house itself had been neat and rather cozy. And although the ad had anticipated the modern rage for remodeling, the house gave no impression of neglect apart from the sag of the front porch, and the need for some aesthetic updates. The banister, the mantels in the two fireplaces, the dining room, and the kitchen cupboards—although an unpleasant shade of green— were undamaged, and clearly made with skill and a fine sense of aesthetic balance. Fiona could see herself alone there, and it didn't fill her with dread, as it might have done, but with a deep sense of rightness, as if it were already home. If there were any ghosts, apart from the chicken carcass, they were surely benign.

The ferry engines shifted for the impending arrival on the mainland, and passengers began to return to their cars. Fiona took a last deep breath of the lake air, and turned from the railing. It was a long drive back to Ephraim, and for the first time, it didn't feel as if she were heading home, but leaving it. She turned on the ignition of the car, waited for the gates ahead to open and her turn to join the line of cars winding their way back to civilization. Her mind was filled with happy thoughts of paint colors and gardening, and a growing feeling of glee in anticipation of telling the others.

As so often happens in life, however, that particular joy did not play out as she had hoped. Elisabeth was not answering her phone—the signals, were, as usual, intermittent anyway—and Coffee was locked and dark, although, even in its desertion, the scent of coffee hovered protectively around it like a guardian spirit. Her own spirits undiminished, Fiona returned to her own small cottage and poured herself a celebratory glass of scotch. She was buying a house. Her first house.

After a frenzied series of phone calls to the owner, Marcy had announced that there would be no objections to Fiona's more or less immediate occupancy as tenant until the sale went through. Although this would be unheard-of in most places, things here were more casual and based on a simple trust in other people. Fiona had been in Door County long enough to find this unsurprising. Sipping her scotch and humming to herself, she began to assemble a list of necessities to bring along, and of tasks she would need to accomplish.

After he left Elisabeth's, Roger drove slowly back to Ephraim. He always drove slowly—"like a little old lady," Terry had once observed—and long lines of cars tended to build up behind him wherever he went on the Door. It was probably just as well that he didn't go any faster, since he was no more conscious of his actions than he was of his whereabouts when he drove. Capable, as he was, of a physicist's intense purpose and concentration, driving was another opportunity for Roger to think, and the more he thought, the more slowly he tended to drive. This was the case now, as his line of thought intensified, and his ancient Jeep dawdled along the narrow curving road.

By the time he'd reached the village, a long line of cars trailed behind him, some frustrated to the point of shouting within their cars, and others—mostly tourists—content to use the opportunity to gaze around them in wonder at the beauty of the scene.

As was the case with many of the Peninsula's villages, all built along the shoreline, a steep hill lined with woods descended into Ephraim. Before the descent, it was just possible to catch a glimpse of the white steeples and red roofs of the little town nestled against the bluffs on the other side of Eagle Harbor. At the bottom of the hill, at the entrance to the town, the harbor, on the left, was mostly hidden by lakeside cottages on thin slices of land not much deeper than the buildings themselves. With the exception of a small public beach, only tantalizing flashes of water could be seen. On the other side of the road were myriad small white buildings: shops and hotels and inns, most set back a bit from the road.

It wasn't until the road wrapped around the far edge of the harbor, a mile or so along, that the rest of the village came again into sight, its pristine nineteenth-century charm almost shocking in its purity. Up the steep bluffs to the right was the village proper, and the main road, curving around the harbor very close on its left, was the state road that led further north to Fish Creek, Sister Bay, Libertyville, Gill's Rock, and at the very tip of the peninsula, Northport, where the Washington Island Ferry docked.

It was here, along this road, that Coffee was located. Seemingly ideal in its positioning, it was, for Roger, an inconvenience to be so visible to the tourists whom he detested. Their business was both Coffee's lifeblood and the bane of Roger's existence. No one had ever dared to ask what had possessed Roger, with his philosophical eschewing of even the most minimal human interactions, to go into retail business. Fiona had frequently pondered Roger's suitability to the laboratory, where isolated and uninterrupted he would have been able to pursue his own idiosyncratic path. If asked, Roger himself might not have been able to answer the question. But he had come here, he had started the business, and it was there, a fait accompli. Like everything else he took on, he pursued it with a dogged persistence.

Tonight he turned into the parking lot next to Coffee utterly unaware—as usual—of the frustration and helpless anger he had left in his wake. The drivers of the cars behind him rolled their eyes to Heaven, breathed prayers of thanks, and accelerated a bit too rapidly in their eagerness to be gone. At least the first few did. The rest were reduced to slumping in their seats and seething as the ancient pale green Impala driven by an eighty-year-old farmer's widow halfway down the line of cars, continued on its steady pace toward home.

Roger's mind was on his evening's plans. Terry's comments about lighting, seemingly ignored, had been heard and deeply pondered. Roger had no qualms about working with electricity whatever. He figured he could install the track lighting he'd purchased earlier that day in plenty of time before the shop was scheduled to open tomorrow morning. Taking a moment to turn on some inspirational music, he pulled the boxes out of his car and got to work.

Chapter Seven

T he narrow straits that separated Door County from Washington Island had been known since the time of the Potawatomi as the place of death, so sudden and violent were its storms. Entire flotillas of canoes had perished here, and the spirits of those lost souls were said to wander still. The French explorers, including Robert de LaSalle, who had visited Washington Island, had called it Porte des Morts, the Door of the Dead, and the county took its name from this cheerful allusion. Death's Door was the common name for the straits, used so regularly that its meaning had been dulled to residents.

Fiona, however, found it best not to dwell on this particular piece of lore at the moment. The changing seasons brought unstable weather. It was raining off and on, thundering occasionally, and windy. She had never had a rough passage on the ferry, but those occasions were legendary. Regulars told tales of winter trips when sheets of ice covered the deck of the ferry, waves breaking over the bow to coat the windshields of the cars with an inch of ice to be scraped away on the other side. Rough seas and high waves were accepted as a fact of life by local people, but Fiona had not yet developed the sanguine view of a native, if, in fact, they were sanguine about these things. Today the water looked choppier than she had seen it from a ferry, so it was with a little trepidation that she squeezed her car into its designated place and pulled very hard on the handbrake.

Most people sat in their cars for the trip. A bit nervous, and feeling somehow safer out of the car, she passed the cabin on the cargo deck and followed some of the walk-on passengers up the narrow stairs to the enclosed main cabin with its upholstered benches and tables, and then, pulling her hood up over her hair, she mounted the outer steps to the observation deck. The rain had stopped for the moment, but the bench seats were wet, so she leaned against the railing. The wind bit against her, and she tightened the hood strings of her jacket. No one else had a taste for the weather, so she found herself quite alone, except for the big blond man in the pilothouse whose rear window was about even with her knees. He was engrossed in his task and did not appear to notice her, but Fiona was intrigued to see that he was writing.

Fiona was careful not to appear too nosy, fully aware that she was exactly that. Feeling that she could look without seeming to, Fiona was able to see that he had a spiral notebook filled with his handwriting. It didn't look like a ship's log. "But, what," she thought, "do I know about it?" She would have thought he'd have been busy reading charts or something marine-related. But then, she supposed, he probably had piloted this course thousands of times. In a few moments he was joined by another crewman, and she noticed that he tucked the notebook carefully away on a shelf in the corner before engaging with the others and performing his other duties.

The engines fired up, and even on the open deck in the wind, she could feel their pulse, like the heartbeat of the ferry. It was heartening, she thought, that the crew seemed unconcerned, and Fiona felt a moment of admiration and gratitude for the human ingenuity that made the engines and the ferry and the navigation systems they were all about to depend on, and for the valor and optimism of human beings who strove to conquer the natural world. It was something that mattered in the vastness of the universe. Oddly comforted, she turned her face toward the wind, and stood against the railing as the ferry made its way out of the harbor and turned northeast, toward the Island and home.

The sky had cleared, and it was sunset as Fiona found herself standing alone for the first time on her porch, the key in her hand. The house was not yet hers, but ownership was a formality now. She had possession, whatever papers were yet to be signed. With trepidation, she noted now the bounce of the porch floor, the curious angle of the storm door, and the small brown stain running along the ceiling's inner edge. Across the street at the Albatross, all was silent, and Fiona noticed now that she was ravenously hungry.

She had brought with her the mere rudiments of occupancy: a coffee pot, two mugs in case of company, an inflatable bed and bedding, several lamps, a flashlight, a small stool, and one book, *Meditations of Marcus Aurelius.* In her innocence her first goal had been to paint, but Terry's visit this afternoon had forced her to shift her priorities a bit: she was beginning to realize now that the most important piece of equipment she had brought along was her checkbook.

She had called him with her news, and feeling gleeful, had asked him if he could find time to look the place over for her. He had agreed cheerfully, and Fiona knew that it was as much out of curiosity as friendship. He arrived smiling in his ancient but meticulously maintained van, pulled a tool kit from the back, and stuffed a grubby yellow flashlight in his back pocket.

His mood had changed rather quickly. "This here is what you'd call a pig in a poke," said Terry. He was crouching on the dirt floor of the crawl space under Fiona's new house.

Fiona noted that he was not smiling.

"See that over there?" He ran the beam of his flashlight along the floor joists above his head. "See that? See how the floors are sagging up there? He moved the light down. "See those wooden posts? They're called piers. They are what's holding your house up. They're sitting right there on the dirt. No concrete. It's kind of amazing this place has been standing as long as it has." He flicked off the light and looked at Fiona. "You got an inspection contingency, right?"

Fiona hesitated.

Terry dropped his chin and looked at her over his spectacles. He spoke slowly. "You didn't put a contingency in, did you?"

Fiona looked at him and smiled weakly. There was a silence as they regarded each other, and Terry sighed the sigh of the master at his delinquent apprentice.

"Who'd you buy it from? Who's the agent?" Terry asked. "If there's no contingency—"

"Marcy Landemeier was the agent."

"Ah," said Terry. "Well, Marcy'd know better than to—" he

paused, interrupting himself. "Better get those papers out. Let's have a look at them."

It had been a humbling afternoon, with phone calls to Marcy, who made phone calls to the owner, who was unavailable, but who made his own phone calls later, with more calls from Marcy, who made calls to contractors, to inspectors, the bank, and probably the ferry line, thought Fiona, just to make sure they could handle the traffic.

Crouching on a black vinyl sofa in the realty office, she idly recalled the lobby of the hotel in Chicago, its lush silence and yellow damask, its carefully inattentive waiters, its scent of lilies and of luxury. In her mind she played over and over Champagne Man's crisp salute, and drinking burned coffee from a plastic mug with the logo of an insurance agent, she pondered the vagaries of fate.

Terry had finished some hours later, and Fiona had felt a note of panic as he tossed his tool bag into his truck. He was the last connection to the ordered routine of her life.

With his departure, she was cut adrift in an alien world. "Is there anything that doesn't need to be fixed?" she asked, feeling as if she were clinging to the arm of a departing protector.

"Well," said Terry, frowning as he thought about his answer, "the roof's probably ok." And with that, he said a cheerful goodbye and drove off to catch the late afternoon ferry.

Resignation had replaced Fiona's anxiety during the frantic activity of the afternoon. But now, alone and facing an empty house—standing on nothing but wooden piers and dirt—she felt the anxiety return and the need to replace the urge to flee with action. Like it or not, she told herself, she was committed, and the only thing to do now was to move forward. Hovering in her mind's eye was the look on Terry's face as he slowly shook his head, realizing he had failed to convince her to escape from the deal. Turning the key in the lock, she opened the door, and stepped across the threshold into her new house.

E lisabeth spent a quiet day at the gallery. There was little business on a weekday at this time of year, and it was a good opportunity to deal with the mundane realities of office work. She didn't mind these kinds of things. Elisabeth was a born organizer, and enjoyed the satisfaction of accounts that reconciled and papers that were neatly filed.

The gallery business was one of revenue ebbs and flows, and fortunately, Elisabeth's family trust neatly covered her lean times. While realizing how lucky she was, she did not take her circumstances for granted, but she had never had sufficient need to be able to fully appreciate the difference between the circumstances of her life, and those of most of her acquaintance. Fiona, she knew, lived hand-to-mouth, but she did not complain or seem to scrimp in any way. On the contrary, it seemed that when Fiona had money, she spent it cheerfully.

Elisabeth was frugal by nature, however, and except for occasional ventures into couture fashion, rarely spent unnecessarily. She lived comfortably but simply, drove an older car, and felt no sense of denial. She had traveled a great deal when she was younger, but no longer felt any particular urge to do so, preferring to stay where she was content, mingling with old friends for dinner or coffee, and happily lounging at home with the devoted Rocco at her feet.

She would have been fooling herself, however, if she had tried to ignore the growing longing she felt for companionship and love. She had, like most women, always intended to marry and have a family, but somehow, she had never met a man she had felt she could live with. She had fallen in love, briefly, with a wholly unsuitable academic in college, but their fundamental incompatibilities would have led to a lifetime of mutual misery, and the end of their romance, while painful at the time, had been a mercy. There had been others, but no one after that had truly captured her heart.

Living here in Door County limited the prospects of romance merely by the size of the population. The odds were simply against the likelihood of meeting a soulmate, however kind or decent or well-educated the general populace. Up until recently, Elisabeth had felt reconciled to this. She was not the kind of woman who would settle, and life with someone not wholly beloved was inconceivable. It was better to be alone.

It was early afternoon when Elisabeth reached a stopping place. She shut down the computer, turned out the lights, and locked the door of the gallery behind her. Calling cheerfully to Rocco, the two of them climbed into the car and headed down to Egg Harbor. Elisabeth was in the mood to cook, and Egg Harbor was her favorite place to buy groceries.

By the time she returned home it was approaching four o'clock, and the dreariness of the day had changed to blue sky and the red slanting light of an autumn afternoon. She found herself eagerly scanning the porch chairs as she pulled up, but they were empty. Disappointed, but still hopeful, she unloaded the car and carried her bags into the house. Rocco bounded around her, as enraptured to be home again as he had been to go in the car.

Elisabeth put on some music and hummed to herself as she put away the groceries and began her preparations for dinner. She was a gifted cook, and she enjoyed the process of cutting and chopping, sautéing and mixing. As dinner simmered on the stove, she set the table in the dining room, taking care to seem not to care too much, but nevertheless lighting two pairs of fat white candles, one set on the table and the other on the sideboard. She opened a bottle of wine, decanted it, and left it to breathe while she went outside on the porch to enjoy the evening, Rocco following to make his nightly explorations of the property.

After some time, he returned and settled with his head on Elisabeth's feet. They sat together, Elisabeth rocking, and Rocco dozing, as the light faded.

It was eight o'clock when Elisabeth went inside with Rocco and turned off the music. She poured herself a glass of wine, put away the uncooked vegetables, and fixed herself a plate of boeuf bourguignonne from the casserole on the stove. Carrying her dinner with her to the living room, she sat down by the fire to eat with her plate in her lap, the candles in the empty dining room still burning.

Rocco looked up at her, his intelligent face filled with love and worry, his ears moving with each new thought. After a moment, he laid his head down again on the rug, his big yellow eyes focused on Elisabeth's face, canine empathy resonating from deep within his blameless soul. His distress for his mistress notwithstanding, however, Rocco had a healthy sense of self-interest, and he was comforted by the knowledge that he would be dining well, and very soon.

If Fiona's goal was action, there was no shortage of things for her to do. She had decided to occupy the south bedroom on the second floor while she painted. It was the largest of the three rooms upstairs, with a bank of tall narrow windows, and a fireplace whose utility Fiona rather suspected was no more than aesthetic at this phase of its life. It was surrounded by red brick, with a wide mantel and dentil detailing. The walls of the room were white, but in need of a fresh coat of paint, and the wooden floors, though old, were in good enough condition. She tried peering up the flue to see if it was open, but all she could see was blackness. Something for another day.

Leaving a pile of her things in the front hall, she went up and quickly swept and mopped the floor in her new room, noting a bit nervously the number of spider webs. She inflated the bed and made it, and set up the small lamp on the wooden stool she had brought. As she worked, she noticed gaps between the toe moldings and the wall, the inevitable result of the settling of an old house. The thought of the house's settling was a sore point, but she refused to dwell on it at the moment. If she landed amid the rubble somewhere in the basement overnight. Well, so be it, she thought to herself. The house had stood for more than a century; it wasn't likely to collapse tonight.

Feeling satisfied upstairs, she returned downstairs to the kitchen and bathroom. As she opened drawers and cleaned the pantry shelves, it was increasingly obvious that the house had not been completely unoccupied. Evidence of mice was everywhere, and somewhat more profuse than she might have expected. Even after disinfecting every surface she could find with bleach, she did not feel it was an excess of caution to put all of her food in the refrigerator. She was not quite sure how she wanted to address the mouse problem, but she wasn't particularly happy about sharing her food with them.

Looking around with a sense of accomplishment, she mentally listed her next tasks. This wasn't so bad, she thought. Just some paint, really, and it would be completely charming. Optimism surged through her as she poured herself a glass of very nice scotch—another of the bare necessities brought from the mainland—and went out to sit on the porch. The sun was setting earlier now, and its last light slanted through the trees across the road. Fiona leaned against a column and sighed, feeling the warmth of the scotch suffuse her limbs.

She made herself a dinner of cheese, olives, and bread, eaten in a private picnic on the porch as the evening deepened. It had been a stressful day, and the prospect of painting tomorrow and the warm relaxation of the scotch made her think with pleasure of the clean, newly made bed waiting for her upstairs, the coziness of the little lamp, and the lure of her book.

As she entered the hallway, she felt rather than saw, something move out of the corner of her eye. Turning swiftly and instinctively, she scanned the hall and the entry to the main room, but she saw nothing there. Her own hair brushed her eyes, as she turned. Shrugging and smiling at herself, she went to wash her face, and then retreated gratefully to the sanctuary of the bedroom.

As she entered the room, she had again the sensation of movement at the edge of her vision. Again she turned, but there was nothing. Used to living alone, Fiona would not have described herself as jittery, but there was a certain edge to spending the first night somewhere new, she told herself. She would get used to it soon enough.

Lying against the fresh, white pillowcases, she settled back to read one of her favorite books. It was a source of comfort to find that the anxieties and pleasures of her own life were neither new nor uniquely hers. To contemplate the immediacy and humanity of someone who had lived nearly two millennia before-helped Fiona to have a calmer view of herself in the universe. She had, of course, read other diaries and biographies, but she always found them strangely sad and discouraging when the protagonists inevitably died in the end. *Meditations*, on the other hand, comforted her. "The first rule is to keep an untroubled spirit. The second is to look things in the face and know them for what they are," she read.

"I live in the wilderness," thought Fiona. "I am vulnerable to stupid ideas. My footings are on bare dirt."

Wrapped in the silence of her reading, a sound began gnawing at her consciousness. Pausing, she frowned as she realized that what she heard *was* gnawing. More of a crunching, really. Fiona put down her book and listened. The sound, which appeared to be coming from somewhere just above her ears, could not have been produced by any mouse. No, she told herself. These were the crunchings of something with a much larger jaw

Fiona sat up straighter in bed. This, she had to admit to herself, was unsettling. There was clearly something there, in the wall. "You can't look things in the face if they're on the other side of the wall," she thought grimly. The crunching stopped when she moved. Barely breathing, Fiona waited, listening for movement. After a pause of a minute or so, the crunching began again. There it was, yes, in the wall. And it was definitely not a mouse. The crunching was accompanied by what could only be described as cracking. This was not mere gnawing away on something as a recreational activity. No. This was serious chewing. Eating, perhaps.

Fiona sat thinking. She wasn't frightened. Animals, she felt, were less frightening than insects, and far less frightening than people. On the other hand, she was acutely aware of the, well, precariousness wasn't the right word, she told herself, but the, perhaps, vulnerability of the house's structural underpinnings. It wouldn't do to have something chewing away on the beams. Bad enough that the pilings or whatever they were called, were sitting on plain dirt. No, clearly this was a situation she could not allow to continue. This was a matter of some urgency. She stirred uncomfortably as the crunching continued with an air of business as usual.

But what should she do? There was no one to call in the middle of the night—exterminators probably did not make emergency calls—at least not on Washington Island. How could she get through the night? Assuming that she could actually sleep through such a racket—and it was pretty loud, she thought—would it be some kind of moral failing on her part to just pretend it wasn't there for now and to deal with it in the morning? More than likely, whoever was in there chewing had been doing it for some time before she, Fiona, had appeared on the scene. What harm was there in just leaving it for the night? "Face things as they are," she said to herself.

But it was disquieting—both literally and figuratively—to sit idle while some creature sat on the other side of the wall busily eating away the rafters. Fully aware of the futility of her actions, she reached out and pounded her fist on the wall from which the sound was emanating. Three times, she pounded. The crunching stopped. Was this, she wondered, a stoic's approach?

In her mind's eye, a large glittering-eyed creature sat back on its hind feet and stared at the wall, just as Fiona sat up in her clean white bed, staring from the other side. A minute passed, possibly two. And then, with what might have been a shrug of resignation from the chewer, the crunching began again. Again, Fiona pounded on the wall, and again, the crunching stopped. But it was a much shorter time before it began again.

Now thoroughly awake and alert, Fiona pounded a third time. This time the crunching stopped for, perhaps, thirty seconds before it started again. The situation was escalating, she thought. Visions of herself, barefoot and armed with a broom, came to her mind, and possibly to the mind of her invisible adversary. Just as she had resigned herself to retrieving the broom from the kitchen, the crunching stopped and was replaced with the sound of scrabbling. Clearly the creature was on the move, looking for a quieter place to dine, or gnaw, or whatever it was up to.

"Out of sight, out of mind," seemed to fit here. This was a problem, she told herself, she could address in the morning. After five minutes or so of tense waiting, silence reigned. Settling herself back into her pillows, Fiona began again the calm progression of Marcus Aurelius's observations. Sighing, she reached for her glass and a final sip of scotch before finishing the page and turning out the light. Outside, there was no sound of traffic. Only the waves of the lake, a short walk away, and the slow, resolute singing of the season's last crickets. She felt a deep inner calm descending, of the kind she felt while floating at School House Beach.

Drifting off to sleep, Fiona was walking along a long hallway lined with old paintings. It was a pleasant place, if a bit dusty, and there was a stream of yellow light shining through each of the many doors along the passage. She longed to see what was in the rooms, but each time she meant to turn toward one, she found that she wasn't quite near enough to it and had to continue walking. In this manner, she continued down the hall, and yet, not down the hall, trying repeatedly to reach the beams of light, where, she felt sure, she would see a sunlit ocean. As she tried for the third time to reach one of the doors, she felt something gently brush her face. In her dream, a small bird was flying near her head. It seemed to be circling around her, its soft wings touching her skin as it passed.

Suddenly she was awake and sitting straight up in bed. It was completely dark in the room. There was no golden light, but something had moved near her face. Fiona sat dead still, trying to calm herself against a rising panic. "It's nothing," she told herself, "Only a dream." She consciously adjusted her breathing to long, deep inhalations. "There's nothing there." Gradually her heartbeat slowed.

Then she felt it again. Nothing touched her, but the soft rush of air as something flew just past her head. Fiona uttered a small scream in spite of herself, and hurled herself toward the lamp by the side of the bed. Instead of turning it on, she knocked over the small stool, sending the lamp crashing to the floor, where the scotch glass shattered into a thousand pieces. Alcoholic fumes permeated the air. An odd clicking noise filled the room.

She felt again the soft rush of air. Fiona heard someone yelling and realized it was herself. Following the only instinct she had to draw upon, she pulled the covers over her head and lay there, breathing hard, thinking many thoughts. "Next steps?" She asked herself aloud. "Ok. Next steps. Analysis: I am barefoot, in the dark, with shattered glass everywhere and something flying around my head. And now I appear to be talking to myself."

Still keeping her head covered, she tried to locate her cell phone from somewhere around her pillow. At least if she opened it, she would have some light. Locating it at last, her heart once again pounding, Fiona slowly emerged from under the covers, turned on the phone, and shone the blue light onto the floor. She needed shoes first.

One arm over her head holding the blankets for protection, Fiona lay on her stomach and hung over the edge of the bed using the phone as a flashlight. She felt gingerly for her shoes, hoping they weren't full of broken glass. Finding them at last, she shook them upside down as well as she could, hoped there were no lingering shards, and sat up, her head still under the sheets as if they were a tent. She slipped on her shoes with trembling hands. "Now," she said, with a sense of resolution.

Throwing off the covers, she stood from the opposite side of the bed. There was no overhead light, so she needed to get to the hall, where she could flip on the switch. Crouching, as if under enemy fire, Fiona ran toward the door and into the hall. She slammed the bedroom door shut behind her and leaned against it breathing hard, like the heroine in a melodrama. "Why," she asked herself, "are you panting? Geesh."

Collecting herself, she found the switch and flipped on the light. A dreary glow infused the atmosphere that reminded her of film noir. In the deeper part of her mind, where we observe ourselves as if from a long distance while doing other things, Fiona made a mental note to scour the house for compact florescent bulbs and remove them.

Suddenly she felt something fly past her face. She jumped and screamed again, briefly, and then mentally castigated herself. Taking a deep breath, she calmed herself and looked around. Above her head, around the edges of the ten- foot ceilings, a small brown bat flew frantically in circles around the room. She heard again the unfamiliar clicking noise, and realized suddenly that it was coming from the bat.

Fiona had seen bats before, but never indoors. As a Wisconsinite she had come to appreciate their value in mosquito consumption, but it was appreciation from a distance. One didn't contemplate close personal relationships with them. She slid down the door and sat on the floor, watching the small creature's rapid circling overhead as it clicked incessantly. She hadn't known that bats made this particular sound, either. And, in any case, what was she going to do about this?

Fiona recalled stories from the men at the coffee shop, using tennis rackets and brooms to kill errant bats. This approach did not appeal to Fiona. For some reason, there was something pathetic and frightened about the little creature that aroused sympathy rather than animus. After all, they were just small furry mammals with wings and bad teeth, she told herself. In any case, the bat clearly was displeased by the circumstances as much as she was. But, she wondered, how many were there? Just this one? Or a colony of them somewhere in the attic?

She watched the bat above her, still circling. But behind the door she could hear, quite distinctly, the rapid series of clicks that she had heard a moment before. Fiona frowned. The bat seemed to respond in another blast of clicks. Suddenly light dawned. No longer frightened, she stood up and opened the door. The hall bat swept into the bedroom clicking, and then, in only a moment, two bats flew into the hallway, one larger than the other, but identically colored, and the sounds of clicking filled the air.

Feeling oddly delighted, Fiona sat down again, and watched as the mother and baby swirled together above her head. After a few moments, they disappeared into the darkened and empty back bedroom.

Mentally balancing the risks of more bats flying in than out, Fiona nevertheless followed them in, and, somehow no longer concerned about their flying around her head, crossed the room to open the top of the window where there was no screen. She stepped back against the corner of the door to watch. In only a matter of the briefest time, they located the opening, and clicking rapidly together, they flew out into the night air. Fiona closed the window, and stood there for a moment, assessing what was left of her mental resources.

Without bothering to find her bathrobe, she went downstairs to retrieve the bottle of scotch. Returning to the bedroom with a flashlight—about which she felt incredibly smug for having packed—Fiona discovered, to her delight, that the lamp was unbroken. Ignoring the shards of broken scotch glass, she righted the table and the lamp, and got into bed from the other side. Picking up her book, now slightly wet around the edges, the scotch bottle nestled firmly against her side, she thumbed a bit stickily through the pages to find her place. She sighed and settled back into her pillows.

Across the room, an earnest crunching began. Fiona pulled the stopper from the bottle, took a long swallow of scotch, and turned the page.

"Do the things external which fall upon thee distract thee?" she read. "Give thyself time to learn something new and good, and cease to be whirled around."

"Well," she said to herself, "At least I've got the whirling part covered." She nestled the stopped scotch bottle against her side and turned the page.

Chapter Eight ✣

F iona woke to the dawn's first tentative bird call, and rolled over to cover her head. The insistent singing of the birds, combined with a long habit of early rising, however, led her soon to sit up and take in her surroundings. A sticky and aromatic pool of broken glass lent something of the air of the corner barroom to the atmosphere, but aside from that, the first shafts of sunlight streamed in from one east window, and the white room shone golden in its glow. More birds joined the chorus, a multiplicity of squirrels chattered, and the lake waves, sounding slow and gentle now, broke against the beach down the block. Mercifully, she thought, nothing gnawed. At least, not audibly, she corrected herself.

It had been a long night. Each time she fell asleep, the crunching had begun again, and her intermittent and increasingly violent poundings had apparently been received as a mere addition to the regular environment. Nothing worth concerning one's gnawing about.

Unwilling to encounter any more of the house's other inhabitants until fully awake, she lay in bed taking a personal inventory. The slightly sick feeling in the pit of her stomach had diminished but still lurked in the background. "What," she asked herself yet again, "have I done?" Bats, clearly multiple mice— and something much larger than a mouse—and God knew what else she would find, all cavorting freely around the place. How would she ever begin to stake a claim among so much competition? She rolled out of bed, uncharacteristically and immediately putting on her shoes—after first checking carefully that they were unoccupied—and descended the stairs as loudly as possible, hoping to give fair warning of her presence.

More shafts of light shone through the kitchen windows, and the simple appeal of the room surprised and comforted her. In that moment, her anxiety about her purchase vanished, and she experienced again the sense of belonging which had impelled her to this ("harebrained" as she had mentally labeled it) decision in the first place.

Feeling unaccountably cheerful, Fiona began to plan her day. It was strange how, in the bright light of morning, the night's happenings seemed dreamlike and far away, as if they'd happened in another world or another lifetime, and were no longer terribly important. But the broken glass and spilled scotch—very expensive scotch, she thought later, as she swept, then mopped the floor— were concrete evidence that she had not been dreaming.

When she had finished cleaning up the night's debris, Fiona sat down to look through one of the seven phone books which had accumulated in the house over a remarkably short period of time. There were, apparently, no exterminators on Washington Island, which she found something of a relief. She had to admit to herself that the idea of killing an animal went against her nature. She couldn't help feeling that she was the interloper here, not It—whatever It was. Since Terry's ominous warning about the foundation, though, the fragility of the house had loomed large in her mind, and she knew she had to do something. Perhaps

someone nearby could help her cope with her unwanted roommate. She would ask next time she went to the hardware store.

Elisabeth decided that it was time to take matters into hand.
She had allowed herself to drift along, but it was time she let
Roger know that she was more than a passive recipient of his
visits. She needed to make sure he knew that she was interested.

After several cups of coffee on the porch, she took a deep
breath and made the call. Roger had no cell phone, only the
land line at Coffee. But where else would he be in the morning?
She still hadn't quite decided what she would say. She would figure it out as she went. A few miles away in Ephraim, the phone
began to ring. Elisabeth took another deep breath. Three rings,
five rings, eight. Roger did not have anything as newfangled as
an answering machine. Disappointed, she hung up the phone.
Time, she thought, for a distraction.

When Elisabeth called, Fiona found herself wheedling as if
she were a child wanting a puppy. "Oh, come on, Lizzie. I want
you to see it."

"Fiona, I think you're crazy. What possessed you to do such
a thing? Did you have to actually buy it?"

Fiona listened good-naturedly, doodling swirling tornadoes
and small houses being swept up in them, as she sat at the little
kitchen table that had been left in the house.

"I recall you saying that only crazed hermits would live
up there. It's completely cut off from the rest of the world, you

said—especially in the winter, you said. Not a single fashion boutique, and you'd have to wear a parka and snow boots, you said, and there's nothing but ice and snow. And where will you get your scotch?" she paused for breath.

"Exactly how is ice and snow and cold any different here than in Ephraim?" Fiona asked, reasonably, if in contradiction to her own previously stated position. "Besides, did you ever hear of the internet? I've already found the greatest boots—very chic and very warm--and a great down parka." She paused. "And they do have scotch. I checked."

Elisabeth took a breath and tried a different approach. "It didn't even pass inspection. The roof could fall in on you during the night."

"It's not the roof. It's the foundation." Fiona heard Elisabeth sigh. "Did I tell you that the Post Office is for sale?"

There was silence on the other end.

"All right. I can see you need someone up there with some sense. I'll be on the noon ferry."

Fiona hung up the phone and danced across the kitchen to pour herself another cup of coffee.

"Well," thought Elisabeth to herself, "there's your distraction."

Roger regarded the results of his work with satisfaction. A series of lighting tracks stretched the length of the counter space and concentrated pools of golden light on the newly hung photos across the wall. There were more lights than there were photographs, and he wasn't completely convinced that the lighting should be focused on the counter itself, where customers' heads would create shadows on their cups. But that, he thought to himself, was a problem to be solved. He looked around the shop with a critical eye. It would be better if there were some interesting thing behind the counter for the lights to shine on. But aside from the menu, there wasn't much else.

Roger frowned. It wasn't quite right. Atmospherics were not his strong suit, he knew. He needed the advice of someone else. He needed inspiration. A spontaneous memory of Elisabeth's most recent visit to the shop came to his mind. She had looked around as she contemplated the color for the first time, and remarked upon an empty length of wall. "That's where the case for local crafts should go," she had said with a curious sidelong smile, looking at him from under her long lashes. "Tourists seem to expect that at a coffee shop." Roger had felt his heart stop. It had not occurred to him that she was teasing. On the contrary, the idea seemed perfectly plausible to him. This, he felt, was an idea he should pursue.

Muttering dire warnings of fallen roofs and broken pipes, twisted ankles from breaking through the porch floors, and the need for exorcisms, or at least some good counseling, Elisabeth arrived a few minutes after the noon ferry had landed. Fiona had been waiting for her on the porch, and she came

down to help carry in Elisabeth's things. Rocco greeted Fiona
joyfully, and Fiona hugged Elisabeth, who then put her hands
on Fiona's shoulders to look into her eyes.

"I hope you know what you're doing," she said, shaking her
head and smiling.

"Me, too," said Fiona.

Together, they unloaded a small overnight bag, a large duffel bag containing another inflatable bed and linens, and a box
filled with paintbrushes, rollers, and other painting equipment.
They all went into the house together, Rocco's intense curiosity
about this new place only slightly greater than Elisabeth's.

"Isn't it perfect?" Fiona asked a short time later. They were
sitting at the kitchen table on two uneven stools they'd found in
the barn (Fiona decided that it must be her lot in life to drink
coffee on wobbly stools) drinking coffee from the only two mugs
in the house. Rocco lay at their feet, having satisfied himself by
thoroughly investigating every room. There were many smells
here which had interested him, and he was tired now, although
not yet completely satisfied that he was the master of all who
resided in this place.

Elisabeth looked around the kitchen thoughtfully. "Well,
not perfect, exactly, but maybe not as bad as I had thought. I like
the light in this room. It feels cozy and warm—despite this awful
green. What do you plan to tackle first?"

"Well, I suppose I should do something about the bats,"
Fiona said musingly. "Probably after that the porch floor."

"Bats?" Elisabeth put her cup of coffee down and stared at
Fiona across the table. "You have bats?"

Rocco shifted uneasily at the tone of her voice and looked at their faces to discern what was happening.

"I did," Fiona said firmly. "At least two. Although I'm guessing that where there are two, there are probably more."

"And I suppose you couldn't have told me this before inviting me to sleep here? And what are you going to do about it?"

"Well, what does one do about bats, really?" Fiona asked.

"One hires an exterminator, is what one does. Honestly, Fiona, what are you thinking?"

Fiona thought about that. She had found the little ears of the baby bat endearing, and felt an empathy for its frantic mother. Like a small flying puppy, she thought.

Were bats endangered? she wondered. She thought she remembered reading something somewhere about the danger of extinction for some particular species. But that was probably in South America or New Zealand or something, and not applicable to Washington Island bats. "I think I might get a dog," she said, her foot touching Rocco's warm ribs. "But only someone Rocco really liked."

"You'd better get one who eats bats," Elisabeth said. "I'm not sleeping here until those things are gone."

"Don't be ridiculous." Fiona stood up briskly and carried the coffee things to the sink. "Let's go to the hardware store and look at paint colors. We can check the board to see if there are any puppies."

Rocco stood up and stretched. He had heard the word "go" and was ready.

Elisabeth sighed and brought her cup to the sink. "All right. But let's do the dishes first. I'll wash. You stand guard against flying mammals."

"Don't worry, I'll just wave the dish towel around your head."

"Great," said Elisabeth. "Then let's get out of here."

Chapter Nine

Roger was later than he had planned to be, and there were very few places left to park. The guys in the orange vests were signaling dully, if a bit irritably, toward the rows in the furthest reaches of the lot, and Roger guessed that there were fewer than fifty places left as he pulled into the space he'd been pointed toward. Never having been to an event like this, he was unprepared for the volume of the crowd. Shrugging to himself, he locked the car and joined the crowds walking into the Green Bay Convention Center.

Roger joined the stream of people entering the convention center. It was a crowd of mostly women, and a few men with looks of resignation on their faces. Not being a sports fan, Roger found that crowds and the mechanisms of large public events were alien to his experience. He was bemused by the masses and puzzled at first at what to do, but found his way to the ticket line and followed the crowds to the entry door.

Cheerful pink T-shirted women stood at the entrances, surrounded by buckets of cut flowers, collecting tickets and handing out roses. Roger allowed himself to be funneled toward a line and handed over his ticket, receiving in exchange his rose and a bright pink card. The ticket lady saw his furrowed brow, and thinking that it was something other than his usual expression, took pity on him, ignoring the press of incoming visitors.

"This is your CraftVenture Card. You take it to each of the vendors on the list and have them sign in the space, like this, see?" she asked him kindly. "And then when you've completed the list you get a gift bag." She smiled upon him and slapped a sticker with a pink bow on his fleece jacket.

"It's for breast cancer awareness," she said, and before he could respond, had turned smilingly to the next person.

The flow of humanity pushed him toward the floor of the convention.

Holding his rose in one hand and his pink card in the other Roger stood on the edges of the crowd. Enormous pink and purple banners proclaiming "Wisconsin CraftVenture" were everywhere; bunches of fuchsia and pink Mylar balloons were bobbing over the doors to the exhibit halls. Women of all shapes and sizes surged past him, talking unceasingly to one another, all seemingly delighted and certain of their direction. The cavernous space was chilly at this time of day, and there was a smell of popcorn in the air, and perhaps a whiff of coffee and something greasy on a griddle.

When Roger didn't know something, he looked it up. So confronted with the unknown world of crafts, he fell upon his habits of research. When his on-line searches revealed an upcoming crafts fair in Green Bay, he had, in his surly innocence, assumed that this would be the answer to his dilemma. Roger didn't do crafts. He didn't know anyone who did crafts. He was fairly certain that he didn't want to know anyone who did crafts. But Roger had made the mistake of conflating the hand-thrown-ceramic-coffee-mug kind of craft with the make-a-scrapbook-of-your-granddaughter's-life kind of craft. The distinction for any woman was clear and unmistakable. But Roger was in alien territory; subtle distinctions were not part of his philosophy. In his world, facts were facts. Ions were ions. A craft was a craft.

Frowning, Roger studied his CraftVenture Card. An MIT-trained scientist, Roger found himself unclear as to the procedure. A more sensitive or emotionally attuned man might have thrown up his hands and raced for the nearest exit. Roger, however, was generally immune to environmental intangibles, and was therefore unfazed by his surroundings. He had come to this thing to learn about crafts, and he would therefore stay and learn about crafts.

A woman in a lavender sweatshirt jostled him accidently. "Excuse me!" she said, and went on with her nonstop stream of conversation.

The loudspeaker cut through the din of female voices, all raised to make themselves heard. "Ladies, don't forget to complete your CraftVenture card! Gift bags only go to the first five hundred visitors!"

Roger looked again at his card. The first vendor on the list was something called Pure Romance. Looking up, he saw the booth besieged by women, all holding their CraftVenture cards aloft. Roger was nothing if not competitive. If this was a contest, then he would win. But clearly, he needed a strategy if he were to complete this challenge. Instinctively acting on his contrarian nature, he decided to follow the list in reverse.

Elisabeth watched Fiona all day for signs of madness, but was forced to come to the conclusion that she was at least no crazier than usual. Although Fiona's utter lack of practicality did not bode well for her long-term survival on the Island, Elisabeth felt, she could always leave if things got too bad. Assuming, of course, that her stubbornness wouldn't override her judgment.

That day they had played more than worked, finding paint swatches, going back and forth over colors—all shades of white with poetic names—making multiple trips back to the hardware store for things they had forgotten and inevitably being side-tracked there by the attractive nonessentials of equipping a new household. They had gone out for lunch, set up Elisabeth's bed, gone for a walk, and shopped for the necessities of a nice dinner.

Elisabeth was pleasantly distracted and managed to think of Roger only every half hour or so. She did not discuss him with Fiona, nor did Fiona ask any questions. But the situation gnawed at her. Although she had not admitted this to herself, Elisabeth's anxiety was fed by a deep suspicion that Roger was up to something. She spent a great deal of mental energy trying not to contemplate the idea that was pushing its way toward the surface: Roger's improvements to the shop and his odd behavior were perfectly explicable if he were preparing Coffee for sale. Maybe what she had thought was newly acknowledged affection had been his odd way of telling her good-bye. Firmly taking control of her emotions, Elisabeth pushed these thoughts away no matter how often they reappeared.

Fiona, meanwhile, basked in Elisabeth's companionship, her appreciation enhanced by awareness of her impending loneliness.

Rocco followed wherever they went with the focused attention that was his profound expression of love. He was a shepherd, and his job was to be with his flock. Like all intelligent creatures, the fulfillment of his purpose filled him with contentment. Besides, there was always the prospect of ice cream. He could be patient.

They were on their third trip of the day to the hardware store, looking for a particular size of screw to repair a broken drawer in the hall linen closet. With more hope than understanding, they walked up and down the fasteners aisle, waiting for Tom to finish with another customer.

"Have you thought of naming the house?" Elisabeth asked as they idly opened little plastic storage drawers. "I notice that a number of people have done that here."

"I've thought of it," said Fiona. But I've come to the conclusion that unless you're a native or absolutely everyone does it, it just seems pretentious. What's the difference between a wood screw and a metal screw?" she asked, frowning.

"They have different threads."

"Ah," said Fiona, unenlightened, and closed the drawer she was looking in. "Besides," she added after a moment, opening another drawer, "every name I come up with—if it isn't unutterably cloying—sounds like either a cemetery or an insane asylum."

"That could work," Elisabeth said brightly.

Fiona looked at her from the corner of her eye and threw a box of picture hangers into their basket.

The next name on the list was PrettyPurse. Roger stepped forward to the pretty young woman at the booth, whose bright red hair had an oddly purple sheen in the light. The sign behind her offered free purse analysis. What, he wondered, could that possibly mean? Did they test them for water resilience or fireproofing? How could they conduct an analysis without doing damage to the material? He didn't pay attention to fashion, but he had gathered from overheard conversations between Elisabeth and Fiona that women paid a lot of money for their purses. Silently and unsmiling, he handed her his CraftVenture Card.

"Don't you want an analysis?" she asked teasingly as she stamped his card in the designated place. Fortunately, it was a purely rhetorical question, so she did not pause for Roger's response. "We can tell you what kind of person you are by what you have in your purse. I mean, I know you don't have one, but I bet I can tell something about you by what you have in your pocket!" She smiled again at him.

Roger frowned and pursed his lips. Slowly, as if at the point of a gun, he emptied the pockets of his jeans and down jacket, scowling in his most endearing fashion.

"You can put it all right here!" said the red-haired woman, indicating a hot pink tray on her display table.

Warily, as if something were about to attack him, Roger put his belongings on the tray.

"Well, let me see!" she said playfully, looking at the wad of keys, miscellaneous coins, the chocolate wrapper, the pencil stub with the carved end, the wood screw he needed to match, and several weeks' worth of crumpled receipts from gas stations and ATMs. "I can see at once that you're the strong silent type!

Not a man for joking around, either! You see what you want and go right for it." Undeterred by his expression, she looked up at him from under her lashes, just as Elisabeth had done. "I'll bet the woman in your life has no doubts about your intentions!"

A low sound emanated from Roger which might have been words.

Undaunted, she continued. "Now you just gather up your things, and I'm going to give you a little something for her." She handed him a little pink card with elaborate laser cut edges. She seemed to speak in exclamation points, as if her own enthusiasm could be transferred to her listener. "You tell her she can use this card for twenty percent off on anything we sell! Or you can choose a gift for her! Our website is right there on the card! She'll just love it!"

She smiled brightly at him, but Roger, his brows furrowed, simply shoved his belongings back into his pockets, snatched the CraftVenture card, and moved off. Instinctively he knew that neither Fiona nor Elisabeth would be moved by a gift from PrettyPurse.

The woman's cheery farewell receded into the noise of the crowd. Roger checked his list for the next stop. It was becoming clear to him that this event was a waste of his time, but possibly the coffee booth would be of interest.

It had been a full afternoon of painting. Fiona and Elisabeth were seated in the kitchen with their coffee. Fiona was making a list for another trip to the hardware store—"the Mercantile," as it was known on the Island—while Elisabeth ruefully examined the effects of paint on her nails. The telephone rang, and Fiona got up to answer.

It was a longish conversation, and as she sipped her coffee, Elisabeth found her gaze wandering around the room to the built-in china cupboard on the other side, which still needed to be cleaned out. It was expertly carved with the kind of craftsmanship she supposed was of another century. Clusters of grapes and leaves on the vine curled around the upper corners. The perfectly dovetailed door frames, and—judging from their luster—solid brass pulls and hinges could not be hidden by the years of grime that had accumulated. The wood was unpainted, but thick dust, some rather magnificent cobwebs, and a couple of cracked and unmatched dishes remained from the previous occupancy.

Just as her mind was shifting to the interesting question of tonight's dinner, a small movement caught her eye. Elisabeth peered toward the cupboard. Surely not, she thought, even as an instinctive shiver of fright shook her. She looked again. Was it real? No. She froze, and drew a deep breath.

Never had she seen a spider this big inside a house. It was poised, frozen like a Halloween toy, upon a piece of flowered china. Its thick black body was easily two inches in diameter, and its long legs were covered in black hair. For a moment, Elisabeth caught the blue gleam in its eyes. She shivered again.

Fiona, engrossed in her conversation, did not, at first notice Elisabeth's frantic pantomime. Fiona frowned, shook her head, and turned her back on Elisabeth as she struggled to concentrate on what she was hearing from the other end. Elisabeth, with an increasing sense of urgency—who could sleep with such a creature in the house?—tapped Fiona again on the arm, and pointed toward the cupboard. Fiona glanced toward the cupboard, rolled her eyes at Elisabeth, and continued to talk. She gave her friend a look of school-teacherly disapproval. It wasn't like Elisabeth to play juvenile tricks. Must be the result of all those brothers.

At last, Fiona hung up the phone and turned to Elisabeth with her hands on her hips. "Really, Liz?" she asked, the disapproval dripping from her voice. "That was the editor of that new journal I'm writing the article for. He had to hunt me down, and was none too pleased about it. The least you could do—"

Elisabeth interrupted her. "It's no joke, Fiona. Take a look."

"Ha. Ha," said Fiona, and turned to get herself another cup of coffee.

Elisabeth grabbed her arm.

Fiona turned her gaze toward the cupboard. There is no way that spider could be real, she thought, as she studied it. It was like something in a cartoon. As she stared, the spider moved. In one voice, Elisabeth and Fiona screamed and jumped back toward the table.

There was silence.

"Ok, ok, ok. Let's be calm," said Fiona. "We're bigger. And presumably smarter. We just need to figure out what to squash it with."

"What if it jumps?" asked Elisabeth, her voice sounding squeaky.

"Jumps?" asked Fiona, skeptically, finding it helpful to calm her nerves with utterly false bravado.

"Yes. Spiders jump. Tarantulas can."

"It's not a tarantula," said Fiona, not sounding particularly sure of herself. "There are no tarantulas in Wisconsin. The spiders to be wary of around here are Brown Recluses. They are very small and unremarkable looking." She paused. "And I doubt it can jump. Very far," she added, quietly, almost to herself.

Elisabeth did not look convinced.

"Look," said Fiona reasonably, "We have to kill this thing, or neither of us will get any sleep tonight. We need a plan. Otherwise, it will run into a corner somewhere and lurk in the dark." This complete about-face from her previous views of non-extermination she managed without a twinge of conscience. The spider, she felt, must go.

The two women were silent for a moment as they each imagined a night in the house, in the dark, with the spider. Bats seemed infinitely preferable.

"Ok," said Elisabeth. "What, then?"

Fiona pondered. They had paint rollers and brushes, and a hammer, but nothing that might be considered a useful weapon. And the location inside the cabinet eliminated the effectiveness of mere bludgeoning. The spider would move quickly, probably into a corner and down the tiny cracks where the wood joined, never to be seen again. Until, of course, it was seen again, probably in the dark. "Any ideas?" she asked Elisabeth.

Elisabeth was silent, thinking. "Do you have any of that spray bleach left? We could stun it with spray, first, then squash it."

Fiona looked at her friend with respect. "Splendid," she said.

Armed with the bleach and the hammer—there being no

better squashing tool at hand—they approached the cupboard.

Still holding a somewhat bedraggled rose, Roger had completed the last three booths on the list. His pink carry bag bulged with coupons and literature. He had sampled chocolate in the shapes of flowers, had a chiropractic analysis and chair massage, and participated in a demonstration of cookie cutting. He had tasted flavored instant coffees—for those moments of escape from the demands of the day, he had been told—had his hands rubbed with scented lotions, his aura analyzed, and accepted a free greeting card. A display of multicolored hangers had baffled him, and he had won a free closet organizing consultation.

Making his way toward the gift bag table, Roger joined the line. He could see the empty cartons lined behind the booth. The stock was dwindling, and the last of the gift bags were meticulously set out in rows behind the display table. He reached the booth and surrendering his CraftVenture card with a certain reluctance, redeemed it for his gift bag. It was the second to the last one. Next time, he thought to himself, he would have to move faster. It had been the chair massage that had set him back.

He stood looking around, trying to get his bearings in the cavernous confusion of the convention center so he could head out from the same door he'd entered. At midday the crowd was thicker than ever, and the noise of the PA system, the music from different booths, and the ubiquitous chatter of thousands of female voices combined in a hubbub that had begun to wear on even Roger's iron nerves. He had definitely had enough. The memory of the last peaceful evening with Elisabeth came unbidden to his mind, and he looked forward to seeing her on his way back up the peninsula from Green Bay.

Newly motivated, he was moving determinedly in the direction of the door through an aisle of food purveyors, when he saw it. Roger stood transfixed. The noise of the crowds receded from his awareness as he gazed upon the centerpiece of one of the vendors' booths. An enormous coffee machine of copper and brass rose like a monolith behind the bustling servers, its Italian name gleaming proudly along the top. He watched as the servers expertly pulled the levers to release the intensely aromatic coffee into cups, twisting nozzles of steam into pitchers of milk, their hands protected by pristine white cloths. The smell of the coffee filled his senses, so rich and powerful as to make his own coffee—which was excellent—seem weak and anemic by comparison. He watched for some five minutes, jostled by the crowds, before he got into line. What, he wondered to himself as he looked up at the offerings, was a macchiato?

The next trip to the hardware store had a smaller list than usual; however, Fiona found it necessary to inquire about someone who could replace broken glass. "Is it a window?" asked Tom, his pen poised above paper covered with various calculations. Elisabeth and Fiona exchanged glances.

"Well, no," said Fiona. "A cupboard door. We had a little incident."

Tom jotted down a name and number and handed it to her.

"Thanks," said Fiona, and went to see if there was Borax in the laundry aisle. She had learned that it was toxic to spiders.

Chapter Ten ✳

Despite dire warnings of the results should she encounter any wildlife—and the spider incident notwithstanding, since, as Fiona very sensibly remarked, you could have spiders anywhere—Elisabeth stayed for three days without the sighting of a mouse or bat, and the anonymous gnawing creature remained mysteriously silent.

They took down the faded and outdated curtains and washed the grimy windows, and laughing and cursing, ripped out the dated and filthy blue carpeting on the stairs and in one of the bedrooms. With the help of good food, long conversations, wine, and late nights, together they were able to paint the kitchen and all its cupboards, the living room, and one bedroom. Elisabeth was particularly good at cutting in, and she worked the edges of the rooms and the moldings, while Fiona filled in the large spaces with a roller. They also succeeded in slaying three of the spiders they now referred to as "zip code spiders," since they were large enough to have their own postal designations. On the sighting of the fourth, Elisabeth had calmly retrieved the spray bleach—now considered an indispensable household commodity—and the hammer, and dispatched the creature herself.

By the time Elisabeth was ready to return to the gallery, the newly painted rooms of the little house gleamed with white walls and sparkling windows. Elisabeth promised to bring potted mums for the porch when she returned. No puppy listings had been found at the hardware store, however, so Elisabeth determined that Rocco should stay behind and keep an eye on things.

"Don't be silly," argued Fiona. "Do you think I can't stay alone here?"

"No, of course, not," lied Elisabeth. "But he'll be good company until I get back. And besides, you'd be doing me a favor. I have to leave to meet my brothers at the end of the week. School has started, and Patty and her family are gone back to Chicago, so I'd have to take him to that kennel in Sturgeon Bay. They are good to him, but Rocco pines there. He would be much happier here with you, and, frankly, you could use another living thing around here." Elisabeth paused as she realized what she had said. "An intentional one, I mean. And, don't forget, I'm going to need you to take him when my brother's new baby comes in December. I've promised I'd come and stay with the girls."

She departed with a kiss and a wave, and Fiona and Rocco walked together back into the little house. It seemed desperately quiet. Fiona put her hand on Rocco's head, and he sighed, leaning against her leg. "It's ok, Rocco," she told him softly. But Rocco could sense the anxiety that buzzed around Fiona, and he nuzzled his head closer to comfort her.

Shaking off her mood, Fiona turned her attention to the day's task of patching some small holes and cracks. She had already planned her work, but as so often happens in renovation projects, she had no sooner begun than she realized that she didn't have the one thing she needed, in this case, an extension cord for the palm sander she was using. Why, she wondered, did appliances and tools these days have such short cords. Who sands only things less than twenty inches from the wall? Irritably, she changed out of her paint clothes—which were too disgraceful to contemplate even a trip to a lightly trafficked hardware store—instructed Rocco to mind the house, and headed up the road to the general store.

Elisabeth's drive home from the ferry required that she pass Coffee on the way. With some effort, she convinced herself not to stop in. The gallery had been closed for three days, and she would be leaving again soon for an even longer time away. There would be mail to open, and messages to answer, and all the minor but necessary details of life that accumulated when one was away. The powerful inner discipline that governed her life would not allow her to put pleasure first, but she couldn't help glancing at the shop as she went by. The parking lot was empty. Everything was dark. A sharp point of anguish pinched her heart.

Fiona, easily distracted at the best of times, and now a regular customer, found herself wandering the aisles of the hardware section with rather more interest than usual. Perhaps because they reminded her of Saturday afternoons with her father, Fiona was always comforted by a hardware store; by the smell of metal things and fertilizers, by the shiny screws and nails in their bins, the beautiful order of the place, the mysterious tools for things she didn't know how to do, and perhaps by the atmosphere of nonchalant competence which permeated the place. She needed light bulbs, she remembered, and a smaller Phillips head screwdriver, and probably some finer sandpaper, while she was at it. In the process she also found a fire extinguisher and another flashlight.

It was while she was examining the smoke alarms, and pondering whether she really needed one which talked in two languages, or whether the standard non-talking kind would do, that she was joined in the aisle by another customer, who seemed interested in cabling. He looked familiar, but since Fiona knew hardly anyone on the Island, she was briefly puzzled. He was a tall, broad man, with blond hair and rosy cheeks, probably in his forties. He looked up, with that sense people have of being looked at, and smiled at her. The light dawned.

"You're the ferry captain," she blurted out.

His smile broadened, and he nodded. "Ver Palsson," he said, putting out an enormous hand. "Everyone calls me Pali."

Fiona introduced herself.

"You're a writer, aren't you?" he asked.

Fiona, although accustomed to small town life in Ephraim, was nevertheless astonished at how quickly information about her had circulated. "That's true," she admitted.

"I write a bit myself," he said more quietly, as if he were confessing a personal vice.

"What do you write?" asked Fiona, remembering the notebook she'd seen on the ferry.

The look on his face suggested an inner conflict. The truth was that Ver Palsson wanted desperately to talk to someone about writing, even though this was a perfect stranger, and he was sensitive to the teasing he often received. He was no coward, however. He paused only briefly before answering. "Poetry," he said.

Fiona was reminded of someone saying somewhere that if you wrote poetry as a teenager, you were an average adolescent, but if you write poetry at forty, you're a poet. "I don't know many poets," she said, smiling. She tried to think whether she had actually known any at all since college.

"Me either," he said sheepishly. Fiona knew better than to ask whether he'd been published.

"I haven't really published anything," he said, as if reading her thoughts. "I guess I'd rather not know if it's lousy."

Fiona laughed. "I know exactly what you mean," she said. "That's why I have friends read things over for me. They're harder on me than any critic."

"It's hard to find friends who will tell you the truth," he said. "They don't want to hurt your feelings."

Fiona smiled. "I guess you have nicer friends than I do."

He smiled back. "Could be. You can find out for yourself. Some of them are going down to Nelson's for All-You-Can-Eat Spaghetti tonight. You should come down. It's good to know your neighbors—and my wife says it's good to have someone else do the cooking."

Fiona laughed. "That's especially true when you've been spackling all day. I would love to."

Fiona left the hardware store feeling rather like a sixth grader who'd been asked to sit with the cool kids at lunch. It would be fun to have Island friends, and especially fun to know the ferry captain, who would doubtless have stories to tell.

Fiona worked steadily all day, stopping only to eat a piece of cheese and bread while standing over the kitchen sink. She did, however, allow time after she had cleaned herself up to take Rocco for a long walk. He was joyful, as always, and his good spirits made Fiona happy, too. After a necessarily circuitous route they ended up, as they almost always did, on the beach, and Rocco didn't find it too cold to swim. Fiona threw sticks for him, and breathed in the air.

Nelson's, home of the Saturday night All-You-Can-Eat Spaghetti Dinner, had been built sometime around the turn of the twentieth century. It was a large barn-like structure covered in white clapboard, with an old-fashioned painted sign. Like most old buildings, it was built close to the road, and there was only room for one line of parked cars along the front of its old porch. Big old trees hung over the building and its tiny parking lot. On busy nights—which was almost every night—latecomers parked along the road, and the line of cars stretched along both sides of the street for some distance. There were two entrances, dating, Fiona guessed, to the times when nice women didn't go into bars. One opened directly into the bar, and the other to the dining room. On warm nights, only the screen doors stood between patrons and the mosquitoes. As she got out of her car, the sounds of conversation, laughter, and television sports drifted out from the building.

She found Pali, his wife Nika, and three other couples already seated at the bar. Pali was a big cheerful man in his forties, handsome, with blond hair and cheeks rosy from the weather. One of several captains employed by the ferry line, he was a native Islander. He had gone away to the marines as a young man, but married a local girl, and after they had been away for a few years, they felt the Island call them home.

His wife was slightly younger, tiny and blonde, too. They were both of Icelandic descent, as so many Islanders were. Open and cheerful, kindly but not so much as to be dull, Fiona found them a delightful pair. Like so many Islanders, too, they could turn their hands to almost anything, and their self-sufficiency filled Fiona with awe. She found herself wondering how it was that this hearty, hardworking, outdoors man had come to writing poetry. "Not," she told herself privately, "that there's anything wrong with that." But she would have to ask him, and to find time to talk to him about his work. She didn't expect that it would be great poetry, but she admired his commitment to his writing.

They introduced Fiona to their friends. There was Lucas, a carpenter, and his wife, Amy, who was a teacher at the school. There was Erik, who also worked for the ferry line, and his wife Kristine, who was raising their children and working part-time at the Island library; and Mark and Diana, whose marital status was vague, but who worked together in some kind of internet business, whose details Fiona was also vague about.

The bar was dark and narrow, with the original ornate woodwork. Black-and-white photos from the Island's history covered the wall opposite the bartender, showing horses and wagons, enormous snow drifts, the island's high school sports teams, and Model-T Fords parked alongside ten- or twelve- foot snow drifts. On the ceiling were hundreds of dollar bills, attached by thumbtacks. Fiona found herself pondering how this had come about, and what kind of beer-induced bar game had led to it.

The group had been waiting for her, and they chatted

around the bar for only a few minutes before moving into the dining room. Erik and Lucas stopped for a moment to talk with someone else at the bar, but it wasn't long before everyone was seated around two tables that the waitress had pushed together for them.

The food was the kind that Fiona remembered from her grandmother's house. She imagined that her old Chicago friends would have turned up their noses because the spaghetti—the "pasta" as they would have insisted—was not *al dente*. But it was a homemade sauce, with seasoned meatballs and garlic bread, and there was a big salad bar with cottage cheese and pickles and bean salad and pickled beets. It was delicious and comforting, and from an era long gone. And everyone was happy, not harping on the service or critiquing the food. They all seemed to know the waitress, a young and beautiful girl with an Eastern European accent, and they joked with her and chatted with her as a peer, not—as was so often the case in Chicago—as if she were a menial.

It was this kind of homey atmosphere and food, combined with the remoteness of the place, which no doubt limited the Island's appeal to Chicago tourists and to their money. And while Fiona was secretly pleased by this fact, she was nevertheless acutely aware of the tenuous economy of everyone who lived there, and how much every single visitor mattered. She listened to the conversation of her companions, in which was embedded an implication of many different jobs and tight budgets.

But everyone at the table had come to—or stayed—on the Island by choice, and they seemed, if not content, which implied, Fiona thought, some complacency, then cheerful, willing, and uncomplaining. They had chosen to be here, and this, she had to admit, Fiona shared with them all.

Upon her return to the gallery and more consistent cell signals, it became apparent that Roger had not called once during the three days she had been at Fiona's. Elisabeth churned with disappointment. Everyone knew that Roger had no known romantic history. Perhaps he had changed his mind. Perhaps he hadn't intended romance at all. Perhaps he was only being friendly and she had misread him. Or maybe he really was moving. Elisabeth found the suspense of not knowing nearly unbearable. And besides, she missed him.

Elisabeth's hand trembled slightly as she dialed the phone. She hit the wrong number and had to hang up and try again three separate times before she finally succeeded in getting it right.

She had argued with herself about what to do all day before she finally determined on the proper course of action. She would call and invite him to dinner. It would be simple and it would be definitive. She could not bear another evening of waiting and hoping. It was too stressful. She had to know. Making this call was a confirmation to herself, and even knowing this, she surprised herself with the intensity of her emotions.

Roger's laconic hello caught her off-guard in her ruminations. If he had merely answered, "What?" it would have had the same tone.

"Roger?" Elisabeth's voice had become slightly breathless in her nervousness. "It's Elisabeth."

"What's wrong?"

Elisabeth felt even more flustered than before. "Wrong? What's wrong? Nothing. Nothing's wrong. I just wanted to ask you if you wanted to come for dinner." There. She had said it.

"I can't."

"You can't?"

"No. I can't."

He didn't sound disappointed or regretful or wistful. He sounded like, well, like Roger, brusque and businesslike. There was no trace of warmth or friendliness in his voice. Elisabeth was in no state to feel comforted by the ordinariness of his demeanor. Instead, she was suddenly overwhelmed with jealousy. He was seeing someone else, she thought to herself. He doesn't want to tell me. Her mind raced over the single women who could possibly be the candidates for Roger's attentions.

If her usual common sense had prevailed, Elisabeth would have been well aware that this was unlikely, bordering on the impossible. She had, however, reached that stage of besottedness in which the beloved's attractions become so magnified that he appears to have become irresistible to hoards of rivals. Her heart pounded as she clutched the phone. She paced the kitchen.

The pause on the line had lengthened to some seconds. "Hello?" said Elisabeth, wondering whether they had lost the connection.

"Hello," said Roger. There was another pause.

Elisabeth wanted to ask where he was, but it seemed presumptuous. If he had wanted her to know, wouldn't he have told her? "Ok, well, I guess I'll see you another time," Elisabeth said, hoping he would prolong the conversation.

"Ok," said Roger, and hung up.

Elisabeth looked at the phone in her hand, and sat with a thud on a kitchen chair. Her heart was still pounding, and she was breathing heavily. She put her hands out on the table to steady herself. Had she been there, Fiona would have been astonished to witness it for the first time in her experience, but Elisabeth—cool, calm, imperturbable, and gracious Elisabeth— was hopping mad.

R oger looked at his phone for a moment before placing it in the gray plastic bin next to his jacket. Both hands and his full attention were required to navigate the intricacies of airport security. He bent and began to unlace his sneakers.

Chapter Eleven

iona sat idly at the kitchen table, drinking her coffee
and watching the mouse that sat up on its back feet
like a dog, in the middle of the floor. Rocco lay at her
feet, but it was clear that he had noticed the mouse.
He looked from Fiona to the mouse, his ears pricked and shifted with his eyes watching with all his attention, but waiting for
Fiona to give him the permission he so earnestly desired. The
mouse seemed utterly unconcerned at their presence, merely
interested in the smell of toast, it seemed. Fiona sympathized,
and couldn't help but notice, with a certain tenderness, the little
feet ("little lizard feet"—was that Roethke, she wondered?) and
the dainty movements of its head. Voices not her own chastised
her for her complacency, but Fiona was unable to rouse herself
into an anti-mouse state. A sense of common cause with a fellow
(non-spider) creature was her dominant emotion, and so she sat
regarding the mouse, as the mouse, rather deliberately, Fiona
thought, avoided regarding her. The mouse had the air of someone with a routine—clearly one established long before Fiona
had arrived on the scene. So, in a sort of companionable silence,
Fiona drank her coffee and contemplated the day to come while
the mouse delicately washed its face and hands and perhaps
contemplated its own.

Despite the long list she had of things to do, and the up-

coming housewarming she was planning, Fiona was restless and
unfocused. She missed Elisabeth's company, and the silence of
the house was beginning to weigh on her. She had not yet met
her immediate neighbor, who was apparently away from the Island on a trip of some kind. She was a single woman, Fiona had
been led to understand, who put a great deal of time and energy
into her house and garden. Fiona looked forward to her return,
and to the prospect of, if not friendship, then at least a civil acquaintance. The loneliness of life on the Island was beginning
to nudge at her a bit.

It was a beautiful day, and warm for September. Fiona had
spent very little time acquainting herself with the Island. She
had no idea what lay beyond the inn on the coastal road, and,
given the dire tales of winter she had heard, there would not be
many more beautiful days before the snow came. Leaving her
house to Rocco and her new companion, she decided to rent a
bike at the general store, and go exploring.

She was standing by the door when the proprietor unlocked
the store for the day's business. He was, Fiona thought, surprisingly young, midtwenties at most. She had expected that the
majority of the residents here would be elderly—although she
was unable to explain to herself why this should be so. He was at-
tired like many of his generation in slim jeans and a close-fitting
T-shirt over his muscular body. A set of small studs decorated
one ear, and an elaborate tattoo which looked like a tree with
eyes, covered most of his arm. Fiona had never ascertained the
etiquette—if there was any—of observing people's tattoos. Was
it rude to look? Surely it had been chosen to be decorative, and
people were intended to see it? Or were strangers supposed to

avert their eyes? Was it like the visible underwear, so fashionable now, which one was apparently supposed to accept without noticing, as a matter of routine? The young man moved with an easy confidence that would have looked at home in the midst of SoHo.

"Good morning," she said smiling. "I'm Fiona. I just moved in up the road."

He gave her a beautiful warm smile and reached out his hand. "Tom," he said. "The Goeden place, right?" he asked. "I was wondering when you'd turn up. Got the whole Island talking about you."

He had blue-gray eyes which seemed to be expressing an opinion even though he said nothing. She felt, rather than heard, his evaluation of her. She felt old.

He put the packages he'd been carrying on the counter as he spoke. "How's the old place?"

Fiona tipped her head on one side considering how much to tell. She was not interested in being the subject of stories of the greenhorn woman who bought the Goeden place. Not, she realized, that anything she did or said could actually stop those stories. "Mmm, guess I've got my work cut out for me," she said lightly. "It's nice here, though. Quiet."

"Not always. Wait until a busload comes through. Fall color." He nodded toward the merchandise. "I'm running a little late this morning, if you want to look around, I'll get things opened up."

Fiona drifted off toward the hardware section while he moved around the store, turning on lights and getting ready to open.

"Where you from?" he asked, conversationally, when they

met again at the register.

Fiona knew the right answer. "Well, most recently from Ephraim, and before that Milwaukee, and before that Chicago…she paused. "Depends on how far back you want to go. My friend and I have always loved to come up here to School House Beach, and I developed an affection for the Island. It's so peaceful here." She smiled at him. "Thought I'd rent a bike today and get to know my way around a bit." She dumped her armful of odds and ends on the counter, and began to rummage in her bag for her wallet.

Obligingly, the young man rang up her sale and helped her fill out the rental paperwork. When they'd finished, he took her out to choose from among the line of brand-new bikes lined up along the front of the store.

"Need a map? Know where you're headed?"

"I thought I'd head out along the harbor road, toward the dunes, and explore a little." Fiona gathered up her packages and her helmet, checking her shorts pocket for her sunglasses.

"Well watch out for Piggy. He lives up along that road."

"Piggy?" Fiona asked, pausing in her preparations to leave.

"Piggy," he said, firmly. "You'll know him when you see him. He's one of those dogs who looks as if he had his face kicked in and has never gotten over it. He's not big, but he makes up for it. He runs loose up there around the point. If he comes after you, put the bike between you and him and back away, because he'll rip your leg right off." Tom grinned at her. Fiona studied him for a moment to see if he were joking.

"Seriously?" she asked, a small smile on her face.

"Seriously," he said his eyes meeting hers. "I'll bet he bites a couple of tourists every year, and then I end up having to go get the bikes." He smiled at her and shrugged, and turned to get back to his work. "Have a nice ride," he said without irony.

Fiona thanked him, somewhat dubiously, and Tom turned and went cheerfully back inside to finish unpacking his merchandise. Fiona wheeled the bike into the parking lot, and stood for a moment, gathering her energies. It was a beautiful morning, crisp and sunny, the sky that intense deep blue peculiar to autumn. It was bound to warm up, but not too much. She took a deep breath of air and pushed off.

It had been a long time since she had ridden a bike, but Fiona found herself remembering the long summers of her childhood, riding her purple Schwinn bike around the dirt roads of her rural neighborhood. She felt an almost physical ache of longing for the warm nights, the idleness, the freedom of long unscheduled days, the opportunities to build things and play games, the gentle swooping arcs she had made then, and was making now, sweeping from one side of the empty road to the other. She coasted down a gentle hill feeling the same kind of joy as a wheeling nighthawk must, circling in the air. She felt childish in the best sense; free, uninhibited, and simply joyful.

She thought with pleasurable anticipation of her two ham sandwiches, her apple, her cookies, and her thermos of lemonade. She drew in the scent of the fields along the road, spicy with Queen Anne's Lace and chicory, and something unidentifiable which smelled like fall. She noticed the gravel along the edge of the road, and recognized the calls of a blue jay, a red-winged blackbird, a phoebe, and a meadow lark. She felt proud to know their songs. She wasn't so much a city girl as Terry thought.

The signs to the sand dunes led to a crowded car park, and Fiona dutifully left her bike on the rack before unloading her backpack and following the wooded path to the lake. No one stole things on Washington Island. There was no need to lock it. Mosquitoes buzzed and whined around her face, and she slapped at them impatiently, moving as quickly as she could over the already sandy, hilly path.

As she crested the hill, the dunes spread out before her. She was surprised at how small they were, and how swampy the water was. It annoyed her that the shallows were allowed to grow over with cattails and grasses, and that the beaches were not kept clear. But she sighed, and finding a soft place in the sand, slightly shielded from the wind in the lee of a dune, she spread out her blanket, took out her book, and made a nest for herself in the warm sand. There was something about the fall air, the water, and her solitude, and Fiona had a hard time concentrating on her reading. She felt past emotions and experiences wash over her like smells on a breeze—again, that almost physical sensation of nostalgia. She remembered faces and moods, the texture of grass against her cheek, the sharp intake of air into her lungs after a whole day swimming, the sound of the beach from underwater.

Fiona found herself thinking of friends she hadn't thought of or seen in twenty years, friends she had played with every day until dinner and every night until dusk. They had walked to school together, been in the same classes, and known each other's secrets. She thought of the navy windbreakers which had been her unfailing summer uniform—best because you could hide under shrubberies at night without being seen during capture the flag—and the importance of the right sneakers. She was walking along the dusty lane in her mind's eye, heading home after a day of summer play, singing to herself, when she fell asleep.

Fiona woke to the sound of shrieking gulls, feeling cold and rather stiff. She tried, at first, to warm herself by shifting in the sand, but the dampness had crept through, and she sat up, instead, wrapping her hooded sweatshirt around her shoulders. She rummaged in her bag and found her lunch, and ate both her ham sandwiches hungrily and without chewing. She ate two cookies, letting them melt in her mouth in a slow buttery way, but saved the rest with the apple, and drank part of the lemonade, even though it made her feel colder. She wished she had brought coffee, and she longed for the company of Rocco's massive presence—his furry warmth and his companionship. She had left him in the yard sleeping in the sun and looked forward to going with him for a walk. What would she do without him when he went back home?

After lunch, she tried to read for a while, but it was too cold to concentrate. She decided it was time to go home. Fiona considered her day's inactivity. There was some inner chart she kept which made any day spent outdoors—even while sleeping—count more fully in her life than days spent otherwise. She could not account for this perspective, but it was a strong underpinning of her values—one she only occasionally became conscious of. By this reckoning, despite her dozing, the day had been a success, and she felt a deep sense of belonging to the world as she shook out her towel, and stuffed it and her book and leftovers into her backpack. It wasn't a long ride home at all. Just enough to wake her up. She trekked up the hill to the wooded path, turned to look once more at the lake, and plunged into the mosquito-infested woods.

Fiona pedaled dreamily back toward home, her mind on the curious combinations of dreams and memory she had felt. It was warmer away from the lake, and there was very little traffic, since, after all, it was a Thursday afternoon. And, of course, it was Washington Island.

She was startled out of her reverie by a shrill, chattering bark coming from the farmhouse to her left. Before she could fully register what was happening, a small, ugly dog who looked as if his face had been flattened, came hurtling toward her across the yard and down to the road. He had no leash, but a collar. His muscular barrel-shaped body and stubby legs did not seem to impede his ability to move in any way. Snarling, snorting, and drooling, his small black eyes filled with malice, his bark shrill, angry, and piercing, he made a streak toward Fiona with evil in his heart.

Fiona continued to pedal at a slightly faster pace, but he was extraordinarily fast and coming from an angle, and she quickly realized that the animal would soon quite literally be nipping at her heels. She swung her left leg over the bike, dismounting horseback-style, and found herself face-to-face with genuine menace. Fiona adored dogs of every variety, but at this moment she found herself wondering if this creature could possibly be a member of the same species. Piggy lunged toward her.

Remembering Tom's warning, her heart pounding, Fiona kept the bike between her and this snarling mass of fur and spit. The little beast took hold of the spokes on her bike, bending them with an aggression so determined that Fiona began to wonder if she could hold him off. It was like something out of a nightmare. She pivoted with the bike, keeping her eye on Piggy as he tried to get at her through and around it. She was wondering what she could lay her hands on to use as a club when she heard a woman's voice, shrill with saccharine affection, calling from the direction of the house.

"Piggy! Oh Piggy-dog! Where are yooouuuu?" she called.

Piggy-dog, unaffected by the sound of his mistress's voice, bit through a spoke, and Fiona heard the soft hissing of air as he punctured the rear tire.

"Oh there you are Piggy! You bad doggie! Don't worry, ma'am. He won't hurt you!" This last was addressed to Fiona, who was too busy holding Piggy off with an increasingly diminished steel frame and tires, to answer. Feeling the heat of Piggy's breath on her shins, she was unconvinced of his benign intentions, and given the circumstances, she felt unequal to a discussion about the relative import of Piggy's life goals. She gripped the bike frame and held it like a chair before a lion, and with the same intensity of purpose.

The woman stood, rather stupidly, Fiona thought later, at the edge of the grass and called to her dog. "Piggy! Piggy-dog, you come away from there! Come away now!"

Her admonishments did no good whatsoever because Piggy, having punctured the rear tire, was now working devilishly at ripping apart the front. Fiona had a sense of unreality as she staved off the dog's bites, wondering whether this woman would simply stand in her yard and watch as the dog ripped her legs off. At the moment of her despair, there was the sound of a truck

engine, and Fiona recognized instantly the distinctive rumble
of the blue pickup she had seen many times around the Island.
The driver, a woman, hit the horn a few times in a fruitless attempt to distract the dog, and drove up just behind and to the
left of Fiona and her bicycle, which she now held before her like
Agamemnon with his shield.

"Forget the bike! Quick! Get in!" The driver had pushed
the passenger door open, and idled the truck nearby. Without
a moment of hesitation, Fiona dropped the bike, leapt into the
seat, and slammed the door shut. The driver gunned the engine,
and they took off in a cloud of dust.

Piggy's owner stood looking after them for a moment, and
then crossed into the street to fetch her dog. "Poor Piggy-wiggy,"
she said. She knelt down to the slavering dog and kissed him on
the cheek.

As they sped off, Fiona took a quick silent inventory. Bike
gone, limbs intact, heart racing. She turned to look at her res-
cuer, who was driving the narrow country road with the lack of
attention born of long familiarity. Here was that rare thing: a
Washington Island native. Her simple forthrightness was sup-
plemented with a survival instinct which suffered no fool and
minced no words. Not entirely sympathetic, but undoubtedly
honest. She was, Fiona felt, a force to be reckoned with.

"You all right?" she asked, looking briefly over at Fiona to as-
sess her condition. "I'm Nancy Iverssen. Live up near the School
House. If you don't mind my saying so, you look like you could
use a drink. My place isn't far."

Gratefully, Fiona agreed, pleased to have the conversation,
if nothing else. They drove the few miles in silence. Nancy

drove up the long bumpy drive to the farmstead, and parked the truck by the door.

"Come on in. Place is a mess, but there's no one but me, so I only have to please myself."

Nancy led the way into her kitchen, tossed her keys and her broad-brimmed hat on the counter, and immediately began to busy herself around the kitchen. Fiona followed her in, and stood for a moment taking in the room. It was probably not the original kitchen of the century-old farm house, but its pine cabinets and yellowed fir tree wallpaper dated from a bygone era. A pile of mail and newspapers on one counter and a coffee cup in the white enamel sink were the only mess that she could see. The room was otherwise neat, suffering only from decades of daily use. There was an ambient smell of wood smoke around Nancy, and Fiona recognized that this would be inevitable, since the house, too, had the smell, reminiscent of summer camp and family vacations.

"Have a seat," said Nancy, indicating the pair of battered armchairs pulled up to a stone fireplace on one side of the room. "What do you want? I have gin, whiskey, and brandy. Also beer, if you prefer that."

"I think whiskey is called for," said Fiona, sinking into a chair.

"Soda?" asked Nancy, turning briefly to look at Fiona.

"No thanks. I'll take it neat."

Nancy was a brisk woman of, perhaps, sixty, Fiona guessed. She was lean and tall, and wore hiking boots, jeans, and a work shirt with a blue fleece vest thrown over it; her graying hair was pulled back into a ponytail. Her brown eyes had a look of intelligence, and her face and hands were tanned and wrinkled from an outdoor life. She moved with the speed and ease of a much younger woman, her energy fairly vibrating as she poured and served a whiskey for Fiona and one for herself.

"Skal," she said, using the Icelandic toast, as she settled herself in the chair opposite Fiona and raised her glass.

"Thanks for the rescue," said Fiona, returning the gesture. "I'm not quite sure what I would have done if you hadn't come along when you did."

"Probably be nothing but a pile of bones by now, in some corner of the Shoesmith's property. That dog is a damned nuisance." Nancy took a swallow of her drink and put her glass down. Fiona had the impression that sitting was not something that Nancy did much.

"Can't think why no one's done anything about him. Terrorizes the entire Island. Although," she mused, "Marilyn Shoesmith is not the brightest bulb, and I suppose it's out of some misplaced sensitivity to her feelings." She stood, knelt in front of the fireplace, and began to crumple newspapers for the fire. "You're not the first biker he's gone after. There'll be a lawsuit one of these days."

"Well, I can't say I wasn't warned. Tom at the hardware store told me about him this morning. But I was daydreaming and had forgotten all about it—and frankly, I didn't take it that seriously."

"Well, now you know."

"I'm worrying about the bike," Fiona said, watching with admiration as Nancy built the fire with a skill bordering on artistry.

"One of Tom's?"

Fiona nodded.

"No problem," Nancy said briskly. "We can stop by there when I run you home. Isn't the first time. Won't be the last."

"Can't be good for the bike rental business," observed Fiona, her mood beginning to melt into the whiskey.

"Well, it's not as if tourists run off and write to the *New Yorker* about it." Nancy lit the fire and returned to her chair with an air of accomplishment.

"That's better," she said. "Starting to feel the autumn in the air." Nancy settled back into her chair and picked up her glass again. "So what possessed you to buy the old Goeden place?"

With difficulty, Elisabeth decided to refocus her mind. Her trip to her brother's to stay with her little nieces would be fun, and completely distracting. She was haunted, though, by a sense of loss. She had never wanted a life alone, but here she was, unmarried, in her thirties, and clearly unable to attract a man. Her life, her comfortable home, her gallery, usually so completely right, suddenly felt small, limited, and inadequate. Like herself, she thought. Just like herself.

Her assistant at the gallery greeted her with enthusiasm on her return, but secretly thought that the trip had not done her employer much good. Elisabeth looked pale and listless, and seemed distant and distracted. It wasn't like Elisabeth, whose tranquil good humor always set the mood for any room she was in.

Elisabeth, for her part, turned to the operation of the gallery and the preparations for her time away not as the usual pleasures, but as heavy obligations, joyless, and requiring stern self-discipline. She crossed the drive from the gallery to the house in the evening, and the empty porch rockers struck her heart. She wished Roger had never come so she would not have to have these associations. She had no interest in cooking, in reading, or in the snug comfort of her surroundings. She made herself a pot of tea and spent the evening moving restlessly from room to room.

It felt strange to come home to an empty house; Rocco's absence was a hole in her comfort. She missed his warm presence, his affection, his watchfulness, and his intelligent companionship. Elisabeth had been around dogs all her life, but Rocco was once in a lifetime. She sighed. As much as she loved him, Rocco's attention was not enough. Well, it would have to be, she told herself. She must stop thinking about Roger. She would not call him again. His limitations were too much, and his heart was locked away. From her at least. Still, she wondered, where was he? What was he up to? Resolutely, she pushed away her questions every time they arose. It had become a full-time occupation.

Nancy's friendship quickly became a mainstay of Fiona's new life. They met, usually by accident, at Mann's or at the post office, or Nancy would be driving past while Fiona was in the yard, and she would stop for a lengthy chat through the car window. Nancy's knowledge of Island history and mores were essential guidance for Fiona in this new culture, and it was a means of survival in her solitary state.

As time went on, the thing that Fiona found hardest to adjust to was the silence. Fiona was too particular about her own mood to like to listen to random music on the radio, and there weren't many choices. The television was equally unsatisfactory, its inane babble more irritating than companionable.

After the first week of incessant use of her iPod music and her audio books, the yammering began to wear on her nerves, and so, in a moment of exasperation, she switched it all off. The silence engulfed her. It drifted through her mornings; no cheerful morning media voices to chat about the traffic or the latest world disaster, no singing ads, not even the well-modulated and brilliantly varied voice of a book narrator. The silence seemed, as in some latent line of poetry she recalled, to come down upon her, and she felt her soul absorb it, even as she squirmed and resisted its amplifying silence.

Her dreams became more memorable and haunting. She returned to the experiences of them frequently during the day as if remembering an odd trip she had taken. Her own feelings and desires, so long baffled and suppressed, began to surge forward, magnified and overwhelming. It was an awkward, uncanny, and uncomfortable feeling. But she allowed the silence to continue to penetrate her heart, and gradually she found a gentle equilibrium, not unlike the feeling of lying on an inner tube, allowing the waves to gently carry you with the current. In this way, after a misery of resistance and anxiety, Fiona began to settle into a great depth of peace.

Chapter Twelve ✳

Her newfound calm notwithstanding, Fiona approached her first big encounter with Island society with a great deal of trepidation. She could not, in fact, recall having been so nervous about anything in quite a long time. Pali and Nancy had each separately encouraged her to attend the potluck at Nelson's, pointing out that these parties were key elements of Island social life. It was to be a benefit for the Island dental office.

As the day of the potluck approached, she worried for days about the right thing to wear—wanting to strike exactly the right note of casual not trying-ness, and also not wanting to appear a rich city-slicker, or worse—a tourist. She was none of these things, she knew, but it could be so easy to offend in a small town. On the other hand, she would not feel comfortable in a Packers jersey, either. The compromise was between comfort and blending in.

Since it was a potluck, it was necessary to bring food, and this, too, was the focus of Fiona's thoughts that week. No goat cheese, she thought, nor mango salsa, nor, Heaven forbid, cilantro—but then, a bag of chips and salsa wouldn't do, either. It wasn't as if gourmet food wasn't eagerly offered and enjoyed here as anywhere, nor, as she had discovered, were the Islanders in the least unsophisticated in their tastes, but it wouldn't do to try too hard. Still, it had to be something good. Finally, she settled on lemon pound cake, as something neither pretentious, nor effete, and always appealing. She hoped she could negotiate the vagaries of the ancient oven whose thermostat, she had discovered, veered toward the eccentric.

The Saturday of the party was another splendid autumn day, the air crisp and dry, the sky a brilliant blue. Fiona dressed in jeans, a white shirt with a blue sweater, and her favorite Italian leather sandals. Her shirt was crisply starched and ironed, even though ironing was something Fiona detested.

Her lemon pound cake was actually the second one she had attempted, the first having burned a bit around the edges. It was a tiny bit uneven—one side having risen faster than the other in the ungovernable oven. Nevertheless, Fiona felt some pride in it; when she had licked the whisks, the batter had been delicious and thick with beaten eggs, lemon juice, and a pound of butter. All was in order as she walked to Nelson Hall down the street. The trees were at their peak, dazzling with brilliant yellow and orange or a flash of red. The sky was a deep, almost glowing blue. She took deep breaths and savored the smell of the lake, lingering subtly like the undernote of perfume.

The Albatross was closed for the season, and Fiona felt both relief and regret as she walked past. It was sad to see the little place dark and desolate, its cheery yellow sign in the window—*Thanks for a great season!*—a reminder of the many winter months to come. It had been a little too convenient to run across the street for a burger, though, and Fiona had realized early on that she would have to be disciplined about living so close. She had been struggling with her own rule, allowing herself ice cream or a burger once a week. Period. Anything more than that and she'd have been sinking the ferry within six months, she reminded herself.

When she entered the hall, the crowd was already quite large. Fiona felt the shyness she always felt walking into a party, heavily exacerbated by pound cake nerves. She recalled the school bake sales where she had been mocked by the other children for her mother's delicious, but carelessly decorated cakes. For some reason, this had left a deep trauma on the child Fiona, one which now took the form of excessive pound cake anxiety. Her own patience with herself was limited. It annoyed her that this should make her uncomfortable.

She looked for Nancy and Pali, but there was no one she knew, just a sea of indifferent strangers. She took her cake over to the table where a staggering assortment of casseroles, platters. and cake dishes were collected. There were chicken dishes and beef; platters of ham and turkey and pork; bean salads and tuna salads and pasta salads; homemade pickles, pickled onions, pickled herring, and pickled beets; and vegetables of every description, including plates of roasted peppers and squash. Breads and rolls of every shape and variety filled basket after basket. An entirely separate table housed the desserts. There were dozens of kinds of pies and brownies and blondies, delicate lace cookies and robust oatmeal raisin cookies, lemon bars, and a lot of things with chocolate. There were layer cakes, and Bundt cakes and angel food cakes. Along one end was a row of beautifully golden brown pound cakes, some with marbled chocolate, some with fruit glazes, others with caramel dripping down the sides and enormous roasted pecans arranged enticingly along the top all perfectly symmetrical. Fiona thought of the drooping side of her lemon pound cake, its long slope down the one end. She thought of the two dozen eggs, the two pounds of butter, and the optimism which she had spent in baking the first and then, with her hopes only mildly diminished, the second of her own creations. She looked down for a moment at her Italian sandals, and then looked again at the glittering desserts arrayed in splendor before her. Fiona sighed. Then, checking around to see whether anyone was watching, she moved casually toward the large plastic trash can at the far end of the table, and with one more casually furtive glance to ensure that she was unobserved, she swiftly dropped her second lemon pound cake into the black depths of the can, and moved away.

Thus relieved, she made her way toward the bar, where she ordered her usual neat scotch. Fiona stood shoulder to shoulder with the press around her, a sea of Packers green and gold, and caught the eye of the man standing at the other end of the bar. He was sixty-ish, with a potbelly, not much taller than Fiona. He had nice brown eyes, and a twinkle. He raised his glass at her and smiled, and Fiona, feeling pathetically grateful, did the same. She saw a small plump woman with dark brown hair approach him. He spoke to her and although it was too loud to hear them, Fiona could tell they were talking about her, because they both glanced up at her and smiled, and continued their conversation. In a moment she could see that they were coming toward her, and Fiona felt happy. The loneliness of life on the Island was beginning to tell, and she had realized last night with a kind of wonder, that she hadn't spoken to anyone in two days. She hoped her voice wouldn't croak.

"You must be the one who bought the old Goeden house," said the man, smiling at her. "I'm Jake Sinclair, and this is my wife, Charlotte."

Fiona shook hands and introduced herself, her voice coming out normally.

"Are you settling in?" Charlotte asked above the din.

"I think so. There have been a few surprises here and there, but I didn't expect it to be perfect." Understatement, she felt, was preferable to gossip.

"No. When a place has been empty that long—of regular owners, I mean—there are bound to be things that need fixing. When we bought our place, twenty-seven years ago, we spent months getting it to where we could move in. And even then, we couldn't do it all. You just do a little at a time, and eventually you get it to where you want it." She paused. "But then, you're never really finished with a house, are you?"

"No, indeed not." Fiona happily settled into the commonplace of human interaction.

As they chatted, Fiona reveling in the company of human beings, someone bumped into her, spilling a little of her drink. She turned around, and found herself facing a woman with the most malevolent eyes she had ever seen. At the sight of Fiona's face, the woman's eyes narrowed and she simply stared without a saying a word. Instinctively, Fiona stepped back.

"Oh, Stella. Nice to see you. Haven't you met? This is your new neighbor, Fiona. Charlotte turned to Fiona. "Stella lives in the little purple house next door to you."

So this was the long absent neighbor. Her hopes of friendship undiminished, Fiona decided to ignore the distinct signals of unwelcome being put out by the woman, and smiled, putting her hand out. "Nice to meet you."

The other woman shook hands, and nodded once without smiling. Inured to bad behavior by continual contact with Roger, Fiona was undeterred. She tried again.

"I can see you've put a lot of work into your house. Have you been there long?" Fiona's words had been carefully chosen. It was true that the house had had a great deal of attention, much of it too twee for Fiona's taste, with ruffly curtains, a complex and vibrant paint scheme, an elaborate birdhouse with gingerbread trim colors and paint to match the house, and so many garden gnomes that Fiona suspected they might have been placed to frighten the squirrels. Fiona herself found them vaguely disquieting in the early morning.

Stella hrrumphed, or grunted—Fiona wasn't sure which.

"Long enough," she said. She paused for a moment, and looked down at Fiona's feet. "Those are fancy shoes, aren't they?" she said, her voice loud to carry above the music.

There was a sneer in her voice. Fiona paused and unconsciously raised her eyebrows. Really? she thought. My shoes? My shoes are offensive? "Do you think so?" she asked aloud, wondering if perhaps this woman was insane. She could be, probably, although her hair was in order, and she seemed neatly dressed. Shouldn't crazy people have wild hair and stained clothing? Surely they wouldn't wear Lifestrider sandals and sweatshirts with cardinals and little sparkles on them? But then again….

Jake broke into Fiona's ruminations.

"Stella here's been on the Island her whole life. Went to school with Charlotte." He spoke to Stella, as if he weren't quite sure of the details, which Fiona was certain was not the case. Stella ignored Jake as if he hadn't spoken.

"I don't know who you think you are, but if you're not from here, you'll never fit in." Her eyes sparkled with malicious pleasure.

Fiona had no intention of letting this woman get the better of her. "Fitting in has never been a particular goal of mine, so that works for me."

Stella looked at her for a moment, then turned her back on them all, and started to walk off. She stopped, and turned back, her eyes burning into Fiona's. "I saw what you did," she hissed, and stalked away.

Fiona was utterly confused. What on earth was she supposed to have done? She pondered over whether the woman had actually curled her lip. She had read of this in various novels—so-and-so's lip curled in malice—that sort of thing, but she had never actually encountered it in real life.

"Charming," said Fiona, watching Stella's progress through the crowd.

"Don't mind her," Jake said, cheerfully. "She's a mean one. Always has been. I think some folks are born that way." He paused, looking around the room. "There's Jim. I think you better meet him, just to take the edge off."

Fiona gripped her scotch, which was already working to remove any edges, but she didn't correct him. And she did mind Stella. She really did. It would have been nice to have a neighbor who was civil, whom one might invite, from time to time, for a cup of coffee or, better yet, a scotch. She had imagined herself chatting happily over the fence—and, admittedly, there was no fence, which kept this, she supposed, firmly in the realm of fantasy—about what flowers to plant, or the amusing typos in the Island paper. Fiona realized that she had lost track of the conversation.

Charlotte was murmuring soothingly. "She's all prickles and bumps, but she'll get used to you."

"Hey, Jim!" Jake's voice carried remarkably well as he waved his arm, gesturing to someone to come over. A deeply tanned man who appeared to be in his thirties nodded in response, and crossed the room to them. He had blue eyes and an angular face, and was dressed in jeans and blue sport shirt.

It's the Marlborough Man, thought Fiona.

Charlotte leaned closer to Fiona and said in what passed for a whisper, "That's Jim Freeberg. He's a ranger at the state park." She looked sideways at Fiona. "Bachelor. Nice looking, isn't he?"

Fiona smiled vaguely, still feeling a bit off-balance by the encounter with Stella, but she had to admit that he was handsome. He looked like a ranger cliché, she thought, with eyes that seemed both intense and focused on something in the distance.

Jake and Jim shook hands, and Jim said hello to Charlotte. Jake presented him to Fiona.

"I just introduced Fiona, here, to Stella DesRoisiers, and figured I'd better find someone normal for her to talk to, just to make up for it." Jake smiled happily at them, clearly pleased with his arrangements.

Fiona put out her hand to Jim, and they shook hands, thinking as she did so that he was really rather extraordinary. "His hands are nice," she thought instantly, and then mentally told herself to back off. "How lonely are you, really?" she asked herself. Sheesh.

"Stella trying to scare you off? She is one prickly pain in the ass, if you don't mind my saying so."

Fiona smiled and shrugged. "Based on the two sentences we've spoken, I'm thinking you're probably right. I understand she's a regular part of the welcoming committee?"

"She's been charging around the Island insulting people for going on forty-five years, now, I'd guess," said Jake.

"She's not so bad when once you get to know her," said Charlotte, kindly. "She just doesn't know how to behave with people."

"You're too nice, Char, honey. That woman is the closest thing to Satan I ever want to meet. Glad she's your neighbor, not ours. But don't you worry, Fiona. She's just a spiteful, mean woman. No harm in her so long as you don't listen to what she says."

Jim laughed. "That's no mean feat, Jake. But he's right. Once you get used to her cranky ways, it's easy to just let it go in one ear and out the other. Don't pay her any attention at all. "

"I think I'm going to have to work on that." Fiona smiled at him, already well on her way to not caring about Stella.

"Can I get you another drink?"

Fiona looked down at her empty glass. Did it matter, really? She was walking. "Sure, thanks."

"Have you tried the Island specialty yet?"

Fiona turned her head slightly to the side, puzzled. "A specialty? Like Island Wheat Beer?"

"Nope. Worse than that. But as long as you're here, you're going to have to try it, and you might as well get it over with."

And with that, he worked his way over toward the bar.

"What's he talking about?" Fiona asked Charlotte.

"I probably shouldn't say, since he'll want to tell you, but it's bitters. Angostura bitters. It started during Prohibition. There was a lot of bootlegging going on up here.

"Not a whole lot of Feds way up here." Jake jumped happily into the conversation. "So no one did much to enforce the law. But can you imagine a winter up here with no booze?"

Fiona shook her head, appalled.

"So anyway," said Charlotte, her look daring her husband to interrupt, "Bitters were considered medicinal—for stomach complaints—and not illegal. Back in the day this place was owned by a pharmacist named Tom Nelson, and he discovered that there was an epidemic of stomach ailments among the residents up here. "

Jake jumped in. "No problem for a pharmacist to order bitters for medicinal purposes. Did a roaring business all through Prohibition. They're something like ninety proof."

"Really?" Fiona asked. "Ninety proof?"

Jim appeared, holding a glass of water in one hand, and another shot glass of what looked like deep rose-colored syrup in the other. He handed the small one to Fiona and took her empty glass.

"Ever had bitters?"

"I've had a champagne cocktail, but that's about it." She held the glass up to the light, and marveled at its viscosity. "What's in this stuff?"

"It's herbal. But the exact recipe is a secret. Like Coke. Only a handful of people know what's in it."

Fiona sniffed cautiously at the glass and tried not to wrinkle her nose. "You want me to drink this?"

Jim was unoffended. "It's traditional. All newcomers have to drink a shot. We sell more bitters here on the Island than anywhere else in the world."

Fiona looked around at the group, sighed, and raised her glass.

"Here's to neighbors," she said, and inexpertly tossed back the shot, just to get it over with.

The others laughed and applauded, and laughed more when Fiona followed the shot with a long drink of the water. There was a pause.

"Does Stella drink a lot of this?" she asked.

Jim gave her a high five and Fiona, in her ignorance, nearly missed his hand. High-fiving was not a normal part of Fiona's routine, but she made a mental note not to be so geeky about it in the future. Perhaps she could practice with someone. Roger? No, clearly not. Terry. He would be the one. Meanwhile, Charlotte patted her arm, and Jake offered to get her a beer.

"You're gonna need something to chase that down besides water."

"Don't worry about having too much," said Jim, seeing her hesitate. "I'll take you home. We've actually got two sources of evil around here. Stella's the human one, but the other one is canine, and I wouldn't want you to run into him on your own in the dark."

"You mean Piggy? We've met. And I'm not so sure I want to run into either one of them," said Fiona, "even in broad daylight."

Charlotte playfully punched Jim's arm. He was irresistible

to everyone.

Fiona began to feel that her first entrée into Island society was a success.

"So tell me," Jake asked loudly amidst the hilarity. "Why'd you throw away that cake?"

Stella got up in the morning and was nasty. She appeared to get her own particular pleasure in her nastiness, and seemed even to enjoy it. In her view, life was a choice between being petty or vicious. And though her approach was not universally applied—she generally operated on only a few well-chosen targets—it was universally observed.

Islanders didn't try to analyze why Stella was mean. She was merely a fact of life like weather, or sunspots. You didn't try to change the weather or to understand it. You bemoaned it occasionally, or hoped that it would change, but you didn't waste time trying to improve it. You didn't think back over what you had done to make it rain so hard when you wanted to sit in the sun; you didn't analyze your most recent conversation to see whether your poor choice of words had brought on fog or hail. And you didn't toy with the idea of baking a slightly uneven lemon pound cake in order to calm the wind. You simply accepted whatever was happening and made the best of it, even when it sometimes meant a change in plans.

Although Fiona did her best to adopt this philosophy, it went against her nature. In her innocence of small town life, she interpreted the lack of open warfare with Stella at the moment as a period of inactivity. And even so, not yet aware of Stella's unfolding plan, she knew she had to accept the current situation not so much as a cessation of hostilities, but as a spell of calm weather which, while pleasant, would simply have to end sometime. Even knowing this, she still found herself spending too much time wondering what she could do to make things better.

Compounding the situation against Fiona, was a simple but virulent reality.

A government of the people, while delightful in theory, is inevitably hampered by the fact that it has to be made up of the people who come immediately to hand, and in the case of local government, this truism is boiled down and concentrated into prescription strength. Whatever personal relationships, grudges, or idiosyncrasies that may exist among the community's inhabitants are packaged inextricably with the bearer, whose character, for good or ill, is magnified and carried out in the everyday activities of public office. No one understood this better than Stella.

As the evening wound down, Jim insisted on driving her home. Actually, as she thought about it, Fiona hadn't allowed him to reach the point of insistence, feeling that it would be rude to refuse, and also that she'd had more to drink than she was actually accustomed to. A ride would be welcome.

Jake and Charlotte had exchanged knowing glances, and she had seen Jake give Jim a man-club punch on the arm. But their brief drive to Fiona's was friendly and utterly uneventful.

Fiona had her hand on the truck door as she thanked him, but he was already turning off the engine and getting out. "You don't have to do that," she said, feeling awkward.

"Actually, I do," he said. My mom would kill me if she heard I'd sat in the truck and let you walk to your door alone."

"She wouldn't hear it from me," said Fiona, smiling.

"Maybe not, but she'd hear just the same. Probably before I got home."

Together they walked up the steps to the porch.

"Really?" Fiona asked, her hand on the door.

"Yeah, pretty much. We'll be engaged and married by the end of the day tomorrow." He grinned.

Rocco, just inside the door, had awoken, and he stood just inside, his pointed ears visible above the door's divide, his deep bark sounding scary through the door.

Jim seemed unfazed. "I've seen your dog. He's a beauty."

"He's not mine; he's just visiting. Would you like to meet him?"

"Sure. So long as he's ok with it."

Fiona opened the door, and Rocco rushed out. He immediately inserted himself between Fiona and Jim, and began to investigate this new person before he'd be allowed to get near Fiona again. Jim stood patiently and allowed the big dog to get a sense of him. Fiona noted the calm that seemed to emanate from Jim. Clearly a man at ease with animals. And with himself.

"It's ok, Rocco. He's a friend."

Rocco, not entirely convinced, moved warily next to Fiona and sat beside her, his eyes focused on Jim's every move.

Fiona wondered if she were expected to invite him in. She was exhausted, and could think of nothing but getting into her bed, but she didn't want to be rude.

"Well," said Jim, just as these thoughts were in her mind, "I can see you're in good hands." He indicated Rocco with a nod. "It's been nice meeting you. I'd better be off."

"Nice meeting you," said Fiona. "Thank you for the introduction to the Bitters Club."

He was already down the porch steps and striding toward his truck. "It's a lifetime membership," he said, over his shoulder. "Once you're in, you're in. See you!" And with that, he was in his truck, and drove away.

Fiona met Nancy the next day at the Mercantile as she was buying some chicken wire and a chain for her saw. Nancy's usual raw energy blazed around her, making Fiona, who had a bit of a hangover, feel distinctly lackluster in comparison.

"I looked for you last night," Fiona said after they had nearly bumped into one another in the nail aisle.

"Well, I had some pump problems out in the cider house, and figured I'd better take care of it. Anyway, I hear you went home with Jim." Nancy was nothing if not direct in expressing her thoughts.

Fiona paused in her search for the right size of nail and looked up.

"Where did you hear that?" she asked, astonished.

"From Charlotte. Ran into her after church." Nancy looked Fiona over appraisingly. "Is it love?" she asked facetiously.

Fiona was speechless. She just looked at Nancy with her mouth slightly open. Nancy grinned.

"Not quite used to the grapevine, eh? Not to worry. You'll hear ten different versions of your own story by the end of the week. None of 'em true."

She lowered her voice and leaned closer.

"But you could do worse."

She raised her eyebrows meaningfully and smiled again.

"Got to get back. Did some shanty-Irish repairs on that pump and got to get my handyman, Nils, to come take a look at it. Said he'd be by this afternoon. Don't be a stranger."

And she strode off to the register to make her purchases, leaving Fiona standing in the aisle.

Chapter Thirteen

T he pot luck had been the icebreaker, and from that moment, Fiona was on the social circuit.

To her surprise, everyone she met embraced her with the pleasure of discovering a new dancer at the ball. Invitations to events and to membership in various organizations were tendered at the hardware store, at the grocery store, and at the liquor store which, in addition to some very fine scotch, also sold moccasins and did appliance repair; officially named Petersen's, it was known locally as "Shoes and Booze." The invitations were polite, and generally insistent, and Fiona recognized that refusal was something to be saved for rare occasions. She knew instinctively that to avoid these events would be churlish, not to say stupid. In a community this small, interdependence was survival. One befriended one's neighbors both for the assurance of mutual companionship, and as insurance against unforeseen disaster. Besides, she was lonely.

The Island's culture was profoundly interesting to Fiona. She had never lived in a small town and was surprised by the interest that Islanders took in their neighbors and the ways in which they amused themselves. Left, for most of the calendar year, to their own devices, isolated from mainland amusements and society, the Islanders' regular round of events kept everyone busy and connected.

There were spaghetti nights and nature talks, historical events and fish derbies, potluck dinners, and even a performing arts center which hosted touring plays and concerts. Fiona particularly looked forward to the activities of the local dramatic society, which met monthly during the winter, and held extemporaneous play readings, in which everyone was welcome to participate. There was no social hierarchy here except native Islanders and nonnatives. The multimillionaire obsessed with astronomy and the ferry hands, the bartenders and the Ph. D.'s, the truck drivers and the teachers, the storeowners and the farmers, the postmistress and the ministers, the screenwriters and the novelists, all mingled and chatted happily together wherever they met. They were neighbors, united in the common cause of Island life. Everyone knew it and acted accordingly. Everyone, that is, except Stella DesRoisiers.

Having gotten off on the wrong foot with her neighbor, Fiona thought it would be wise to make another attempt. She was under no illusions that the lady would become a dear friend, but it would be better if their relationship were less antagonistic. She wasn't entirely clear on how to proceed, but she remained alert to the possibilities.

One sunny morning, as she sat at her kitchen table drinking coffee, she noticed Stella struggling to get something out of the trunk of her car. Fiona's natural good manners would have obliged her to offer help in any case, so she put down her coffee and headed out toward Stella's garage.

"Good morning!" she called. "May I give you a hand?"

Stella, looked up with surprise, but her face quickly changed to a sneer. "Aren't you the good little girl scout," she said with the singsong taunting quality of the playground. Fiona had not expected a welcome, but Stella's nastiness was on a level she had not encountered outside of grade school.

"It's a sincere offer," she said, calmly. "We are neighbors, after all." Stella snorted a false little laugh and turned back to her car. "Get lost," she said.

Fiona stood still for a moment, her lips pressed together. Then she took a deep breath. "Ok, then," she said, as if talking to herself, "Good luck." And with that, she turned and went back into the house. Her outward calm did not reflect her pounding heart or the tight knot in her stomach. Fiona detested conflict. Stella's behavior was inexplicable and her rudeness appeared impenetrable. Fiona determined not to let Stella bother her. But it was going to be difficult; that much was clear.

Elisabeth returned from her trip abroad—as she thought of it, although she had only been to Madison—in a happy mood, but tired.

Her time away had given her a chance to get some perspective on things with Roger. Her anger had dissipated with time and distance, but she still felt unsure of her standing with him. Her own feelings were less nebulous, but she had decided that pursuing them was like trying to tame a wild animal. She would leave things to develop in their own time. If he was interested, she would know. It wasn't an ideal circumstance, but she had determined her course of action, and she would stay with it.

She walked across to the gallery within an hour of her return. Like the house, it would need airing, and she wanted to be open in case a shopper happened by. She carried smaller items for the tourists who might not have thousands to spend, but who wanted something beautiful to remember their trip by. The carefully lit glass cases with jewelry and other small handcrafted things were immediately visible to anyone who walked in. There were other small metalwork things for the table or the house displayed nearby, and some relatively inexpensive photography, framed and signed, by local artists. You had to venture deeper into the gallery to find the more pricey items, the paintings and sculptures of the sort only the rich or the passionate collector might buy.

Restored to her natural self, Elisabeth enjoyed the gallery, and it felt as much like home to her as the house. Her generous nature was expressed in her opening of this place to visitors, for she felt delight in other peoples' pleasure and enjoyment. She flipped on the lights and turned on the stereo, checking as she did so that the alarm had been turned off. This was a superfluity, since no one stole things much in Door County, but it was required by the insurance company.

The environment tended to, it didn't take long for her to become engrossed in the mundane office work that had accumulated in her absence. There was mail to be opened and some small bills to pay, and some messages to be noted in her voice mail to be returned later. She heard the chime on the door as she was finishing her tasks, and she carefully arranged her papers for her assistant to file later. A professional smile of welcome on her face, she stepped out of her office to greet her customer.

She could hear by the creaking of the old barn's floorboards that he or she was overhead, looking at the portraits there, and she climbed the twisting stair in the corner, rather noisily, so as not to startle her guest. Roger stood with his back to her, gazing at a painting of a storm over Lake Michigan. It was one that Elisabeth particularly liked. There was a particularity about this storm, with the sunset behind it, that made her feel that she remembered the day it had happened.

She came and stood next to him and they stood together looking at the painting, neither speaking for some long time. At last Roger looked at her, and she turned and smiled at him. Roger put his hands in his pockets, sighed a deep sigh, and smiled back.

They spent a long afternoon in the gallery, moving together from painting to painting, talking little, but simply standing side by side before the art. It felt to Elisabeth as if they were receiving a benediction, and she thought she saw on Roger's face a similar feeling.

When they had gazed at the last painting, they walked together downstairs and out into the cool autumn twilight. Roger's pickup was parked uncharacteristically close to the porch, and as they approached, Elisabeth noted a grocery bag standing on the porch near the door.

Roger nodded in the direction of the package. "That's for you," he said. And without another word, smile, or wave, he got into his Jeep and drove off.

Elisabeth stood watching the Jeep disappear down the drive, then bent down to pick up the bag from the porch floor beside the bench. She wasn't completely certain whether Roger had intended it for her or for Rocco. It was surprisingly heavy. She set it on the bench, opened it, and drew out an oversized book. In the dwindling light, she could just barely make out the words, but she recognized the title immediately. It was a lushly photographed depiction of fifteenth- century Venetian glass, written in Italian by a leading expert, and, as she well knew, shockingly expensive. She looked down at it, stunned, and then toward the darkness where Roger had disappeared, her brows ever so slightly furrowed. She sighed. Then, neatly folding the bag and tucking it under her arm, she went dreamily inside, her treasure firmly held in both hands.

The routine of making dinner restored Elisabeth to a more ordered state of mind. It wasn't until later, when she was cleaning up the kitchen, that she went to put away the bag on the pantry shelf. She was happily looking forward to making herself a cup of tea and curling up to savor her new book. As she turned the paper bag to tuck it next to the others, she noticed that it wasn't completely empty. She unfolded it and peered inside to find what appeared to be another small book.

She reached in and drew out a little yellow packet of postcards. Elisabeth stared at it in surprise. There were probably fifteen in all, attached in a long, folding strip. She opened it, studying the familiar photos of gondoliers, the Bridge of Sighs, and Piazza San Marco, a little frown of confusion gathering on her face. There was nothing unusual at all about the pictures, a common enough souvenir. In fact, she probably had one herself somewhere. But somehow she couldn't imagine Roger buying postcards. When had Roger been to Venice?

Pondering, she folded the length of pictures, tucked their covering tab back into place, and went to pour herself a glass of wine. You can't drink tea with an Italian book, she decided. As she settled in happily with her book and her wine, she felt a momentary pang, first for Rocco, and then for the empty chair across from her.

Not long after her induction into the Bitters' Club, Fiona got a call from Jim. Full of apologies for taking so long to call, he explained that he'd been off the island at a Department of Natural Resources management course. Would she and Rocco like to go exploring? Fiona had no idea what this meant, exactly, but the splendid autumn weather continued, and it was too nice to stay inside. A little voice in her head told her that she was putting off her writing assignment for far too long. It was to be a serious piece on the national defense for a public policy magazine, requiring a great deal of research and intellectual heavy lifting. But she decided to go anyway. Deadlines, she thought, be damned.

Roger eyed the copper machinery in front of him with satisfaction. He had spent most of the night checking its connections, practicing, and testing its product—which explained the sleeplessness—and now felt confident that he understood its operation. The company representative who had installed it yesterday had assured him that they would respond promptly to any malfunctions—even, as he had pointed out helpfully—way up here in the outer reaches of civilization.

Since his epiphany at CraftVenture, Roger had done his usual extensive and meticulous research on the machines. This was an Italian model, its unpronounceable name prominently displayed across the front of its hammered copper urns. The price had been astounding, but Roger was nothing if not a man of determination, and his conviction that this was the best of its kind had lent him an almost cavalier attitude toward its cost. And anyway, he had a fondness for apparatus of all kinds, probably related to life in a physics lab. He looked forward to working with it.

It was not yet six a.m. when the door of the shop jangled with an early customer. Roger came out from the back room wiping his hands on a white towel, and gazed with a kind of welcome at the tourist couple who had entered. Not having been to bed, his hair was even more disheveled than usual, although his T-shirt was clean, and fatigue made his expression somewhat milder than his customary scowl. They were middle-aged, dressed in expensive casual wear, and murmuring to one another a conversation they had started earlier. The man spoke, with the experience of a long relationship, knowing exactly what his wife would want. "A medium double latte and an espresso, please."

Roger was unfazed by this heretofore unfamiliar terminology. He had done his homework.

"Regular latte?" he asked, his tone almost friendly.

"Nonfat," the woman replied, as her husband had strolled over to examine the photography displayed on the wall.

Roger poured the milk into the stainless steel pitcher that had been part of the machine's equipage. He put the pitcher under the tube, opened the steam valve, and gently began the up and down movement of the steam in the milk. He carefully, methodically turned the valve off before removing the tube from the pitcher, wiped the tube gently with a clean white cloth from the counter, and poured the milk over the two shots of espresso he had already added to the cup. He handed the cups across the counter, completed the transaction, and watched with a sense of accomplishment as his customers left the shop. This, he thought, was going to be easy.

Having made some reasonable progress on her article, and having reached a point of fatigue in painting and repairs, Fiona decided to take the day off and head over to the mainland. It seemed like a lifetime since she had been down to Ephraim, and she looked forward to breakfast at Coffee with happy anticipation. With Elisabeth out of town she'd had no urgent reason to make the rather tedious drive down, and anyway had been happily—mostly—occupied with her house. But now Elisabeth had returned, and it was time to take Rocco home.

Reasonably sure that she had removed most of the paint from her hair—and from Rocco's—they boarded the early ferry. Pali was not on duty that morning, but the crew knew her by

186 North of the Tension Line

now, and nodded their greetings as she walked from the car up to the observation decks.

She and Rocco stood together at the prow of the boat, enjoying the wind, the late autumn sun, and in Rocco's case particularly, the watery scents of fish and birds and diesel. Rocco was not allowed in the cabin, but it was warm enough to stand on deck, and being together made them both happy. Fiona, longing for coffee, had limited herself to just one cup that morning, in order to preserve the pleasure of drinking a cup at Coffee.

The plan was to have a leisurely breakfast—arriving at the time when Mike and Terry should be in—do a little shopping to replenish the supplies of coffee beans and cheese, and to pick up a few items of hardware which were not in stock at the Island general store. Then, lunch with Elisabeth to effect the dog swap, a quick stop at the used bookstore, and then a late afternoon drive back up to the Island with a stop or two at various shops along the way.

Painfully aware of the thin economic line trod by her neighbors on the Island, Fiona did her best to shop with local merchants whenever she could. Between Island commerce—Fiona had quickly developed a relationship with the proprietors of Shoes and Booze—and the internet, she had been able to acquire most of her needs, and had racked up a shocking total on her credit card to boot, but it was still pleasant to browse here and there, and perhaps, to chat with a clerk or fellow customer. Fiona enjoyed the combination of community and solitude on the Island, but there were times when a little broader society was necessary.

Standing on the ferry deck, Fiona mulled the question of

Jim as she absorbed the scenery with her usual deep sense of inner unwinding. He had been attentive and thoughtful, although Fiona didn't flatter herself too much. There were not, after all, many single people on the Island, and those who were got to know each other pretty quickly. In any case, she liked him. He was intelligent, well-read, and had a gentle and knowledgeable way with Rocco. But there was no particular spark between them. She turned her mind away from her memories of Chicago. There was no point in dwelling on lost opportunity, she told herself. But there was a part of her that grieved.

What was it, she wondered, that drew one human being so immediately to another? Was it, as scientists had suggested, something so elemental and immutable as pheromones? Did the smell of someone really draw you to him unconsciously? Fiona revisited the night in Chicago, and tried to remember how he had smelled. He had been close enough that she might have smelled him before he spoke in her ear. The memory of his closeness was delicious, but she could not remember anything other than the usual smells of cocktail parties at Chicago clubs: the mingling scents of flowers, food, and alcohol, and the occasional whiff of someone's heavy perfume. Certainly he had not smelled of cologne. She would have remembered that.

The changing sound of the ferry engines interrupted her thoughts, and her hand placed on Rocco's head for comfort, they walked together back to her car to disembark and begin the drive to Ephraim.

Fiona met Mike and Terry in the parking lot of the coffee shop. Her own delight was more subdued than Rocco's, who spun in circles when he saw them, and ran from one to the other, trilling with excitement, unable to decide whom to greet first. Mike crouched down in the middle of the drive, and rubbed the big dog's head with both hands while Terry patted Rocco's back with affection, the powerful tail thumping against his legs while he and Fiona exchanged pleasantries.

"I'll be ready to have an open house soon," said Fiona. "I plan to have lots of food and lots to drink, and there will be space to stay over so you don't have to drive home."

"Will we be expected to work?" asked Terry, teasing. "Or is everything already finished?"

"Not finished, but no, of course you won't have to work." She paused. "Unless something goes wrong—which isn't completely unlikely."

"Well you tell us when, and we'll be there," said Terry. Mike nodded and smiled. "And now, let's get on inside. I'm overdue for a cup of coffee. Place has been closed for days."

This was news, but Fiona was pursuing her own line of thought. "Do you think Roger would come?" asked Fiona as they approached the door, the enticing scent of coffee beginning to wreathe around them.

"Well, now, I don't know," said Terry.

Mike smiled his cherubic smile. "Depends on whether Elisabeth is there."

"Coffee smells better than usual, wouldn't you say?" asked Terry as he opened the door for Fiona and Rocco to go in. But as they entered, all conversation ended.

Confronting them in gleaming copper and brass was the largest and most complex coffee machine that Fiona had seen outside of New York or Italy. It perched behind the counter with the regal air of an exotic bird. It seemed out of place for a little coffee shop in Ephraim.

Terry gave a low whistle. "This is an upgrade," he said, stepping around Fiona to take a closer look. "Bet this set you back a few. Whew! And smell that coffee!"

Mike settled himself at the counter, his keen gaze taking in the full effect. "Nice metalwork, too. That copper will be delicate, though, as you know, Roger. Better keep the oxalic acid in that cleanser away from it."

Roger nodded seriously. "They give you a special cleaner for it so you don't ruin the lacquer, but they say it shouldn't need much more than an occasional wipe down with a damp cloth."

By now Terry had settled himself beside Mike at the counter, and Fiona, too, had sat down, but busied herself with arranging Rocco's lead and her handbag in order to gather her thoughts.

"Well," said Terry, "guess we'd better get down to it. I'm not much for fancy, generally speaking, but I think I better try whatever that thing's brewing. What do you recommend, Roger?"

Roger thought for a moment. "I'd say an Americano," he said with authority. "It's milder than a straight espresso, and more like what you'd be used to."

"I'll try that, then," said Terry. "Mike, what about you?"

"I'll have a cappuccino," said Mike confidently. "Don't get to have one of those much, but I always order them when I'm in Europe."

"Fiona?" Terry looked down the counter at her.

"I'll have a latte," she said and paused. "With soy milk, please."

"Coming right up," said Roger, and turned to busy himself with his new machine.

Chapter Fourteen ✳

It was a gray Monday morning when Stella DesRoisiers walked into Mann's Grocery Store and got a cart. She strolled idly along the aisles adding a few things here and there to her basket as if she had all the time in the world. In fact, however, Stella was a woman with a purpose. She had driven past the store several times over the course of the last week, looking for just the right cars to be in the parking lot at the same time. Stella had a plan, and it was important that the right people be available to help her, however unwittingly, to put that plan into action.

By the time she reached the meat counter, her cart had what might be an expected number of items, and a nice conversation had already begun among the regulars who congregated there. Instinctively, if not consciously, Stella knew that conversations have a rhythm and momentum which need to be respected if you want to join in. It was a bit like the jump rope games of her childhood, where little girls would sway with the movement of the big rope before leaping in and joining their friends in a game. Stella had been a champion jumper, but she had never been successful in gaining the affection of the other girls. They all knew that she would trip them if their jumps came close to her record, or pinch them under almost any circumstances at all. She had not been a particularly well-liked child.

Her popularity had not improved with age. Stella knew she was disliked, and if somewhere in her heart this bothered her, it would have been difficult to observe in her conduct. She had never done much to endear herself to her neighbors. Nevertheless, Stella was a longtime member of the community, and in a small town even the least beloved are accorded a modicum of everyday civility.

A chorus of good mornings, made with well-moderated enthusiasm, greeted her. Stella nodded graciously, and pulled her cart up alongside them. The conversation quickly shifted, as she had known it would, to the topic upon which Stella could be considered an expert: her new neighbor.

"So what do you think, Stella? Must be nice to have that house occupied after all that time." This observation was made with a sly wink at the others. Everyone knew that Stella had been waiting for the price to drop on the old Goeden place so that she could adjoin it to her own property. Fiona's impulsive purchase, made so innocently and with such delight, had earned her a bitter enemy before she had so much as signed the papers. The fact that Fiona was an outsider made the situation so much the worse. The fact that she was a beautiful single woman had sealed her fate.

Stella shrugged at the question. "Can't see as how it does much to improve the neighborhood. Not sure we need someone of that type around here." This was her first cast. She sent out the line gently, and with only a subtle lure.

Her neighbors would not take long to rise to the bait.

"Seems a nice enough woman," said one. The others nodded, being careful not to jump too hard. They all knew Stella's nature.

"Not terribly bright, maybe," offered one.

"But always smiling," said another.

Stella shrugged and made a face. "Maybe. I just wonder what kinds of people are going to be coming around now."

There was a slight shifting among the group. "Well, city people aren't so bad, now are they? And anyway, I understand she'd been in Ephraim for a while." Several heads nodded. They had heard this, too. Someone who'd already been living on the peninsula wasn't a complete outsider.

Stella snorted. "There are city people, and then there's her kind of people." A veteran fisherwoman, she was beginning to feel the pull on her line. "I'm not sure you'd be so easy if you knew what she is."

Again, there was some movement as people exchanged looks. Who would be the one to come right out and ask? After some moments the bravest of them ventured the question.

"What do you mean by that, Stella?"

A look of smug satisfaction crept across Stella's face. "Well," she paused, as if she hadn't practiced this line in her sleep for weeks. "Well, you know that she tells everyone she's a writer, don't you?"

There were nods and the beginnings of some frowns. This sounded true.

"But," continued Stella, "do you know what kind of writer?" They all looked blank.

"Do you know what she writes?" pursued Stella, somewhat irked by their slowness. But she had them now. Everyone was focused on her, hanging on her every word. She lowered her voice and they all leaned in.

"*Pornography*. That's what she writes. "And," she lowered her voice further. "It's the hard stuff." Stella paused. "That's what I'm told anyway."

She allowed a note of piety to creep into her voice as she delivered her final line. "Of course, I could be wrong."

There was stillness among the group. No one wanted to acknowledge any familiarity with the topic, but each mind was racing to determine the definition of "hard stuff,"and then, to ascertain the likelihood of truth. It certainly seemed possible… single woman… said she was a writer… no obvious means of support…and then, of course, there were her looks; no one could deny that she was a stunner… The collective conclusion was easily reached.

"Well," said Stella brightly, as if she was awakening from a trance. "I shouldn't stand here gossiping." And here she delivered her coup de grace.

"Maybe nothing to it, anyway. I'd better get on; day's a-wasting!" And she turned from them toward the checkout, a slow smile of satisfaction creeping across her face.

Fiona had been looking forward to her housewarming party since the moment she had bought the house. It would be fun to show everyone around, to open the doors of the little house to company. The house, she knew, would not be perfect, or even close to perfect. But it would be presentable and welcoming, filled with candlelight and flowers, her furniture in place, with perhaps the odd mouse or bat thrown in here or there. She was grateful that after the first four, there had been no new spider sightings. She hoped it wasn't because they had gone into hibernation somewhere in the cellar.

Fiona had thought about inviting Jim to the housewarming, but had decided that it would be better not to combine her Ephraim friends with the Islanders. At least not yet. There was something about the mix that felt like a clashing of worlds, and she didn't feel quite up to it. In any case, she knew that her friends—the women particularly—would have interpreted Jim's presence as significant, and she was not in any way prepared for that kind of reaction.

Fiona had not yet discovered the identity of the nighttime gnawer, as she had come to think of it. Its appearances, if she could call them that, were sporadic but loud. She had almost come to the point of not being terribly concerned about it, but she knew that sooner or later there would have to be a reckoning of some sort, whether with the creature or with the repair bill for the damage it must be doing in some invisible place. Probably both, she thought. She had begun to contemplate the possibility of a cat to help her to deal with the various intractable residents of the house, but she had not yet been able to bring herself to this final—and to Fiona—drastic step.

The final papers signed and the painting completed, the moving of her furniture and household goods had gone relatively smoothly. She had been able to hire some young men from the Island and their truck to take the heavy things: her couch, her bed, and her bookcases, mainly, and to arrange them in the house. Terry had suggested someone on the Island to work on her foundation—and the problem had been dealt with competently, if not inexpensively.

Fiona had learned that along with tips for hiring the right workmen, the place to hear the latest gossip was at the meat counter of the Island's sole grocery store. Rare was the time she would stop by that she would not encounter some earnest or fiercely intense conversation about school governance, or the dumping ordinance, or the failing wall at the newly built arts center. She made a mental cautionary note that nothing one did in the remotest corner of one's own home was secret, and that although Islanders could tease one another face-to-face about their mistakes and foibles, it was essential to understand that whatever you said about someone would be repeated to them within a matter of hours.

On the Saturday of the party, she spent the morning hanging pictures and picking the last of the autumn flowers. After making herself casually presentable, she sat down on the porch swing to wait. About ten minutes after the arrival of the two o'clock ferry, a small caravan of cars pulled up in front of the house. There was Terry and his wife, Anne, in his ancient but shining van; then Mike and his wife, Ella; and Elisabeth with Rocco. Fiona felt a brief moment of disappointment. She had hoped that Roger would come.

She walked down to the road to welcome her guests, hugging them and leading them into the house.

At the first moment she took Elisabeth aside. "Where's Roger?" she asked in a low voice.

"Oh, he's coming," said Elisabeth. "He said he'd be a little late. He had to pick something up along the way and was going to take the later ferry."

The two of them carried a tray of drinks into the living room, and the volume of conversation escalated at a rapid clip. The party was in full swing when a knock at the screen door signaled Roger's arrival. Fiona went to answer, glass in hand. She smiled gaily as she swept open the door. "Welcome to the project!" Roger, stared at her coldly, his customary look of greeting.

"Come in; come in," said Fiona, waving her glass at him. "The party has already started." Roger paused and cleared his throat. Speaking never came naturally to him.

"I can't come in yet. I have something for you. You have to come out."

Intrigued, Fiona put down the scotch and came out onto the porch. "You have something for me? Really? Roger, I'm—you're full of surprises."

Fiona was genuinely moved. A gift from Roger. This was a momentous event.

"You wait here," he said, and disappeared around the side of the house.

"What's going on out here?" Elisabeth had followed them out. "Is that Roger?" Rocco padded out beside her, a protective shadow, full of intelligent interest.

Fiona turned to her and beckoned. "He's brought me a present." And then, sotto voce, "Can you believe it?"

Elisabeth called back into the house to the others. "Roger's here. Come see what he's brought. He has a present for Fiona."

At this moment, Roger reappeared, holding what appeared to be a long, thick, leather leash. Rocco's ears pricked forward, and deep in his body, he began to make a rumbling sound so low that it was almost inaudible. Embarrassed, Elisabeth shushed him and made him sit, but he shifted uneasily, his ears at full alert, and the hair on his back standing up as he stared toward the corner.

Fiona stepped down from the porch. The leash trailed behind Roger some seven feet or so, so there was a brief delay before the other end of it came around the side of the house. Fiona had the experience of stepping out of time as the object at the end became clear. Stepping daintily, with an air of malevolent condescension, a large black and tan goat made its way along the path.

The screen door on the porch slammed, as Mike and Terry came out, followed by Ella and Anne, still deep in conversation.

Elisabeth stood frozen, her mouth in a perfect oval "oh." Rocco stopped rumbling and began to growl until Elisabeth told him "Enough." She took hold of his collar just in case, and he strained a bit at her command, nose quivering and face full of concentration. The goat was taller than he was.

Roger came toward Fiona and extended the lead to her.

"It's for you."

Fiona took the lead in silence, unable to take her eyes off her gift.

Roger looked up at the group on the porch.

"My brother had him. Got him in one of those internet deals. But he can't keep him. You're the only person I know who might be able to have a goat, so I figured. ..." here his voice trailed off reflectively.

"Him?" Terry asked. "It's a male goat? It's not even a milking goat?" Roger ignored this.

Mike looked on in bemused silence.

"Where did your brother get it?" he asked, curiously.

"Craigslist."

There was silence as they all digested this information. Fiona watched the animal nibbling, with the greatest concentration, a delicate corner of the porch railing.

After a long pause Elisabeth broke the silence.

"What's his name?"

"Robert," said Roger. "His name is Robert."

Unable at first to take her eyes away, Fiona watched as Robert moved his attentions to the rose bushes. She kept her face and eyes completely still, and thought carefully about what she wanted to say. At last she turned to Roger, and touched his arm.

"Thank you, Roger," she said seriously. "What a truly remarkable gift."

Roger bowed his head patronizingly. "You're welcome."

The party had taken on an odd quality after the arrival of Roger and his goat-gift. None of them had had any notion of the correct approach to goat care, and out of some kind of distantly recalled social obligation on Roger's part, and sympathy on everyone else's, they had trooped out to the barn, glasses in hand, to watch as Robert was settled into his new stall, his pail filled with fresh water from the faucet in the corner, and his trough filled with food. It was Purina goat chow, in a big green bag. "I didn't know Purina made goat chow," Elisabeth had commented to Fiona.

Mike's gentleness had calmed the goat in its new surroundings, and he stroked its neck, rather absentmindedly as Anne

held the lead. While Roger moved the animal into its stall, Terry
helped to fill the trough, and had turned on the valve to the water
faucet so it could be used. Ella, not quite certain of her feelings
about this creature whose malevolent eyes and cloven hooves
emanated evil, stood aside in silence. Elisabeth had sipped her
wine and made occasional warning commands to Rocco when
he seemed about to move in the goat's direction. Fiona hung
back from the activity, watching with a small smile that made
her look as if she had just been checked into an asylum.

The need to catch the last ferry had meant an early departure for everyone. After settling Robert into his new ac-
commodations, they had left Fiona standing alone on her porch
looking small and tired. Elisabeth had taken her aside to ask,
briefly,

"Are you ok?"

And Fiona had shaken her head as if coming out of a trance.
She smiled and squeezed Elisabeth's hand. "I'm fine. Just a bit…
shocked."

She grinned, looking more like her usual self, and Elisabeth
had had to content herself with that. "I'll call you tomorrow," she
said, and ran out to her car, where the men were waiting.

They had lined up together to board, Roger's truck first,
then Mike and Ella, then Terry and Anne in his van, and Elisabeth last. Their vehicles tightly, but efficiently arranged on deck,
they had reconvened in the passenger lounge before departure,

the bright light of the ferry's public spaces casting a pallor over their faces, and creating a feeling of a hospital waiting room. Elisabeth wondered if they were all a bit in shock.

There was silence for a long time as the ferry pulled out of Detroit Harbor and began the short trip across Death's Door. Ella and Anne continued their genial chatter, while Mike and Terry joined a desultory conversation of the Packers' season with a man in the next seat. The conversation became more animated as the prospects of tomorrow's game were discussed.

Elisabeth turned to Roger. "Let's get some fresh air." And without saying anything he had stood up and led the way out of the lounge, up the stairs to the open deck beneath the pilot-house.

It was cold on the water, and Elisabeth shivered as they leaned on the railing, looking back at the wake of the ferry and the sparse lights of Washington Island moving further away. Elisabeth thought of Fiona, of how small she had looked as they said good-bye, of how alone and untethered from the world she was in the little house on the dark Island. Untethered. What did that remind her of? Elisabeth remembered with a start. The goat, she thought to herself. There was a goat. She sighed and looked out of the corner of her eye at the man standing beside her. Tentatively, Roger reached out, and put his hand over hers.

The friends parted company as the ferry chugged into Northpoint, each heading to their cars for the trip home. Elisabeth had said a reluctant good-bye to Roger, and his response was unsatisfactorily typical. She smiled to herself, content with the memory of his hand on hers, and sang along to the radio all the way home.

Passing by Coffee on the way back to his place, Roger spotted an enormous crate on the asphalt near the building. He slowed the car and pulled in next to the object. Bad timing. But it was what he had been expecting and watching for since he had placed the order some four weeks previously. He checked his watch. It was late, but with luck, he could have the job finished by morning. He parked the car and began rummaging in the back for his tool box. There was no need to call anyone. He could take care of this himself.

Chapter Fifteen ❖

No sooner had Fiona acquired a goat than she began plotting ways to get rid of it. The problem she
found, was rather complex. As impervious to emotion as he might appear, she had no intention of
offending Roger, particularly since this was the only gift she had
ever known him to give. Furthermore, while not enamored of
her new pet, she felt some compunction as to what might befall
him in other hands. The usefulness of goats—particularly male
goats—seemed to Fiona somewhat limited, but she had no intention of allowing her ignorance to lead in any way to harming him.

The morning after the party she sat drinking coffee in her
small, sunlit kitchen, pondering her dilemma and watching
Robert wandering along the end of his tether. She had risen
earlier than usual, awakened by a feeling of anxiety which, for
a moment or two she had been unable to pinpoint. It was when
she had remembered Robert, that she had sat up in bed, fully
alert. A goat. An animal who needed water and food—which
Roger had included as part of his gift—and God knew what else.
She had dressed hurriedly, and gone down to the barn to find
the goat—Robert, she corrected herself—patiently chewing the
wooden pegs on the side of his stall.

He lifted his head when she entered, his yellow eyes glittering in the dusky morning light of the barn. She approached

him cautiously, and put her hand out to him over the stall. He ducked and backed away, but after a moment he approached her hand. Slowly and warily, Fiona began to touch the side of his neck. He was softer than she'd thought he'd be, and he seemed fairly calm. She gently stroked the place where his neck met his shoulders, and he leaned into her hand. Perhaps he would like some fresh air and sunlight, she thought, and carefully attaching the leather lead he had come with, she'd brought him out into the side yard, tethering him where she could see him from the house. Now he was there, chewing grass in his morose fashion, and managing somehow to convey the impression that he was waiting for her to look away so that he might get up to something.

Robert did not, she thought, resemble the sort of boutique-y goats she had seen on websites for artisanal cheese. Those goats had a quality and facial expression whose benignity reminded her a bit of Springer spaniels. One saw the pictures and thought: how sweet to have a goat! But there was nothing sweet about Robert. The deep tan stripes slanting across his black face gave him a sinister look, and his coloring suggested something more menacing than a spaniel—more like a Doberman. Although for the most part, his long ears and hangdog expression created an air of melancholy which surrounded him like a cloud, there were moments when she caught a look of malevolence in his yellow eyes, which made her think he might be contemplating her demise. At least, she thought, he had no horns.

As Fiona drifted in her thoughts, a screen door slammed, and Stella made an appearance in her backyard. Robert stopped his chewing and looked up. The slow fluidity of his movements made Fiona think of the villain in a bad movie. At the same time, with that sense people have when they realize they're being looked at, Stella glanced over in Robert's direction. Fiona watched as Stella's movements, too, became slow and deliberate. She turned to face him, her hands on her hips and just stood there, gazing at what appeared to be a goat in her neighbor's yard. Fiona was reminded of old cowboy movies where the gun duelers turn toward one another, their hands poised beside their holsters, each waiting for the other to make a move. Later, Fiona would look back on this moment both as an omen, and as an indicator of some form of character judgment lurking in Robert's mind.

But slow motion clearly was not Robert's preferred mode. He lurched forward in Stella's direction—stretching his tether to its furthest length—he seemed to prance, kicking his hind legs up, and then his front legs, pulling as hard as he could. His enormous pink tongue lapped hideously from the side of his mouth, and a manic gleam was in his yellow eye. Fiona reflected later that it was easy to see how the myth of satyrs had evolved, so perfectly did his face resemble a caricature of human lechery. She squeezed her eyes shut against the memory, realizing in a flash that the licking of Robert's lips had reminded her of Anthony Hopkins in the fava beans scene of *Silence of the Lambs*.

At the moment of the crisis, however, a feeling of impending disaster filled her, and Fiona froze as Robert, his desperate leaping at last succeeding in breaking his tether, lurched delightedly toward Stella, tongue lolling, nostrils flaring, and saliva splashing, all the while emitting a series of wet-sounding snorts.

It was Stella's screaming which broke Fiona's paralysis, and she flew from the house to capture the delinquent. Fleeing to the safety of her kitchen door, Stella ran inside and slammed it, screaming steadily as Robert pursued her up the wooden porch steps, and playfully (Fiona hoped) butted his head against the door. With screaming still coming from the house, Fiona reached the stairs and grimly gathered the broken tether. She tugged hard, pulling Robert back down the steps, whether from a surge of adrenaline or the miracle of gravity, she didn't know. Robert continued to prance and turn, until, seeing her, the look on his face changed in an instant. The very picture of decorum and great good sense, he tossed his head once, then turned and sedately allowed himself to be led back to the barn, his head held high like an aging dowager duchess. Fiona nervously secured him in his new stall, checked the latch, and closed the barn door, sliding the long wooden bolt behind her. "Fiona Campbell," she thought to herself. "Goat wrangler."

Taking a deep breath, she crossed the yard, and went up to Stella's door to apologize. All was silent within. Fiona knocked. She heard a series of quick footsteps before the door was flung open, and Stella's scarlet face appeared before her. Fiona opened her mouth to speak, but it was too late.

"How dare you?" Stella hissed. "How dare you allow that… creature…to attack me? How dare you?"

Fiona's eyes widened and she opened her mouth to speak, but before she could summon her thoughts, Stella began a wild rush of words which she spat out. In an oddly detached way, Fiona found herself noticing Stella's pink fluffy slippers, slightly dirty around the edges. They didn't seem to be the slippers of someone who could be so angry. "Fluffy slippers should be for happy people," Fiona thought, irrelevantly. "Why don't I have fluffy slippers? Am I not happy enough? But then, clearly, that's not actually a qualification." Catching herself, Fiona drew her attention back to Stella's face. Her eyes were narrowed to slits; she seemed almost gasping with fury. Fiona had to coach herself not to look away. It seemed almost intrusive to witness a stranger in such an intimate state of anger.

"Do you think you can get away with this? Do you think you can keep a vicious animal here? What kind of idiot are you? Don't you ever EVER allow that THING to come near me again, EVER. Do you hear me? EVER. Now get out of here. GET OUT!"

And with that she slammed the door. The door popped open, and she slammed it again, harder.

Fiona stood for a moment, stunned. Turning slowly she descended the steps and returned to her yard as if in a daze. Never could she recall having been spoken to in this way. During her days at the newspaper even the rudest lout among her former editors had been mild in his tirades compared to this. Granting that Stella had had a shock—which Fiona most certainly allowed—and that Robert was not a step forward in neighbor relations—which she also allowed—still, the intensity of the scene made Fiona feel that Stella had merely been waiting for an excuse.

Once safely inside, Fiona stood in the middle of her kitchen, uncertain of what to do next. Her heart was racing too hard to allow for any more coffee. She sighed. It was eight o'clock on a Sunday morning. Outside of a P. G. Wodehouse novel it was probably too early for a scotch. Could she leave Robert? What did she even know about the care of goats? Nothing. And she hadn't had her internet installed yet, either. Clearly the necessity of clarifying Robert's needs loomed large, but not nearly so large as Fiona's need to find a new home for him. A screaming and hostile Stella was not going to be an asset. And who, thought Fiona, despite her own responding anger, could really blame her?

She thought for a moment. Surely Robert could be left alone for a few hours if the barn door were latched firmly. She would leave him food and water, and catch the next ferry to the mainland where she could scope out her options. If all else failed, the Sister Bay Library would be open, and she could do some goat research. The thought occurred to her—again—that she could pile Robert into her car—he'd just fit—and show up at Roger's door. She reviewed the firm, but polite speech she had already composed last night as she lay in bed. It was good.

"*Roger,*" it began. "*I can't tell you how truly touched I am by your gift. To know that you value our friendship means the world to me, and I look forward some day to being able to show you just how much…*" no, that could be misinterpreted… "*I hope someday I can find a gift that will be even half as meaningful match to others…*" a bit thick, there, she'd have to work on that part. "*But a living thing is a responsibility I don't feel up to, and I just don't think that it would be fair to Roger*—oops—*fair to Robert to keep him in that barn all alone. It just wouldn't be right.*" At this point Roger's stony look would be drilling a hole in her head. And her heart, too. No. Fiona knew she couldn't do it.

Quite apart from anything else, she felt responsible now for Robert's well-being. She couldn't risk him being foisted off on someone and coming to some harm, evil benighted beast though he was. Cursing herself, her conscience, Roger, and the world at large, she went upstairs to get her bag and a jacket for the ferry. It was always cold on the water. On the other hand, maybe the ferry would sink on the way over and solve the whole problem. Fiona sighed. Who needed Bertie Wooster? There was always scotch. Thus comforted, she headed for the dock.

After she had spent several fruitful hours at the Sister Bay Library, Fiona felt she had what she needed. She had an armful of books, copies of several articles, and a sense of something close to complacency about the prospects of goat care. She could do this, she had decided, at least for a little while. At least until she had figured out the right way to get rid of him. She corrected herself. To re-gift.

Pleased at a morning well-spent, she left the library, and headed south to Ephraim, and to Coffee, where she could be sure of finding some pleasant conversation, and also Roger. As she turned in, Fiona caught a glimpse of what looked like Mike and Terry standing and staring at the front of the shop. Pleased to see them, but puzzled, she parked and walked across the drive to join them. They all stood together and looked up. No one spoke.

The familiar crooked letters on the door were gone. Above the length of the plate glass window hung a gleaming new sign. It was black, with professionally painted gold letters, shadowed in red. Ground Zero, it said. And on either side of the words was the silhouette in gold of a coffee cup with a mushroom cloud arising from its depths.

There was silence. The sun sparkled on the freshly cleaned windows and caught the gold of the lettering, making it seem to shimmer. Roger, seeing them there, came outside to join them, the door jangling behind him as he came, wiping his hands on a clean white towel. The dark circles under his eyes indicated that he had been working late the night before, but his T-shirt was clean, and his hair freshly rumpled. A penetrating breeze stirred the leaves around their feet, and there were white caps on Eagle Harbor. A seagull uttered a raucous cry.

They all stood looking. Roger spoke first. The look on his face made it clear that he was utterly unaware that the name could cause offense, but then, Roger's social antennae were not finely tuned. It was a physics term to him, and it had not occurred to him that anyone could have a different association.

"I've ordered an awning, too," he said, gazing at the sign with an air of satisfaction. "The name will be across the front along the edge." Silently, they all turned with one movement to look at him. "It's yellow," he added.

They all turned back, looking up.

Fiona opened her mouth to speak, caught Roger's face, and stopped, biting her lip as she gazed back up at the sign.

After some moments, Terry spoke.

"I don't know about you all," he said, slowly. "But I think I better sit down."

And with that, they all followed him silently into the shop, Roger standing aside, proudly holding the door for them to enter.

It wasn't until that night, as she was about to get into bed, that Fiona realized that for the first time in many weeks, she hadn't thought once about Champagne Man. Maybe there was something to this goat business, she thought. And picking up the book she was reading from the nightstand, *The Idiots Guide to Goats*, she settled in for the night.

The next morning was Monday, and Fiona was up early to wait for Luke, an Island carpenter who had come highly recommended. Work was in short supply on Washington Island, and she had quickly discerned the importance of using local labor. Fiona had originally planned for him to work on the front porch, but Robert's presence and subsequent activities demanded some remedial work be done to contain him. When she heard the knock on the front door, she went to get it cheerfully. To her surprise, she opened the door to see the Island's policeman, Nils Johnsson, standing there.

"Miss Campbell?" he asked, in that combination of authority and respectfulness so carefully cultivated through police work.

"Yes, Sergeant Johnsson. How are you? Would you like to come in?" Fiona was wondering where she had left her checkbook, since he must be selling tickets to a benefit of some kind.

"Thank you, ma'am," he said, ducking his head to enter the front doorway. He must have been six feet four inches, with the blond hair Fiona had come to expect on this Island full of Icelandic settlers.

He seemed very serious and professional, not the jovial fellow she had encountered several times down at Nelson's or at the church supper last week. He was looking down at her from what seemed to be a great height.

"Would you like a cup of coffee?" asked Fiona, gesturing toward the kitchen.

"No, thank you, all the same. I'm afraid I'm here on business."

Something about the way he said it make Fiona's stomach lurch, and without his saying another word, she knew what was coming.

"There has been a complaint about a domestic animal. A goat. We've had a report that it has been wandering."

There was a brief silence, and Fiona sighed. "Thank you, Stella," she thought.

"I'm afraid that's true," she said. "He's…new…I just got him, and he got away yesterday. He broke his tether."

"Well, as you know, the owner is responsible for the ani-mal at all times, and since the incident"—Fiona winced at the word—"was reported to the police"—Fiona felt her stomach curling into a tight little knot—"I'm afraid that I will have to issue a citation for 'animal at large'. Goats, as you know, can be quite dangerous. Particularly male goats, as I understand this is." Sergeant Johnsson regarded her dispassionately.

"Yes," said Fiona quietly.

"It's a $300 fine. If you dispute it, you must appear in court on the date noted. I must also inform you that if there are mul-tiple complaints, the animal could be confiscated."

"Could you take him now?" Fiona asked, eagerly.

Sergeant Johnsson frowned. "I'm afraid this is not a joking matter."

Fiona thought she had never felt less like joking in her life.

Suitably chastised, however, she fell silent, and watched as he wrote busily on his metal clipboard. The sergeant looked up at last, his pen poised.

"May I have the correct spelling of your last name, please?" Fiona could see Luke's truck pulling up behind the patrol car in front of the house.

She took a deep breath. "C-A-M-P-B-E-L-L."

After Sergeant Johnsson had left and Luke had begun his work, whistling cheerfully, Fiona searched out her checkbook with shaking hands, determined to get this unpleasant task out of the way. She had no doubt that the citation was out of the usual realm, having heard many stories of the Island's performing arts center, when patrons would leave a performance only to find Petr Gulbrandsen's cows wandering among the cars. She was quite sure that he had not been issued citations.

No, this was Stella's act of war, and Fiona had no illusions whatsoever about that.

Later that afternoon, after Luke had gone, Fiona took herself resignedly out to the barn to feed Robert the goat. The late sun slanted through the windows and reflected the bright new wood that Luke had used to build out one of the stalls and strengthen its door and walls. He had done good work, Fiona thought, running her hand over the edge of the door brace. The bill for the barn, however, had meant that the porch repairs would have to wait.

She looked at the goat who was wholly engrossed in discovering the last nugget of goat chow in the bottom of his bucket. Fiona sighed as she dug a scoop into the big metal can that held more food and carried it to the stall. Instantly, the animal was on alert, and he stood watching her, his yellow eyes glittering, and a long strand of saliva glistening from his lip.

"Here," said Fiona. "I'll give you more, but you have to try not to spit on me."

The goat stamped his foot and snorted, leaving wet spots on Fiona's sleeve and shirt front.

"Yuck! Robert! That's disgusting!"

"HAHAHA!" said Robert.

Fiona stopped and regarded him frowning. "Well, that was disturbing," she said out loud.

"WHAT?" asked Robert, now fully interested in the conversation.

There was a long silence as each looked at the other, expecting some explanation.

"Did you say something?" asked Fiona, finally.

"WHATWHATWHATWHATWHAT?" said Robert.

Fiona studied him, frowning. It was becoming clear to her just what impact a lonely life could have on the human mind. "Just what I need, because my life hasn't been complete until now," she said.

Robert bared his teeth in a goatly smile. "Uhuh, Uhuh, Uhuh," he said cheerfully.

Fiona filled the trough without taking her eyes from him. "You creep me out, Robert," she said.

The goat chuckled to himself from the depths of his feedbin.

"I'm leaving now. You'll have to talk to yourself." There was silence in the barn as Fiona latched the door and walked slowly back to the house, trying to remember what her life had been like.

Impending winter in Door County brought out a universal desire to soak up the last remaining dregs of sunshine. The waning warmth of autumn days was something to be savored and remembered, stored up against the long cold months to come. Roger and Elisabeth went for a walk in Ephraim, first in the golden lanes in the bluffs above the town, but as the sun went down and the temperature fell, they found themselves walking along the edge of the harbor. It was getting cold, but they were still unready to give ground to the season.

They sat side by side on the grass along the water, and watched the sky. A slight wind was coming up; Elisabeth buttoned her jacket, drew her knees up and put her arms around them.

"You know, I've been meaning to ask you something," she began.

Roger shifted nervously, but did not look at her.

"Ok," he said.

"What…" Elisabeth hesitated over her choice of words. "…inspired you to give Fiona a goat?"

"Oh," he said, obviously relieved. Elisabeth wondered what he had thought she was going to say.

"Well," he hesitated. "You did say she would be lonely."

Elisabeth was somewhat taken aback. Although she had no doubt that she had made a remark of this kind, she was reasonably certain that a goat had not been the kind of society she would have suggested. She maintained a bemused silence. Was Roger, in his own unusual way, becoming thoughtful?

Roger began to relax in what he felt was an outflowing of approval. "He should make extremely good company, too. He talks."

She gave him a skeptical smile. "Haha," she said.

"No, really," said Roger, turning to look earnestly at her. "He talks."

Elisabeth was puzzled. Roger was not a man given to flights of fancy.

"Seriously," he said. "He makes these extremely loud noises that sound like words, and it's really quite convincing."

"But," said Elisabeth, unwilling to play the fool, "We were all there, and he didn't make a sound."

"He's shy."

She studied him for signs of joking, but he was completely serious.

"What kinds of things does he say?" she asked finally.

"Well," said Roger, frowning into the distance. "I don't really know his full range. I've only heard him once. My brother said it takes awhile before he gets comfortable around someone, but once he gets going, it's kind of repetitive. I guess he says something that sounds like 'WHAT? I'm not sure what else." Roger paused. "And he also says 'BOB.' It's kind of eerie, actually."

"Bob?" Elisabeth said, musingly.

"Yeah. That's why his name is Robert."

"Oh." Elisabeth frowned at the sunset, still puzzled.

"But you still haven't answered my question."

Roger looked surprised. He thought he had. "I haven't?"

"No. Why did you give him to Fiona?" She turned to look at him again, a small smile on her face. "Did you really think he would be good company?" Roger shrugged.

"He was driving my brother crazy," he said, looking back off toward the water. He paused thoughtfully. "And Fiona just seems like someone who would appreciate a talking goat."

Elisabeth squinted at him for a moment in silence.

"You know," she said slowly, I think you might actually be right."

His face expressionless, Roger stared in silence off into the distance. Slowly, as if it had a will of its own, his arm went around her shoulders. Smiling to herself and unhesitating, Elisabeth laid her head against him.

It was almost dark when they got up to go home.

The $300 check had been painful to write, but it added motivation—if any more were needed—to Fiona's growing goat-related desperation. Despite Roger's claims as to the difficulties of getting rid of Robert, Fiona felt she had to try. She was surprised, however, when within twenty-four hours she received a response to her ad on Craig's list.

Healthy male goat.

Unneutered.

Black and tan.

Cannot keep.

$100 OBO.

She'd had no idea what a goat was worth, nor did she particularly care. But Fiona had a fundamental philosophy that people valued things they paid for. She would have been uncomfortable offering a free goat, not knowing what kinds of people might be eager to accept such an offer. It was a gamble in any

case, but she wanted to tip the odds at least a bit toward the side
of good stewardship.

"I could use your goat," said the e-mail. "When can I get
him?"

Hastily, Fiona wrote back, and arranged for the transaction
to take place on Saturday. She felt a tiny twinge as she hit send.
That had been almost too easy. But she chided herself to take
yes for an answer.

It was just after three-thirty Saturday afternoon when an old
truck with a trailer rattled up and parked in front of the house.
When the driver emerged, Fiona went outside and down the
porch steps.

"You the goat-lady?" the man asked.

Fiona inwardly shuddered. "It's come to this," she thought.
But she nodded.

"Yes."

"I come about the goat, as you see," he said, nodding
toward the trailer. "Hell of a ride over here. Lake was windy as
all get out."

"It can get a little rough at this time of year," Fiona acknowledged. There was a pause.

"I suppose you want to see him?" she asked.

The man shrugged. "I come all this way; doesn't matter one
way or another what he looks like."

A sudden suspicion crossed Fiona's mind, but she quelled it.

"If you'll wait here, then I'll go get Robert. The goat," she
corrected herself. Somehow she didn't see this man as the type
who would name his animals.

The man nodded, pulled out a crumpled pack of cigarettes

and lit one, cupping the lighter in his hand to protect the flame. Fiona headed toward the barn. She didn't like the look of the man. And she didn't like the look of the trailer, which was filthy and smelled. She could picture, in her mind's eye, the condition of the barn this man kept, and the kind of care he was likely to give to his animals. She thought of Robert, of his malice, and of his mischief. "Nasty creature," she thought. But she wasn't sure if she was speaking of the goat or of the man.

Fiona stopped in the middle of the yard and turned around. The man had his back to her, smoking and squinting off into the distance. She definitely did not like the looks of him. "Do you want to be the goat-lady?" she asked herself. No. The answer was definitely no. Strengthened by this inner conversation, she turned back toward the barn and attached the thick leather lead to Robert's harness.

Surprisingly docile, for once, he submitted to her tugs, and followed her like a big dog across the yard, the bell on his neck jangling loudly.

When he saw the trailer, Robert stopped abruptly. Sounding, for once, like an animal, he bleated loudly and backed away, his head up, sniffing the air.

"Come on, Robert," said Fiona firmly. "You are going for a ride."

Reluctantly, Robert followed Fiona across the yard and to the waiting trailer. The man threw his cigarette onto the ground and came toward them to open the trailer gate. As soon as he saw the man, Robert jumped and tried to skitter away. Fiona held firmly to the lead.

"Robert! Come on!" she said loudly, pulling him hard toward the trailer ramp.

"BAWB!" said Robert, all four legs stiff as he balked at the ramp.

The man came behind and tried to push Robert's hindquarters. Before Fiona could give a warning, Robert's sharp hooves flashed back in a swift kick, and the man fell backward into the street. Robert pranced and bucked like a horse, as Fiona tried hard to hold onto him.

"Goddammit," said the man. There was a sharp, ugly anger in his eyes that Fiona could feel simmering across the ten feet that separated them.

"Are you hurt?" she asked, although she secretly found it difficult to care.

"Nah, I'm all right. That damn animal is lucky, this time, though. He'll learn a thing or two; that's for sure."

"Here, give me the lead." He put his hand out to snatch away the lead as Robert continued to pull and buck. Fiona stood still for a moment. Sensing her calm, Robert, too, became suddenly still, and he stood quietly, but alert at the end of the lead.

Fiona took a deep breath.

"I've changed my mind.

"What do you mean, 'you changed your mind'?"

"I don't want to sell him."

The anger in the man's eyes reappeared.

"I just came all the way up here with a trailer on the ferry. And you've just changed your mind?"

Fiona met the man's eyes and spoke quietly.

"I'm sorry."

The man's eyes now narrowed into slits. He opened his

mouth to speak, but Fiona continued, undaunted.

"I'll pay you for your time and trouble, and for the ferry. But I'm afraid he has to stay." With Robert tagging along, his bell dangling madly, she ran up the porch stairs to the house and grabbed her wallet from her purse hanging near the door. She ran back, Robert gamboling cheerfully behind her, and handed the man the $100 she had meant to spend on airfare for Thanksgiving.

"One hundred dollars doesn't even cover it," said the man, sensing opportunity. He didn't know anyone who kept $100 bills lying around. Where there was one, there were likely more.

"Take it or leave it," said Fiona, instinctively accessing her city demeanor. "The goat stays."

And with that, she turned on her heel and walked Robert back toward the barn. Behind her she heard the man curse and spit. But he got into his truck, slammed the door, and drove away. Fiona waited behind the house until she heard the engine fade into the distance. It occurred to her that he might come back when he realized that she was a woman alone. But this was one case in which the Island's remoteness was an advantage.

Fiona walked out to the barn and pushed open the door, Robert, now tranquil, following behind. The space was filled with great slanting shafts of afternoon sunlight, clean hay, and with clean water in the trough. Fiona had done all this first thing, cheered with the knowledge that it would be for the last time. Tonight she would be goat-free, she had told herself.

Robert looked up at her as they entered and stomped his feet. A sardonic sneer crossed his face and he tossed his head. Fiona looked into his glittering eyes and mentally replayed the events of the past half hour. She had just paid $100 for a goat. A goat, what is more, that she neither wanted nor liked. It was only slightly less than she had been paid, after taxes, for her last article, and judging by the property tax estimate she had just received, it would probably mean that a Thanksgiving trip to see her father was out of reach.

"You have no idea," she said aloud to him. "You just have no idea at all."

Robert snorted and tossed his head again, waited while she opened the gate for him, and walked contentedly into his stall. Fiona threw another handful of goat chow into his bucket, and went back to the house.

That night Fiona lay in bed reading *The Idiots' Guide.* "Goats," said the book, "are nervous creatures. Talk or sing to your goats to calm and soothe them, and they will come to trust you." Fiona looked up from her reading and imagined herself singing to Robert. It was not lost on her that the book made no reference to the goat talking back.

Nor did the author appear to have observed that the effect of goat conversation on the stress level of the owner was exactly the opposite of comforting.

Chapter Sixteen

Each morning he walked into his shop, Roger had a fresh jolt of surprise. Mentally, he was still expecting the familiar white, utilitarian interior, with its bright laboratory lighting and the vaguely burned smell of coffee sitting on a heating plate. The changes made it feel as if he were entering a new place, and Roger wasn't entirely convinced that it was better. It was alien to him. And somehow the color, the lighting, the pictures, and the new music seemed like distractions; unnecessary embellishments on something that had been complete in its simplicity.

Generally speaking, second-guessing decisions was not his way. When he chose to do something, he did it and moved on. But the pace of this change was troubling him. Not the most emotionally attuned person, Roger nevertheless had his own intuitions. And this discomfort he was feeling meant something. He noted it in himself, as of an observation in the laboratory, and set it aside to be considered. Turning on the lights, he set about the routine for opening up the shop, but this morning, he left off the music. He was comforted by the simplicity of the silence.

L ars Olafsen was a man who took his responsibilities seriously. He had grown up on the Island, he knew his neighbors, and he had been raised to treat others with respect until
they proved that they deserved otherwise. As the chairman of
the town board, his diligence manifested itself in an outward
slowness which was occasionally aggravating to his fellows, but
no one ever thought to accuse him of unfairness.

When his phone rang one autumn evening, he answered
with an unconscious singsong that betrayed the legacy of gen-
erations of Swedish spoken in the home. The inflections of
that influence, nearly forgotten and now directly transcribed to
English, were there for the discerning listener, and added to the
quality of lilting obstinence that could so easily appear to be
mocking.

His wife, Katherine, was putting away the dinner dishes, so
he took the call in the den, away from the clatter.

"Hallo?" he sang.

"Lars? This is Stella."

Lars didn't groan. He was too polite for that. But he knew
well enough that a call from Stella meant a headache for himself
and for the board. Stella had a well-known tendency to be high-
handed, insistent, and, he had to admit, rude and petty. Once
she had chosen to be outraged about something—and it could
be anything—there was no stopping her until she got her way.

Lars dwelled for a moment upon the six months of his life he
had spent mediating a dispute between Stella and the supervi-
sor of the town dump. She had insisted that she was in the right
demanding curbside pickup of her refuse, even though everyone
else on the Island had to go to the dump themselves. In the end

she had won as she always won: by wearing everyone down to the point that they would do anything just to make her go away.

"Yes, Stella," he said calmly.

"What are you going to do about that woman?"

"I'm sorry, Stella, but what woman?"

Lars knew perfectly well what woman. He would have had to have been living under a rock not to know what woman.

"You know perfectly well, what woman, Lars Olafsen," fumed Stella. "The one with the goat."

Lars did not answer immediately. He was, in his steadfast Skandinavian fashion, envisioning the long painful path that stood before him. It was the path of Stella's obdurate ruthlessness, which would lead, inevitably, to that nice young woman—if, in fact she was nice, which some seemed to question—moving away from the Island and taking her money—and her free-spending, perhaps morally questionable friends—with her. And, he thought sadly, the town board had just finished its strategic visioning, led by a high-priced consultant, during which had figured predominantly a lament about the inability to draw people to the Island to live and to spend, building the fragile economy. Bang, he thought, goes that real estate sale; bang goes all that lovely ferry trade; bang go the carpenter, the plumber, the mason, and all the other tradesmen who hoped to get a piece of that falling down wreck of a house. Lars, if he had been Irish, would have sighed.

But Lars was not Irish, or he would have started drinking earlier in this phone call.

"HELLO?" yelled Stella into the phone.

"Yes?" asked Lars calmly.

"I asked you; what are you going to do?"

"And I," said Lars composedly, "asked you: What woman are you talking about?" Delaying tactics were futile, he knew, but they offered some momentary gratification.

"Lars, I demand that the board take action. That woman has a goat. A *male* goat," she added significantly. "And it attacked me. I have a police report. That animal is a menace. It's a danger to the community and if anything happens, I will hold you personally responsible." Stella paused to take a breath.

Lars replied, without one note of exasperation. "Stella, you know the procedure. If you have a complaint about a goat," and how many opportunities does one have to utter that sentence, he thought, in a rare moment of flippancy, "you must write a letter to the board for our consideration. We will consider it in due course."

In a conversation with a normal person he might have paused here, but since it was Stella he went on, and consequently found himself talking at the same time as his irate constituent.

"In due course?" she yelled. "In due course? I'm telling you that that animal is dangerous. Someone could be injured."

"The board," repeated Lars, "as I was saying, has a number of issues pending on the docket. We must take things in order. In any case," he said, treading dangerously close to democracy, "we must allow the owner of the goat an opportunity to respond. This," he added, with well-hidden satisfaction, "could take some time."

"Well I don't intend to wait around to be attacked," said Stella, in cold fury. "If you will not act, I will not be responsible for the consequences."

Before he could respond, she hung up.

Lars stood for a moment holding the receiver. He checked his watch. That had gone well. He'd only missed five minutes of his favorite show, and although he needed to call the other members of the board to warn them, he hesitated now that prime time television was in full swing. Lars went out to the kitchen to urge Katherine to finish up.

Stella hung up feeling some satisfaction. She had no doubts whatsoever about where this was going. It might take some time, but the board would rule in her favor, and when that happened, she was pretty sure, that stuck-up woman would have to get rid of the goat. And when *that* happened, she was also pretty sure, it would only be a matter of time before she, Stella, could find something else to make her neighbor decide that leaving was a whole lot better than staying. Stella really didn't care about goats one way or another, but that woman had to go.

The use of the law to intimidate her neighbors was a method Stella had employed with success in the past. It was true that she had created lasting animosities, but if this bothered her, she showed no sign of it. Since, generally speaking, when a method is effective, it tends to be used again, Stella's resourcefulness in the use of municipal code was wholly predictable. In any case, the rules were quite clear: first, the keeping of domestic animals was restricted by zoning, and second, if they were not under control of the owner, they could be confiscated, and, if dangerous, killed. Municipal code 65; section C, paragraph 3.

Chapter Seventeen ❖

E ach day Fiona was discovering more of Robert's vocabulary. His conversational inclinations were sporadic, but when he felt like it, he was quite capable of
carrying on a lengthy exchange. Fiona began to look
forward to their little chats. There were days when these were
the only conversations she had.

It would have been a mistake, however, to confuse these interactions with developing feelings of affection. Fiona was careful not to turn her back on Robert when he was out of his stall,
and even when he was in it. Looking in his eyes, it was difficult
for her not to imagine that he had plans for mutiny, or possibly
assassination.

Elisabeth had a gallery opening scheduled for Friday evening. Since the ferry schedule, now in its abbreviated autumn
form, would not have permitted her to stay for the reception,
Fiona had been invited to spend the night. Nancy had kindly
volunteered to oversee the care and feeding of Robert, but Fiona
felt a twinge of guilt, like an exhausted and long-suffering parent
who had been at last relieved by a responsible baby-sitter.

The show was a hometown tribute to the work of their
friend, Mike, whose reputation in the outside world had continued to grow. He had had a review in *The New Republic* six
months back, and it had created a cascading demand for his

work and his time. Elisabeth, who had scheduled the show two years before, was now facing the complications arising from his popularity. Retrieving his works from previously cooperative fellow gallery-owners and collectors, and responding to inquiries from the press in places like Chicago, Milwaukee, and Minneapolis—and even as far-off as Tokyo—had made demands on her time she had not fully anticipated.

Fiona had been looking forward to the opening. Stella's antagonism had begun to wear on her, and it would be a relief to escape the mild paranoia she had developed whenever she was in her yard. It wasn't that there were any overt incidents; it was merely the knowledge of Stella's presence, her rancor simmering behind the windows, that colored Fiona's days. It was as if there were an evil spell brewing next door, targeted directly at her.

Even had she had the best of neighbors, however, Fiona had not been a guest at a cocktail party since the wedding in Chicago, and after weeks of having dust, paint, and caulk in her hair, she was happy to have an occasion to be clean and, she hoped, fashionable. She was delighted, too, for Mike, whose newfound status as an art world demigod would only mean good things for him.

It was a golden morning. The yellows, reds, and oranges of the trees made the Island seem to glow in the sunlight. Fiona felt happy as she drove along the road to the ferry dock amid the flutter of falling leaves. Pali was the captain, and she was prepared when he invited her to the pilothouse; armed with her own thermos, she presented the crew with a box of doughnuts. Their cheerful round of coffee made the ride across Death's Door seem shorter than usual. There was a cold wind on the water, in spite of the sun, and the warmth of the little cabin was delightful, filled with the smell of coffee and cinnamon. As the ferry approached Northpoint and the crew dispersed to their duties, Fiona returned to her car, and waved good-bye to them as she drove onto the dock. Her mind filled with the anticipation of the weekend, she zoomed happily along the road's slalom-style curves which she imagined had been installed to slow down traffic rather than to encourage speed. She looked forward to her excursion with the enthusiasm of a small child.

Knowing that Elisabeth would be preoccupied with the more important work of installing the exhibition, Fiona had volunteered to be in charge of the reception, a task she looked forward to. She stopped at Fish Creek to select sausages, cheeses, crackers, and pâtés, and at Egg Harbor for fruit, wine, beer, and soda. There would be glasses, not plastic cups, and she would use some of Elisabeth's beautiful pitchers and platters. As she turned north again for the gallery, Fiona drove further inland where she could forage illegally along the roadside for wildflowers, branches, cattails, and grapevines to use for decoration.

Being back in her old territory inspired Fiona to draw contrasts between her new life and her old. Life on the Island was quieter and more solitary. As she passed one of her favorite restaurants, whose bar she had regularly visited, Fiona realized suddenly that she hadn't had a drink in a very long time. She had expected that the loneliness of life on the Island would have led her to increase her scotch consumption. But the opposite seemed to be the case. The Island seemed to have eliminated her need for other kinds of relaxation, and the new bottle of ruinously expensive single malt scotch she'd purchased was still sitting unopened on the living room shelf.

The loneliness itself seemed to have lessened rather than intensified. Despite Stella's almost palpable belligerence, Fiona walked in a serenity she had not experienced before, as if cloaked in a shield of invisible protection. Fiona pondered this as she waded through an open field, cutting clusters of wild asters, their variegated shades of purple and fuchsia in vivid contrast to the gold of the tall grasses they were growing among. Bees buzzed around them, relentlessly pursuing the last tastes of summer. It was not as if she didn't want company—far from it—but she was comfortable in some new way that she couldn't explain even to herself. Or, even, especially to herself.

Fiona placed her harvest into the trunk of the car, and set off down the road to Elisabeth's. She parked in a customer space and gathered her first load of cargo to carry to the house. As she walked up the path, Rocco, who had been frantically barking from inside, at last escaped and ran to greet her, twirling in loops of joy, trilling and barking. He had been taught not to jump on people so he leapt in the air, running away from her and returning in a frenzy of excitement. Her arms full, Fiona put down the bags of groceries and sat on the ground to put her arms around him and to whisper in his ear. Instantly Rocco sat and settled his big head against her shoulder, his chin fitting perfectly against her neck.

"Hey, Rocco," she said softly. "I'm glad to see you, too." He purred like an enormous cat and nuzzled closer.

After a few moments Fiona gathered up her packages, finished unloading the car, and put the flowers in buckets of water on the porch, and the food in the refrigerator. She looked down at Rocco's expectant face.

"Now?" She asked him, looking into his golden eyes. Rocco barked once in direct response.

"Ok, let's go see Elisabeth!" said Fiona.

Rocco gave a soft song of pleasure, and together they went across the driveway to the gallery. Elisabeth was on the phone, and looked up and waved as she continued her conversation. The smell of oil paint, varnish, and floor wax permeated the air. Packing cases were everywhere; two young women were measuring the placement of a portrait, which Fiona recognized immediately as someone she knew. Rocco, familiar with the chaos of an opening, greeted his friends, then found his favorite corner and lay down where he could watch without being stepped on. Mike stood off by himself in a corner, his placid countenance exactly as always. When he saw Fiona, a beatific smile spread across his face, and he came to meet her.

"Hi, Mike," she said, hugging him. "How's it going?"

"Oh, about as always," he said, still smiling. "But Elisabeth is a wonderful organizer with a great eye." His eyes crinkled as his smile deepened. "And no one can ever say no to her. She will have everything perfectly placed and in order before the doors open."

Fiona glanced over at Elisabeth, whose conversation seemed to have taken a slightly contentious tone.

"Anything wrong?"

Mike shrugged and shook his head. "There's a shipment of paintings that was supposed to be here from San Francisco, and they haven't arrived. It's not the end of the world, probably, but I would have liked to have had them here."

They both turned to look as Elisabeth could be heard saying in a firm voice. "I am sorry, but that is not acceptable. You will need to send someone to get it."

Mike looked at Fiona, and indicated Elisabeth with a slight nod of his head.

"As I say, no one can ever say no."

They smiled at each other.

"Do you have time to show me some of your work?" Fiona asked.

"Absolutely. Come over here and let me tell you about this portrait of my good friend, Ed."

They walked together toward the stairs and Mike led the way to the second floor of the exhibition.

An hour before the opening, Fiona made a last trip through the gallery to see that everything was ready. The bars had been set up in two rooms, staffed by two amiable college students; the tables with the pâtés, sausage, cheese, and fruit platters were on the open patio between the two buildings to keep the traffic flowing. Her field harvest of autumn flowers and grass were dramatically displayed on the food tables and bars, and tucked in several small niches of the gallery.

Elisabeth and one of her assistants were adjusting the lighting for the last painting from the shipment that had been personally delivered less than an hour before, and a second assistant had cleared away the last of the packing and was sweeping the gleaming wood floors. Mike had gone home to rest and change.

The galleries consisted of a converted barn and outbuilding, connected by a covered walkway to one another, and surrounded by gardens, patios, and gravel walkways lined with sculpture. The barn had two floors, with a narrow winding stair connecting them. The need to connect the different areas had made the floors in the various rooms at slightly different heights, varying here by an inch, there by an inch or two. These small steps, that were not quite steps, could be hazardous to the unwary, and Elisabeth had marked them with large signs commanding people to look down, the result of both common sense and the advice of her lawyer.

Fiona was wearing a simple silk dress the color of the lake at midday, and her Italian sandals, whose slippery thin leather soles and heels made walking just a little precarious. It felt odd to be wearing something other than shorts or jeans and a T-shirt. She felt lighter, and looked forward to the evening and conversations with friends.

At five o'clock people began to arrive, first in a trickle, and then in an advancing wave. The big field beyond the drive was filled with cars, and the rising murmur of visitors filled the gallery and its gravel paths. The bars and appetizer tables were busy. Ice had sloshed over onto the floors, the food supplies were diminishing, and the ubiquitous yellow jackets, even at this time of year, persisted in their pursuit of cheese and fruit on the tables outside.

A press of people surrounded Mike and Elisabeth, everyone eager to offer their congratulations, and to demonstrate to their friends that they were special friends of the artist. In Door

County, it was likely to be true that they were at least acquaintances. But people in groups inevitably follow the same patterns, Fiona thought to herself that it was no less so here. An event like this attracted nearly everyone in Door County from all walks of life. The wealthy visitors from Milwaukee and Chicago, local artists, but also the permanent residents: the owner of the grocery store and other businesspeople, members of the fire department, teachers, carpenters, and farmers—it was hard to find any segment of the community not represented. Fiona flowed with the crowd, stopping to chat with Terry and his wife, Anne, and other acquaintances, finding small opportunities here and there to take in some of Mike's work when there was an opening in the crowd, occasionally replenishing or refreshing a tray of food.

It was in the midst of this last activity midway through the evening that Fiona spotted Roger leaning uncomfortably against a column. He was alone. His rumpled hair had been slicked back and Fiona was astonished to see that he was wearing a sport shirt rather than his usual white T-shirt. His sleeves were rolled up and he looked hot and miserable. Crowds were not Roger's preferred milieu. Fiona went and stood next to him.

"What do you think?"

He glanced at her scowling. "I've seen his work before."

"Ah," said Fiona. "Did you just get here?"

"No."

"Did you have something to eat?"

"No."

The conversation limped, as conversations always did with Roger, and Fiona wasn't sure if she should leave him alone or whether he would feel abandoned if she did. She could never read Roger. But, perhaps, she thought, no one could. She gazed at him as he stared off into the distance, and realized suddenly that with the press of people surrounding Elisabeth, Roger was cut off. It would not be within his powers to elbow through a crowd. She felt a wave of empathy for him.

"Have you spoken to Elisabeth?"

"No." He continued to look away.

"Come on," she said, not daring to touch his arm. "Let's go find her. She must be desperate for a break."

He followed her silently through the crowd of people like a big sullen dog. Elisabeth was standing with her back to them, chatting with an elderly couple. Fiona went up to her and touched her arm without interrupting the conversation. As Elisabeth turned, Fiona gestured to Roger, and leaving him there to suffer or bask, she moved away.

It was as she drifted toward the landscapes in one corner of the gallery that Fiona felt the sudden jolt of dismay that came from recognition. Standing in the corner with another woman, was Stella. She was wearing a purple quilted jacket with flowers appliquéd on the front, and a smear of lipstick in an unflattering color. Fiona, who had hoped for an escape from Stella and her malice, was about to turn away when a portion of the conversation carried. "She's a stuck-up bitch." It was clearly intended for her to hear. Fiona detested confrontations, and this was not the place anyway. She kept going. "Did you hear me?" Stella repeated. "A stuck-up bitch." Fiona swallowed hard and pretended not to hear. She would not be goaded, and she would not spoil Mike and Elisabeth's evening.

"Some day she's going to wake up and find that goat with its throat slit."

Fiona froze. The crowd seemed to disappear. There was only the lights and sound and the pounding of her heart. She was no longer thinking, just reacting. Slowly she turned around and walked up to Stella until she was leaning into her face. Stella was smiling.

Fiona took a deep breath and spoke very slowly in a low voice. "If there is ever even so much as a hair disturbed on that animal, I will see to it that you spend a very long time in jail. Do you understand me?" And without waiting for a reply, she turned her back and strode away.

Fiona was in a white fury. Blind and deaf to everything around her, it was as if she were propelled by rage. The nerve of that woman, she thought. Robert may be a nuisance, and God alone knew she would be happy to see the last of him. But to suggest such a thing. And in such a way. And in this particular circumstance. It was ghoulish. What a black heart the woman had.

Turning on her heel, Fiona forgot the slickness of the polished wood floors, and the tiny two-inch step from one section of the barn to the other. She forgot the thin leather soles of her new Italian slippers, the newly waxed floors, and the spilled ice around the serving table. Striding blindly toward the exit, her foot slipped, and she caught at a railing just before she hit the floor, hard, landing with her feet in opposite directions.

There was a moment's silence before concerned witnesses hurried to help her up, exclaiming, asking if she were all right, and no doubt, exchanging knowing looks above her head. Humbly, Fiona accepted their ministrations with as much grace as she could, and escaped as quickly as possible to the comfort of the solitude and darkness outside the gallery.

She seated herself rather gingerly on a bench along the path, brushed herself off, took a brief inventory of her wounds, and examined her ruined heel. A crunch on the path alerted her to company. Looking up, she found Mr. Ingersoll, the kindly machinist from down the road gazing at her with concern.

"You know," he said without preamble, "my old father was an alcoholic. Never would admit it. My mother suffered something terrible by it, and us kids did, too." He paused, nodding, and looking deeply into Fiona's eyes. "You're a nice young woman. Take my advice, as a voice of experience. Stay off the stuff. You'll be the better for it." And patting her gently on the arm, he moved away.

Recovering what she could of her dignity, Fiona made her way across the path to the house. Fumbling with the screen door, she let herself into Elisabeth's kitchen where Rocco was waiting to greet her.

It was getting close to sunset when Nancy set off to Fiona's to look after her goat. Nancy was one of those people who could put her hand to anything. She had no arrogance about this; it was merely her view that if something needed to be done, you did it, brushed off your hands, and went on to the next thing. Most people, in her view, dithered unnecessarily. "See it; do it"; that was her motto. She would never have put it this way, but there was a kind of purity in the way she lived her life. It was both uncomplicated and necessary, and it suited her.

As she walked around the back of Fiona's house she noticed that the door to the barn was open. Nancy frowned to herself. Had she forgotten to close the door? She wasn't usually careless about such things, but she had been getting rather absentmind-ed lately. She shrugged to herself and went into the barn.

Robert was nowhere to be seen. His stall gate was closed, but Nancy quickly saw that it was unlatched. At first she dared to hope that he might have dug himself into the straw in his stall, but it didn't take her long to find that he was not there. Begin-ning to worry, she went out into the yard.

The gallery opening was winding down, but the last lingerers were still clustering around the wine and cheese. Her ser-vices would not be required until everyone had gone, and Fiona decided she had time to take a walk to soothe herself. Changing swiftly into jeans, she left a note for Elisabeth in case she should return first, summoned Rocco, and slipped out of the house, heading up the path from the house toward the small wooded ridge nearby.

It was just sunset. The orange light still penetrated the trees, the air was cool, and the smell of fallen leaves filled the air. The two of them crunched along the path. Rocco snuffled urgent-ly in holes and around trees, wandering off the path and back again when he felt she was getting too far away.

Her encounter with Stella had left Fiona disturbed and agitated. The strangeness of her new life; the sudden shift in routines and responsibilities, all of which had seemed perfectly acceptable and pleasant for the most part, suddenly loomed above her, insurmountable. All of her newfound tranquillity was gone. Her recent humiliation had triggered this mood, and she was exhausted, she knew. She was suddenly tired of everything being so hard. She wanted to just go home. But where was that now?

Her precipitous escape from Chicago to Ephraim had been a desire to explain her life to herself, to get away from the superficial hamster-wheel quality that her days had acquired. But Ephraim had been a more acceptable transition, somehow; more reasoned than the Island. It bore at least some resemblance to what she thought of as her real life.

What explanation did she have now? She hadn't chosen her circumstances so much as allowed circumstances to choose her, reacting to other people's views of her—to a dare, for God's sake—impulsively purchasing the house on the Island, with no real friends, no support network. And a goat! She had a goddamned goat!

"And not even a decent freaking shoe store," she raged at herself. No place to go to soothe herself with the comforts of civilization, no windows to stroll past just to enjoy the beautiful displays. Fiona, never much for crying, now felt like sobbing in frustration. Why had she done this to herself? Why could she never just let things be comfortable? Why was she living next door to this…she struggled for the word and grasped what came first…psychopath? Why had she stuck herself in the middle of nowhere, when she could be in Chicago, reachable, knowable? Where someone could find her if he wanted to? Near… She stopped herself. The hair rose on the backs of her arms and she began to shiver.

From the depths of somewhere—whether it was in her mind or in the woods, she couldn't be certain, a faint sound began. Fiona stood motionless, filled with a paralyzing fear she had never known before in her life. She felt herself surrounded by something that rose and swirled around her. At first it was like wind whistling, then singing, and then screaming, and all at once wailing, high, mournful, unearthly songs. She could not run or scream; she could only listen, her mind and ears straining. Rocco, beside her, froze and stared into the woods, his fur standing straight up; his body beginning a long, low vibration of warning, running like a counterpoint to the rushing sound. The sound seemed to spin and soar, and like a distant star that disappears when you look directly at it, suddenly shimmered, swirled, and died. Then it was gone.

Fiona stood for a long moment. What had just happened? Had anything happened? she wondered. How can something you didn't see and didn't hear have happened? Or had she heard it?

She looked down at Rocco. The hair on his back was still standing up. Had he heard it? Or was he reacting to her? Rocco's golden brown eyes searched her face. He pushed his nose against her hand. She reached down to touch the warmth of his head, his ears. He turned back down the path toward the house and stopped to look back at her, clearly urging her to follow. Fiona looked uneasily into the shadows. It was almost dark.

"You're right, Rocco," said Fiona, suddenly recovering her wits. "Let's get the hell out of here." They ran all the way back to Elisabeth's house.

The next morning Fiona described her experience in the woods to Elisabeth as they sat together drinking coffee. "I know it sounds stupid," said Fiona. "But I felt suddenly, acutely mortal. As if I were going to die."

"Did Rocco hear it?" asked Elisabeth.

"I'm not sure," said Fiona.

They both looked down at him and he looked back, wagging his tail. He had heard his name. Were they going to give him toast?

Elisabeth broke off a piece of her buttered English muffin and gave it to him. He smacked his lips happily, and looked for more.

"My Irish grandmother would have said that they were banshees, come to warn you," she said, getting up to make more toast.

"I think he wants jelly on it," said Fiona, reaching for the jar on the table. "Warn me of what?"

Elisabeth looked at Fiona and frowned.

"Did you know that feelings of foreboding or impending doom are a recognized symptom of heart attack in women?" she asked.

"No," said Fiona. "But since I frequently have feelings of foreboding, how would I tell if this were routine, everyday foreboding or symptomatic foreboding?"

Elisabeth looked at her calmly.

"It hardly seems routine. Are you depressed?"

Fiona pondered this question for a moment. "No. I wouldn't call it that."

"Do you think you have a fever?" she asked.

"No," said Fiona. "No depression. No fever. Just banshees and nonspecific foreboding."

"You're fine," said Elisabeth firmly. She paused.

"But maybe you should lay off the scotch." She went to get more butter for Rocco's toast.

Fiona drove home that afternoon by a circuitous route. She felt the need to console herself, and that generally meant that she wanted to buy something. Her favorite antiques store was a bit off the beaten path—"What wasn't?" she asked herself—a cluster of several small houses linked by gravel paths and exuberant gardens. It always pleased her to wander its cluttered rooms gazing at English armoires and desks she could never afford and the broaches and lamps and new French table linens that she occasionally could.

As she dallied in the shop, Fiona thought it would be an idyllic life to be a clerk in a little store and spend all day making beautiful displays of things. You could have calming music on that you liked, and occasionally a customer to have a happy, meaningless chat with, and then you could go home to other things, leaving the worries of business to the manager. Probably not much, either, in the way of banshees, nor other manifestations of a mind trembling on the edge of sanity. "Although," she thought, "possibly the occasional haunted armoire."

Fiona bought a blue and white tablecloth, a small white lamp, two scented candles, and a little box of letterpress stationery. She had a happy meaningless chat with the shopkeeper, and went back to the car. It had been a pleasant diversion to visit the little store, but it hadn't shifted her mood. Stella was beginning to make her nervous. Was the woman completely unstable? Should she start locking her doors? And what about Robert? Was she really a threat to him? These were things Fiona needed to know. She wished there were someone she could talk to about these things, but she was worried that the Island grapevine would spread anything she said. It occurred to her that Nancy might be a good choice for solid advice, but she also seemed to share the Island love of a good story.

In the midst of all of this, the thought of driving away from her friends on the mainland left a little nub of pain in Fiona's chest. She still wasn't sure about what had happened out in the woods, and she was a little afraid to think about it. It had felt real. She headed north to the ferry. She had developed a more casual approach to the schedule and had cut things a bit close. A small line of cars preceded her.

It wasn't long before the ferry appeared suddenly over the horizon, and Fiona watched from the warmth of her car as it pivoted, docked, and unloaded the few vehicles it carried. In a remarkably short time the crew began waving the next passengers on. Driving onboard, the car made its familiar bump over the metal ramp to the ferry deck.

Fiona felt a wash of relief flooding over her. Pulling the brake, she left the car and walked upstairs to stand at the deck in the open air. The wind was still soft, the water was smooth, and the late autumn sun sparkled on the lake. As the engines started up, a deep sense of well-being filled her, and the little ferry started on its way, pointing its face toward the Island and home.

As she drove up to her house, Fiona noticed a number of cars parked in front. She recognized Nancy's and Jim's, but it was the presence of the fire engine, the fire chief's car, and the Washington Island police car that made Fiona's heart stop. There seemed to be a commotion going on around the back of the house. Fiona pulled the handbrake unnecessarily hard and ran.

A group of a dozen people were standing clustered around the big maple tree in the back of the house, including two firemen with long heavy ropes and what looked like a folded tent and fishing net. A ladder leaned against the side of the back porch, and a third fireman was standing on the roof, where several sturdy branches of the tree, still covered with brilliant red leaves, were overhanging. Several Islanders, including Nancy, stood nearby, all looking up.

"Careful!" Nancy was saying. "If he moves away from you too suddenly he's going to fall."

"Wait until we get the net set up," Jim was saying to some invisible person apparently above their heads.

Fiona followed their gaze. About twenty feet up, standing nonchalantly on a very small and delicate-looking branch, Robert was nibbling daintily on the red autumn leaves. Out of the corner of his eye he observed the activities going on around him with a look of weary cynicism. Robert saw Fiona before anyone else did, and he paused, a small branch of leaves sticking out of his mouth. He made a noise that sounded like "AHA!" the leaves falling from his mouth as he did so.

"AHA AHA AHA AHA AHA AHA AHA!" he repeated.

The activity of the people around him ceased as everyone stared first at Robert, then at Fiona, then back again to Robert. Fiona felt as if she had been caught doing something suspicious.

"Hi Robert," she said, resignedly.

A piece of leaf clung to his lip as he leered down at the people clustered below him. He looked Fiona in the eye. "BAAAW-WWWWWWWWWB!" said Robert. He seemed to be enjoying himself. "BAAAAAAAAWWWWWWWB!"

"Funny," said Jim. "Almost sounds as if he's talking." One of the firemen made a rude remark, and the men chuckled, glancing over at Fiona and Nancy to see if they'd heard.

Nancy came over to stand near Fiona. "He's been up there since yesterday," she said quietly. They stood side by side looking up as they spoke, as if watching a particularly riveting film together. "I knew he was ok, so I figured I wouldn't bother you. But then, when I realized he was stuck, I couldn't reach you. Cell phone signal," she added, apologetically.

"BAAAAAAAWWWWWWWWB!" said Robert.

"Has he been making all this noise?" Fiona asked, distractedly.

Nancy hesitated. "Well, no. Not until you got here."

Fiona digested this information in silence. She stood watching the activities of Robert's rescuers, nodding her head ruefully, her lips compressed into a line.

Sergeant Johnson drew out his ticket book and began writing. "I'm sorry, I've forgotten," he said. "What is your middle initial?"

"But he hasn't left my yard," said Fiona, frowning slightly.

"He did, actually," said Nancy, rather guiltily. "That's how he got up in the tree. We found him on Stella's garage roof, and in the process of trying to retrieve him, he managed somehow to get from there to here."

"Or from here to there," offered Jim, who had come over to join them. "It's hard to see how he could have jumped onto the roof without starting from the tree here. You can see how that larger branch would have made it pretty easy for him to get up there."

Sergeant Johnson stood patiently through this conversation, his pen poised over the book.

Fiona hadn't quite realized that goats could climb trees, although, as she thought about it, she realized that this had been a rather obvious omission. They climbed rocks. Why not trees? "Did he do any damage?" she asked, with what she thought was remarkable calm. She was thanking God that Stella had been off the Island during this episode. Not, she reminded herself, that Stella wouldn't hear about it. Probably before she got off the ferry.

"No," said Nancy.

"Not that we know of," said Jim. "But, of course, we won't know that until Stella gets home," he added helpfully.

"It's A," said Fiona turning to Sergeant Johnson. They all looked at her inquisitively.

"For Ainsley."

"HAHAHAHAHA," said Robert.

F or the next forty-eight hours, Fiona waited uneasily for the demanding knock on her door that would signal Stella's arrival. She found herself checking the windows, and jumping at small noises, and even began to wonder whether it would make sense to think about methods of protection. When it came right down to it, she realized, the only thing standing between her and someone who wanted to hurt her or Robert was a shovel and a bottle of spray bleach.

But even though Fiona could not see it, she was right that Stella was on the offensive. As a longtime resident, Stella was well acquainted with the methods she had at her disposal, and she was already in the process of deploying a tactical weapon. If the more subtle strategies were not sufficient to drive that woman out, Stella would invoke the next level of intervention.

Stella's spitefulness was a deliberate tactic for getting her way, and it was a pretty effective one. Generally, Island people had a "live and let live" philosophy, and were unlikely to interfere in anyone's business. Its officials, however, like people everywhere, had a regrettable tendency to do what was easiest. And not crossing Stella was always easier than getting in her way.

Even if they were uncomfortable with her methods, going along with her was the path of least resistance for members of the Town Board and its various committees. Much better to keep her off your back, even if it meant upsetting that nice new woman who didn't seem to know much, whose occupation was… questionable, and who probably wouldn't try to defend herself. Politics gets done this way everywhere, and Washington Island was no exception.

There was therefore an inevitability—a forces of the universe quality—about the outcome. Stella was a believer in the letter of the law, not the spirit, and she was expert in finding ways to apply that letter to her own benefit. Armed with two municipal citations against her neighbor, Stella would demand eviction of that animal. She had the evidence in her favor and she would win.

"Then," she said to herself, "we'll see how long that stuck up city girl lasts in town, knowing that everyone is against her."

Chapter Eighteen ✦

Fiona had made some dramatic changes in her schedule to accommodate her goat responsibilities. She had never been a late sleeper, but now found herself rising with the sun, and even before her first cup of coffee, pulling on her jeans and trudging out to the barn to make certain that there was food and water.

She made at least two trips to the barn daily, made sure he had access to the out-of-doors in fair weather, and arranged her outings to coincide with his feedings. The amount of time required in attending to what she had come to think of as goat slavery, seemed to be growing on a daily basis.

Robert, despite all Fiona had read about goats' needs for sociability, showed very little interest in her company, with or without singing. Most mornings when she arrived he didn't even look up when she entered the barn, rather like an aristocrat who felt no need to acknowledge a servant. Fiona recognized these signs of entitlement early on. This, she felt, was simply another aspect of her thralldom. Dutifully, she talked and sang to him, feeling particularly foolish when he stared silently at her, his yellow eyes glinting. Occasionally, he would make a remark, and inevitably, Fiona found herself puzzling over how he always seemed to find the appropriate word.

Fall had begun its shift from October's idyllic golden days

to the stark outlines and harder cold of November. The meadow grass, the scrub brush, the harvested fields with their long rows of stubble, the bare trees and even the sand and water seemed to have been infused with purple, and they glowed with it, even in the overcast days. Fiona loved the raw quality of the bare landscape; it seemed purer, stripped to its essential shapes as if it had been drawn with a few sharp lines. The fallen leaves that remained, one on a branch or skittering across the road in the wind, became symbols of another time.

She also loved the solitude. Whatever tourists the Island could glean in the final glories of fall had drifted away from this harsher world. The ferry runs had dropped to two a day; sufficient to supply the needs of commerce merely. Traffic dwindled to almost none as the number of residents fell to a few hundred. Fiona took ever longer walks along the empty roads, greedily drawing in the bitter air, infusing herself with it to such an extent that she could still smell it on her hair and clothes, many hours later. Gradually, her anxious mood had lifted again, and her fear of harm from Stella faded away. It had all been just talk. Fiona felt somehow as if she had expanded into herself, not as if she were lighter, but actually weighted and steady, like a ship taking on ballast to find its balance. She felt happier and simpler than ever before in her life.

It was while returning from one of these walks, refreshed and happy, that Fiona decided to make the day's last visit to the barn. She and Robert had sunk into a comfortable routine, and she was feeling more sanguine about his presence. The time will come, she thought, when I will tell this story over dinner, and we will all laugh. She could see herself in the future, blissfully goat-free.

It was late in the afternoon, and dusk came early. The western sky was pink, and there were blue-black stratus clouds portending rain or possibly snow. Fiona could see her breath in the lavender light of early evening, and strolled blithely toward the barn, her hands warming in the pockets of her suede jacket. She was already contemplating the warmth of the house, and the glass of Bordeaux she would drink with bleu cheese and one of the perfect pears she had brought home that morning from Nancy's orchards.

She pulled open the barn door, and peered in. "Hello, Robert!" she called jauntily. "I'm back!"

She was late, but Robert did her the honor of looking up from his meal. He was munching hay methodically, long shafts of it sticking out from either corner of his mouth. His fiendish yellow eyes seemed to glow in the dim light of the barn. Fiona chatted gaily as she checked his goat chow and made sure the water was flowing into his trough. She had ordered a trough warmer as advised by *The Idiot's Guide*, but it hadn't yet arrived. This was apparently a proven means of achieving warmth for goats during the winter. She had already installed a small double metal dish that held mineral salt and baking soda for Robert to nibble, two essentials, she had learned, to goat health.

Her obligations fulfilled, she leaned against the railing of his stall. Robert was chewing his last mouthful of hay, his eyes fixed steadily on Fiona. They regarded one another dubiously.

Robert finished chewing and seemed to freeze. "WHAAAATTTTTT?" he said loudly.

Fiona straightened herself, and half-smiling peered over at him, her head tilted to one side. "Did you say something?" she asked, rather drolly, she thought.

"WHAAAAAAAAAATTTTTT?" said Robert again.

Fiona gazed at him, a small smile on her face. "What?" she said back at him, conversationally.

"Whaaaaaaaat?" He seemed intrigued by the discussion.

"You'll have to do better than that," said Fiona.

"HUH!" said Robert. "Uhuhuhuhuh," he continued more to himself than to her.

"What," said Fiona crisply, "is your point?" And what, she thought to herself, is yours? Is this what your education and ambition have brought you to? You are having conversations with a goat? But she had to admit to herself as she considered it that this was the only conversation she had had all day. "I need to get off the Island," she thought to herself. "I need to make sure I'm all right. I don't even know who I am anymore." But as she thought this, she didn't feel anything amiss in herself. All was suprisingly—and uncharacteristically—well.

"AHA!" said Robert.

She had to admit that his word choices were uncanny. What else did he say, she wondered? And had Roger known of this... skill? She pursed her lips as she considered this for the hundredth time. She'd lay a bet he had.

"BOB!" said Robert.

Fiona studied him. "Bob?" she said. "Did you say 'Bob'?" she asked.

"YAH. BOB! BAAAWWB!" he said.

Fiona sighed. She was suddenly tired and unequal to further goat conversation. It was time for a drink, she felt. "Well, this has been fun," she said to Robert.

"Huh," he said softly, and turned his back on her to peruse the offerings of his trough.

Fiona returned to the house, half entertained and half depressed. "Good God," she thought. "As if having a goat weren't enough; mine has to talk." She poured herself a glass of wine, forgetting the cheese and pear she had planned, wandered into the living room, and plunked down on the couch with a sigh. She picked up her well-used copy of Marcus Aurelius sitting on the table nearby and began to thumb through it. She bet he didn't have anything to meet this particular occasion.

"Has something befallen you?" she read. "Good, then it was your portion of the universal lot, assigned to you when time began, a strand woven in your particular web, like all else that happens." Fiona put down the book and stared off.

"My portion of the universal lot," she said aloud. "A talking goat." She went into the kitchen to pour herself another glass of wine.

Elisabeth drifted through the fall in a romantic haze. Her friends watched in bemusement the shift from her usual brisk practicality into a dreamy, preoccupied vagueness. Roger's visits were frequent, but unplanned and sporadic. He could show up at any time, sometimes more than once a day, sometimes not for several days.

For any other woman—including Elisabeth at any other time in her life—this would have been a sign of inconsideration and selfishness. But Elisabeth knew that with Roger it was really the opposite. His inability to read other human beings was as much a part of who he was was the color of his eyes. He wasn't capable of sensing what someone else might want. His visits were a sign that he was thinking of her, that he needed her company, and that he had transposed that need into the supposition that she must need him, too. So he came. Elisabeth had no illusion that time would soften this quality in him or that his ways would change. It would be like asking someone who was color-blind to see purple. This was Roger. It was all he had. For the moment, at least, it was enough.

It was at about this time that Fiona began to notice that something wasn't quite right. She had been moving along in Island society, beginning to run into people she knew at the ferry parcel pickup desk, or at the grocery store. She hadn't reached anything close to belonging; it was civility, if not acceptance. But a new awareness of exchanged glances and frozen conversations began to dawn on her, and although she wanted to, she really wasn't able to attribute it to her problems with Stella.

She first noticed it at the lecture she attended at the Island Historical Society. Pali, an avid reader of all things historical, was there, as were Nancy, Jim, and Jake and Charlotte, along with a group of about twenty others, or, roughly ten percent of the Island's population. In her previous life, Fiona might have commented sarcastically about there being nothing else to do in the wilderness. But while there was an element of truth in this, there was in the Islanders a fierce pride and loyalty to their homes, which fostered a genuine interest in its history and its commonplace events. In addition to which, as Fiona would have cheerfully admitted, there was almost always cake.

Fiona had spent the day of Indian summer digging in the garden, belatedly planting bulbs and laying out a new bed for spring. It had been only with vigorous attention with a nailbrush that she had been able to remove most of the traces of dirt from under her fingernails despite the highly touted rubberized gardening gloves she had paid almost twenty dollars for. She had been looking forward to this event. It was conversation after a long day of silence, and the chance to have someone seeming pleased to see her.

She entered the hall, noting the hand-lettered sign on the wall which never ceased to annoy her. *Your entering a public building. Please be respectful of others.* Saying something to someone about it was out of the question, of course. It would be seen as the worst kind of affront, not to mention snobbery. Fiona made a mental note to carry a marker with her in case she should ever find herself in the hallway unobserved.

When she entered the fluorescent glare of the community room at the Municipal Hall, there had been a barely perceptible gap in the conversations. Although her friends greeted her, in a small place in the back of her brain there was a very faint awareness that the other people in the room were trying not to look at her, or stealing glances sideways. When she approached a group, conversations froze for the briefest, almost imperceptible moment before diving into the normal round of greetings.

Innocent for the moment, Fiona joined in cheerfully. The speaker was a particularly knowledgeable historian of the Great Lakes, who had gripping tales of shipwrecks, storms, and survival. His talk was welcomed with genuine interest, and afterward, he mingled dutifully with the audience over the cake and coffee. Great Lakes historians are always cheered by enthusiasm for their subject.

Stella, of course, was there. Fiona made eye contact with her but did not speak, and Stella looked back with a certain smugness. Fiona wondered whether she should feel sorry for such a clearly unhappy and unpleasant woman. Perhaps she actually had some form of illness that made her so miserable and mean. In the midst of these thoughts, Pali tapped her on the shoulder.

"Did you learn anything?" he asked with his usual cheer. The Styrofoam coffee cup he held was dwarfed by his large hands.

Fiona smiled. "It's all new to me. I was especially interested to hear about the Christmas tree ships to Chicago. That's a rough time of year to be traveling the Great Lakes. " As they engaged in conversation, Fiona was aware that there were looks being exchanged. She put it down to ongoing curiosity about a newcomer.

Nancy, Jake and Charlotte, and Jim all said their hellos, and a conversation over the merits of yellow cake or chocolate, mixed with some shipping history, carried the remainder of the evening.

Tired from her day of labor, Fiona said her good nights early. Jim had offered to walk with her to her car, and they left the overheated municipal room together. The warmth of the day had shifted dramatically and the crisp autumn night was scented with the smell of wood smoke from many chimneys; the frost was already settling. In the parking lot, a pair of women whom Fiona vaguely recognized were engaged in an animated conversation near one of their cars. Seeing Fiona and Jim, they fell silent, exchanged looks and good-byes, and then hastily parted to their cars.

Fiona couldn't put her finger on it, but something hadn't felt right that evening. Jim looked sideways at her, as if making up his mind about something. Fiona caught the look and tilted her head up at him as they walked.

"Something on your mind?" she asked, wondering as she did so whether it had been wise to ask. What if he were contemplating some heavy relationship question which she felt unequal to dealing with? He hadn't seemed terribly serious or devoted, but you could never really be sure.

Jim shrugged and smiled. "Nothing really. I guess I was just wondering about something."

She looked at him quizzically.

He laughed. "Don't mind me. My mind is always wandering. It's got nothing much to do with anything." He paused, and then confessed. "I was thinking about your writing."

Fiona felt vaguely flattered. "My writing? What about it?"

"Well... ." he paused and seemed embarrassed. "I guess I was just wondering where you published it."

"Are you interested in my work?" she asked, feeling even more flattered.

"Well. I, uh, just felt that, I should, well...Since we're friends, I thought..." He paused again, struggling for his words.

Fiona smiled at him. "You feel obligated to read my stuff?"

Jim frowned briefly. "Not obligated, no. No that's not it. But...curious, I guess." They had stopped next to her car. He seemed to be struggling with something. Jim looked at the ground and then lifted his head and looked directly into her eyes. "Does that make you uncomfortable?"

Fiona grinned at him. "Why should it make me uncomfortable? I'm flattered. But…" she hesitated a moment. "It's kind of intense, really. Very technical. I've been doing it for years, and become a bit of an expert." She gave him a quick sidelong look. "But now that I'm developing a specialty in goats, maybe I should switch."

"Gosh." said Jim. And there was a silence.

Fiona sensed some inner tension that she couldn't understand. Probably, she thought to herself, I shouldn't even try to be funny.

After a long moment when he seemed to be wrestling with some inner turmoil, relief burst from Jim's face and demeanor. "I guess I should have known you'd feel that way. I mean, after all, it's your work, right?"

"Well, yes. And I guess I think it's pretty good. Most of the time, anyway." She was smiling at him. Suddenly he seemed something more than merely likable. "Would you like me to autograph one of my books?" she teased. "I can sign it 'To Jim, my favorite ranger.'"

"Oh wow," he said, running his fingers through his hair, with what seemed to Fiona very much like nervousness.

Did he think she was making a pass at him? For a writer, she certainly could choose the wrong words sometimes.

"Uh, that would be great. I could show it to the guys at work, right? I mean, I probably wouldn't want to leave it lying around where just anyone could see it. Especially if you…" He seemed to be searching for a word "...pursue this goat thing." He smiled again. "My mom still snoops when she visits."

After they said good-bye and she was driving the short distance home, Fiona pondered on this remark. But what an odd thing to say, she thought to herself. Was there some political thing he disagreed with? Something to do with war or the national defense? Oh well. Maybe Jim wasn't all that great at word choices, either.

She let herself into the house, poured out a small glass of scotch from the decanter on the side table, and went contentedly, if wearily, to bed.

She hadn't noticed—and no one had thought to point out to her—the posting on the town bulletin board near the door of the hall, the one that gave official notice of town meetings. Wisconsin law was strict. Any meeting of a quorum of public officials required public notice. The next meeting was scheduled for January. Among its topics: domestic animal complaints.

Roger's discomfort with the strange new circumstances of his life continued to grow. He was on a path that he had not foreseen, and what's more, that only a few months before would have been anathema to his entire sense of the world and his place in it. He was not a coward, but he was in uncharted territory and the choices were risky and undetermined. He was unaware of any experiments that could be performed to formulate a theory or predict the outcomes. He was gradually and reluctantly coming to the realization that in life, as in the laboratory, sometimes you had to guess.

Fiona would have been shocked to learn that, at least among those who were skeptical of Stella's propaganda, the Islanders generally shared the view that she was well-meaning, but clueless and charmingly inept. The possibility that she might not be entirely proper, enhanced her status among the men, but had a more generally negative impact upon the women.

Most of the Islanders, in their turn, would have been surprised to hear that Fiona was anything more than what they saw: a woman alone, from Someplace Else who had been duped into paying full price for the old Goeden place and didn't have her full share of common sense.

The Islanders' general lack of motivation to oppose Stella was enhanced by their conviction that Fiona wouldn't last long on the Island anyway. Unless, of course, Jim Freeberg got some sense and married her, they told themselves. She wasn't bad looking, for all her foolishness—"if that's all it is," commented one elderly woman tartly—and attractive single women were in short supply, particularly ones with questionable morals.

"Nice legs," one of the guys at the bar had commented as he watched Fiona leave Nelson's Friday Fish Fry one evening, and his companions had nodded their agreement. "Hear she's seein' Jim Freeberg," one of them remarked, and there was silence as each followed this information along his own mental path, taking a swallow of beer or brandy before the conversation could begin again.

An observer of university politics once remarked that in any dispute the intensity of feeling is inversely proportional to the value of the issues at stake. But in a small town, whose population may be even smaller than that of a university campus, there is an accelerating quality in this minor truth. Fiona, who had moments of being nearly as clueless as the Islanders supposed, was unaware that Washington Island had apparently volunteered for a study on the subject.

It was entirely normal and predictable that Fiona only heard about the agenda for the town board after the wheels had been set in motion. And she heard about it one cold morning when she went to Mann's and stopped to chat with the group at the meat counter.

Fiona's shopping cart was full. She had been writing all week, and hadn't been out to shop. It was only when she had used up the last of the coffee that morning that she had recognized dire necessity. She rounded the corner toward the deli counter, hoping that the freshly baked bread was available that day, and encountered the little group. Conversation ceased when she appeared. But after the usual pleasantries—the wind was coming up, and winter was surely coming; too bad the Bjornstads were moving to the mainland, they would be missed—they got down to business.

"So are you planning to contest?" asked one woman, whom Fiona recognized as being a member of the Historical Society, treasurer of the PTA and president of the Washington Island Christian Women's Association. Even as a mere member she

264 North of the Tension Line

ruled with an iron hand, and although no one could doubt her Christian morals, there were those who wondered about how she applied them.

Fiona's confusion was duly noted by observers. The look on her face was that of someone who suspects a joke is being played on her, but who has confidence in its good nature.

"Contest?" she asked, innocently, her eyes sweeping the faces before her.

Several of the women in the group shared smug sidelong glances, shimmering with superior knowledge. All of the men felt sympathy. She might be a trollop, but they could see that she was genuinely sweet-natured. Her experience was, they couldn't help feeling, an asset.

"The ordinance," said one of the kindlier ladies. "Your goat. The board is being asked to have him removed."

"Or destroyed," added one of the other ladies helpfully.

Fiona froze, her eyes on the face of the woman who had just spoken.

"What do you mean, 'destroyed'?" she asked.

"Slaughtered, dear," said the most elderly lady. "If the board rules against you, he may have to be killed."

Fiona looked from one to another, her face a mask of calm. They all looked back at her with varying degrees of sympathy and glee. In that moment, the realities of small town life and the raw ugliness of human nature became clear to her. Chicago might be big and cold, but Fiona could see now that small and cold was infinitely worse.

She left Mann's with her groceries, feeling shattered. It wasn't just her concern for Robert—"DAMN Robert!" she thought—it was the realization that she was not among friends. Not at all among friends.

That night in bed she drearily paged through *Meditations.* "The object of life," she read, "is not to be on the side of the majority, but to escape finding oneself in the ranks of the insane." Fiona closed the book with a snap and turned out the light.

"Maybe," she said to herself, "I should just buy a romance novel."

November had reverted to mild autumn weather. Fiona sat one late afternoon on the steps of her porch watching the setting sun. The Canada geese were moving south, and their calls could be heard for miles as they approached and departed, their great V-shaped formations shifting as they flew. As one flock flew low over the house, the usual cacophony was inexplicably stilled, and she could feel more than hear, the beating of their wings, like the heartbeat of one large creature. Fiona watched in silence until they were gone.

On this side of the house she was less likely to encounter Stella, and Fiona had taken to sitting here by the street rather than on the quieter, more private side of the yard. Nearby, a red squirrel chattered aggressively. "Probably the last warm day of the year," she told herself. A cold front was predicted tonight, sweeping away the Indian summer with winds and storms. Soon winter would force her, like everyone else, to retreat indoors to the warmth and isolation of the house. It occurred to her that less contact with the town would probably be better anyway.

The prospect of the town meeting had shaken her deeply. Despite her new friendships, Fiona had begun to feel that she was surrounded by unseen forces working against her. Combined with the small town grapevine, everything contributed to a growing sense of paranoia, which she was struggling furiously to resist. She had bought the house. She lived here. And she would not let anyone scare her off.

She hoped.

The irony of having to defend Robert was not lost on her, but she could not give in. No matter how annoying, troublesome, and malevolent he was, she was nevertheless responsible for him. And even though he neither knew nor cared, she was not going to shirk her responsibility to protect him. Besides, giving in to Stella was not an option. No. She had to figure this thing out.

Fiona sighed. On top of everything else, she had accepted a dare. And she was damned if she were going to give in. It might be childish. But she knew if she failed, she would never be able to live it down. Not even with herself.

Especially not herself.

Among her many miscalculations, Fiona had not counted on the reluctance of the house's original inhabitants to give way. That night, the invisible chewer made another appearance. Fiona had allowed herself to be lulled into complacency by its absence, hoping that it had somehow decided to take up residence elsewhere.

The gnawing was, if anything, louder than before, and Fiona could have sworn that the creature—whatever it was—sat just on the other side of the wall next to her head. She had long since given up on wall-pounding, since it made no difference whatsoever.

She reached for her music, put on her headphones, and covered her head with the pillow. Somehow, even with these measures, the chewing seemed even more resonant, as if it were being transferred through the bedsprings. She tried to convince herself that the steady rhythm was part of the music, and slowly, with many false starts, she managed to fall asleep.

She had been away. Somewhere undefined. Maybe a city. Maybe not. She needed to get back. Back to the Island. But for some reason, she hadn't been able to find her car, so she had taken the train and a bus, and hitchhiked, and now was walking along a road that should have been the way to the ferry, but it wasn't. She had thought she was on the Peninsula, but now she wasn't sure. There was a smokestack over in the distance. There were no smokestacks here. Could it be a ship? No. Ships don't have smokestacks like that. It was brick. There was a dark cloud of smoke in the air. The road was paved, but it was crumbling. She trudged alone. No cars passed. There were no houses, no gas stations.

Until now, her trip had been peopled by faceless fellow travelers. Not literally, but simply unnamed, unspecific, unfamiliar people. They had ignored her, as she had them. She longed to talk with them, but something held her back. She spent a long voice-less train trip struggling to think of some way to achieve human contact with the man next to her, but unable to find the means within herself. She longed to take his hand, but she was afraid he would mistake her intention. And she wanted only to touch someone else, to be comforted by the warmth of another person's hand. To know that someone else was beside her in her aloneness. And now somehow she was on this road. She had to get back to the ferry. There was only one more today, and she didn't want to spend the night here, alone along the road. But where was it? Where was she?

At last, along the road ahead, she saw a reddish golden light, and the deep bending S curves of the road to Northpoint. Eagerly, she ran along the road, dropping a heavy bag as she went. Nothing in it mattered, only the ferry, only this last chance to make the ferry.

The last small hill before the steep incline toward the water was before her. With every ounce of her strength she ran, gasping, to reach the top. Triumphant, she crested the hill and looked down over the dock. The road was empty. The ticket booth was closed.

It was too late. The ferry was chugging off, a hundred feet away from the dock, its white decks glowing in the deep rose light of the last sun, its stern flag whipping in the lake wind. It seemed very small against the lake, but it moved with a steady determination against the waves, heading sturdily across Death's Door toward the Island. Fiona could see the profiles of a few passengers through the lighted windows, some talking, some not. They seemed comfortable and complete. They were headed out across one of the most notorious passages of the Great Lakes, but none of them seemed to mind. They were leaving the world behind. They were going home.

Fiona stood on the bluff as the ferry grew smaller, dwarfed by the lake as it continued its small, urgent journey. In her dream, she watched it until it was out of sight.

Chapter Nineteen ✳

The change from soft autumn weather to winter had been swift and brutal. One day in late November had been fifty-seven degrees, and the next it was thirty-four with a brisk wind and an inch of snow. Fiona had been procrastinating about making a major pre-winter shopping trip to Green Bay, but realized she couldn't put it off any longer. Her household really hadn't been properly outfitted for winter, and while she could buy most necessities locally or online, there came a point at which she just wanted choice, and to see something before she bought it.

As usual, she preferred to ride the ferry outside the car, and before the ropes had been pulled in, she had climbed the stairs to the upper deck.

Ice had begun to form along the edges of the water, but Fiona was snug in her new hooded parka. She leaned against the railing of the ferry *Arni J. Richter*, watching the heavy mist rising from the lake as the much colder air hit the water. The lake had taken on the gelatinous quality it acquired before ice began to form, and it moved thickly as it gleamed in the early morning sun.

"Hey Fiona!"

She turned to see the guys in the pilothouse waving to her.

"Want to come up?"

Happy at this sign of acceptance, she climbed the few steps to join them, and pulled the heavy steel door closed behind her.

It was comforting and warm in the pilothouse, and it smelled like coffee. She saw Pali's thermos tucked into a corner, so used and battered it looked as if it had been dropped from a roof onto asphalt, run over a few times, and left out in the rain for the summer. There was a pile of tickets waiting to be counted on the small desk behind the captain, and a half-eaten box of chocolate doughnuts sitting open. The pilothouse was as clean and well-maintained as the rest of the ferry. The console's wood and metal shone, and Pali stood with his hands on the wheel, and his eyes on the road. At this time of year it was a quiet sea with no traffic visible for miles.

"Want a doughnut?"

Young Joe, as he was affectionately known by the crew, held the box out to her, and she took one shyly, feeling a bit in the way. He was barely twenty—if that—tall and almost painfully thin, and in contrast to his laconic, easygoing captain, vibrating with youthful energy. He fidgeted with the tickets and the cash-box without accomplishing much, and his restlessness seemed to be temporarily soothed by eating. "Growing boy," thought Fiona.

"Have a seat," said Pali without looking back.

She sat on the inner corner of the blue upholstered bench seat behind the captain, her back snug against the window. The lake spread out before them, the old coast guard station on Plum Island perched on its northern edge. A bald eagle whirled and spun above the Island. There was a nesting pair, Fiona knew, and some immature offspring who lived there. Two mute swans were diving for breakfast along the western edge of Detroit Island, and a flock of some kind of ducks took off in front of the ferry, disturbed from their morning swim. Fiona sighed with pleasure.

They traveled this way for some moments, each absorbed in thought. It was Fiona who broke the silence.

"Thanks for inviting me up. This is great."

Pali chuckled. It's pretty comfortable," he said. "Mostly."

Fiona nodded sympathetically. "Gets a little rough sometimes, I bet."

"Well, yeah," said Pali. He paused, clearly considering what to say. "But that's not what I mean."

Young Joe started laughing. "Hey Pali. You're not going to tell her that, are you? She'll think you're off your nut."

Fiona was puzzled. What, then? "Too many visitors crowding in?"

Young Joe's cell phone rang, and he left the cabin to answer it, bouncing like a puppy with a new toy.

"Well, that, too," Pali said. "Some of the Islanders think they can just ride up here, and just come on in without asking. Sometimes there's no room for the crew." There was another long pause, and Fiona could tell that Pali was wrestling with something. "That's not what I meant, either, though."

The silence seemed to go on to the horizon with the lake. Fiona decided not to guess, and Pali kept looking straight ahead, clearly choosing each word before he spoke. At last he said, without turning, "It's the ghost."

Fiona's heart beat twice in the silence. Through the window she could see Young Joe talking animatedly on his cell phone.

"The ghost." Her statement was flat without understanding.

Having told the secret, Pali's reserve was gone. "It's haunted. I know it sounds crazy, but the pilothouse is haunted. There's a ghost."

Young Joe came bursting back into the cabin. "He tell you about our friend?" he asked, cheerfully.

Fiona began to wonder if this were some kind of hazing ritual. Tell a tall tale to the foreigner and see if she'll buy it. She could imagine the laughter around the bar. "I suppose you'll tell me next that you have Yeti hiding in the woods."

Pali compressed his lips in a rueful half smile, and Young Joe hooted as well as he could with a mouth full of doughnut.

"I know what it sounds like," Pali said.

"We're not supposed to tell anyone in case the tourists freak out," added Young Joe helpfully.

"I would think it would attract more people than it would discourage," said Fiona blithely, still not convinced that they weren't teasing her. "You could have special moonlit ghost rides, like the tours they give in Gettysburg. Although, the more I think of it, the more tasteless that whole thing seems."

"Well, I don't know how tasteful it is or isn't. All I know is, some weird things happen here. And I don't know any other way to explain them." Pali delivered this statement calmly without looking back. He certainly didn't seem to be joking.

Fiona, still frowning slightly and trying to strike the balance between being respectful and being a sap, sat back on her seat. "What kind of weird things?" she asked at last, turning to Young Joe. There was a gleam in her eyes, and she smiled a small smile, her face a study in skepticism.

"Things get moved," said Young Joe. "We'll leave things in one place, and when we come back, they're someplace different. Not like they've fallen, but moved to a different shelf."

This did not sound particularly convincing to Fiona. "Does this tend to happen around April first?" she asked

"No," said Young Joe, finally serious. "Happens pretty regular." He looked at the captain for confirmation, who nodded. "We've all seen him, though," said Young Joe. "We've pretty much all seen him."

Fiona looked at him quizzically, no longer smiling. "You've seen him? You've seen the ghost?"

This time Pali looked back over his shoulder at her and nodded. "Everyone but me." His stolid, sincere nature reminded her briefly of Rocco.

"Yeah, but you're the one who knows him, Pali. The first time; that was the most intense," continued Young Joe. "You tell her, Pali."

Fiona sat quietly, bemused.

Pali took a deep breath and began his tale. "We were coming back on a last run. It was October, two years ago, and it was a pretty light load. There was a storm watch, but nothing definite, and even though it was a little windy, there didn't seem like anything to worry about. The lake was kind of choppy, nothing bad, but enough to bother some people. Fortunately, we only had locals, and they're mostly used to it."

Fiona had, by now, the understanding that if a ferry captain says it's kind of choppy, it was a very rough ride. Pali took a hand off the helm and ran it through his hair. She noticed again how blond he was, even the faint stubble on his cheeks.

"I had the radar on, making sure there was no small traffic, and the guys were on the lower decks. We were taking the eastern route around the back edge of Plum Island, trying to avoid some of the larger swells. Everything was normal. We were about halfway across when the waves started rising, and I sent the guys down to make sure everything was secure."

"He was up here," Young Joe jumped in. "It was dark on the deck, but it was lit up in here. Bright as day."

"We had rounded the Island, and were heading out into the crossing. All of a sudden, I felt as if someone had taken the wheel from me. It was turning against me, and at the same time this big swell hit us from out of nowhere."

"Georg and me were coming up the outside stairs and we almost went down backward," said Young Joe.

"That was the first time I felt his hand on my shoulder," continued Pali calmly. "Right here," he nodded his head to his right. "As clearly as if you were to put out your hand right now."

Fiona was watching him intently as he spoke. She had only known him for a few months now, but she had little doubt about his character. Pali was not a liar. His eyes were straight ahead, scanning the lake.

"It lasted for about a minute, but it felt like ten." He looked back briefly at Fiona. "And that was it."

Young Joe jumped in like an eager puppy.

"That wasn't the strangest part, though. Just before the wave hit, I looked up and saw somebody standing up here next to Pali. I didn't really think much about it, but when I come up later, I was surprised that he was gone. I asked Pali who it was, and he didn't know what I was talking about."

"There hadn't been anybody up here," said Pali seriously. "I'd been alone the whole time."

"Georg saw him, too," added Young Joe.

There was a long pause.

"Lots of times now, I'll be standing here alone, and I'll feel a hand on my shoulder," said Pali.

Fiona was at a loss for what to say. "At least it doesn't sound terribly sinister," she said, finally.

"Oh no," he said. "You can't say it's sinister; If anything, it's…" he searched for a word and failed. "He…it saved our lives." He took a swallow from the bottle of water sitting nearby, still watching the seaway ahead. "But it's damned disconcerting; I can tell you."

Fiona could imagine that this would be true.

A deep silence fell over the pilot house, as the waves and the engines continued their steady sound.

They were approaching the breakwater.

"Well," said Young Joe. "Guess I better get down there."

"Guess so," said Pali. He shifted the engines downward, followed Young Joe out, and walked over to the port side of the stern, where he opened the small white box on the corner so he could control the rudders with a clear view of the dock.

Fiona, left alone in the pilot house, sat for a moment, absorbing what she had heard. She had no sense of a ghostly presence. It seemed odd, though, to stay in the pilot house without the crew, so she gathered her gloves, checked her pocket for the keys, and stepped down to the observation deck, closing the door behind her. With a smile and wave to Pali, she headed back down to her car.

"See you later," she said.

"Yup," said the captain. See you later."

Off and on throughout the day, Fiona returned to Pali's story, turning it over in her mind. She was still not completely
convinced that this was not an elaborate joke the crew played on
newcomers. The fact that both Georg and Young Joe had seen
someone when no one actually was there was pretty difficult to
explain. The veracity of the tale notwithstanding, Fiona had to
admit to herself that she was pleased and touched that she had
been trusted. It helped a little bit to soothe the sore places made
by Stella and her conniving. And this story was clearly not the
kind of thing you could tell everybody.

Fiona found it interesting, too, that the ferry line had determined that it should be kept quiet. Probably they didn't
want anyone to question the integrity—or, perhaps, the mental
state—of their captains and crews. She sincerely believed, however, that the line had gotten it exactly wrong. A ghost story,
however loudly people claimed not to believe, was a surefire
way to draw a crowd. And crowds, of course, meant revenue.
For everybody.

After a successful day of shopping, the car piled high with
the essential and the frivolous, Fiona reboarded the last ferry for
the trip back to the Island. Pali and Young Joe were still on duty,
but too busy to chat. She hunkered down in the car, closed her
eyes, and listened to a Beethoven sonata. The car rocked with

the ferry, and Fiona drifted off into a gentle dreamless sleep.

She woke with the sound of the engines throttling back, and the soft bump of the boat against the dock. She made the short drive home in the dark, unable to make sense of the story she had heard, and too tired to care.

She had just settled into bed with a book and cup of tea, her mind wandering over the events of the day, when it occurred to her that her life now included a goat, a crazy neighbor, a ghost, and possibly some banshees. It was as she mused upon these things that the sound of gnawing began in its usual place, directly above her head. She lay back on her pillow and carried on a silent personal debate as to whether her list of oddities should be alphabetical or in order of personal peril. "B for Banshee," she decided. She was beginning the third page when she fell asleep, oblivious to the scampering in the wall behind her head.

Fiona's off-Island foray to the gallery night had made it abundantly clear that leaving Robert in someone else's care was not an option. After two municipal citations and a looming town meeting, she knew that she had no margin for error. Robert, in his unfathomable goat mind, had assigned Fiona to his department. No one else would do. Thwarting his schemes would inevitably lead to some new disaster, she knew, and Fiona was simply not up to it. Comforting herself with the prospect of saving a little money, she grimly determined to stay on the Island during the holidays.

She celebrated Thanksgiving with Pali's family, and came home from the noise and cheer of the gathering feeling the silence of her house more than usual. She had become accustomed to living alone, but the contrast made the empty house seem almost oppressive. Before undressing for bed, she went out, as always, to check on Robert, a practice that had become more essential as the weather got colder. She switched on the single bulb that lit the barn's entry and peered into his stall.

Robert's yellow eyes narrowed when he saw her, glinting wickedly in the dim light.

"I came to make sure you were still here," Fiona told him. "But, on the whole, I think it would be better if you weren't." Unbidden, an old voice in her head spoke the words of her grandmother's homespun philosophy. "Be careful what you wish for." She shook her head and smiled at herself.

Robert's ears flicked warily, and he grunted, watching her intently as she watched him. Fiona had always felt a comfortable communication with animals, and with Robert it was no different, really, except for the fact that the messages she received felt more malevolent than she would have hoped. They stared at one another for a few moments, and then, with a toss of his head, Robert went back to scrounging in his hay.

Wearily, she turned away, and closed up the barn for the night.

Elisabeth's new nephew was born three weeks early, and true to her word, she made the trip to Madison to help with her little nieces. Elisabeth felt some regret that she hadn't had a chance to say good-bye to Roger, despite his rather withdrawn demeanor of late. She had planned to leave Rocco with Fiona, but her departure was so hurried, that she was forced to bring him with her. Her sister-in-law, who was not a dog person, would not be thrilled, but, thought Elisabeth, they would all have to make the best of it. Rocco was delighted to go in the car, and, except for those occasions when they wanted him to wear a hat, always thoroughly enjoyed having the little girls to romp with.

During this season of family gatherings, Fiona felt wrapped in a mantle of loneliness. In defiance of herself, however, she went out into the cheer of Christmas preparations around the community. She bought crafts from the church bazaars, attended the school's Christmas program, contributed to the many charitable funds, and enjoyed several parties at Nelson's and at the homes of new friends. Jim invited her to a showing of It's a Wonderful Life at the community hall, and it had been so long since she had seen it that she was caught up again in its homely charm.

The Christmas decorations that were part of the Island tradition delighted and intrigued her. Each wooden electric post had a steel frame erected at the top. Thinking at first that this was some necessary technological innovation, Fiona was captivated to discover that they were actually tree stands, and a living Christmas tree perched atop each one, lining the main street. She guessed that this was related to some Scandinavian tradition she had never heard of. In their presence it was, in any case, impossible to pretend that you were anywhere else but on the Island.

From time to time, she remembered the upcoming town meeting with trepidation, but she did her best to shove it out of her mind. She could not control the result, she told herself. She could only present her side of the story, and let the process play itself out. It was, nevertheless, the thing she thought of when she woke in the middle of the night, and it filled her heart with dread.

Chapter Twenty ✤

It was early in the new year when Elisabeth returned to the Peninsula, and on the first morning, she decided to make a rare early visit to Ground Zero. It was barely light out, but she wanted to catch Roger before the morning rush began. She had a Christmas present for him, and despite a few unremarkable e-mail exchanges, had not been in touch with him since she left.

The bell on the door jangled as she entered, and Roger came out from the back scowling in welcome. Elisabeth thought that there might be a softening in his expression when he saw her. "Good morning," she said, somewhat formally, not quite smiling at him but searching his face for some response. Roger bobbed his head in what passed for an acknowledgment. Tenderly, he placed a cup of coffee in front of her on the counter. It was the best he could do. Elisabeth gazed hopefully at him, but he did not look at her. Rocco settled under Elisabeth's seat and sighed. He expected this would be a long stop.

As Elisabeth was sorting the tangle of words she wanted to speak, the bell jangled again, and a tourist entered. Roger rearranged his features into his public face and went to wait on his customer. Elisabeth used the opportunity to compose her thoughts, watching silently as he poured more hot coffee into her mug and then turned his attention to making the egg sandwich that had just been ordered. Rocco, who had looked up briefly when the door opened, now determined that there was nothing here of interest and put his head down again. He had been just about to begin a dream about swimming.

The man at the counter looked over at her and nodded civilly, and then opened the newspaper he had laid on the counter. There was a pleasant silence in the little shop as the egg sandwich sizzled on the griddle. Roger was not one for idle chatter as he worked, as Elisabeth well knew, and he dealt with this by standing with his back to the counter, fully focused on his cooking. It was easy to imagine him standing over a laboratory experiment in the same way, the extraneous details of the world closed off from his awareness. Under the counter, Rocco's legs began to move as he dreamed of retrieving Frisbees at School House Beach. There would be ice cream next. The man at the counter sneezed.

"Bless you," said Elisabeth, looking over at him with a small smile. The man smiled back. It was unusual to see a man traveling alone in Door County. It was the place people went for romantic weekends or family vacations, generally not business trips. He was rather attractive, she thought. A quiet air of graciousness surrounded him, although how she had perceived this, she couldn't quite identify.

"Thank you," he said. He nodded again, smiled briefly, and went back to reading his paper. Elisabeth observed him covertly and almost unconsciously. He looked expensive. He wore jeans, a sweater, and hiking shoes, all perfectly ordinary. Maybe it was his haircut she decided. And his watch. He looked up again when Roger put down his egg sandwich. At this moment, the door opened again, and the vestrymen from the church down the road walked in. The calm of the shop turned to bustle as they laughed and talked with one another and placed their orders. The man at the counter returned to his breakfast and his paper, and Elisabeth came to the belated realization that she was not going to have the conversation with Roger she had hoped to have. There was a lot of work to be done at the gallery after her Christmas trip to her family. She sighed inwardly, and took out her phone to check the weather. She needed to get back.

Fiona left the house feeling virtuous. She had spent the morning working on her article, and had made great progress. She needed a little fresh air now and some companionship, so she headed over to Mann's for some groceries and a little conversation over the pork chops.

The store was disappointingly empty. Fiona gathered her few necessities and lingered over the rest, idly reading packages and comparing prices. She enjoyed grocery shopping. She took some time debating the myriad tea possibilities and then stopped to study the coffee filters. After a brief comparison she reached for the least expensive package, ignoring her revulsion at its name, "Because You Care." One eyebrow raised, she studied the lengthy apologia of earth-friendly pretensions on the side. "Thank you for caring" it said after a full essay on the product's green ambitions. "I don't, actually," said Fiona out loud, throwing the package into her cart. This was not strictly true, of course. But she was skeptical about the influence of her coffee filter choice on the earth and she resented both the preaching and the coy cuteness of the package's pretensions. Were there people who wanted lectures even on their coffee filters? she wondered. What was it about the culture that made it simultaneously superficial, bossy, and ill-informed? "Not an ounce of humor to be discerned anywhere," she thought, and rolled her eyes at her own earnestness.

By the time she reached the last aisle, she had filled the cart.

Ingrid, the store's longtime employee, was at the checkout. She had heard the stories about Fiona, but as the clerk in the Island's only grocery store, she found it best to get along with everyone.

"Stocking up for the storm?" she asked as she rang up Fiona's purchases.

Fiona looked up from digging in her handbag for her wallet. Purchased as a convenient and utilitarian leather pouch, it was extremely frustrating to use, since everything fell into the dark depths of the bag, and the opening was too small to open it up and look in. Fiona had begun to feel that she spent twenty percent of her day rummaging in its depths to find one thing or another. A new purse was on the top of her shopping list during her next trip away from the Island.

"I haven't really been paying attention, to tell you the truth," she said, her hand still groping into the depths of the bag. "What's coming?"

"They're saying we're right in the path of two converging Alberta Clippers, and they're predicting a full-scale blizzard with up to twenty-four inches starting tonight, then another storm with sixteen inches right on its heels. That's if," she added, struggling to get the smug coffee filters to scan, "these weather guys actually can predict anything. I find it amazing that they can be so consistently wrong. It's mind-boggling."

Fiona felt relief as she located her wallet and smiled at this universally expressed view, which she shared. "Assuming they're right, what will that mean? Will they shut down the ferry?"

Ingrid shrugged. "Hard to say, but whatever happens, I doubt the ferry will be out of commission long. If it's a real blizzard and big waves, they will shut down for a run or two probably. We haven't really had a big storm in a few years." She looked at Fiona and smiled as she handed her the receipt. "It will be a busy day around here." There was a note of weariness already in her voice.

"Hold on," said Fiona, as she was about to leave. "I'd better get some batteries and extra butter. I like the smell of cookies baking during a snowstorm." She disappeared back down the aisles behind the cash register to the dairy case.

Fiona left the store thinking through what else she might need. She liked snowstorms, and felt a sense of happy anticipation only slightly mitigated by her regret at not yet having had the fireplaces checked. It would have been cozy to have them working, but she supposed that candlelight would suffice.

As she drove she switched on the radio to join in the communal excitement of impending Armageddon and learned that there was, apparently, no other news worth discussing. An official warning had been issued, which seemed a realistic indicator that something was coming. This was the first time she could recall the National Weather Service, which normally spoke in mind-numbing bureaucratese, slipping into human language. Its usual "blizzard-like conditions" had changed to a brusque and simple, "Blizzard warning. Do not do any unnecessary driving," for every county in Wisconsin.

Humming cheerily to herself, she went to the gas station to fill the car, bought extra wiper fluid, and paid an extra visit to Shoes and Booze to stock up, even though she didn't really think she needed anything. Her last stop was the library. Snowstorms were a good time for classics. She came away with three Jane Austen novels and a biography of Paul Revere. "That should do it," she thought, and feeling prepared for all eventualities, she felt she had time before the pending disaster, to stop at the bar for a burger.

Christmas decorations, once cheery but now vaguely sad, still adorned the mirror above the bar. A few regulars were there, mostly retirees who came for some company, just as Fiona had done. The conversation was entirely about the coming storm. Memories of storms past, of power outages, of cars buried in snow and ships sinking, were all examined, and prognostications of alternating doom and skepticism were offered. The television was on in the background, and there was a pause in the conversation when the weather forecast came on.

The graphics showed big blue arrows and satellite photos with swirls of clouds over Canada, along with the obligatory live shots of reporters in front of waiting snow plows and mountains of blue road salt. "Here in Brown County, the snow hasn't started yet," chirped one young Green Bay reporter. Fiona rolled her eyes to herself.

"These darn guys on the TV never get it right," said one

elderly gentleman, whose reddened cheeks and rough hands tes-
tified to a life spent outdoors and possibly of afternoons at the
tavern.

"It's all in Green Bay anyhow. There's no guarantee it'll
come our way," said another patron, whom Fiona thought she
remembered as an excavator. "Not much digging going on at
this time of year," she thought to herself. He seemed cheerful
enough, and well-fed, but she wondered how he survived the
slow seasons.

"Fifty, hundred miles makes a difference in these things,"
agreed his companion.

"Remember the year they said we'd get some snow in the
grassy areas?" asked the proprietress, who turned to speak over
her shoulder as she flipped their hamburgers on the grill. "Closed
down the entire northeastern part of the state for three days."

There were a few chuckles, and then a lengthy debate over
the year in which this had occurred, and a recollection of the
time the ferry had been stranded on the ice and the passengers
had had to be snowmobiled to the Island, while their cars had
been left on the ferry for almost a full week.

"Arvi wanted them to let down the ramp so he could drive his
truck across the ice, but Sven talked him out of it, remember?"

They did.

Fiona sat eating her burger and listening. There was no one
here she really knew, and without any Island memories of her
own, she had nothing to add. Her outsider status was less uncomfortable now, and she was able simply to observe and listen,
accepted, but still not one of them. It was almost enough, just
to be around other people. She would never have admitted it

aloud, but the silence at the house had begun to wear on her. It would have been good, she thought, to have been with her family and friends over the holidays, to hear cheerful voices and to be among the crush of Christmas noise and activities. Christmas alone had been an experience she did not want to repeat.

She left the tavern with a feeling of regret. It would have been fun to have someone to spend the storm with. She wished she hadn't waited to buy a puppy, which would have offered company and a cheering routine. She had a brief mental image of herself curled up in her favorite chair with Robert standing nearby in the living room. She shrugged to herself and headed home to unload all her groceries.

To Elisabeth's surprise, the gallery did a brisk business that day. Elisabeth had sold the usual small things she kept for the sake of the casual shopper, but also two quite expensive pieces: a painting and an outdoor sculpture. The commission on the two would pay for her overhead for at least a month. She was tired when she turned out the lights and locked up. She walked with Rocco across the drive to the house, hoping against instinct to find Roger waiting for her. But the porch was unoccupied, and the dark empty house was oppressive. She thought that his lack of communication this morning must mean something, but she was tired of guessing. Rocco walked across the kitchen to his bowl and looked back at her expectantly.

Elisabeth set out his dinner and debated. Her usual pleasurable anticipation of an evening at home eluded her, but she wasn't sure she should go out. Winter storm warnings predicting Armageddon were the talk of everyone that day. The storm wasn't expected to begin until around midnight, and anyway, storm predictions were so often exaggerated, she told herself. She absentmindedly wiped off the kitchen counter. She could go out, she decided. There was bound to be someone she knew at the supper club in Fish Creek, and it would be a pleasant way to spend the evening. She was not going to sit home waiting for something that might never happen, she told herself, pretending that she meant the storm.

As she began to change her clothes to go out, Elisabeth thought for a moment of Fiona, alone on Washington Island and waiting for the blizzard. She made a mental note to call her, and then promptly forgot as she stood in front of her closet trying to decide whether she should wear fashionable boots or ones for snow. Despite her skepticism about the forecast, Elisabeth was a native. She chose the snow boots.

Fiona stood in her kitchen looking around and mentally checking off a list of things she should do for the blizzard. She was more aware than she had expected, to be of her solitary state. There were neighbors, of course, and people nearby she knew she could call if there were an emergency, but the need for self-reliance was stronger here than she had ever experienced.

Robert was her first thought. She had plenty of hay and goat chow in the barn, so she wasn't worried about running out. She decided to make sure he was taken care of first.

Robert looked up as she opened the door, his yellow eyes glittering. He had been drinking, and the warm water was dripping from his black snout. "Hello, Robert," said Fiona, resignedly. She always felt resigned about Robert. He looked at her as she spoke to him, and she thought she could see his eyes narrow, but he wasn't in a talking mood.

Nevertheless, he came to the edge of his stall when she approached and suffered her stroking of his neck. Fiona eyed him leerily as he eyed her back. Despite the insistence of the *Idiot's Guide* that goats were social creatures who enjoyed company, Fiona had yet to discern any real appreciation of her attention. She paid her respects daily, and even went so far as to feel guilty about his solitude. For his part, Robert always seemed to view her as if she had interrupted something. Possibly, she thought, he's building a conspiracy to take over the Island.

Robert pushed his head against her hand and stomped his foot. He uttered something that sounded like a small curse under his breath, turned his back, and began to chew a mouthful of hay.

Thus rejected, Fiona went about making sure the water was running clear, his stall was clean, and sprinkling the supplement she had been urgently assured was essential to his well-being over his goat chow. Robert eyed her suspiciously as he chewed.

"Don't worry," she told him. "I'm reserving the cyanide for later."

As she finished her goat ministrations, she found herself recalling the Great Plains blizzards of the Laura Ingalls Wilder books in which Pa runs a rope between house and barn so he won't be lost in the storm. She wondered briefly whether she even had a rope, and then laughed at herself and settled for bringing the snow shovel up from the shed to lean against the front door. She might as well shovel from there in the morning.

Fully aware of the anachronisms, she charged her cell phone, her notebook, and her iPod, then set out the lanterns and matches, and filled the bathtub, the sinks, and three pails of water in anticipation of losing power. She made herself a lovely stew with shallots and mushrooms and wine and set it to simmer in the oven. Feeling that she had done all she could, she bundled up and went for a long walk. The sun shone brightly, and there was no indication of a change in the weather. Fiona breathed deeply. She missed Rocco's good company.

When she returned, she noticed Robert standing idly in his pen outside. Their eyes met, and she felt his reproach. Wondering whether she should invest in a talisman against whatever curse he was calling down on her, she went in to make herself a cup of tea and settled in for an afternoon of *Mansfield Park*. The house was filled with the aroma of her dinner cooking. There was nothing to do now except wager on the accuracy of the forecasts, but Fiona had no one to take that bet. It had occurred to her that the storm might delay tomorrow's town meeting, but no one, she thought, could be that lucky.

The supper club was not busy that night. There were a few tables of diners, and as predicted, familiar faces at the bar. Elisabeth decided to join some friends for a drink before dinner. She enjoyed having company around her, but dining alone in a restaurant was one of life's great pleasures. She would be sociable now, and again after dinner, but she would order her steak at her own table.

She was laughing with her companions over a story when she caught the glance of a man at the other end of the bar. She felt a twinge of recognition. He had been at Ground Zero that morning. He nodded to her and raised his glass in her direction. She raised hers back, and then, feeling that she was somehow hosting a party, she gestured silently with an open palm toward her group, inviting him to join them. He left his seat and came over.

"Hello," he said, extending his hand. "I'm Pete."

A light flurry of snow had begun to fall when Fiona went to bed that night with her book, snug under her comforter, a cup of hot tea at hand. It was still ridiculously early when she became too drowsy to keep her eyes open, so she tucked her book under one of the pillows and turned out the light.

Inevitably, the crunching began. This time it seemed to be coming from the ceiling and accompanied by occasional thumpings. Fiona pondered whether these were from feet or tail, but could not reach any conclusion. It was with these thoughts that she finally fell asleep.

Elisabeth and Pete Landry were sitting over their coffee, the empty bottle of wine on the table. Over the course of the meal they had covered the basics of their lives. He worked for an international oil company and his job required that he spend much of his time roaming the world, something he enjoyed for the most part. She gathered from his business card that he spoke Mandarin, Italian, and Portuguese. He was born in India to a British father and an American mother; he was single and an Oxford graduate, and had served in the United Staes Navy. His skin was tanned and slightly wind burned, and his eyes crinkled when he smiled.

Their conversation had shifted to their travels, and she was telling him about her last trip to San Francisco. Laughter and loud conversation still came from the bar, and Elisabeth was looking forward to a nightcap with everyone before heading out into the cold. Outside the windows, the first flakes of snow had begun to fly, but she wasn't worried. Her car was practically invincible in the snow, and she was a confident and experienced driver. Wisconsinites who let the weather determine their business, were in danger of never venturing out at all in winter.

It had been an enormously pleasant evening, far better than she could have anticipated, and Elisabeth did not repine for the solitary meal she had planned. Pete had been charming, and although her heart was engaged elsewhere, she thoroughly understood his attractions. In the way of strangers thrown together they had confided in one another, telling more than they might have had they been old friends. "What woman wouldn't want this amusing, considerate, and intelligent man," she thought. He had offered some masculine perspective for her to contemplate, and she felt a new glow of optimism.

Engrossed in their conversation, a lull in the noise from the bar drew her attention, and Elisabeth looked up. Standing in the door of the dining room stood Roger. She saw him take it all in: Pete's relaxed pose at the table, his laughter, the remains of a happy dinner, the empty bottle of wine. Their eyes met for several long seconds, and then, before Elisabeth could speak or move, he turned and was gone. Frozen with dismay, she could see him from her table through the window, heading toward the old jeep across the street, his bare head and shoulders hunched against the blowing snow.

The snow was coming down sideways when Elisabeth and Pete said good night and headed out to their respective cars. Neither of them had noticed the looks exchanged at the bar as they left, but Elisabeth was distracted by thoughts of Roger, and from the moment they left the restaurant, the weather drove everything else from their minds. Even within the shelter of the high bluffs above the town, the wind slammed against them. In the hour or so since it had begun, there were already five or six inches of snow. The county plows had been through once, but their priorities would be keeping the main roads clear. The side streets were a vast covered field of snow. By now, there could be no doubt that travel would be a challenge. The forecasts seemed to have been on the mark.

Pete's rental car was closest to the restaurant. Elisabeth urged him to forego chivalry, pointing to her own car across the street, and the piercing wind made their good-byes brief. Shivering, she started the engine and let it run while she brushed the snow from the windows in her usual meticulous fashion. That rental had not looked very storm-worthy. From across the street came the familiar sound of inadequate tires on snow trying to gain traction. She finished her windows, walked across the deserted street to his car, and rapped on the driver's window. He rolled it down, a sheepish look on his face.

"Guess I should have sprung for the four-wheel drive."

"Need a lift?" she asked. "It could be hours before a tow truck gets to you."

"Thanks," said Pete Landry cheerfully. "I think I do."

Fiona had been asleep for some time when she woke with a start. It took a moment for her to get her bearings, confused by the noise. The crunching had stopped, replaced by a deep howling roar. The storm slammed against the little house making the windows and doors rattle, and the wind wailed in the trees and eaves. She slipped out of bed and went to the window. The trees bent and swayed, and the snow fell sideways so thickly that Fiona could not see across the street to the shuttered and silent Albatross. Standing in the draft from the windows Fiona felt goose bumps rising on her arms.

Despite her love of the snow and its beauty, she felt a quiver of fear. There were no lights nearby; there were few houses in sight. If there were to be some medical emergency, no one could come to the rescue. The hospital lay eighty miles away in Green Bay as the crow flies, inaccessible except by helicopter, and no helicopter would fly tonight. She wondered whether even the fire department or the Island's several policemen would be able to reach anyone in need. She thought of Nancy, of Jim, of Pali and Nika, of Jake and Charlotte and of her friends on the Island, safe, she hoped, and warm, and of her friends on the mainland, who, even if they were beneath the same storm, at least had the protection of the land around them, not the Island's unyielding blockade of wind and water.

Never in her life had she been so completely isolated from the rest of the world. She realized, as she looked out, that she should be able to see three different streetlights from where she stood, but there was nothing but swirling snow and darkness. The power was out. Fiona stood at the window for a long time before she noticed that her toes were icy cold on the bare floor.

Trying not to think about the morning, she ran back across the room, leapt into bed, and pulled the covers up to her chin. This time, the weather guys had got it right.

Pali woke with a start when the wind began; it struck hard, roaring like an airplane landing. He checked his reliable battery clock by the bed; 12:21. Normally he'd be up at four o'clock on a winter's day to get the crew working to shovel out the decks of the ferry. With winds like this, he knew that the waves would be too high for a crossing. As captain, normally he would consider it his duty to go down to see for himself before he made the decision to cancel. And the decision was his to make. He could get up at the usual time, or he could wait for the ferry line's owner to make the decision and call. Either way, he had no doubt what the decision would be. Nika lay sleeping beside him; school would be closed. He wouldn't mind staying in bed this morning. He pulled the covers higher over his massive shoulders and rolled over closer to the warmth of his wife.

Pete was staying at an inn in Egg Harbor some miles past Elisabeth's, not terribly out of her way. But as they made their way cautiously south, she began to wonder how far they would get. The snow was falling so heavily that without the wind it would have been difficult to see the road. With the wind, it was nearly impossible. Even long familiarity with the route was insufficient for Elisabeth to feel any confidence that she knew exactly where the road was.

The snowflakes made a hypnotic kaleidoscope pattern in the headlights, and the road was covered. A faint path of the plow gave the sole indication of where to point the wheel. In the car there was no sound but the frantic beat of the windshield wipers as both passenger and driver concentrated on discerning the way ahead. Moving painstakingly forward, they left the last lights of Fish Creek behind them. Elisabeth felt a knot of anxiety in her stomach, only some of it related to the road conditions. She saw nothing but darkness ahead.

Fiona could not sleep. Every moan of the wind sounded to her like the plaintive calling of Robert. She had done the best she knew how, but why hadn't she thought ahead to what would happen in a big storm? Evil he might be, but she could not bear to think of his suffering in the cold. It was some hours before she wore out her worries and fell back into a restless sleep.

The twenty-minute trip had reached the ninety-minute mark as Elisabeth and Pete approached the small hill leading to her own intersection. She breathed a silent prayer as she gently built some speed to get up the hill. Under ordinary conditions, she never even thought about there being a hill here, but even on this gentle incline, she felt the wheels slipping.

Elisabeth was considering her options. The road beyond the gallery to Egg Harbor and Pete's hotel was a long, gentle but twisting slope down through the woods. The prospect of spending at least another hour driving there and back—assuming that they didn't end up in a ditch—was not appealing. If they did end up in a ditch, they would have to stay there until they were dug out. Probably not until morning. As much as she sought another choice, Elisabeth's common sense told her that continuing was pure stupidity.

"We're not going to make it to Egg Harbor," she said at last. "I grew up here and I've never seen anything like this." She paused, mentally rehearsing what a terrible idea this was—he was a complete stranger—but she was unable to come up with a sensible alternative. "I'm terribly sorry, but I think you're going to have to stay with me. In my guest room," she added hastily.

The windshield wipers filled the silence. This was not an appealing option to either of them. Pete thought of his hotel room with privacy, his things, a TV, and a minibar. After a moment he slowly nodded. "I see your point." They were silent for a few minutes. He looked over at her as he spoke. "It's a bit awkward, isn't it." He said it as a statement, not a question. "I'm sorry to inconvenience you like this. No doubt you are wishing you hadn't offered me a ride."

"Don't be silly. It's not a big deal," said Elisabeth, resolutely cheerful. "But you may wish you'd brought more luggage. From the looks of things, you may have to stay for a week."

"I've done worse. I once had to stay at a Howard Johnson's in Newark."

They stopped laughing suddenly as the car began to skid. Elisabeth brought the car under control and resumed the conversation.

"Well fortunately, I have a well-stocked pantry. And liquor cabinet," she added.

"We could probably use another drink after this," said Pete.

"At least," she agreed, as she tried, as gently as possible, to slow the car without breaking for the turn ahead. She wasn't even certain at this point whether she could have found her way home walking across the fields. In a blizzard like this, it would be easy to set off across familiar territory only to be lost in the whiteout.

They had to abandon the car at the end of the driveway and walk up the fifty yards to the house. The drifts were already above the wheels, and the snow pulled the sturdy little Japanese station wagon with an inexorable certainty. The car slipped into the ditch with a small thunk, and Elisabeth and Pete sat for a moment in the silence, the windshield wipers still moving, but the car most certainly stopped. They turned to look at each other with rueful smiles. She took a deep breath, actually relieved to be finished driving.

"Sorry I can't drop you at the door," she said, sincerely.

Pete shrugged and zipped up his jacket.

"The good news is that I have no luggage."

Grateful for her snow boots—even though they were well short of the depth of the drifts—Elisabeth was nevertheless exhausted and slightly uneasy as she trudged up the small hill to her house. He seemed like a decent enough guy, and he had good references, and, of course Rocco was there at the house. She had a mental image of gentle Rocco tearing Pete limb from limb. She checked her thoughts and gave her attention to plodding ahead. Luckily, there was a fence along the drive to help them find their way. The wind blew snow into her eyes and nose, her legs were wet through her jeans, and it was bitter cold. She tried not to dwell upon the unknown character of the man

sludging through the snow behind her. She just hoped she knew
what she was doing.

Fiona woke in the dark and icy cold air of her room with the
sound of the wind still roaring outside. She looked at the
clock next to her bed and saw its blank face. The power was still
out. She lay in bed for a while, torn between its warmth and the
thought of coffee.

The loss of power was an inconvenience, not an emergency.
Fiona, alerted by the locals to the frequency of power outages,
had a propane gas stove, a perfectly serviceable fifty-year-old oil-
burning furnace—both too ancient to have the electronic ignition that would be useless without power—radiators, and most
important, a coffeepot that worked on the stove. These were the
true essentials, all unimpeded by a lack of electricity. Ultimately,
the yearning for coffee won out, and Fiona wrapped herself in
sweats and warm socks to descend to the kitchen.

She gazed out the window as she waited for the water to boil.
Even in the darkness she could see there was at least eighteen
inches of snow on the ground, and it was falling heavily, sideways from the wind. She could barely make out the outline of
Stella's house, but she felt no comfort knowing that Stella was
nearby.

"Roger."

She had said his name out loud. Elisabeth sat up in bed and remembered her dream. Roger had been lost in the storm, wandering in hopeless circles, blinded by the blowing snow, and calling to her. From her house she could hear him calling, but she could not get out to find him. Anguish and self-recrimination filled her heart. She had awakened from a vision of his face, wind-bitten, bewildered, and accusing.

She looked at the clock by the bed. 5:30. The wind was blowing as hard as before. Rocco, hearing her stir, came to the side of the bed and rested his chin next to her pillow. Elisabeth patted the bed, inviting him to come up, and he leapt with the grace of a cat, if with somewhat more impact. Shivering more from nerves than from cold, she nestled back down under the blankets, comforted by the big warm dog who lay nestled nearby, and gradually fell back into troubled sleep.

Fiona's one big worry was Robert's water supply. The well pump wouldn't be working, and the electric heater she used to warm his trough, would be off. The slow trickle of the running water in the shed normally kept the pipes from freezing, but without electricity to run the well pump, there would be no trickle now. She wondered how long before the power came back on and felt sympathy for the men who would be out in the storm even now, struggling to make the repairs that everyone on the Island was depending on.

As she looked out the window again, she realized that Stella's house had disappeared. Suddenly, yesterday's idea of the rope between house and barn didn't seem quite so silly. Fiona transferred one of her buckets of water rather sloppily into a big soup pot and turned it on to boil. Somehow, she would have to carry it to the barn without spilling it all over herself and thaw the ice which must have begun to form by now on Robert's trough. She supposed that would have to be after she had shoveled the hundred feet or so to the barn. Carrying her coffee with her, she went upstairs to dress.

When she stood on the porch a little while later, her anxiety for Robert rose further. It was much colder than she had expected. Would he be warm enough? Not having other goats to create and share warmth was a disadvantage for him—although, as Fiona was fully aware—a blessing to herself. She had thought about this, and planned for it, but she realized she had not considered the prospect of not having the warmed water. This had been stupid, she told herself. But it was too late now. The snow was still falling heavily, and, if anything, the wind had picked up. She decided that she should not take the time to clear the path to Robert, but to trudge through. The snow was blowing fiercely.

Fiona went back in to get the water, which she had mixed with molasses. The sugar would help to keep the water from freezing, and would provide extra calories to keep Robert warm. Fiona pulled up her hood, put on her mittens, and headed out into the storm.

When Elisabeth woke later that morning, it had just begun to get light. She noted with relief that the clock was on, and the small hall light she'd left burning still shone under the door. They had power. And, she thought, "Pete didn't turn out to be an ax murderer." Somewhat cheered, she got up, showered, and dressed. The emotional remnants of her dream still haunted her, though, and she longed for the comfort of coffee on a snowy morning.

She moved quietly down the hall to the kitchen so as not to disturb her guest. His door was still closed. She would make something lovely for breakfast. Maybe that would help her mood.

At 7:15, the owner of the ferry line made his second call to Pali. "I'm shutting down for the day. We have twenty-foot waves and swells much higher. That won't be changing until the wind lets up."

Pali could sense the stress behind the calm voice. The well-being of the Island depended on the ferry, but it was a business that ran a very fine line between red ink and black. Every day down meant a loss of revenue and a step closer to ruin. There would be trucks with deliveries at Northpoint, waiting to load their goods for Island commerce. There were oil trucks and grocery supplies. There was mail. There were people who would be wanting to get to the airport for a sunny vacation; people who wanted to keep their appointments. Nancy Gunderson was scheduled for chemo in Green Bay today.

Keeping the ferries running was a capital-intensive business. Along with regular maintenance, there was always some mechanical problem that needed attention, fuel costs were rising, Environmental Protection Agency and Wisconsin Department of Natural Resources mandates forced extravagant—and highly impractical—alterations in piers and equipment, and everyone knew that as tourism dropped and more and more residents were forced to move away to find jobs, their tenuous connection to the mainland kept getting thinner. The ferry was lifeblood; there was no getting around it.

"John Eisely's going to be pissed off that he won't be getting that boiler," commented Pali.

"Well John's just going to have to get over it," said the owner. "Can't be helped."

Fiona stood before the barn door with the bucket of water, her head down in frustration. It had not occurred to her that the deep accumulation of snow would blockade the barn door. There was no way she would be able to open it without shoveling, and that would be a major undertaking. The door was six feet wide, and its path would have to be cleared at least enough to open it so she could squeeze through with the bucket.

The only other way into the barn was through a window. But

she could not see any way she could pass the bucket through to herself. "No," she thought. "There is no way out of it." Turning, she trudged back to the house to retrieve the shovel, recalling how blithely she had dismissed Jim's urging that she purchase a snow blower.

By the time she finished shoveling, the water was cold again. She was about to dump it when she remembered the molasses. It could be days before the store opened or the ferry could bring supplies in. This was a precious commodity not to be wasted. Wearily, Fiona lugged the bucket back to the house. "At least," she thought, "I'm spilling less this way." Her anxiety for Robert buzzed in her head.

At Ground Zero, everything was closed and dark. With only a short drive for coffee, the wild snow was insufficient to deter the intrepid natives, for whom habit and a nonchalance about Wisconsin winters occasionally overruled common sense. Several cars sat in the parking lot, waiting for Roger to show up. The electric grid was far less susceptible here than on the Island, and everyone looked forward to the smell of coffee and cinnamon, and the new halogen lighting that gave a cheering warmth to the shop on a dreary day.

Terry saw Mike's truck idling in the lot and ran through the storm to jump into the passenger seat. "Well, how about this?" he asked, without preamble. "What's happened to Roger, do you s'pose?"

Mike frowned slightly and shook his head. "Couldn't say. Not like Roger. Weather doesn't stop him."

Terry pursed his lips and nodded. It was strange. "Wouldn't think we'd have to worry about Roger. Fiona's the one I been thinking of."

"How do you suppose she'll do?" asked Mike.

Neither admitted that their fears for her had been in both their minds since the night before.

Terry frowned, shook his head, and raised his eyes to Heaven. "Power's out on the Island and she hasn't got the sense God gave a goose. Probably out wandering the beaches or some such nonsense, getting lost in the snow."

Mike nodded. "Yes," he said, frowning again. "I'm worried."

Terry stared out the window at the parking lot where the snow still swirled madly. One of the other cars had given up and was pulling away. "Well, looks like there's no action here this morning. Better get on with the day." He put his hand on the door latch, turning back to Mike. "Drive safe."

"Will do."

Terry slammed the door and, ducking his head against the wind, dashed across the lot to his truck.

Fiona put the bucket down and looked around. The barn was colder than she had expected. Unthinkingly, she reached for the light switch. It clicked pointlessly; there was sufficient light, however, from the east windows. A thickening film of ice was forming across the trough. Robert was nowhere to be seen.

Covered with melting snow, Fiona pushed her hood back from her head and carried the bucket to the trough. Using a broom handle, she broke through the film of ice and poured in the warm water, stirring it to mix in the molasses. She had no idea how effective it would be in delaying the freezing, but she had a childlike confidence in the *Idiot's Guide*. She heard the vague snorting sounds that indicated Robert's presence and saw him rising from beneath a pile of hay. He shook himself like a dog, and came to hang over the edge of his stall, straw still clinging to his head. Despite his ridiculous appearance, the intelligent comprehension in his eyes was disconcerting.

"Are you warm enough?" she asked him. He looked at her. Fiona reached out to touch his ears, and he bent his head. Robert liked having his ears stroked. They were soft and still warm, which Fiona took to be a good sign. She wondered what she would do if it got much colder. He ambled over to his trough to drink, looking at her out of the corner of his eyes as he did so. Clearly, he found the molasses a welcome innovation.

His stall was clean enough for now, she decided, and she recalled an old farmer's advice. "Don't be in a big hurry to clean out the barn in the winter. The manure helps to keep things warm."

Fiona added more hay for Robert in one corner, filled his bucket with goat chow, and added his supplements. He had eaten a lot since last night. Robert watched her activities with an imperious air, his expression implying criticism of her bumbling methods. "If you think you can do it better, by all means," she told him. Robert made a rude noise.

Chores finished, Fiona lingered awhile, leaning against the edge of the stall. He was, for the time being, the only creature she had contact with. But at last the cold began to sink in, and she began to long for another cup of coffee. "Ok, Robert. Carry on," she said and turned to leave.

"WHAT?" said Robert.

"I'll be back later."

"WHAT?"

As she closed the door behind her, she heard him kick the side of the stall.

Chapter Twenty-One ✤

Pete appeared in the kitchen as Elisabeth was putting scones in the oven. He was showered, and neatly dressed, albeit in yesterday's clothes. Elisabeth thought again to herself how attractive he was. Rocco bounded across the room to him, as if they were old friends. Pete rubbed Rocco's ribs with both hands and spoke affectionately to him. "The cups are over there," Elisabeth said. "Help yourself."

Pete poured his coffee and stood looking out the window with Rocco seated beside him, having his ears scratched. A shrewd judge of character, Rocco had already determined that Pete was all right. "Doesn't seem to have let up at all, does it?" commented Pete, gazing at the whirling snow.

"No, if anything, I'd say it's a little worse. Looks like you're going to be stuck here for a while."

Pete shrugged and smiled.

"It does. So what can I do around here to make myself useful? I know how to scramble eggs and make toast, I am fond of hedge trimming, and have been complimented on my fire-building. Which reminds me, I noticed that your wood pile is low. Do you have a supply somewhere? I can do some chopping for you."

"Maybe you can scramble eggs later," said Elisabeth. "And there's wood in the shed across the driveway," she added. It's cut, but I'd be grateful if you could bring some more in. Even if we don't really need it, it's cozier to have a fire going." She motioned him toward the table. "I'm not sure I'll have an opportunity to evaluate your hedge-trimming, however," she said, putting the coffee pot on the table.

"We should also see if we can get your car out of the ditch without a tow truck. Although I think it's unlikely."

"Well have your coffee and some breakfast first and we'll figure it out. Under the circumstances, there's no point in rushing."

"True." Pete poured himself another cup of coffee and rubbed his stubbly chin with some embarrassment. "I'm afraid I don't generally pack my shaving kit when I go out to dinner."

"Oh, that's ok," said Elisabeth. "I have a fresh razor you can borrow. I'll get it for you and you can shave while breakfast is cooking." She disappeared for a moment and reappeared with a package of disposable razors. Pete accepted a pink one, and went off to the guest bath to shave.

While he was gone, Rocco began to stir and growl. Elisabeth frowned and shushed him. "Rocco! Be quiet. There's no one out there." But Rocco was at the door, his ears standing straight up, and his hackles raised. Suddenly Elisabeth heard footsteps on the porch. Without thinking, she went quickly to the door and flung it open. There, his face red with cold, and wet from melting snow, his blue jacket so crusted with ice that it was nearly white, stood Roger.

He stepped into the kitchen at approximately the same moment that Pete appeared, freshly shaven, his coffee cup in hand.

Elisabeth wanted to fling her arms around Roger in relief, but in the split second when she turned to see Pete, reconstructed the scene to fit what Roger must be seeing, and turned back to explain, he was already out the door again. Blindly, Elisabeth grabbed her jacket from a hook and started to go after him, but Pete was faster.

"Wait here," he said. "Let me go." And grabbing his own jacket, he ran out into the storm.

"Oh, Rocco," said Elisabeth. Together they sat on the kitchen floor with the big dog's head against her cheek.

After a long ten minutes, Elisabeth heard footsteps on the porch, and Pete entered the kitchen, bringing snow and cold with him. He looked chagrined.

"I tried to catch him, but in the wind I doubt he could hear me, and he was moving fast. He was parked near enough that he just drove away before I could reach him." He sat down next to her on the floor. He didn't want to mention his own thoughts about the likelihood of Roger's winding up in a ditch. "I'm sorry," he said.

Two big tears rolled down Elisabeth's face. "Thank you," she said, trying to keep her self-control. Rocco leaned closer and licked her tears.

"Come on," said Pete, standing and holding out his hand to help her up. "Judging from the smell, I'd say those scones are burned. And you look like a woman who could use some scrambled eggs on toast."

At noon the storm was as fierce as ever and the Island's power was still off. As much as twenty-four inches of snow was expected over the course of three days. The accumulation—though record-setting—wasn't the whole problem; it was the drifting. The plows had been by, but the road was snow-filled anyway, with drifts almost as high as Fiona's head. It would be difficult to keep up with it for a while.

In Wisconsin, snow removal is swift and efficient. Within twelve hours of a storm, the highways are generally clear and dry. Few inhabitants allowed a storm or cold weather to impede their plans; they simply carried on. To do otherwise was viewed as weakness.

This, however, was out of the ordinary. The radio announced a civil warning, urging the need for everyone within hearing to stay at home. The National Weather Service announced "life-threatening conditions." The governor had declared a state of emergency. I-94 was closed from Chicago to Milwaukee; I-43 was closed from Rock County in the southwest near the Iowa border to Brown County, home of the Green Bay Packers in the northeast. The National Guard had been called out to patrol the highways looking for stranded drivers. It was the worst blizzard in living memory; no one had seen anything like it.

It was time for Fiona to go and check on Robert again. She was reluctantly aware of his dependence on her, and she wasn't completely sure that she knew what to do. How on earth had she ended up taking care of a goat, anyway? The thermometer was dropping; she could only guess what the barn would be like. As she waited for the bucket of water to boil, she drank the dregs of the morning's coffee reheated in a little pan on the stove, and then bundled up in her parka warm from the radiator, but still damp. She was on her way out the door when she noticed a brown puddle on the kitchen floor. Fiona frowned. What was that from? Oh well, she would take care of it when she got back. Pulling her hood up over her hair, she went out into the storm.

The path showed no signs of her morning trek to the barn. The snow was now well over the tops of her boots. She felt as if she were being beaten by the wind, and reached the door with a feeling of relief.

When she entered the barn this time, Robert was waiting for her, standing where had he been when she left, one piece of straw perched rakishly behind one ear. He eyed her from head to toe. Fiona eyed him back.

"Don't you start with me," she said.

She poured more water into the trough. He must like the molasses quite a lot, because the water level was low.

"Here's your tea, Majesty," she said.

When she got back to the house, Fiona decided it was time to take action to protect her food. The freezer, she knew, would be ok for a day or two if she didn't open it. But the things in the refrigerator needed help. She piled a few things into plastic grocery bags, and set them, along with the milk and covered stew pot in a neat line along the porch wall. Inside, she had commandeered every container, pot, pan, or jug she could find and filled them with melting snow. Robert was going through a lot of water, and the results of one bucket of snow were rather meager. She felt pleased with herself. Despite the predictions of the Ground Zero crowd, she was doing just fine.

When Fiona returned that afternoon, the cold in the barn was penetrating. Robert emerged from his hay at her entrance, and came to see her. Fiona realized that she didn't know what an acceptable temperature would be for a goat, but he had no one to warm up with, so there was a thinner margin for error. What was she going to do? She could not allow an animal—not even Robert—to freeze. Although, she reminded herself, he did have hellfire on his side.

As she worked, she thought about the problem. Her own inexperience, she knew, gathered the odds against Robert's survival. If only she had some way of covering him. A blanket would never work. She wouldn't be able to keep it on him, and besides, he'd probably eat it. A vision of Robert in a sweater came to her mind. She dismissed it with a small laugh at herself, but she started thinking. "Armholes would help," she thought. After more thought, she decided she had to try something.

Her new down vest, keeping her warm under her jacket, had been a purchase she had made specifically for the Island, and she found that it was extremely effective in keeping out the cold. Brushing her hands off on her jeans, she took off her coat and then the vest. Still slightly damp from the snow that had melted on her, she began to shiver. She hurriedly got back into her coat and held up the vest to look at it. It might not be big enough to fit around his chest. Ideally, she needed something man-size. But it would be better than nothing.

Getting it on him was going to be the most difficult part of the problem. She stood for a moment looking speculatively at Robert. His eyes met hers, and as if he could read her thoughts, he began backing away. Fiona laid the vest on the floor as flat as she could and went to get a handful of goat chow, which she placed on the floor above the vest. All she needed, she hoped, was one leg in the right place. The vest would then be covering his chest, which should work, but how would she keep it on him, since the snaps would not reach to close? Robert, whose willingness to cooperate on new ventures was not well-known, walked straight to the goat chow and miraculously put one foot in each armhole. Fiona reached to pull the vest up, and he danced away. She went for more goat chow.

The next time, Robert was standing on the wrong place. The time after that, he turned sideways on the vest to face her. The time after that, he stood on the vest and crumpled it between his feet.

After the third try, Fiona decided to sit down in front of the vest while she offered the goat chow. When he approached— with somewhat less enthusiasm after so much goat chow—she reached gently and slowly to move the vest into position before he put his feet down. She got one foot in, but it was the wrong foot. This might work better than her original plan. If he wore the vest around his back it would easier to keep it on him and it would still help keep him warm.

Slowly, cooing to him the entire time, which, as she thought to herself, would make anyone suspicious, not just Robert, she pulled the vest up and around him. Robert seemed completely unconcerned. He nudged her hand with his nose purposefully. Did she, in fact, have any more goat chow? He wanted to know. She reached for more. Fiona feared she had made a strategic error. How was she going to get the second foot into the second armhole? She began to understand the wisdom, so widely shared among farmers, of building trust with your animals. If they know you and know your intentions (at least, for the most part, until you butcher them, she thought), they were more likely to allow you to do things like this. Fiona had to admit that she had seen no evidence in the literature that this applied to putting clothing on them, but the principle she felt, was the same.

She stood next to him holding the vest up over his back. This was not quite the arrangement she'd been going for. Her fingers and toes were getting painfully cold. She let go of the vest and went for another handful of goat chow, which she put into her pocket. As soon as she was close, Robert began nuzzling aggressively at her pocket. The vest fell down and he stepped delicately out of it.

With more patience than she felt, Fiona began the process again. She laid the vest on the straw once more, sitting at its neck. This was not as easy as before since Robert was heavily involved in trying to eat the goat chow in her pocket. He stepped inadvertently into one armhole. Just as Fiona was reaching to pull the vest around him, he bent his knees and lay down in front of her, his head in her lap. This was not the charmingly affectionate gesture it seemed; it was merely a more comfortable way to get the goat chow out of her pocket. But Fiona saw her opportunity. Maneuvering the vest around him as she tried to push his surprisingly heavy head out of her way, she pulled the vest around him once more, breathing a prayer of thanks once again that he had no horns. Then, with infinite care, she slid the other sleeve of the vest over his bent foot. "Here, Robert," she said, and reached into her pocket for the goat chow. He ate it sloppily, and after determining that there was no more on her person, he rose to leave. Fiona pulled the vest triumphantly over the rest of his leg, and gazed proudly at her well-dressed animal.

Unmoved, Robert turned his back on her and went to get more molasses water.

Relieved, cold, and covered with goat spit, Fiona zipped up her coat and trudged laboriously back through the wind and snow to the relative comfort of the house. It was still snowing.

As she entered her kitchen and slammed the door against the wind, she felt a bit guilty at how good the heat felt. She hoped the vest would be sufficient. It didn't cover Robert's chest, but the insulation of the down around most of his torso should help to keep him warm enough. She pondered the fact, gleaned from *The Idiot's Guide*, that goat body temperatures were higher than humans. That must mean that he would be more susceptible to the cold rather than less. "He's a GOAT," she told herself out loud. "He lives in a BARN." But he was a solitary goat in a big barn, without the heat generated by other animals.

Fiona kicked off her boots and stomped sock-footed toward the stove to make some tea. Feeling that her foot was wet she looked down, suddenly remembering the strange yellow-brown puddle. What was that? She didn't remember spilling anything. It was an odd color. More like tea than coffee. She shrugged, got a paper towel to wipe it up, and went upstairs to change her socks. Cold, tired, and feeling inadequate in her goat-tending duties, she found the appeal of her bed irresistible, and she lay down to take a nap.

It was late afternoon when Pete returned to the house, stomping his feet and brushing the snow off his shoulders. Rocco came in behind him, his fur covered with ice balls.

"You should have enough wood to last you for a month up here on the porch. I moved one of the rockers, and extended the pile to the edge. Rocco was good company, weren't you, Rocco?" He scratched the dog between the ears as Rocco looked up at him adoringly.

"Thank you," said Elisabeth, beginning to rub Rocco down with a big beach towel, which he gleefully interpreted as a wrestling match.

"That would have been a weekend of work for me, carrying up little piles, the way I do. It's very nice of you."

Pete shrugged modestly. "Keeps me busy. I went down to look at the car, by the way. It's hopeless without a tow."

"Everyone's probably busy with real emergencies right now, but it wouldn't hurt to get my name on the list," said Elisabeth. "I'll call." She suddenly noticed how wet his clothes were. "You are soaked to the skin."

Pete looked down at himself and made a face.

"Here," said Elisabeth, hanging up the towel, and pouring

another cup of coffee. You sit down and try to get warm, and I'll go see if I can find something for you. Maybe one of my brothers left something somewhere."

Pete sat down at the kitchen table with the coffee, and stared out at the swirling snow. Rocco came and lay contentedly at his feet, his big head resting on Pete's foot, steam rising from his damp fur.

Pete hadn't bargained on the storm being this intense. He had had only a few days before his obligations would require his return to the city, and under normal circumstances, that should have been enough. But, he told himself, he had to accept that his plans were going to have to be postponed. He felt a twinge of frustration and dismissed it. There was time. He could be patient. And at least he knew now what he was looking for. "Or, more precisely," he corrected himself, "where to look."

When Fiona awoke, it was nearly dark. There was no sunset, just a vague light in the clouds to the west. The storm still beat hard against the Island, and Fiona felt mentally battered by the sound of the wind. It wouldn't be so bad, she thought, if she could stay safe inside, baking cookies and reading; if she weren't responsible for Robert. She remembered, with no small bit of irony, the pity she had always felt for dairy farmers and the unrelenting drudgery of their daily care for hundreds of animals. Sundays, holidays, birthdays, sick days, and days when you just didn't feel like it. It wasn't like a dog who was with you and a member of the family. "I am not a farmer. I've never wanted to be a farmer. What," she asked herself again, "am I doing with a goat?" She sighed. It was time to go make sure Robert's water wasn't frozen. Or Robert himself, for that matter.

Feeling better for her nap, she went almost cheerfully downstairs. She had enough to eat, she was warm, she had coffee, milk, and if necessary—and it certainly was, she felt—scotch. Robert would be fine. She could solve whatever came her way. Walking into the shadowy kitchen, she stepped in something wet. What was on the floor? Her first instinct was to reach for the light switch, but she caught herself and went to light her big lantern instead. Suddenly she realized that she would have no light in the barn. How would she find her way in the dark with no path? How would she carry a flashlight and the big bucket through two feet of snow? How would she see anything in the barn? Stunned by this realization, Fiona sat down on the floor as she contemplated this new wrinkle. Why hadn't she thought of this before?

And more important, why was she sitting in water?

She stood up hurriedly, and peered through the lantern light at the floor. A yellow-brown puddle shimmered in the candlelight. Fiona realized now where she had seen a puddle like this. Last year in Ephraim, when her cottage roof was leaking. She held the lantern high and looked up. In the diminishing late afternoon light, it was still possible to see the growing brown stain on the ceiling. It was a slow dripping leak, but it was not a small one. She could see that from the damage to the ceiling. Momentarily stunned by this development, Fiona stood staring up, and then shook herself into action. She would have to deal with this later. Right now she had to get to Robert and solve the lighting problem. It was almost dark already. In a flash of overdue inspiration, she grabbed her backpack. She added a jar of molasses, a battery lantern—purchased on one of her meandering trips to the hardware store—and her biggest flashlight. She put the water on the stove to boil.

Hurriedly, she ran up to change her wet clothes and then came back down to prepare for the weather. She was running out of dry jeans, and was forced to switch to sweatpants. She pulled on her boots over tights and added two pairs of thick socks; over her cotton turtleneck she added a hooded sweatshirt, jacket, scarf, hood, insulated gloves, and mittens. It was a little tricky pulling the backpack on with all those layers, but when she was ready, she picked up her bucket and stepped outside.

Elisabeth had spent the day trying not to show her feelings in front of her guest. She had kept busy by making a big pot of minestrone and baking bread, and she planned a nice dinner. The burned scones had been thrown out to the birds and squirrels.

Pete had offered to try to find a way back to his hotel, but Elisabeth had urged him to stay. "Why should we both sit alone—you in a hotel room—when we can be perfectly comfortable here together? After all," she added, with her first trace of humor since that morning, "our reputations are already ruined."

Pete gave her a look of sympathy. "I really am sorry about

this. Once he calms down he'll see reason. You'll be able to explain it to him."

Elisabeth started to look tearful again. "I'm not so sure. You don't know Roger. Anyway, I e-mailed him, trying to explain."

Pete looked at her hopefully. "And?"

"Nothing. It says it hasn't been opened."

Fiona was unprepared for the temperature. The bite of the wind almost knocked her back. The snow swirled, seemingly from everywhere. With every breath, her nostrils stuck together; with every step her boots squeaked on the snow. Her eyes burned. The paths she had made in her travels to and from the barn had been obliterated, and she struggled through snow now nearly two feet deep and drifted in some places almost to her waist. She recalled lectures from well-meaning friends when she had first moved north from Chicago about how in frigid temperatures it never snowed.

"So much for that theory," she said aloud.

Her mind filled unbidden with images of Chicago on a winter night. She remembered stepping from a cab in Italian heels and a cashmere wrap to dash elegantly into a restaurant or hotel bar. She recalled the warmth and scent of flowers and food that filled the senses after coming in from the cold; she thought of the hushed tones, the professionally polite waiters, the hilarity of slightly inebriated colleagues. She remembered how it had felt to be noticed and admired as she entered a restaurant. Her thoughts were interrupted by a sound she could dimly hear through the muffling of her hood. She stopped for a moment and listened. There it was again. She pushed the hood off to hear better. It was a sound she knew well.

From across the yard Robert was calling. "BAAAAAAWB!" he yelled. "BAAAAAAAAAAAWB!"

Why was he calling? Was he cold? Was his water frozen? Was he bored and lonely? Frightened by the sounds of the wind? Or merely being annoying? His distress nevertheless struck pity in her heart. "Hey Robert!" she called. "Don't worry!" Trying to hurry without spilling his water, Fiona struggled through the still deepening snow.

By the time Fiona had gotten through the snowy path and pulled open the door, much of the water had spilled and all of it was cold. How many times was she going to have to do this during the night? Robert was wailing in a way that might have been hysteria in some other creature, but finding him unfathomable, Fiona was unsure of his actual state. Seeing her made no difference. If anything, it made him louder.

Fiona approached the stall and for the first time that she could recall, he came immediately to her hand.

"BAAAAAAWB! BAAAAAAAAAWWWWB!" he yelled.

It was frigid cold in the barn. She stroked his nose and his neck for a few moments, and then felt his ears. They were cool. A sudden silence descended, and Fiona looked into the eyes of this odd creature. Their yellow light seemed somehow dimmed. She sighed the way she always did when she had made a decision, and her long slow intake of breath seemed to interest Robert. He moved his face closer to hers and belched.

Fiona sighed again, and moved to check his trough. It was nearly empty again, but she didn't want to fill it now so it could freeze. She poured the bottle of molasses into the remains instead and mixed it around.

"Whatwhatwhatwhatwhatwhat?" Robert said comfortably, now rummaging in the goat chow.

"Don't talk with your mouth full," said Fiona irritably. Satisfied with the molasses mixture, Fiona pulled her hood up in preparation for the walk back.

"Don't go away," she told Robert. "I'll right back."

She stomped laboriously up to the house to do what she had to do, piteous cries of "BAAAAAAAAAWB! BAAAAAAAAAAAWB!" drifting back to her from the barn.

The wind was still howling as Pete and Elisabeth sat down to dinner. She had lit the candles in the dining room, and opened two bottles of wine, a white and a red. There was a fire roaring, expertly built by Pete, and the air was filled with the smell of veal, rosemary, and orange casserole; brussels sprouts; and *potatoes boulangere.* The room was as perfectly cozy as could be, made even more so by the storm that beat against the house. Privately, Elisabeth wondered if she could eat at all, but she felt she needed to put a good face on the circumstances.

In the aftermath of Roger's departure, she much preferred having Pete there than being alone. She had gone over and over in her mind how things could have turned out differently. It all came down, she told herself, to things beyond her control. She could not have left Pete to cope with a stuck car. She did what she should have done. And in time, she hoped that Roger would come to see that. But all of the calm reasoning in the world did nothing to quell the knot in her stomach, nor to assuage her worry over Roger's safety. No matter how experienced the driver or reliable the car, this was dangerous weather to be driving around in.

There was also, if she was completely honest with herself, a part of her that was angry. She was angry that Roger didn't trust her, and angry that he had allowed their relationship—if that's what it was—to drift so aimlessly as to make this kind of misunderstanding possible. Yes, she thought in her more militant moments, this was Roger's fault, not hers.

She had moved away into these thoughts, but was called back to the present by Pete's voice. He raised his glass to her. He had been going to say "to absent friends," but he didn't want to start her crying again. "Living well is the best revenge," he said, instead.

Elisabeth's eyes sparkled and she smiled as she raised her glass.

"Revenge," he thought, noting the smile, "can be just as warming as romance." Rocco, who had been lying asleep by the fire, raised his head at the shimmer of emotion he felt in the room.

Fiona stood back and looked for anything she might have missed. The little kitchen was wrapped in plastic painting sheets, all duct-taped to the floor. The counters were cleared of everything. The kitchen table and chairs were moved into the dining room. The lower cabinet doors were blocked by the ladder that was laid lengthwise in front of them and held in place by two cinder blocks from the pile in the basement that had been annoying her since the pier work had been finished. The upper cabinets were held closed with fine floral wire twirled around the knobs in a way Fiona knew would be the very devil to remove. The curtains had been taken down, rolled into a haphazard ball on one of the relocated chairs. Rocco's plush bed lay on the floor near the window. The dripping from the ceiling, now in four places in the kitchen and four in the front hall, was going to contribute to a horrible mess, but she couldn't think about that now, nor about the pleasant evening she had planned, curled up with a plate of cookies and a book. She nodded to herself, struggled back into her parka, and went back out to the barn in what she hoped would be her last trip of the night.

It should have been awkward or uncomfortable to spend so much time with a stranger, but Elisabeth found that Pete was good company He was helpful, undemanding, interesting, and self-contained. She did not feel that she needed to entertain him, nor did he seem to require constant conversation. Whatever his moods were, he kept them to himself.

After dinner they carried their wine into the living room and sat across from one another by the fire. Rocco came in from the kitchen, where he had been licking veal gravy from his bowl, and lay down in front of the fire with a thump and a sigh.

They chatted amiably for a while, until they were both stifling yawns, and Elisabeth stood up to say good night.

"If the weather clears, I'm going to have to try to get back tomorrow," Pete said. "Do you think my rental car is still where we left it?"

"Probably buried under fifteen feet of snow."

"Ah well," said Pete. "We'll figure it out in the morning.

He had taken a Winston Churchill history from the bookshelves. "Do you mind if I take this to my room?"

"Of course not," she replied. "Take any book you like." And with polite wishes of pleasant dreams, they each went to bed.

Standing some ten feet apart, Fiona and Robert looked at each other across the kitchen. Robert maintained an ominous silence, his eyes glittering dangerously in the dim light. He seemed neither confused nor grateful for his new circumstances, merely imperious, as if this…hovel…were not quite up to his standards.

"Where," his look implied "is the crystal ballroom?"

Fiona calmly regarded him from the door. She was comfortable with this decision. It was too cold to leave him alone in the barn, and the low ceiling and dirt floor of the cellar meant difficulty in tending to him and an impossibility in ever removing the scent of goat from the house. The kitchen was scrubbable, warm, and accessible. It also meant that she didn't have to get up every three hours to make sure his water hadn't frozen. It made sense in its own utterly weird way.

"Good night," she said. "Don't eat the kitchen."

"WHAT?" said Robert.

She went upstairs to bed wondering what she would find in the morning.

It was, she felt, more a Marcus Aurelius night than a Jane Austen one, and she settled under the covers with a sense of entitlement. By her side was a flashlight and a mug of hot brandy with sugar and ginger. There was still the leaking roof to contend with, but she felt relief from anxiety about Robert's well-being. "As to his behavior well," she thought, "how bad can it be?"

"Accept the things to which fate binds you, and love the people with whom fate brings you together, but do so with all your heart." Fiona hoped that this dictum applied exclusively to people. From the kitchen she could hear a distant thumping sound. She switched off her flashlight and buried herself under the covers, too tired to read or worry or care. She was asleep in one minute.

Fiona dreamed that she was in the blizzard struggling to find Robert. She could hear him bleating, sounding in dreams more like a goat should sound, but the wind and snow had blinded her. The horror she felt at being responsible for the death of an animal so wholly dependent on her was consuming. Calling him, she struggled in Italian heels along a path that led dangerously along a snowy cliff face decorated with crystal chandeliers, uncertain with every step of exactly where the land ended and a long fall began. Her fingers and toes were numb, her shoes were slippery, and she felt certain that she would die. A cocktail party going on somewhere nearby carried the sounds of glasses and people chattering and laughing. But above this she could hear a strangely labored breathing. Was he dying nearby?

Suddenly her brain switched to reality. She was awake. In her bed. A deep animal fear struck her in the chest. She could hear the sound of stentorian breathing. Someone was in the room. Heart pounding, unable to breathe, she lay frozen in blank terror and focused on the sound. She heard a knocking on the wood, and then a familiar smell.

"Robert!" Fiona sat straight up in bed, her breath coming now in great gasps as she recovered from her fear. He emerged from the darkness with tentative steps, his cloven hooves knocking on the wooden floor. Still breathless, she shone the flashlight into Robert's face.

"How did you get here? Did you eat the door?"

Robert looked at her. "Whatwhatwhat?" he said softly.

A vision of the destruction he must have left downstairs came to her with devastating clarity just as the nausea of unspent adrenaline swept over her. Fiona made a loud and inarticulate protestation and slid down into the bed, pulling the covers over her head. She felt Robert's head nudging her, and heaving a sigh, she pulled off the covers and reemerged. Their eyes met, Robert's usual satanic gleam somewhat ameliorated by his delight in himself.

"AHA!" said Robert.

Fiona, exhausted by the worry and physical exertion of the day, was too tired to bother. She recalled a story—probably apocryphal—about Winston Churchill being asked whether he had difficulty sleeping during the dark days of World War II. "No," he had reportedly said. "I simply say, 'To hell with everybody' and go to sleep."

This, thought Fiona, was as useful a piece of philosophy as she had ever read. Pulling a pillow over her head, and rolling over toward the middle of the bed, she made haste to follow the prime minister's advice.

Chapter Twenty-Two

Fiona woke just before dawn to the sound of the plow dropping at the intersection. It was remarkable because the sound carried, unmuffled. The wind had stopped, but she could see that snow was still falling. The blank face of the clock told her that there was no power yet.

The sound of hooves stepping and sliding on the wood floor approached her bed, and she sat up so as not to have her face drooled on. The feeble light of the early morning showed Robert as he stood regarding her with an expression as cheerful as she had ever seen.

A brief glance told her that he had been busy during the night. The new fleece jacket she had left carelessly on the floor lay in tatters; the decorative basket of birch twigs by the fireplace had been eaten, only crumbs of twig and basket left to indicate where it had been; it looked as if the corner of one of the windowsills had also received his attention. Other signs of his presence contributed a barnyard atmosphere to the room.

Fiona took all this in with a philosophical grimace. "'Leave another's wrongdoing where it lies,'" she quoted aloud. She doubted whether Marcus Aurelius had ever had goat droppings in his bedroom.

"Come on Robert," she said, getting out of bed and pulling on an old sweater. "Let's go get some breakfast." Robert butted her from behind. Fiona paused, squared her shoulders, took a deep breath, and kept moving.

"Don't get used to this," she told him over her shoulder as they went down the stairs to the kitchen.

He managed the stairs with goatly agility, the sound of his hooves resonating in the quiet house. "Whatwhatwhatwhat-whatwhat?" he said to himself, as he minced happily along behind her.

Fiona had one of those moments of seeing herself as if from a distance, a bedraggled woman in sweatpants and a ratty sweater, followed through her house by a large goat. Images of her future, gray-haired and surrounded by cats and ceiling-high piles of newspapers flashed through her mind. Desperately working to apply the principles of stoicism to this terrifying vision, Fiona went in search of coffee.

She had thought herself prepared for what she would find in the kitchen. But she was wrong. The first thing that hit her was the smell. Robert's indoor habits were not of the first drawer, and evidence of his bad manners was in abundance. This was combined with the brown water of the leaking roof, which had spread and run across the slanting ancient floors to every corner of the room. The plastic, which Fiona had so carefully laid and taped to the floor had been torn and clearly chewed. Great strips of it lay randomly scattered, and gaping holes left the floor unprotected. Rocco's soft bed, left for Robert's comfort, had also been chewed to smithereens, leaving piles of polyester stuffing and microsuede floating everywhere, mixing together with the various other elements on the floor in a manner reminiscent of a prize-winning modern art installation. A corner of the kitchen counter had been nibbled, and an end strip of the Formica was gone, leaving the particle board underlayment gaping unattractively. The bucket of goat chow was miraculously upright.

Fiona stood in the door trying to take it all in. Chortling contentedly, Robert butted her from behind, and pushed his way past her into the kitchen, going straight to the goat chow.

"Hahahahahaha," he said softly to himself as he ate.

The power on Door Peninsula was more reliable than on the Island, and houses were warm and well-lit. Even though the snow still fell, and the weather service was predicting more to come, as soon as the wind had died, people began to come out into the world again and carry on with life. The plowing and shoveling of driveways and parking lots began in earnest. The air was filled with the sound of plows dropping to the ground, their chains clanking, and of engines moving forward and backward at a rapid clip, their OSHA backup beepers shrill in the predawn darkness, all with a background of the buzz of dozens of snow blowers. Men walked indoors smelling, not of fresh, cold air, but of small engine exhaust.

Just after dawn, Mike and Terry pulled up to Ground Zero at the same time, but finding the lot unplowed and everything closed up and dark, they stood in the chill air for a few minutes talking. The remains of the first round of the snowstorm lay around them in towering piles of snow at the edge of every street and every parking lot. The cold temperatures had not permitted much melting on the black asphalt, and a thin layer of packed snow covered even this. The temperature that morning, hovering at a balmy zero, was not expected to rise until the front came in that afternoon bearing another foot or so of snow. Ground Zero's untouched blanket of snow made it look desolate and abandoned.

"The thing is," Terry was saying to Mike, his hands shoved into the pockets of his big parka, "it's not as if he's the type to just take off. He's a bit of an odd duck, but he's always been steady enough."

Mike nodded seriously, considering. "I drove past his place, just to be sure things were all ok, but the truck was gone."

They paused, pondering the mystery. Terry was the first to say the hard thing they had both been thinking.

"I suppose there could have been an accident."

Mike nodded again. "No way we could know, really," he said. "Not until something showed up in the newspaper."

They stood in silence for a moment.

"I just can't see him taking a vacation," said Terry. "It's not his style."

"No," said Mike, frowning. "Anyway, how could he get anywhere in this weather?"

They paused again. Both thinking the same thought.

"You seen Elisabeth around lately?" asked Terry.

"Well, no," admitted Mike. "But I know she's here. She was at the supper club last night."

A pair of crows called to one another from a tree on the bluffs, their rough voices carried with crisp clarity in the winter air. Mike recalled the Nordic myths of the two crows who were messengers of the god Odin. He shivered. He was feeling the cold more this year.

"I'm wondering whether we should make a report. Just in case." Terry's voice trailed off.

Mike nodded. "It's a thin, line, you know. He would not appreciate anyone butting in."

"On the other hand, if he's lying in a ditch somewhere...." Terry left the sentence unfinished.

Mike nodded again. "I suppose," he said, doing a calculation of the possible scenarios, "I'd rather have him ticked off than to find we could have done something and didn't."

Terry nodded, suddenly brisk. "I'll give the sheriff a call. See what he thinks. You want to call Elisabeth first and let me know what she says?"

"Guess we'd better," said Mike. "It's gonna worry her, though." He shook his head regretfully. "Suppose it can't be helped. She's an early riser. I'll call in about an hour and get back to you."

"Well," said Terry. "Best get on with it."

"Yup." Mike took a deep breath, frowning.

As he headed to his truck, Terry turned and hollered back. "Sure could use a goddamn cup of coffee!"

"No kidding!" shouted Mike.

The two men got back into their trucks and parted to their respective responsibilities, both more uneasy than either had been willing to admit.

There was no point in making a serious attempt at cleaning while Robert was in the house. "But at least," thought Fiona, "she should be able to tether him to something so that he couldn't spread the destruction further than the kitchen." This was a problem in itself. There was no furniture sufficient to stop him, nor would a doorknob be able to hold him. Besides, he could just chew the wood. As far as she could tell, the only two things in the kitchen capable of holding him were the refrigerator and her ancient stove. And she had doubts about the handle of the refrigerator.

In a sudden burst of inspiration she remembered a length of chain she had purchased on one of her many forays to the hardware store. She had known it would come in handy.

She descended into the cellar to get what she needed, Robert trailing along behind, a sardonic and censorious groupie.

Elisabeth and Pete spent their second day together more quietly. They read, chatted occasionally, and took turns playing with Rocco. Pete kept the fire going, and Elisabeth cooked. She had to admit, it was nice to have someone to cook for. Their relationship seemed to her, not brand-new, but one of long-standing.

Mike's phone call that morning had added new dimension to her worries. She told him she had seen Roger, and when, but her inability to say where he had gone from there, and why he hadn't stayed, had embarrassed and dismayed her. Mike had accepted her sketchy explanation without question.

"Well, you can't tell Roger anything, can you?" he had commented. "I'm sure you tried to stop him from going out."

"Yes," said Elisabeth guiltily.

Robert was not amused by the new arrangements and loudly communicated his views. Fiona had—rather cleverly, she thought—contrived a chain attached to Robert's leather harness on one end, and to the heavy oven door at the other. The ancient stove, lined with fire brick and weighing well over five hundred pounds, was finally proving its value. The clasp on the oven door ensured that, even in one of his mad bursts of energy, Robert could not pull loose. Fiona had left the chain long enough for him to have some movement, but not so long as to trip him or entangle his legs, and just enough for him to lie down. She had even left the chewed-up end of the countertop within reach for his amusement. "Besides," she told herself, she didn't intend for him to be alone that long. She would, after all, be in the house with him. Unfortunately.

She looked out the window at the falling snow. Jane Austen novels and cookie baking seemed like distant dreams.

At around ten that morning, Terry gave Mike a call. "Spoke with the sheriff," he said. "Says there are cars in ditches everywhere, but so far, they haven't found anybody dead or seriously injured, and none of the vehicles matches the description."

"Well, I guess that's good," said Mike slowly. "But it doesn't answer any questions."

"No," said Terry. They were both silent, thinking.

"He's not answering his cell," pointed out Terry. "It's turned off."

"Let's say," said Mike, "that he was able to drive somewhere. Where would he drive to? Could he be holed up with someone somewhere, waiting out the storm?"

There was another silence as they both tried to imagine where—and with whom—this might be.

"I guess one of us should go over and knock on his door," said Terry. "Just to be sure. We could be making a lot of fuss while he's home baking brownies."

Mike chuckled. "Hard to say what scenario would be more unsettling. I'll head over there and see what I can."

"Ok," said Terry. "Call me back."

Fiona had done the best she could with the bedroom. The wide gaps between the wood planks of the floor made it difficult to clean, and she wondered whether she would ever be able to expunge the smell of goat. She decided she needed to tackle a second round, but first she needed to go down to the kitchen and see what Robert was up to.

She opened the door cautiously, as if expecting him to jump out at her. To her astonishment he was standing docilely at the end of his chain. This was so unexpected as to be alarming. What was he up to?

"Robert?"

He turned his head and looked at her with eyes so filled with contempt that Fiona took a step back. "Well, at least he's all right," she thought. And she slowly backed away, closed the door, and went on with her tasks.

Mike opened the door of Terry's woodshop late that afternoon and walked in. The sound of a power saw and smell of sawdust indicated that Terry was there. Mike waited until the saw ceased before halloing and walking toward the back. It was never wise to startle someone with a saw. Terry looked up and took off his goggles.

"Any news?"

"Well," said Mike. "Yes and no. Sounds as if he and Elisabeth had a bit of a dustup. Harvey Wallace and Sue were over at the supper club that first night of the storm, and they had a story that might explain a few things."

Terry looked at Mike over the top of his glasses and leaned back against his worktable. "Let's have it."

A round three that afternoon, Fiona looked out and saw that the snow had become only light flurries. The power was still out—a circumstance whose charm was wearing thin, she felt—but at least there was hope.

It was getting dark, and Fiona was wearily contemplating another night of no power and goat companionship when she heard the sound of a snow blower coming from the side of her house. From what she could make out through the flying snow, it looked like Jim. "How like him," she thought, "to come and help." She realized that she should make him coffee, and—suddenly something else occurred to her: she would have to invite him in. With Robert. In the kitchen. Fiona closed her eyes. It would be all over the Island in a flash. "Oh well," she thought. "It's not as if no one will understand." Washington Islanders certainly knew that necessity trumped style.

Fiona considered her options. Could she invite him into the living room, and keep him there? How penetrating was the smell? It was very difficult for her to tell at this point. Fiona remembered Marcy and her air freshener. Did she even have air freshener in the house? And then there was her own appearance. It was clear that desperate action was necessary. Fiona flew into a frenzy. If she was lucky, she'd have twenty minutes.

"Mind your manners, Robert," she said. "Company's coming." She knocked on the window, waved gaily to Jim, and ran upstairs to make herself presentable. "Sort of," she thought.

When she heard the snow blower engine stop, she grabbed her parka and went out to invite Jim in. It wouldn't do to have him come in through the kitchen. She would bring him around the front.

"You survived," said Jim, smiling, when she approached.

"After a fashion. It hasn't been pretty."

"No. Pretty doesn't count all that much in survival." He took off his hat, and steam rose from his head as he ran a hand through his blond hair, damp with sweat.

"I hear they hope to have the power up before midnight," he said.

"Thank God. Want to come in for a cup of coffee?"

"Sure," said Jim, following her toward the house.

"It was extremely nice of you to help dig me out, but so like you," Fiona smiled at him over her shoulder as they walked up the newly cleared porch steps, the snow squeaking beneath their feet. "I was wondering how many days it would take me to shovel out myself." She opened the front door and gestured to Jim to come in. Fiona noticed with relief that the only smell came from the dish of potpourri on the side table.

As they entered the house, a loud call came from the kitchen.

"BAWWWWWWWWWB!"

Jim seemed to freeze, an odd look on his face. There was a gap in the conversation as Fiona pondered where to begin, not embarrassed, but rueful.

At last, his eyes focused everywhere but on Fiona's face, Jim broke the silence.

"Research?" he asked.

The afternoon light was fading by the time the snow had tapered off to a gentle dusting, and Pete began to make calls to arrange for his departure the next morning.

"Where will you be off to?" asked Elisabeth that night at dinner.

"Well, first to the London office, then to on to parts unknown. Have to see what new crisis they've been brewing for me.

"Is that what you do? Solve crises?"

"Essentially, yes. This chicken, by the way, is delicious."

"Thank you," said Elisabeth. "It was my grandmother's recipe." She smiled at him conspiratorially. There was the comforting sound of a plow outside in the driveway.

"So how long will you be gone?"

"Very hard to say. When things go well, I fly right back. When they don't…"

"Does that get old? All that traveling?"

"Umm, sometimes." He shrugged. "But there's no place that I really come home to." He stopped eating and looked at her. "Home for me is really about the people, not the place."

After Fiona had closed the door behind Jim, she stood for a moment against the door trying to identify what had just happened. The conversation had definitely been strained, and Jim had not seemed like his usual relaxed self. "Did the house smell after all," she wondered? Had she not seemed sufficiently grateful? She had a niggling sense again that something was wrong.

At last she shrugged to herself and mentally shook it off. Jim had been helpful, pointing out that the leaks were caused by ice dams, and offering to solve the problem by raking the snow off the roof in the morning. Maybe tonight, if the power came back, she could actually bring Robert back to the barn. Cheered by this thought, she headed out to the kitchen to see if he needed more goat chow.

"Think you have everything?" Elisabeth asked jokingly the next morning as they drank their coffee together. Pete was waiting for a car to take him back. He was showered and shaved, and, thanks to her brother's bathrobe, wearing his own clothes, freshly laundered. Rocco lay next to the table with his head resting on Pete's foot.

"Everything except the rental car, but they're sending someone to retrieve it." He looked at her affectionately. "Thank you for a very enjoyable blizzard. There aren't very many people it would be fun to be holed up with. You're in a distinct minority."

Elisabeth smiled at him gratefully. "It was fun for me, too." She was quiet for a moment. "I hope this hasn't turned you off of Door County completely."

They both understood the question in her remark.

He stood up at the sound of a car coming up the drive, gently dislodging Rocco's head. He took his jacket from the hook, kissed Elisabeth on the cheek, and patted Rocco. "Let me know about Roger. Oh, and fair warning," he said. "I'll be back soon."

And he was out the door and gone. The kitchen clock ticked in the silence of the house. Rocco threw back his head and gave a deep anguished howl, a mournful dissertation on loss and love. "Wooooe, wooooe, woooooeahhh," he cried.

Elisabeth knelt down and put her arms around him, laying her cheek against his. "I know, baby. I know."

The house seemed empty now that Robert was safely reinstated in the barn and the worst of his redecorating expunged. A faint smell of the barn still lingered in the house, but it was less pungent than before, and might, Fiona hoped, be fading. Her relief was only temporary, she knew. The town meeting would be rescheduled. She would have to check the bulletin boards to see when.

"One damned thing after another," she thought.

She recalled a Chicago friend's slightly condescending question. "What do you find to do up there in the winter? Don't you get bored?" Fiona thought of her three days of uninterrupted goat slavery; the shoveling, the hauling of water, and then, more pleasantly, of the round of community events –town meetings notwithstanding—which could easily fill every night of the week. Boredom was clearly not her problem.

She looked around her goat-ravaged kitchen. She had used an entire bottle of bleach, and the kitchen was, at least, sanitized, if not beautiful. The tattered countertop and the leaking ceiling remained as mementos of the past days. Their repair would have to wait, but at least she now understood how to prevent their worsening. The next storm was due shortly with its predicted twelve more inches of snow. Somehow she could not rouse in herself any enthusiasm for cookie baking. She went into the living room, poured herself a well-deserved scotch, and collapsed on the sofa.

Chapter Twenty-Three

No one knew where Roger was, and although a number of theories were bandied about, and conversations stopped when Elisabeth entered a shop or restaurant, no one had anything definitive to report. Roger had simply disappeared. Ground Zero was locked and dark, and without its usual haze of coffee aroma that had always seemed like a protective spirit. There was no *Closed for the Season* sign; no indications that anyone had been there.

Mike, a member of the town board, noted to Terry that the property taxes had been paid, but since this had been done online, there was no indication of location. "At least," he said, "we know he isn't dead."

"Do you suppose we should tell Elisabeth?" asked Terry.

"What makes you think she doesn't already know?"

The next storm came, and the next, and the one after that. After several years of mild winters, the sheer volume of snow came as a bit of a shock. The necessity of digging out from each successive storm created a state of siege, not to mention fatigue. Island roads were bordered by twelve to fifteen-foot walls of snow. Little-used back doors and many first floor windows were blocked, covered with snow that drifted above the roof lines.

But life went on. School resumed, district officials becoming more sanguine about eight to twelve inches overnight, and less likely to call a snow day; residents remembered to keep their pantries stocked; and local outdoorsmen—particularly the owner of the ferry line—rejoiced in the higher lake levels that would inevitably result.

Lucas, Fiona's carpenter-friend, had been able to repair the ceilings and replace the Robert-torn kitchen counter with relatively little expense. Fiona had asked him to put in butcher block, a less expensive alternative which she felt was an improvement anyway. The little kitchen was once again snug and charming, all traces of Robert's occupation—except, as she told herself, the emotional scars—had been removed.

She had, of necessity, done the ceiling painting herself. This part of the repairs had little cost, since she still had the right paint left over. Nevertheless, the project was another little drain on her precarious finances, and once again she was forced to postpone any work on the fireplaces, and, most important, a much-anticipated vacation away, whose major expense would have been boarding Robert at a farm far away from Stella. Fiona could foresee no respite from the Island, and she faced the coming months with grim resolve.

After weeks of worry and grief, Elisabeth became calmer as the winter wore on. Unlike Fiona, who had to work at it, she was a natural practitioner of stoicism. She had faced the likelihood that Roger was not coming back, and she spent her mental energy reassuring herself of the joys and beauties of her life. Was she in good health? Yes. Did she have good friends and the companionship of the loyal Rocco? Yes. Did she have her lovely home? Yes. Did she have work she loved? Yes. "Well, then," she told herself.

She went about her business and her life just as she had done before. But her defiant refusal of self-pity could not deny what lurked around her heart. Elisabeth knew that whatever else happened, she loved Roger. And, as any good Stoic would acknowledge, his absence or presence could not change this essential fact.

Wisconsin's public meeting laws required that sufficient notice be given before the town meeting could be re-scheduled, and, as Lars Olafsen put it, "what with one thing and another," a date was chosen for the first week in February. This time, Fiona knew to pay attention to the bulletin boards, and she had ample time to prepare herself mentally before being ambushed by the news at the Mercantile.

Snow had been forecast the night of the meeting, and Fiona found herself hoping that it would not cause a cancellation. She was tired of this thing hanging over her. She wanted to be done with it.

Fiona was no coward. Speaking in public and going to public meetings had been a part of her job as a reporter in Chicago, and she took these things in stride. But never had she felt any personal stake in the proceedings, and she felt a new understanding of the participants whose emotions she had viewed previously with detachment and some scorn. Fiona had laughed and brushed off Elisabeth's offer to come, but she wished now that she had accepted. She felt alone.

The possibility that Robert might be declared dangerous, both horrified and infuriated her. She knew—as did everyone else—that the municipal code being cited by Stella had not been intended to apply to domestic animals like Robert. He was a goat, for goodness sake, not a dog. But she had learned to have no illusions about Stella's malignant influence on public life. So much depended upon the decision the board would make. Robert's life may hang in the balance. And although she had no doubt that upon his demise he would go straight through the gates of Hell to stand at Lucifer's side, Fiona felt a fierce obligation to protect him. She was confused. And very nervous.

The village hall was full when Fiona walked in. In the midst of a fierce winter on a remote Island, public meetings were entertainment. But more than that, there was an old-fashioned solidarity among the Islanders, along with a strong streak of libertarian independence, which brought them to take the responsibilities of citizenship very seriously. The town meeting was the crux of a free society, and the source of the American idea. They lived here, it was their Island, and they were not a people to be pushed around by bureaucrats or government officials. Not even the homegrown ones they had had a drink with the night before.

To Fiona's surprise, Nancy and Jim were there, as were Jake and Charlotte, all sitting together in a row toward the front. Nancy stood up and waved Fiona toward the chair they had been saving for her. She sat in it gratefully. Charlotte leaned forward and waved from her seat next to Jim, and Jake winked. Jim smiled and raised his hand over Nancy's head for a high five. Fiona returned their greetings distractedly, but she was nevertheless heartened by their show of support.

"How are you holding up?" asked Nancy, bellowing above the buzz of the crowd.

"I'm fine," lied Fiona.

"Good," said Nancy, giving Fiona a brisk pat on the knee.

"Glad to hear it. No point in letting these things get to you."

Fiona nodded grimly.

A door at the side of the hall opened, and Lars Olafsen, chairman of the Town Board, came out of the little room that was used for committees. He carried with him a brown cardboard legal portfolio, and his coat for a quick escape later. Seeing him, the other board members began to assemble around the long table set up at the front of the room. At precisely seven p.m. the gavel came down and the meeting began. Lars ran a tight ship.

The Pledge of Allegiance was led by a skinny young man who had just been made an Eagle Scout. Pastor Nilsson offered an opening prayer. Fiona felt impatience at these little rituals of village life. Couldn't they just get on with it?

Lars conducted the meeting with skill and an eye on the clock. Several routine matters were dispensed with briskly. Those whose concerns they were, had no sense that they were being rushed or given short shrift, even though, in fact, Lars was moving things along with a shrewdness that would have served him well in any big city.

"We come," said Lars at last, looking down at his agenda, "to the question of a domestic animal violation and a related request for a variance." He looked up over his reading glasses.

Stella was on her feet. "Lars," she called out eagerly.

"We will hear first from the animal's owner," he said dispassionately. "Miss Campbell?"

Reluctantly, Stella sat down.

Fiona, her heart pounding, stood. There was silence in the room. She looked around at the faces of the board, all turned to her. Out of the corner of her eye she could see Stella's face, with its sneering contempt.

"Mr. Chairman," she said in a small voice, and faltered. Someone coughed, and there was the sound of paper rustling somewhere in the back.

"Mr. Chairman," she began again with greater volume, "I would like the Board to know that I have taken steps to ensure that Rob—er—the goat—will not escape again. I have invoices," and here she raised a manila folder with a hand that shook only a little—"to show that I have made improvements to the stall, and to the fencing around my barn. And also," she added, gaining courage, "I would like to point out that there have been no further…escapes…since that work was done."

She took this moment to look around the room, and saw the faces of the people around her. She could not have said that there was universal affection, but the only overt hostility seemed to be coming from Stella.

"I would like to add that he has no horns, and is not, in any way, dangerous." She hoped the disingenuity of this statement would not count as perjury. Personally, she had no doubt that Robert would cheerfully plan for the elimination of anyone who did not pursue his immediate interests. It was fortunate, she felt, that he had hooves rather than opposable thumbs.

"So…" she searched her mind quickly for anything left unsaid. "That's all I have to say." She sat down. Nancy looked at her and gave her an approving nod.

Stella leapt to her feet again. "Lars," she said, with the intentional disrespect of omitting his title. "I am next."

Lars Olafsen looked imperturbably over the tops of his glasses. "The chair," he said, with deliberate formality, "recognizes Miss DesRoisiers."

Stella was gloating with confidence. The Town Board members were useful idiots, all of them, she thought, and Lars Olafsen was no different. "I am sorry to have to say it," she said with mendacious piety, "but it is not true that that animal is not dangerous. It attacked me in my own yard. It—" and here she hesitated very briefly. It would not do to appear ridiculous.

"It charged me, and went so far as to try to get at me through my closed door."

Fiona bit her lip in consternation. This was undeniable, and it certainly sounded bad.

"And on another occasion, it was on the roof of my garage."

Here several members of the audience chuckled. Whether it was at Stella or at the memory of the goat on the roof, it was impossible to tell.

Stella's mask began to slip. Not that it mattered much, since everyone knew perfectly well what she was like. But things were not going as she had planned. Her malice was only thinly camouflaged at the best of times, and it grew more intense when she was thwarted.

"Believe me," she said haughtily, "when a police officer and the fire department have to be called out to deal with something like this, it is no laughing matter."

Here one of the board members interrupted. He was newly elected, and known for his indifference to danger. "Was there any damage to your property?" he asked.

A flash of sharp anger crossed Stella's face and was hastily covered over. She narrowed her eyes and glared at the questioner. "I was terrified," she said primly. "I could have slipped on the stairs. It was a dangerous situation." Now she took a skillfully aimed shot. "Imagine if you had such a creature living next door to your wife and little girl, Arvo. Just imagine."

In his peripheral vision Lars could just see his fellow board members, half on his left and half on his right. He was enough of a politician to realize that he must tread carefully. He needed to get some sense of the prevailing political winds. It wasn't enough to tell their expressions, but he could tell when they were shifting in their chairs. Their restlessness was an indicator of their discomfort. It was not a particularly courageous group, and Lars had little doubt whose side they would take. He felt a pang of sympathy for that pretty young woman.

Stella was still talking. Lars had perfected the art of appearing to pay close attention while his mind pondered other things. It was during town meetings, after all, that he planned his garden every year. The least he could do, he thought, was to slow

down the process a little. Maybe this new woman would figure out the inevitable and sell the place before they had to rule
against her. It was always better to move in the warm weather.

His conscience assuaged by this plan, he waited. It was a
longer tirade than usual. He noted that Miss Campbell looked
pale and nervous. "Ah well," he thought. She was young and
resilient. And, according to the rumors he'd heard around town,
she had many talents. She would rebound.

There was silence in the room. Not a cough or whisper. And
then a small buzz began.

Calmly, Lars banged his gavel again, and the room quieted.

It became obvious that everyone was expecting him to
speak, and Lars realized suddenly that there had been silence
for several moments. He cleared his throat.

"This is a serious matter. The board needs time to investigate and consider the public interest before a decision is made.
I suggest we take a vote on the question…" here he consulted
the papers on the table before him "…in June."

"JUNE?" shouted Stella, leaping again to her feet.

"So moved!" said Tom Sumner, over the noise of the crowd
and of Stella's outrage.

"Second!" shouted Mary Woldt.

"All in favor?"

"AYE," Shouted the board unanimously.

"Motion carries," said Lars simply.

"Move to adjourn," shouted Tom Sumner.

"Second!" said Mary Woldt.

"The meeting is adjourned," said Lars. There, he thought.
I've bought her a little time. He admitted to himself that seeing

the look of outrage on Stella's face was worth the grief she'd be giving him between now and June. He brought the gavel down, gathered his papers and his coat, and moved with surprising speed toward the door, skimming the crowd with the skill of long practice. He was in his car and on his way home before Stella could reach the door.

Fiona left the hall with Nancy and Jim feeling no relief whatever. She could see by their faces that they had no hope of the results, and she noted, too, the conspicuous avoidance of their little group by the rest of the town. Jake and Charlotte had stopped to chat several times and were still in the hall.

"Can I buy you a drink?" asked Jim. He was frowning down at her, looking worried.

"No," said Fiona. "I think I just need to go home." She thanked them both, and said her good-byes. Jim walked her to her car. "I'll be ok," she said, looking up at his frown.

"I know," he said. He bent down to kiss her cheek, waited for her to get into her car, and closed the door for her. He watched as she drove away.

Elisabeth had heard from Pete. He was in Africa, he said, dealing with some kind of negotiations. She wasn't clear with whom or about what, but he didn't say, and she didn't ask. He didn't know when he'd be able to get away, but he would come when he could. This promise was a small bright spot in what, for Elisabeth, seemed a very bleak time.

She wrote back, and tried, in her e-mail, to be cheerful and matter of fact. She felt anything but. Her e-mail to Roger remained unopened.

Rocco was the beneficiary of these hard times for his mistress. She consoled herself with long walks in the woods, which he enjoyed, and indulged him with marrow bones and more leftovers than usual. Elisabeth herself had little appetite, and although she cooked to entertain herself, she frequently ate only a bite or two before she handed down her plate to Rocco.

Chapter Twenty-Four ✳

If there was one good thing about the winter, thought Fiona to herself, it was that she didn't have to encounter Stella very often. There was a good excuse to be home by four-thirty and stay there in the warmth and comfort. Fiona had developed the habit of coming in from her last visit to the barn and putting on her pajamas by seven. She was vaguely ashamed of it, but since there was no one there to see, she chose to please herself.

It was also true that to some extent, Fiona was in hiding. The town meeting had discouraged her and given her a sense that she was unwanted in the community. This, of course, was exactly what Stella intended, as Fiona knew. Nevertheless, Fiona still struggled against the instinct to stay away from public events where she felt it likely that Stella would be. Even though this was ceding ground, she felt the effort of facing the long mean glances that were a Stella specialty, seemed, on many occasions, beyond her. There was also a strange growing sense she had that people were talking about her wherever she went. Living on the Island was becoming more difficult than she had imagined, and even another blizzard would have been preferable to this paranoia and stress.

All of this was one factor in Fiona's invitation to Elisabeth to come to the Island for the week of Valentine's Day. She had, however, been quite candid about the others.

"I haven't got a good excuse not to accept a date with Jim," she told Elisabeth, who had, characteristically, expressed reluctance at the first request. "If you're here, I can say I can't leave you home."

"Why don't you just say no?"

"Because, as I say, I haven't got a good excuse. I don't feel right just turning him down flat. It feels too bald."

"It's honest," said Elisabeth.

Fiona sighed. "I know. I have been impeccably honest with Jim, but I don't know what I feel about him, and Valentine's Day is just too much pressure. I don't want to hurt his feelings. Is that so bad?"

There was silence on the other end of the phone as Elisabeth considered this. "No," she said finally. "It's not so bad."

"Besides, I think you and I will both be in need of consolation, and I can't think of anyone more consoling than you."

"I can," said Elisabeth cryptically. "By the way, do you still have that creature in the attic?"

"Only sometimes."

Elisabeth sighed. "Ok, I'll come. But make sure he stays in your room."

"I will do my best," said Fiona. "But I'm not sure how good that is."

Valentine's Day fell on a Tuesday that year, which meant that the discomfort of being single on this holiday of love was drawn out over a period of nearly a week, while those in the throes of passion—or marriage—were to be seen dining out or otherwise celebrating on any day from the Friday before to the Sunday well after. Valentine's Day was second only to New Year's Eve for its focus on being part of a couple, and those who were not felt their singleness acutely. Even the most independent woman was likely to feel a twinge at the sight of the ubiquitous red hearts and cupids. It was this awkwardness that Fiona and Elisabeth strove to diminish for one another that week.

On Valentine's Day the Island was sunk in an arctic freeze. The temperature stood at seven degrees below zero, and the wind chills varied between thirty and fifty below. The cold was painful, and the wind burned with icy fire. On the bird feeder outside the kitchen window, a tiny chickadee sat frozen to death on the wooden perch, its bright black eyes bulging from its head. Fiona had turned her back on the sight with a shudder of sympathy. Innumerable birds and animals would die in the bitterness. Robert, at least, was not a concern, snug in his new red Thinsulate goat jacket, easily—if not cheerfully—attached with Velcro, his trough warmer filled with a tea of warm water and molasses, and a tall mound of straw to bury himself in.

A golden pink mist, colored by the sunrise, steamed from the lake beyond the thin ice near the shoreline where the water was more than forty degrees warmer than the air. Towering columns of white vapor rose from the stilled waves like a ghostly forest of dead trees. A dense fog surrounded the columns, which merged into a bank of deep blue clouds hovering over the water like a mountain range. The brilliant sun and crystal blue sky deepened the color and changed it with the growing light.

Fiona watched, bundled in her silk underwear, down parka, and what she had come to think of as her Big Fur Hat (or BFH, as Elisabeth liked to call it) as she walked with Rocco, who was also bundled in a jacket much like Robert's. She was struck by the unpredictable beauty of the water, and found herself, as she contemplated the mists, recalling Pali's ghost. The story seemed easy to believe looking out at this alien world. Something strange could be out there. It hardly even seemed controversial to suggest it.

She wondered if these kinds of marine experiences were the reasons for the stories sailors had always told; maybe you couldn't see such beauty and strangeness without believing that even stranger things were there, hidden in the mists. She thought about the combination of fear and comfort entwined within Pali's story. But the wind was too sharp for lengthy contemplation, and Rocco had been out as long as she felt was safe. Quickly they turned, and her thoughts now occupied with the mundane realities of survival, they made their way back to the snug little house, the wind, mercifully, at their backs.

Today was a day to be inside, and Elisabeth and Fiona amused themselves by baking. They spent the morning making a tricky sponge cake recipe and some simpler and perfectly satisfactory butter cookies. Rocco lingered hopefully for a chance to lick the bowls.

During the course of their routine comings and goings from one room to another, Fiona noticed that there was an unfamiliar car parked across the street. A parked car of any kind on this street was unusual, but it was particularly so because the driver had not gotten out. Of necessity in the cold weather, the engine was running. After an hour or so, Elisabeth looked again out the front window.

"You know, he's still there."

Fiona came from the kitchen and they stood together at the front door looking out. "Do you think we should go over and ask him if he's ok?" she asked, wiping her hands on a towel.

"He doesn't seem to be unwell. He's just reading."

"Maybe he's early for an appointment."

"Maybe Stella hired a hit man."

Fiona looked at her, eyes wide. "I wish you hadn't put that idea into my mind."

"Sorry," said Elisabeth, sincerely.

They came out from the kitchen to peer out at him from time to time during the day. It was difficult to tell from the distance and through a car window, but he appeared to be a rather young person with a beard. He didn't look much like a hit man, Fiona thought to herself, but then, with Stella next door, it was hard to be sure. She recalled the signs in airports warning to report anything in the least suspicious. "Do you think we should do something to protect Robert?" she asked.

Elisabeth looked at her. "You can't be serious."

Fiona looked away. "Well, kind of. I mean, he has had threats against him, and we don't know who that is. A stranger on the Island is kind of unusual, especially at this time of year."

Secretly, Elisabeth was already uneasy, but she felt she needed to preserve a veneer of calm.

"I think I smell something burning."

They both returned to the kitchen and to a semblance of normalcy.

The stranger was still there in midafternoon when they sat down to tea. Elisabeth was curled, catlike, in a sunny corner of the couch, one of Fiona's mohair throws spread across her lap. Fiona sat cross-legged on the floor near the coffee table so that she could both pour tea and continue to stroke Rocco's big shaggy head, which lay contentedly in her lap. The perfume of China tea rose from their cups, and despite the cold outside, warm shafts of sun drifted across the room.

The sound of steps on the front porch normally signaled the delivery of the mail, but Fiona was surprised when, instead of the thunk of the porch mailbox, the doorbell rang. Rocco was on his feet first, and she followed him to the door. It was the guy in the car, and he was carrying a small package. Emboldened by Rocco's presence, Fiona opened the door.

"Ms. Campbell?" he asked.

"Yes."

"I have a delivery for you."

Fiona noted that he held it easily in one hand.

"I'll need you to sign" He offered a clipboard.

Fiona reached out to sign her name, then returned the board to him, as he handed over the package. "May I ask you something?"

"Sure," he said.

"Why were you sitting over there for so long? Why didn't you just deliver the package when you arrived? I have to admit, you were making us a little nervous."

The young man looked apologetic, but he laughed. "Sorry. I

was supposed to deliver it at a particular time. It never occurred to me that you would notice I was there."

Fiona thanked him; he waved a cheerful good-bye and went back into the cold. She closed the door behind him and walked back to the living room, studying the package. It was addressed by hand in the kind of graceful copperplate style that had once been nearly universal, and was now almost unknown.

"It's from London," she said. "Supposed to be delivered at a particular time."

Rocco, too was interested, and she showed the package to him so he could sniff it thoroughly. It did not appear to be either animal or edible, and was therefore of much less interest than the cookies on the table. He returned to his post beneath them.

"Something good?" asked Elisabeth, reaching for another cookie. They were impossible to eat singly.

"No idea," said Fiona. "I haven't ordered anything recently. Hang on, I need the scissors."

She disappeared into the kitchen for a moment, and Elisabeth, reaching for yet another cookie, heard the sound of a drawer opening and closing. Rocco, who did not believe in missing any opportunity, leapt to his feet and followed. It might be time for a biscuit, he felt.

They returned, Rocco still licking the crumbs from his lips, Fiona armed with a bright new pair of scissors purchased on one of her hardware forays. She perched on the edge of a chair. She was an inveterate package ripper, but with uncharacteristic caution and almost surgical precision, she began to extricate the contents from the box.

Inside lay a small package meticulously wrapped in brown

paper and tied with string. The care and method of the wrapping made it seem as if it were a time capsule from another century. Gently, Fiona untied the string and undid the paper wrapped several times around the objects inside.

Wrapped in another layer of tissue was a packet of four very old books. They were small, not much bigger than her hand, bound in pale blue, and decorated with an almost modern design of gilt scrolls that seemed to imply movement. The edges of the pages were also gold, and the books, though clearly well-cared for, had also been well-read. A bookmark of brown silk ribbon was placed between the pages of one of the volumes. Knotted on each end were two unpolished, irregular red stones that seemed to glow from within.

Elisabeth sat up and leaned forward to look. "Those are very old books. And what are those stones?"

Fiona, who had barely noticed the stones, rolled them between her fingers. "I'm not sure. They're not plastic—too heavy. Red glass, I suppose." Intent on the book itself, she had barely noticed the bookmark.

"Hmmm," said Elisabeth, leaning closer.

Fiona turned the bookmarked book over in her hands, examining the workmanship.

"It's a first edition. English poetry," she said. Carefully, she began to turn the pages. "1876," she said, in a low voice. "The publication date is 1876."

Who could have sent her such a gift? she wondered. And why specifically at a particular time? She didn't know offhand the prices of books like this, but she guessed it was probably far more than she could afford. Age alone would have ensured that, but the craftsmanship made it more than merely antique.

Gently, she opened to the bookmark and read the poem that was set alone at the top of the page. She knew it well, and didn't need to follow the words to feel their cadence. But she was unsure. Was the poem a message? Or had the bookmark simply been placed without intention within the pages?

"May I see the bookmark?" asked Elisabeth.

Fiona handed it to her, and stared into a pocket of sun that slanted across the wood floor. Who would have sent it? she wondered.

"Fiona," there was a tone in Elisabeth's voice that made Fiona look up.

"I'm not an expert, but I'm pretty sure these stones are uncut rubies."

Fiona frowned. "Are you serious?"

"I'm pretty sure. They're too...deep to be garnets, if you know what I mean. And they're definitely not glass. They wouldn't come near to the cost of the book, but still... ."

Fiona saw her face change and her head come up just slightly as if something had just occurred to her.

"What? What are you thinking?"

A mask slid over Elisabeth's eyes, and she shrugged and shook her head "Nothing. Only...pretty nice gift." She smiled and looked away. She was feeling pleased with herself, and had a growing sense of anticipation. "Shall I refill the tea?" she asked. Without waiting for an answer, she jumped up from the sofa and went toward the kitchen. "At least we know that it didn't come from Stella," she called back gaily.

Fiona sat silent and still, unconsciously rubbing one of the red stones between her fingers as she stared, unseeing, at the little corner of sun on the living room floor. She was thinking with awe of the hearts and minds and long-dead hands that once had wandered the pages of the book that lay in her lap. And of the last time she had thought of the bookmarked poem.

This had been a gift from someone who understood her a little too well. But as she went over the roll call list of names in her life, she couldn't determine who that would be; nor whether the book's arrival on Valentine's Day had been intentional, or just a red herring in a random universe.

It was late afternoon, and the warm gold of the sunset had returned when Fiona stepped away from the bustle she had designed to distract herself and bundled up to take Rocco for a walk. Elisabeth was napping, and while going out into the frigid winds was a chore for her, for Fiona it was a pleasure. She wrapped Rocco in his heavy windbreaker, put some Vaseline on his paws, and they set out for a last foray into the world before the cold of the night lay siege and forced all domestic creatures into retreat behind the walls of civilization. All others would be left to battle on alone.

She tromped along the path through a snowy field, following her own footprints as Rocco ran on ahead, oblivious to the cold. With the bitter wind buffered by the mask over her face and the layers of down and fur and sheepskin and high tech fabric, she felt warm in her core, but she was alert to the danger to the big dog whose delicate ears were thin and exposed, and who breathed the lung-freezing air as he ran.

The bookmarked poem had reminded her of another poem, a favorite, whose power and brevity never failed to move her. It rang in her head in rhythm with the amplified sound of her breath inside her hood, and her boots creaking on the snow.

> *O, Western wind, when wilt thou blow, the small rain down can rain?*
> *Christ, if my love were in my arms and I in my bed again!*

They went only a short way before the cold and a rare sense of prudence drove them back. The small red stones were warm in the palm of her down-padded mitten.

One bitter morning in Valentine's week, passersby were surprised to see that the lights were on and smoke curled from the little chimney of Ground Zero. It didn't take Mike or Terry long to converge upon the shop, each pulling into the parking lot at the same time. It was the reestablishment of their old routine to stop at Ground Zero at the beginning of a day's work. Roger's disappearance had not altered their paths, since they both passed the place many times a day, but they had missed sitting at the counter watching Roger at the grill, his sullen presence adding a note of comfortable familiarity to their mornings. But today, all would be back to normal. The mystery of Roger solved. God was in his Heaven.

They were unprepared, therefore, for the cheerful and unfamiliar voice that greeted them when they entered. A young blond man was standing behind the counter. He had been polishing the copper machinery with a proprietary air. His shining mane of hair reached past his shoulders. He had two piercings in one ear, and elaborate tattoos on both forearms. Mike couldn't help thinking that he looked like an illustration of an angel from a children's Bible—apart, of course, from the piercings and the tattoos. He wondered whether he had ever seen so perfectly beautiful a human face.

The young man smiled benevolently at them as he spoke. "Good morning! I'm Joshua. What can I get for you?"

Mike and Terry exchanged glances, but each felt it would be a violation of some code to show too much surprise to the newcomer.

"Morning," said Terry.

Mike gave his cherubic smile and nodded his greeting.

"I'll have an Americano and an egg sandwich," said Terry, perching himself on his old stool.

"A latte," said Mike. "And an egg sandwich."

"Full-fat, or skinny?"

Mike looked nonplussed. "Ummm...full-fat, I guess."

"Coming right up!" said Joshua cheerfully.

The two friends looked at one another again as Joshua turned his back. Quite apart from anything else, encountering cheer at Ground Zero was an entirely new and unsettling experience. They sat together in not altogether comfortable silence watching their coffee being prepared. Terry was trying to figure out what the tattoos were. They seemed to match, and looked as if they had been inspired by the Book of Kells.

Joshua demonstrated an expertise that bordered on artistry as he brewed the coffee and steamed the milk. Smiling, he placed the cups before them. "Eggs will be right up." And he disappeared into the back.

When he reappeared, he placed the egg sandwiches before them and turned back to wipe the immaculately clean counter behind him. Mike and Terry ate. Joshua, clearly not given to chatter—at least in this he resembled Roger—continued with his work. There was only the sound of Enya in the background.

Fortified by coffee and an egg sandwich, and dying of curiosity, Terry broke the silence.

"So," he said, trying to sound casual, "Where's Roger?"

"Roger?" Joshua looked puzzled and shook his head. "Who's Roger?"

Terry pushed on, his astonishment manfully contained.

"Are you the new owner?"

Light dawned on Joshua's face. "No, no. I'm not the owner. I'm just managing."

"And you don't know Roger?"

Again he shook his head.

"But who hired you?"

Joshua shrugged. "Someone named Tina. I never caught her last name. Just sent in my resume and got called in for the interview. You know the kind of thing."

Actually, Terry didn't. "Where was this? Where was the interview?"

"San Diego."

This time Mike and Terry could not help exchanging looks.

"San Diego, eh?" Terry was fighting back something now more like alarm than curiosity. "How'd you hear about the job?" he persisted, now determined to get to the bottom of things.

"It was on Craigslist. I just answered an ad. Thought it would be fun to live up here." He thought about this for a moment. "For a while anyway."

"So this Tina. Did she work for someone?"

Joshua looked vague. "I guess so. It was a pretty big office. Lots of applicants, though. I was pretty lucky to get it. Not much out there. Especially not for anthropology majors." He shrugged again.

"You guys want anything else?"

Mike stood up and took out his wallet. "I'll take care of it." He paid the bill and put out his hand.

"I'm Mike." Joshua shook it, then turned to Terry. They, too, shook hands.

"Terry."

"Thanks a lot. Maybe I'll see you tomorrow."

He beamed at them, and where his smile fell it was as if a shaft of sunlight had suddenly appeared. His beauty radiated from him.

"Right. See you around." Terry gathered his jacket and followed Mike to the door.

"So long," said Mike.

"And flights of angels sing thee to thy rest," thought Terry, irrelevantly, as they went out the door to their cars.

Chapter Twenty-Five ⚜

There was the Island. There was everything else. It wasn't that Islanders, as a rule, were insular, but something happened here, north of the tension line, that created a sense of what mattered and what didn't. Life wasn't easy here. If anything, it was harder, or at least less convenient. But there was a clarity that came from having to think about what you needed to live. Shipping things over was expensive, and taking things to the dump was a nuisance. What did you need? What did you throw away? What did you hang on to as long as possible to avoid the bother of disposal and the expense and hassle of replacement?

One day in late March, Fiona had taken advantage of the lull in the weather to make a supply run to the mainland, another of many inconveniences. The shortness of daylight and the reduced ferry schedule meant that she had no time for socializing. She needed to be back in time for Robert's feeding, and had crammed her necessary shopping into a brief, frenetic trip.

It was the time of year any resident of northern climates will recognize: the purgatory between winter and spring. The snow piles had become hard, crusty, and black. It was too cold to be outdoors, too warm to snow, and the rain and sleet chilled to the bone. The bleak, muddy earth, the bland gray skies, and the black chill of the water, with great patches of ice still remaining, held neither charm nor hope. Only the branches of the cherry trees, showing red in the orchards along the roads, gave any indication that life might be there beneath the surface, waiting to burst through. Eventually. It was Fiona's least favorite time of year.

She waited now for the last return ferry of the day. The line was not long, and Fiona's was the third car aboard. She had not yet adopted the Islander practice of parking one car on each side of the water, primarily because she could not afford a second car. It made sense, particularly in the winter, when the daily trips were few and reservations might be required for a car, but passengers could always find a place. It didn't matter anyway. She had no intention of being there next year. As far as she was concerned, she had survived the winter, and if she could make it to a year, the bet would be won in September. No one could quibble with a full year. She pulled hard on the parking brake and slid sideways out of the car, the space for door opening being rather limited. It had begun to sleet, but she still hadn't gotten used to sitting in the car for the ferry ride. She pulled up her hood before the wind hit.

As she started up the stairs to the passenger cabin, she heard her name being called. She turned to see Pali, smiling his big smile.

"Must have missed you on the way over. Haven't seen you in awhile. Want to ride over in the pilothouse?"

Feeling happy and childlike, Fiona followed him up, and settled in a corner of the tiny space at the top of the ferry as Pali and his crew went about their preparations. It was warm and comfortable in the pilothouse, and, as always, it smelled like coffee. She looked for a moment or two at the sonar depth readings and the various gauges, but it wasn't long before her gaze lifted and she was watching the horizon where they would be headed, the Island almost black against the water, just visible through the sleet. Even as the shower intensified, the clouds broke, and a brilliant shaft of sunlight slashed down to the water. Mike called this "God light," and she was reminded of one his paintings that captured such a scene.

Pali didn't speak as he piloted the ferry away from the dock. Operating the ferry was second nature to him, but he was—as all intelligent seamen are—a conscientious man, deeply aware of his responsibilities and of the potential for danger which always lurked somewhere near. Fiona felt utterly safe and protected.

She had found herself pondering more and more often the difference between men up here and those she met in the city. She had known powerful and brilliant men, whose confidence and ease were broadcast like signals to all they met, but whose consciousness of their import to others lay close to the surface. The Island men, and the men in Door were, perhaps, sometimes less credentialed, but every bit as intelligent, and they had a different kind of power. It was the kind of confidence that comes from being physically capable, of being able to cope with nature or disaster, of knowing what to do and when to do it, but without arrogance and without any sense of having a special gift. Their power was deeply internal and unshifting, completely unconscious, and unaffected by the regard of others. She felt safe among them, not only because of their competence, but also because they seemed to live under the kind of code of honor one expected from another era. Not one of them would do anything but what he knew to be right. Was it the product of living in a small community, where everyone knew what everyone else was doing, she wondered, knowing that you were always being watched? Or was there some natural integrity that formed within you when you had to face the adversity of weather and the self-reliance of being away from city comforts? Or simply small town virtues, born of a lifetime of churchgoing and family life untainted by popular culture? She was thinking about this, and feeling the slackening of stress she always felt on the ferry heading back. "North of the tension line," she thought to herself. And despite the troubles with Stella, and the looming decision of the Town Board, it was true.

One of her Island neighbors had voiced the same feeling. "It's some kind of purification, an emotional reverse osmosis," she had said. "I step on the ferry, and no matter what the weather is, I feel as if my soul has been purified, and that everything is all right." Fiona settled back on the blue cushioned seat behind the pilot's wheel, and allowed the process—whatever it was—to take its effect. She could worry about the rest later.

Fiona sensed that Pali had sought her out for a reason, that he wanted to tell her something, but was waiting until they were well away. She waited patiently, content to be carried along the water, watching the sky, the broadening clearing of sky and sunlight, and letting the world drop away.

The ferry chugging across the lake, Pali relaxed, too, comfortable in his natural element but fully alert to his responsibilities at the helm. His burly looks disguised his soft heart and childlike nature. He always looked forward to chatting with Fiona about his projects and asking her advice about his poems.

"I've started writing again," he said. "Finally. And I want to show you my latest poem."

There followed a long silence, and Fiona did not feel the need to break it. Pali's eyes were focused on the water ahead; the thrum of the engines filled the space, and they rode in the sound together for a while. Pali steered the little boat toward the western route. It was the first time since fall that she had traveled this way where the route was unprotected, in the open water away from the shelter of Plum Island. Now that the ice was melting, it would be the preferred path for the line. A pair of bald eagles soared to their right. Pali didn't point them out, but she knew he had seen them. The clearing sky was turning peach.

By now they were well away, and the ferry was part of neither the Island nor the peninsula, but its own place, untethered and self-sufficient, somehow freed from the constraints of stationary life. Pali turned to look back at her for a moment over his shoulder before he spoke again.

"I wrote it during the last trip on Friday. We had a full load of cars and passengers; there was nothing especially different about the atmosphere. It was almost dark, the sun had almost set, and the clouds were hanging over the bay, blue-black with golden edges. Normally I work on a poem for weeks—even months—but this one just came over me." Pali cleared his throat. "As I was standing here, right here," he indicated the spot in front of the wheel, "I felt..." he cleared his throat again. "I felt his hand on my shoulder, and then suddenly my mind was flowing with words." He paused. He did not say who "he" was, but Fiona knew. Pali was talking about being haunted. He had had a visit from the ghost.

"I could barely write it down fast enough." Pali was silent

again for a long moment, and then he looked back at her again to see if she believed him. Their eyes met, and she tipped her head to one side, regarding him seriously.

Fiona felt herself unequal to evaluating the scientific truth of the encounter—if there was one—but she believed that he believed. And what's more, she didn't *not* believe. The world was a strange place and ghost legends were as old as the human race, she thought to herself. Who was she to say yes or no; there is a ghost or there isn't? In any case, there was a part of her—and she supposed this was true of most people who told or listened to ghost stories—that wanted to believe it was true, that there was more than this life, that there were great mysteries.

Fiona was silent, thinking, recalling her strange experience in the woods last fall. Quantum physics, she thought, is real, and it is comprised of almost nothing but mystery—much of it less comprehensible and stranger than any ghost. She thought of dark matter, and string theory, both of which she could explain in layman's terms, but which were nevertheless unfathomable to her, and probably to most people. Perhaps, she thought, what we call ghosts are a kind of dark matter, not normally recognizable to us, able to move from one dimension to another, or some manifestation of string theory. Neither the physics explanations nor ghost stories were any more or less peculiar or impenetrable as far as she could tell.

The water was almost still before them as they stood together on the ferry's bridge watching the passage ahead. Fiona hadn't realized that she had moved to stand next to him, and although she hadn't spoken, her willingness to hear him was evident. Now he smiled and shrugged, then gestured with his head to the little shelf to the right. "It's in that blue notebook—where the page is bent back."

Fiona bent to take the notebook and held it up for him to see. He looked up briefly and nodded and turned his attention back to the water. Fiona stepped away toward the window to catch the fading light on the page. "Ghost poetry," she thought.

As she read the poem, she barely knew how to respond. She had been reading Pali's poetry for him almost since their first meeting. She had been reluctant at first, until he had pointed out how much he needed someone who wouldn't be nice. She had been oddly flattered by this remark, but uncomfortable, expecting to have to offend him. To her surprise, she had found that it was all rather good. He had a fine ear, an ingrained sense of traditional froms, and a gift for sharp observation.

She read it again. It was by far the best contemporary poem she had ever read. The words beat an ancient cadence, with subtle, ingenious internal rhythms and a profundity of content which she knew would compel her to reread and ponder. She read it several times, trying out the rhythms on her tongue, reading aloud in a low murmur. She was reminded of the ancient poetry book she had been given, of the way its intricate structures spun words into incantations evoking the longings of human hearts. She held the notebook, looking off at the horizon, but didn't speak, the sound of the ferry engines rumbling beneath them. Then she turned and looked at Pali before she spoke.

"I think it's the best thing you've ever written."

Pali looked up at her quickly and away again. He lowered his voice and said with humility, "I think so, too."

The sleet had stopped as suddenly as it had begun. They

rode together the rest of the way in silence, watching the darkening water before them, as the sun set through the breaking clouds, the deep rumbling of the ferry engines as comforting as a heartbeat. They passed the Tripod, the marker which signaled the entrance to the harbor. Pali pulled back the throttle, turning the ferry into Detroit Harbor and pivoting toward the Island dock. The lights were not yet on at the offices, and a line of cars and bicyclists waited for the return trip—the last of the night. The bustle of arrival descended upon everyone onboard. Knowing that she should not distract him from his work, Fiona put her hand, briefly, on Pali's arm and left him to his duties. She walked slowly back to her car, her mind turning with the cadence of his poem.

As she unloaded her car and put away her purchases, she found herself returning to the question of the difference in male character. "How would Champagne Man have stacked up," she wondered, wishing for the thousandth time that she had at least learned his name. Would he have been comfortable here, where the mantle of financial and corporate power was invisible and out of place? Or would he have been one of those city gentlemen who called on others to do the routine chores that most here took for granted? Would he have been good in a crisis, or rude and irritable when things weren't going well? She was trying very hard to convince herself that he would have been a small man with petty moods and a list of expected privileges; that she had missed nothing, and was fortunate to have been clear of him. But she knew that she had been attracted to him during that brief time precisely because of her sense that he was not like that. His gaiety, his wit and intelligence, his self-possession and graceful humility all suggested something else. And then, there had been that salute. It was a practiced one, and polished. He had been military somewhere along the line, with the supreme confidence and self-reliance that implied.

Fiona sighed, then shook herself mentally. "Stop it. You have taken one meeting with someone and embellished it into legend. Next thing you know you'll have given him X-Ray vision, or the power of interdimensional travel—which, come to think of it—might be kind of handy, actually."

But still, she pined. "A ridiculous state of affairs," she told herself, making herself a mug of hot milk to take to bed to ward off the cold spring night. Utterly ridiculous.

Fiona dreamed that there was someone standing by her bed. She could not open her eyes to see him, but she knew that he was there near her pillow, and he was very tall. She thought she should be frightened, but she was not. She felt some idea emanating from him that she needed to understand, but she couldn't untangle its meaning. Her mind wrestled with it, struggling to resolve her confusion, as if she were trying puzzle pieces one after another that simply wouldn't fit. It was important to know. She had to understand. But it was always just beyond her, further away. It became something she was chasing and unable to catch--a leaf behind a tree, a paper behind a shrub, tumbling away from her as she bent to grasp it. Just as she was giving up, defeated, the tumbling thing became a great black bird, flapping high into clouds lit by the early sun, not soaring effortlessly, but struggling against a heavy wind. She stood watching it, ever smaller as it rose to a great height, until it was a tiny speck, and then, at last, it disappeared.

Standing and staring into the emptiness, all at once a great light dawned within her, and she knew.

In her sleep she shifted and sighed and slipped into a deeper place of the mind.

Chapter Twenty-Six

D espite their odd sense of having stumbled into an alternate universe, Mike and Terry had returned to their daily routine of Ground Zero coffee. Even in the calm friendliness of the new management, they couldn't help feeling vaguely unnerved by the change in atmosphere. There was something more comfortable, and less intrusive in Roger's surly distance. Although Joshua was not exactly chatty, he nevertheless seemed to care a little too much about his customers' welfare.

"That guy smiles too much," said Terry grumpily as he and Mike were leaving the shop one cold, rainy morning. "Sometimes I just want to grab him by the collar and give him a good shake."

Mike was too diplomatic to say so, but he was inclined to agree. On top of everything, they still did not know what had happened to Roger. No one had heard from him. When asked, Elisabeth had politely admitted that she had not heard, either, but she had not elaborated on what had passed between them.

Lack of information, however, did not prevent the community from conjecture, and rumors flew. There was a story that he had returned to his family to care for a sick parent. This kind of caregiving was usually dismissed as being highly unlikely. There was another that he had been offered a post in a university and returned to physics. There was one account in which he had joined a monastery.

In the effort to learn the truth, more than one attempt had been made to discover what Elisabeth knew. These ranged in subtlety from pointed musings about Roger's whereabouts, to direct inquiry. Elisabeth bore most of the probings with her usual grace. But one gray miserable day she snapped.

The weather was getting on everybody's nerves. The incessant snow of winter had turned into the incessant rain of early spring. Not warm rains for growing things, but biting, miserable, icy rains, combined with something the forecasters liked to call "wintry mix." Tempers were running short.

It happened at the grocery store in Egg Harbor. The wintry mix had changed to wind and slanting rain. Reluctantly—and only because she needed treats for Rocco—Elisabeth had ventured out into the weather. She bundled herself into a hooded anorak and boots, and went so far as to put Rocco into his waterproof coat. He didn't mind being wet, but it was bleak enough these days without the house and car smelling of wet dog, she told herself.

Her precautions were in vain. The brief walk to the car left her face and legs wet, and having once arrived at the parking lot of the store, she was unenthused at the prospect of getting out of the car and back into the weather. "You mind the car," she told Rocco. He lay down resignedly in the backseat, put his head on his paws, and sighed. He would have cheerfully gone into the rain if it had meant he could be with Elisabeth.

She was standing at the dairy case studying the cheese selections trying to ignore the rising chill from her wet jeans. Finding consolation was an ongoing struggle for Elisabeth of late, and today she was seeking it in cheese. She was envisioning a cozy fire this evening with Rocco at her side, along with a plate of cheese, some fruit, and as nice a bottle of wine as she could find. She was interrupted in her musings by a familiar voice.

"Elisabeth! How nice to see you out and about."

It was Phyllis Kaffrey. Phyllis was not a native of Door County. She had been born in the East, and after an indulgent upbringing, an Ivy League education, and marriage, had come with her husband to live in Wisconsin. Her voice was drenched with sympathy.

"How have you been? We've all been so worried about you."

"Nothing to worry about. I'm perfectly fine, thank you. And how is your family?" asked Elisabeth, hoping to shift Phyllis's attention to a safer topic.

"Oh, we're all fine. But it's you we should be talking about. You must be so worried."

She waited for Elisabeth to respond, but when there was no answer, she plowed ahead. "I've heard so many terrible stories about Roger. People are wondering what could have happened."

Elisabeth's face was a mask of good manners.

"That's because everyone likes Roger," she said, blandly.

Phyllis looked vaguely surprised. "Oh, yes. Yes, of course, of course," she said hastily. "But what I'm wondering," and here she leaned in confidentially, "is whether he's all right."

Elisabeth turned pale, but found herself unable to summon anything to say.

"I mean, you don't think he could be lying dead somewhere,

do you?"

Without warning—either to herself or others—Elisabeth exploded into tears. Huge wrenching sobs burst from her as if she were seven, not thirty-two. She had a distant awareness that people were rushing toward her, even Phyllis making ineffectual attempts at comfort, but she didn't care.

"Can we help you?"

"Here, come sit down."

"Let me get you a drink of water. Jack! Get some water from the cooler!"

Elisabeth was caught as off-guard by her reaction as anyone, but she had no resources left to feel embarrassed. She was unable to feel anything except the grief and fear that had lain beneath her calm facade for so long. Surrounded by shocked and concerned people here in the dairy aisle, she abandoned all reason, all pretense.

"No! No! Leave me alone! Just leave me alone!"

Shaking off their hands and pushing her way past the startled bystanders, she ran from the store to her car and drove away, not caring where she was going. Even in her distress she knew that she shouldn't be driving, and the violence of her sobs was upsetting Rocco. She saw his frightened face in the rearview mirror, cowering against the seat, not understanding the storm he was engulfed in. His fear helped her to calm herself. "It's ok, Rocco. It's ok," she told him. She found a place to pull over, and, with Rocco standing on the front armrest, his face pressed against her, she cried herself out. At last, her eyes swollen and painful, her weeping subsided, she sat for a while, leaning her cheek against Rocco, looking out at the restless water of the Bay.

When she was calm again, she started the car back up and headed toward home.

It wasn't until she got back to the house that she realized she hadn't gotten Rocco's biscuits. She sat for twenty minutes to regain her bearings. Then she washed her face, and went out into the rain again for Rocco. She drove all the way to Fish Creek to get them, just so she wouldn't have to go back into the store.

Rocco did not seem to mind. But he stayed close, his body touching her, for the rest of the night.

Fiona was finding the daily slog to the barn increasingly burdensome. Unlike the bitter cold, which did not penetrate the depths of down and fur, this damp cold was somehow more miserable. It bled deep beneath the surface and seeped into every tissue. She returned from her goat keeping, feeling as if she could never again be warm, and because she couldn't help herself, she wondered whether Robert was miserable, too.

She did her best for him, despite her distaste for the tasks, and her resentment at the drain he made on her time and energy. She began to wonder if she would ever be free of this responsibility, and occasionally even to suspect that Roger's gift had been a deliberate ploy on the part of her friends to make her time on the Island as unpleasant as possible, and thereby, to win the dare.

But this was only during her worst moments. The rest of the time she was merely dreary. Occasionally, as a tonic to the gloom, she would take out the poetry book with its exquisite bookmark and turn it over in her hands. She took pleasure in simply touching it, pondering why whoever had sent it, had not been willing to take credit for it. She had taken to reading it every night, and it had replaced *Meditations* as her book of choice. Many of the poems she already knew, but there were others that she did not, and she explored these with the pleasure of discovery and wonder.

"Have you noticed that no one has nervous breakdowns anymore?" Elisabeth was talking to Fiona one morning on the phone.

"What do you mean?"

"Well, I can remember my mother's conversations about how so-and-so had a nervous breakdown, and had taken six weeks away. It was fairly commonplace. But we never hear of people having nervous breakdowns anymore."

"Now we just take drugs," commented Fiona dryly.

"I suppose that's true," said Elisabeth slowly. "But I think we're missing something."

"We're missing having nervous breakdowns?" asked Fiona.

"Well...yes." Elisabeth was searching for words. "I mean, I always thought, even as a child, that taking six weeks away from the world, where no one expected anything from you because you were fragile, and needed care, sounded delightful. I always kind of like the sound of sanitariums when I read about them in various novels. People sitting in beautiful gardens on lawn chairs in the sun, with blankets wrapped around them, and attentive staff..." she drifted off into a reverie.

"Are you thinking about checking into a sanitarium?" asked Fiona. "Because outside of a novel, I can't think of a single one. And anyway," she frowned, belatedly alert. "What's all this talk of nervous breakdowns and sanitariums? Are you ok?"

"Actually, I'm not sure."

They were silent for a moment.

"Well, you could go away," said Fiona at last. "It's a perfect time. The busy season for the gallery is months away. And, by the way, I think now the term for sanitarium is *spa*."

Elisabeth didn't need to think about this for very long.

"Would you like to come with me?"

"I can't. I'm an indentured goat servant. Besides, I'm broke, and who would take Rocco?"

Elisabeth was inspired. "Ok. I'm going to look into this. I'll call you back." She stopped for a moment with second thoughts. "Are you sure you wouldn't mind taking Rocco?"

Fiona didn't hesitate. "Of course not. I miss him when he's not here."

"Ok. I'll keep you posted."

After they hung up, Fiona poured herself another cup of coffee and wandered over to the kitchen window to look out. The piles of snow were a little smaller, but still there. It was raining again. But if she looked hard, she was pretty sure she could see a lavender mist along the branches of the trees. It was the first hopeful sign.

Chapter Twenty-Seven

One morning, the rain stopped. Sunlight sparkled in a blue sky, and on that day, at last, it was spring. The dawn song of robins, chickadees, and cardinals joined the cry of gulls and the prehistoric squawk of nesting cranes. Flocks of robins gathered on lawns and in fields. Migrating brown hawks made their ritual passage overhead. The grass turned green almost overnight, and early spring flowers began to thrust their leaves up to the light.

Fiona and Rocco had come back from their morning walk and sat on the front porch enjoying the sun. Robert stood in his pen, bathed in sunshine, carefully masticating a piece of old rope that Fiona had carelessly left within his reach. She chose not to mind. It was warm. "The sun is shining", she thought. "Let him enjoy himself."

They were sitting this way when Jim drove up. Fiona hadn't seen him much at all since February. She guessed she might have hurt his feelings over Valentine's Day. She watched him get out of his truck and come up the walk.

"Hey," she said.

"Hey. Mind if I join you?"

"Please. Sit down. Would you like some coffee?"

"Sure. Thanks."

Fiona got up to get it for him. When she came back, he was

sitting with his chin resting on his hands, staring off into the distance. She handed him his coffee and sat down next to him on the step.

"Guess it's time to get the chairs out," she said.

"About time," said Jim. "Thought we'd never see the sun again."

Fiona smiled. "It was getting a bit claustrophobic."

She could tell he was working his way up to saying something, but she had a feeling she didn't really want to hear whatever it was.

"How's life at the DNR?" she asked.

"Well, let's see. A drowned bear washed up on shore near School House Beach."

"Oh no!" said Fiona, genuinely shocked. "Does that happen often?"

"Every now and then. For some reason they get the idea to swim, and sometimes they make it over, and sometimes they don't."

"That's very sad."

"Yeah. About breaks my heart every time. They're just like big dogs, you know." He looked at her seriously. "I know it's not orthodox theology, but I refuse to accept that animals don't have feelings or souls. All you have to do is look into their eyes."

"I know," said Fiona. "I agree. And what's more, I wouldn't want to be in Heaven if it meant there were no animals."

"No, me either. Anyway, it doesn't make sense. What more innocent heart could you find than a dog's? Far purer than any human being."

Fiona was touched by his fervor.

He looked down into his coffee. "On a happier note, we've discovered a new eagle's nest on the north shore. A young pair, first year together, we think. They mate for life."

"That is happier news."

Jim nodded reminiscently. "Team went up there just the other day to check the nest."

"Really? Aren't they afraid to disturb them?"

"It doesn't seem to bother them. Went up there with a phlebotomist, shimmied up the tree, brought down the eaglets one at a time, took a sample, banded them, shimmied back up and put them back."

"Really," said Fiona, amazed.

"Doesn't hurt them. Although I'd bet it scares them."

Fiona looked at him fondly. "You have a soft heart for a ranger. I thought you were supposed to be hardened agents of officialdom."

"I guess we are, and I guess I do." He laughed briefly. "That's what my mom always said when I was a kid, coming home with some new animal."

He turned suddenly and looked at her.

"Hey, Fiona. I need to ask you something."

She sighed inwardly. "Here we go," she thought. She looked at him expectantly.

"Do you ever regret it? This business you're in? I mean, it doesn't seem to suit you. You seem so…nice….I just…." He trailed off, then looked her directly in the eye. "I don't get it. I just don't get it."

Fiona, didn't get it, either. What on earth was he getting at? She frowned. "What do you mean?"

"Well, I don't mean to offend you. But don't you ever want a different kind of life? Something...more...normal?"

Fiona began laughing. "What would normal be, do you think?"

Jim, who had started out with such confidence, now began to look embarrassed. "Well, marriage, and a family, and...." he paused, clearly struggling for words. "Just...normal." He concluded weakly. He looked at her as if he were asking her for help.

Fiona realized that she needed to be wary. "Sure, I guess. I want those things."

Jim suddenly got angry. "Well, damn it, you have to give it up sometime."

Fiona was completely confused. "Give it up?"

He sighed and slumped a bit. "Look, I'm sorry, Fiona. This isn't coming out right at all. I guess what I'm trying to say is that I have feelings for you, and I want to know where I stand. That's all." He looked at her ruefully. "I'd like to spend more time with you."

A line from Tennyson came suddenly to her mind. "In the spring a young man's fancy lightly turns to thoughts of love." She chose her words carefully. "I like you, Jim. I like you very much." She searched his face. He was watching her warily, as if he were expecting a blow. She tried to soften it. "But I can't return your feelings. I wish I could." This last part wasn't strictly true, she thought. But what she wished for she was unlikely to ever get.

Jim nodded sadly, as if he had expected this answer all along. "But you will give it up? Sometime? Honestly, Fiona, I am worried for you."

Fiona laughed again. "Sometimes I worry for myself. But it's ok. I'm ok, Jim. Don't worry about me. I'll give up this crazy life sometime. I hope."

He looked at her seriously. "Well that's what matters the most to me, honestly." He sighed and looked down at his empty cup.

"More coffee?" asked Fiona politely. She was hoping he would say no, but relieved to return the conversation to something routine.

"No. Thanks. I'd better go." He stood up. "Guess I'll see you around sometime."

"I'd like that," she said, sincerely, standing, too.

He patted her awkwardly on the arm, then turned and ran down the porch stairs, down the walk and to his truck. The engine started, and with a wave, but not a backward glance, he drove away.

Fiona watched him go with regret.

A t sunset that night, the lake was smooth and calm, and in the shallows near the shore the water was the turquoise of the Caribbean. Rocco dabbled along the rocky edge while Fiona sat on a section of soft, dried yellow grass, idly watching. Patches of snow still lay along the beaches, but the hazy stratus of clouds was proof that the seasons were changing. Her conversation with Jim that morning had put Tennyson in her mind.

Here about the beach I wander'd,
nourishing a youth sublime
with the fairy tales of science,
and the long result of Time.

She couldn't remember the rest.

The sun went down in a ball of brilliant pink surrounded by purple clouds with pale peach edges, and Fiona and Rocco walked home, content.

Chapter Twenty-Eight

The Spring Tea Party was an Island tradition. Every year the women of the churches banded together for the event, delighted to have an excuse to dress up and set beautiful tables. Best china, heirloom linens, rugs, and even the good dining sets were arranged on the lawn of Saint Thorlakur Lutheran Church—affectionately known to all as St. Thor—and tickets were sold all up and down Door County to benefit the Island Health Center. The tea party was a community occasion and after the usual snowy Easter, a very much welcome sign of hope for spring. That it took place in June was some indication of just how welcome spring might be.

The planning took months. Calendars had to be consulted and compared against other local events, posters and tickets had to be designed and printed, and committee assignments made. One group of women had to collect the borrowed cups and saucers, tablecloths, teapots, and silver spoons from hesitant owners; one group was in charge of decorating; another was in charge of setup; another for serving; yet another for cleanup. Everyone distributed posters, sold tickets, and baked. The men accepted their role in the proceedings, good-naturedly—for the most part—hauling furniture and rugs, and setting up tents for a gathering they were happy to steer well clear of once it had begun.

While considered an honor, the chairmanship of such an event was a major undertaking, consuming the life of its office-holder and forcing the neglect—and sometimes the indentured servitude—of her family for almost a full year. The job, which rotated among the various congregations, required both patience and tact. But it also required a certain amount of bossiness and a great deal of free time. And this was probably the reason, along with the refusal of the first three nominees, that Stella DesRoisiers managed, at last, to achieve her heart's desire. Or rather, her second heart's desire, after the eviction of Fiona. Patience and tact she did not have. Bossiness she had in abundance.

As chairman of the Spring Tea, Stella was in her element. Even her most ardent critics had to admit that she had an ability to organize that would have been admired by a brigadier general. Every detail, no matter how small, was subject to her scrutiny, and the job descriptions and schedules were planned with the finest precision. Leadership, however, does not suit everyone, and for all her expertise in organizing, Stella had managed to nettle or alienate nearly everyone. Her officiousness, preening, arrogance, and self-importance would have been pathetic if it hadn't been so utterly annoying. But this, too, was enjoyed, since it gave the entire community an engrossing and limitless topic of conversation. All in all, no matter who was doing the evaluation, Stella's chairmanship was deemed a success.

Fiona, whose idea of a good time did not generally involve tea, had dutifully purchased two tickets and promptly called to invite Elisabeth. Elisabeth had just returned from what they both cheerfully referred to as her nervous breakdown, a long luxurious visit to a famous spa. There was a moment of silence on the phone as Elisabeth contemplated the offer. Between the ferry rides and the event itself, coming to the tea party would involve an entire day, and she had been gone for a long time. But she did need to pick up Rocco.

"You could come for the weekend," urged Fiona. "People wear hats. It'll be fun."

"Christine will be gone that week, and I'll have no one to watch the gallery. I really can't close up again." Elisabeth paused again. "But I suppose I could just come for the day. Let me see if Christine's sister is available. I'll call you back."

Roger was not an inconsiderate person. On the contrary, he thought deeply about the feelings of others and how to be kind to them. The difficulty, as he himself was aware, came from his inability to discern what people felt and what they might require. What might be seen as indifference was simply an inability to give and receive signals. It was as if the world spoke some other language, and Roger was trying to guess the meaning.

His awareness of the problem did almost nothing to help him solve it. It required someone else's willingness to understand his underlying good intentions and to accept his behavior. And this, so far in his life, he had almost never found.

Roger did not feel any unhappiness in this. It was simply the reality of his existence which he accepted as he would any other aspect of the natural world. It did, however, pose a number of difficulties, and it was these he pondered as he strolled along the sunlit California seaside.

He observed, with his usual detachment, the other people around him: families with children chattering and bickering; couples strolling, sometimes holding hands, sometimes more alone in their togetherness than if they had been by themselves. The signals of their relationships to one another were there to be read by a casual observer, but to Roger, these people were simply present. Their moods, their relationships, and their interactions were as unintelligible to him as a scientific abstract might be for them.

But there was one person, who did understand; who accepted his deficiencies with grace and good humor. He did not know why this should be, but he knew that it was so. It was his confidence in her understanding that kept him from thinking that he should contact Elisabeth. It did not occur to him that she would worry, or even that she would miss him. He did know, however, that he would be happy to see her again, and he assumed, by extrapolation, that she would be happy to see him, too. He did not know what to think about the man she had been with. But in the weeks since he had seen them together, he had come to believe that he could prevail. Elisabeth loved him. He didn't know much about feelings, but he was certain of that.

It was at this moment that the sparkling of the bright sun in a shop window caught his eye. He stopped to look at the display, and it seemed to him all at once that he was being given a glimpse of something beyond the plane of his intellectual routine. This single shaft of late afternoon sunlight seemed to reveal for him the path that he should take. Like all scientists, he recognized the breakthrough of inspiration and accepted it without question. Stepping out of his months-long bewilderment, he opened the door to the shop and went in.

The morning of the Spring Tea Party dawned with clear skies and temperatures that were downright balmy for Washington Island in June. There were no storms in the offing, and the predictions of mild weather had emboldened the ladies to do some of their preparations the night before—an unheard-of scenario. Nevertheless, there was a great bustle in Island kitchens that morning, and a rising buzz of women's voices on the lawn of St. Thor's.

Stella had risen at 4:00 a.m., after staying up late the night before carefully starching and ironing the ancient handmade lace and linen tablecloth with napkins that were her inheritance from her French great-grandmama, who, although Stella would never have acknowledged this even in the bitter recesses of her mind, had been the source of Stella's own disposition. Great-Grandmama had come from the old country, bearing a few linens, a set of Limoges plates, and a chip on her shoulder the size of Canada. These things she had treasured all her days and left as her legacy to the women who came after her. The plates were now gone, but the lace had endured even the rough life of nineteenth-century immigrants. The chip, if anything, had been enlarged.

The style of the linens was no longer much admired, but to

Stella they were things of great beauty, and she took a deep pride in them. These were to be the center of all eyes at the table set for the wives of the clergy and the few female politicians—or the wives of the male ones—where Stella herself would sit. She intended for everyone to know the value of her possessions, and she also intended to see that whatever photos were taken of the event included both her linens and, of course, herself. She had made a phone call to the reporter from the Washington Island *Observer* and reminded her of the time she had been seen leaving Nelson's late at night with a strange man. It had been entirely innocent, as Stella well knew, but it wouldn't have done to have the story going around. It wouldn't have done. The *Observer* planned a feature story on Stella's tablecloth.

Arriving at the scene, Stella bypassed the committee ladies whose charge it was to set the tables. As Marilyn, from the Catholic parish, stepped forward to receive the revered linens carefully rolled on a covered cardboard tube and swathed in special tissue, Stella put her down with a stare and marched over to the VIP table, her treasures in her arms. No one else was worthy to handle Great-Grandmama's legacy. Stella herself would set the table.

Elisabeth came over on the noon ferry and pulled up at Fiona's house carrying a garment bag and an enormous hatbox. They greeted one another affectionately, but Rocco responded to Elisabeth's return with ecstasy, leaping and trilling, and running in circles around them. With Rocco delightedly trailing along behind, they ensconced themselves in the kitchen for a cup of coffee, and after chatting amiably for a while, they went upstairs to change.

They had agreed not too arrive too early, so when they reached the church there was already such a crowd that they had to park well down the road and walk. Elisabeth wore a rich lavender dress with a matching wrap and a wide-brimmed straw hat which she had to hold down to keep from blowing off her head. She looked impeccable, and, as always, exactly right: not so dressed up as to appear pretentious, but just enough to do honor to the occasion. The combination of holding both the wrap and the hat in the wind, however, suggested that she would not have the opportunity of doing much else with her hands. Fiona, who had no hats except baseball caps, wore a white linen sheath and the most recent additions to her collection of Italian sandals.

Fiona handed over their tickets and they were directed toward the tables by a distracted woman wearing a flowered apron. Every table was full except one, a Sheraton style dining table set near the long row of blooming cherry trees. The sunlight slanted across the white table linens, and the silver serving trays were filled invitingly with tiny crustless sandwiches, miniature cakes, a jar of homemade cherry, a dish of clotted cream, and a vast selection of dainty cookies. They made their way across the lawn, stopping here and there to chat or to introduce Elisabeth, and at last seated themselves with two identical sighs.

They sat side by side, so as not to monopolize the table, and looked out at the tableau before them. Women dressed colorfully in their spring outfits were happily chatting and sipping tea from china cups. The servers, wearing their own aprons, moved from table to table, refreshing teapots and cookie trays, and wearing themselves to a frazzle. Fiona imagined there would be many an aching pair of feet put up and many an Old Fashioned poured that evening once the teacups had been washed and put away. The blossoms from the cherry trees around them gently drifted from the branches in the balmy winds, adding an otherworldly quality to the scene.

Elisabeth bestirred herself from her dreamy mood. "Do you see a teapot anywhere?"

"I think they bring you one so it's hot."

"Ah," said Elisabeth, scrutinizing the sandwiches under their little net insect tent. "In that case, I think I will amuse my-self with one of these while we wait." She reached for the plate, chose one that looked like cream cheese and salmon, and one that was egg salad, and passed it to Fiona. "Mmm, lovely," she said, as she took a bite of the salmon and sighed again. "I am so glad I came! This is delightful."

"It is nice," said Fiona, as she helped herself to several lace cookies and a cherry scone. "I must admit, I did not imagine anything quite so…idyllic." She grinned at Elisabeth.

"Tea on Washington Island. Sounds like the name of a novel."

"Or one of those independent films that have beautiful scenery and too much dialogue."

They smiled at one another and drifted into silence, absorbing the sunlight and blossoms as they ate. Elisabeth blotted her lips daintily with a starched lace napkin and looked around.

"I really could use a cup of tea about now."

"Let's give them another minute to notice us," said Fiona.

"They seem awfully busy."

Elisabeth leaned back indulgently, took off her hat, and let the sun play across her face. "Wake me when it comes."

Fiona reached for another scone. She could never resist cherry preserves.

At this moment, one of the volunteers in a floral apron appeared, her face a knot of anxiety. "I'm very sorry, but this table is reserved," she said, nervously smoothing a corner of the tablecloth and avoiding looking Fiona in the face. "I'm afraid…well, I'm afraid I'm going to have to ask you to move."

Elisabeth was sitting up now, and already reaching for her hat.

"I'm sorry," began Fiona as she got up. "We had no idea. We'll just take our plates and—"

"WHAT," screeched a voice from behind them, "are you doing?"

Elisabeth, thinking that the scolding was intended for the volunteer, turned to placate the newcomer. She was a broad-beamed woman with tiny malicious eyes, dressed in a flowered print that did not flatter her shape. Before Elisabeth could draw a breath, the tirade began. Fiona, her scone turned to rock in her stomach, squared her shoulders, and turned to face Stella.

Stella's face and neck were a mottled red as she hissed invective, and she pushed her face within inches of Fiona's. The volunteer was backing away as several of her coworkers rushed to the scene.

"You think you own everything, don't you?" cried Stella. You think you can just do whatever you want, don't you? You think you are royalty and the rest of us are peasants. Get away from my grandmama's tablecloth. Get away from my table. Get.

Away."

Fiona turned to Elisabeth and spoke in a measured voice. "I see a place at a table across the lawn." She picked up her plate and Elisabeth's and began to walk away.

"Put those dishes down," said Stella, her voice now risen enough to attract attention from several tables away. Fiona, already having started off with Elisabeth right behind, now stopped. She stood for several seconds, with her eyes closed, her head bent as if in prayer.

"I said," repeated Stella, "Put those dishes DOWN."

Fiona's head came up. She turned back to the table, unaware of the collective intake of breaths around her. This was turning out to be the best tea party ever. Would there be a fight?

Her eyes on Stella, Fiona walked toward the table, but before she could reach it, she felt Elisabeth's hand. With her usual poise, Elisabeth draped her wrap on one arm, and passed her hat to Fiona.

"This is your tablecloth?" Elisabeth asked Stella, her voice steady, clear, and ringing. "Your grandmother's tablecloth?" she asked. And without waiting for a response, she took the plates from Fiona's hands, filled with the remains of salmon and egg salad, clotted cream and cherry preserves, and deftly—almost gently—placed them upside down on the tablecloth. She took Fiona's arm, and they both turned and walked away.

A strange strangled cry arose from behind them, inarticulate in its fury. They walked sedately to the car without looking back.

It wasn't until they were some distance down the road that either spoke.

"I have a lovely bottle of cabernet at home," said Fiona.

Would you like a glass?"

"Yes, please," said Elisabeth. "I prefer it to tea anyway."

Late that afternoon, Fiona and Elisabeth sat together at the water's edge, watching the sky change, enjoying the breeze. It was already well past their usual dinnertime, but neither felt any need to stir. The confrontation of the afternoon had receded like a bad dream, but the intensity of it had spurred a particularly deep conversation. It seemed natural, sitting here at what felt like the edge of the world, to talk about life's mysteries. After some time of confidences and silences, Fiona revealed her conversation with Pali and his inexplicable encounters. Elisabeth listened mostly in silence, asking a question now and then. Fiona's voice was low, and she spoke gently, as if there were something fragile about the topic, as if something might break if she handled it too roughly.

After she finished the story, they were silent for a moment, each following the drift of her own thoughts. Elisabeth stared off at the water.

"It's such a cliché," she said at last, "but still surprising when you find out for yourself how much life changes when you've encountered death. You think it's about prizes and headlines and big accomplishments. But really it's about kindness, the first cup of coffee, and a clean kitchen floor. Those are the things that matter."

Fiona was lying on her back on the grass, watching for the

first star. "And having the ferry run on time. That's suddenly become pretty important." She rolled over and grinned at Elisabeth.

"The answer to the ultimate question of life, the universe, and everything, is forty-two.'" she added. Fiona loved Douglas Adams and his philosophy of an inexplicable and nonsensical universe. "That has always seemed about right; don't you think?"

Elisabeth smiled without answering.

"Anyway," Fiona thought to herself, all in a flash, "wisdom is at once more concrete, more attainable, and less understandable than that."

"And once we figure it out," she said aloud, quoting, " 'it will all disappear and be replaced by something even more bizarre and inexplicable.'"

They both spoke at once, their voices rising in the early evening air. "'There is another theory which states that this has already happened.'"

"You know," said Fiona to Elisabeth, "your nervous breakdown seems to have done you a lot of good."

"It has. You should try it sometime."

"Maybe I will. But I should probably sell another article first."

Elisabeth laughed. "The gallery had three major sales this week. Maybe I should go away more often."

Pleased that Elisabeth was cheerful, Fiona rolled over again, and turned her attention to the water, watching as Rocco happily trolled the shallows looking for stones. His tail was wagging, and his energy still high. His exact criteria for selection were not clear to observers, but he seemed to know exactly what he was looking for. Occasionally he would find a fish, and then he pounced, his joy unmitigated by the futility of his efforts. Here, thought Fiona, was the perfect example of a life well-lived: joyous, focused, and unimpeded by failure. The pleasure of simply living was both the end and the means. Fiona knew that her own personality was not compatible with such an approach to life. She worried too much and enjoyed too little. "And yet," she thought, "my enjoyment is still enormous. I have only to push aside anxiety—which surely is not a condition unique to me—and allow myself the experience of daily life. That may not be all we have, but, it's all we can count on."

As an untrained Christian, Fiona wanted very much to believe, but her faithless upbringing and her innate skepticism made her a poor practitioner. After an emotional conversion, she had been baptized as an adult and tried her best to believe, but the native confidence of those brought up in the faith eluded her. Reading, studying, and conversing with those with surer footing did only a bit to bring her closer. She wished she could, but that comfort seemed to be for others. For the most part, she found the person of God so often described by those of her acquaintance simplistic and limited, and she rebelled against the human image represented by so many religious people. And yet, although she frequently frustrated herself with her uneducated theology, she did not find the prospect of God's existence any stranger than the existence of anything else. She had come to be resolved with a lack of resolution. But she could not give up her searching.

Rocco emerged from the water with a rock, and conscientiously shook himself out, splattering them both with cold water.

"Enough" said Elisabeth. "Let's go get some dinner. I don't

want to wait for the last ferry." And together they packed their gear and toweled-off their very wet companion, the comfortable silence of long friendship sufficient for them all.

"Do you think," asked Fiona idly as they strolled back toward the house, "that Stella is capable of murder?"

"Well one thing's certain," said Elisabeth. "If she's counting on the element of surprise, she could never squeeze into your bedroom closet."

"Strangely, I don't find that comforting."

"Neither would I," said Elisabeth.

E lisabeth was just in time to catch the last ferry. It was good to have Rocco back. She kept looking into the rearview mirror to see the big pointed ears in profile against the back window. It made her smile. She opened the rear windows for him, and he put his face out into the balmy evening air.

Elisabeth was feeling more like smiling than she had in a long time. Fiona was right: her time away had done her good—although goodness knew what local gossip had made of her self-described breakdown. She still cringed remembering the scene in the grocery store, but it was past and past fixing. "So there," she thought.

Driving up to the house, she was planning what she would do first. A walk with Rocco, a glass of wine, and a chicken casserole from the freezer. She was in the process of choosing a bedtime book when something jolted her consciousness. From the backseat Rocco was making little cries of excitement. Elisabeth could see the old Jeep parked in front of the porch and a familiar figure sitting casually in the rocking chair. The white T-shirt glowed in the dusk, and she could just make out the tufts of hair standing straight up.

Roger had come home.

Rocco was the first on the porch, and his joyous greeting for Roger was as effusive as it would have been for Elisabeth. She stood back quietly and watched Rocco's spinning and trilling. He had a tendency to forget how big he was, and he nearly knocked Roger over in his enthusiasm.

Roger stood up, and bent to rub the big dog's ears and back, speaking affectionately to him. "Good boy," said Roger. "Good boy, Rocco. I'm glad to see you, too."

It was several minutes before Rocco quieted down again, but he stayed close to Roger, leaning against his leg.

Roger looked up at Elisabeth. He looked the same, but somehow younger. It occurred to Elisabeth that he was happy.

"Are you glad to see me, Roger?" she asked, smiling.

"Yes," he said simply. And when she held out her hands to him he took them.

"I bought you a ring," he said. "I have a plan."

"When can I see it?"

Roger dropped one hand, reached into his pocket and took out a box.

"Let's go in," he said.

Later, Elisabeth mused upon their reunion. It had not been a particularly romantic proposal. She smiled to herself. It was just Roger.

That night Fiona dreamt that she was floating on the lake at night, the stars shimmering above her. She felt cradled and warm and unafraid. She could see the shore lights in the distance, and marveled at the beauty and wonder of being so safe, so perfectly at home in the world. She could feel the hum of the universe vibrating through her soul. Never had she felt so calm, such a sense of belonging. Her entire being seemed to soften and let go.

All at once the lake began to change, the water growing rough and choppy. Struggling to keep afloat, she looked up to see a wall of water—the biggest wave she'd ever seen—coming down on her. She knew that it was over, that she would drown, and fear seized her. Suddenly looming above her, she saw the lighted pilothouse of the ferry, and a shadowed figure at the helm. She felt panic, certain that she would be struck, and then, inexplicably, a hand on her shoulder. She couldn't see the ferry, or the wave, only the night sky and the stars shimmering in exquisite clarity. She was lifted up, tossed and drifted over the wave, her body tumbling, and gently washed ashore onto soft sand. She lay, encompassed by the forgiving dunes, as completely enveloped as she had been in the water. All fear was gone.

Sighing in her sleep, she rolled over and slept deeply.

Chapter Twenty-Nine

As soon as she had awoken, her soul filled with the images of the dream, Fiona had known that today was not a day for writing. Her heart was unburdened. The sun shone, the birds were singing, and the smell of fresh coffee was wafting upstairs from the little electric pot in the kitchen. Today she would accomplish something concrete and physical. There was still the room that needed painting. She could rationalize it by telling herself that her subconscious would be working on the concepts for her article.

Fiona was on the ladder, about an hour into the job, when she became vaguely aware of singing. She stopped for a moment and listened. It was a male voice, untrained, but not bad, and clearly uninhibited. "The one and only cereal that comes in the shape of animals! Tra la la la la tra la tra la tra la tra lalalala!"

With complete disregard for her own status as a newcomer, Fiona had developed a blunt-force distain for tourists. Putting down the brush, she climbed down the ladder, and walked outside to see where it was coming from. She needed some fresh air. In the best-case scenario, maybe the furnace guy had finally put in an appearance. On the street in front of the house, a man was rummaging in the trunk of a car, apparently unaware that anyone was nearby. From this angle Fiona could see that he was fit, and had remarkably long legs.

"The one and only cereal!" he sang again. "Tra la lalalalala-
lalalalalalalalala lalalalalalaLALA! Ouch! Damn it."

He stood up rubbing the back of his head where he'd hit
it on the trunk lid. He looked up suddenly, with that uncanny
awareness that people get when they are being watched.

Fiona stood still. It was him. It was Champagne Man.

He was better looking than she'd remembered him, and de-
cidedly more casual than when she'd seen him last. He wore
jeans and a cotton shirt with the sleeves rolled up, his blue eyes
seemed more intense against the summer color of his skin.

"Ah! Sorry! I was listening to Tchaikovsky driving up, and it
got into my head." He smiled, not in the least embarrassed. His
eyes focused on her face, and he smiled again, looking directly
into her eyes with the full force of recognition.

"Hello," he said as if they had just lost sight of one another
for a moment in a crowd. "Now that I see it's you, I suppose I
should have been singing Noel Coward. An opportunity lost.
Ah well."

Fiona could hardly put two words together in her mind.
She'd heard the term *clashing of worlds*, and now that seemed
perfectly descriptive. What came out of her mouth didn't seem to
be related to anything, but she barely knew what she was saying.

"I thought possibly my house was haunted," she said, smiling, and assuming what she hoped was an air of normalcy. If he
could act as if this were perfectly expected, then she could, too.
What on earth am I talking about? she chided herself. "But I
decided that I don't know any ghosts." As soon as she'd said this,
she thought of the ferry, and wondered if perhaps she did.

"How can you be sure? It could be like that movie with

Bruce Willis, where you don't realize who's a ghost and who isn't."

"Your breathing seems approximately normal."

"Ah. But perhaps I'm merely pretending to be normal. Like John Cleese in the Argument Clinic, I could be haunting in my spare time."

"Possibly. But what constitutes spare time for ghosts?"

"Do you suppose they have schedules? You know, howling at midnight, rattling chains at three, that sort of thing? It's a dreary idea, wouldn't you say? I'd like to think that at least in death we might be free of following routine."

They were facing each other, he leaning against the fender, Fiona squinting slightly against the sun. "What are you doing on Washington Island?" She hadn't wanted to ask in precisely that way, but things just kept coming out of her mouth.

"I'd like to say that I came for the weather, but that would be an untruth." He paused and smiled. "Sorry, I've been rereading Jane Austen lately, and listening to old Monty Python skits on the drive up. It's an odd combination, but the language is remarkably similar, and strangely contagious. It's amazing, really, how many Jane Austen expressions you can work in to everyday conversation."

"No Noel Coward?"

"No. It's one of my personal idiosyncrasies that I only listen to Noel Coward after dark and with cocktails. In any case, I could just as easily ask the same question of you."

"I live here. This is my house." He was even sounding like John Cleese, she thought. Not that she minded.

He looked over her shoulder at the house, apparently sizing

it up, then back at Fiona, in her torn jeans and disreputable T-shirt. She mentally castigated herself for her appearance.

"Would you like to see it? Come in and I'll show you around." She wondered if she could find a pretense to slip away and at least wash her face. Did she have paint on her nose?

At this moment Robert wandered from behind the house, his bell jangling as he moved toward the roses, nibbling intently at the hostas, as if hoping to lure Fiona into a sense of complacency about his activities. His air of sardonic condescension was less pronounced than usual.

"Is that your goat?"

"I'm afraid it is.

"He seems to like roses."

"His palate is rather undiscriminating. He seems to like just about everything."

They stood for a moment in silence, contemplating Robert and his morose foraging.

"He seems depressed."

"Do you think so?" Fiona studied Robert's expression. "Possibly it's indigestion. He's eaten my sandals only just this morning."

"But that's the way it is with goats, I'm told. Although, I can't say I've had much in the way of personal acquaintance with them. Funny. I hadn't pegged you for a goat kind of person."

Fiona thought about asking what kind of person he had pegged her for.

"He was a gift."

"Really?" Robert stopped eating and looked up at them, and they all stood looking at one another for a moment.

"Had you requested a goat?"

"No. No, actually, I hadn't." Fiona sighed. "He had been given to a friend of mine, but he couldn't keep him, so..." Her voice trailed away.

"He's re-gifted?" He asked. "You have a re-gifted goat? Shouldn't re-gifting be limited to things like a box of soap on a rope, or a tie you wouldn't wear?"

"If only I could figure out who to re-gift him to," Fiona said, wryly, "but nevertheless, once you've acquired a goat, it's remarkably difficult to un-acquire one."

"Yes, I can see that it might be. Although you might take a page from the book of the friend who gave him to you."

He gave Robert an appraising look. Fiona had an image of Robert being passed from house to house, like a fruitcake. Feigning unconcern at this interloper, Robert went back to chewing, and Champagne Man looked back at Fiona. He smiled at her as if they were old friends. Fiona smiled back. "Did you say you would show me around?"

"Yes, of course. I would love to." And she wondered if he could possibly imagine how much she meant it. She started to lead him to the house and stopped to turn around.

"I'm Fiona Campbell, by the way."

"Pete. Peter Landry. Delighted to actually meet you."

The kitchen door stood open, the patched screen letting in only the occasional fly, and Fiona stood back to allow her guest ("Pete," she thought to herself) to enter before her. She showed him everything—the broken screens, the nest in the fireplace, the scene of the bat reunion, the charming view from the upstairs bathroom, and the place in the shed where she'd been standing the moment she'd decided to buy the house. He had poked his head into closets, commented on the interesting tile pattern in the bathroom ("They don't do that much anymore, do they?") and gotten on his knees to look up the chimney flue, all the while commenting cheerily on his own house experiences, the beautiful carpentry of the stairway, and the many pleasures of old houses. He had inquired about the neighborhood and small town living, and as they moved from room to room, Fiona found herself telling him the whole story of Stella, the town board, and the upcoming hearings. He listened sympathetically, but without comment. By the time they had made their way back to the kitchen, Fiona was feeling quite thoroughly charmed and schoolgirlish.

"Would you like a cup of coffee?" she asked, gesturing for him to sit at the table.

"Sure, thanks. That'd be great." He seated himself, and looked out the window. A comfortable silence settled upon them as Fiona made coffee and set out a tray of milk, sugar, and mugs. The sound and smell of the coffee brewing filled the tiny kitchen.

"Ummm, about your goat—"

"Robert."

"Er, yes, Robert." Pete paused, and Fiona looked up.

"He seems to be eating a tablecloth."

Fiona ran to the door and looked out. There was Robert, standing next to Stella's clothesline. There was a dreamy look on his face as he slowly masticated what looked to Fiona horribly like the heirloom tablecloth that had graced yesterday's tea party. "Oh God," she said. "What will Stella do when she sees this?"

"Is that her tablecloth?"

"Yes, a family heirloom."

"Ah." He stood up and came to stand next to her, looking across the yard at Robert and the tablecloth. "How do you suppose she'll take it?"

"She keeps mentioning a goat barbecue. This ought to clinch it." Fiona was surprised at her own rising anguish. She had begun to pace. "She will blame me. She will think I did it on purpose."

"Probably," observed Pete, "because she would."

He surveyed the scene thoughtfully.

"I don't like to be unduly pessimistic, but he seems to be at least halfway through the thing. I don't suppose your neighbor would believe that the goat was uninvolved in the disappearance of her tablecloth?"

"No. No, if it isn't him, it will be me. Or vice versa."

"The teeth marks would probably be a giveaway in any case. Do you have many vagrants here?"

"None. None whatsoever. Besides, the coincidence will be too much. She will know it was me."

"So a theft by a wandering passerby seems unlikely?"

"Utterly."

"Any dogs you don't like?"

A faint gleam of hope stirred Fiona's thoughts. "As a matter of fact...." and she told him about Piggy.

"He lives down the road?"

"The yellow house, down the road that way."

"Do you suppose he's at home?"

"Either that or ransacking the village."

Pete thought for a moment, regarding Robert's snacking with a distant expression.

"I think," he said, "that this may be one of the rare cases in which honesty is not the best policy. You're right. She will never believe the truth." He looked at Fiona. "Wait just a moment, I'll be right back." And he slipped out the door and strolled, with an air of insouciance, in Robert's direction.

Robert looked up, his dreamy expression now replaced with glinting wariness, all the while continuing to chew. Pete turned to call back at Fiona sotto voce.

"We're in luck. There's no car in the garage."

At this moment, Robert determined that Pete's intentions were not in the interests of goats, and he began to move away from Pete and the clothes line, sidestepping like a parade horse, his eyes focused on Pete, with the tablecloth, still attached to the clothesline, firmly in his mouth. Pete, with an expertise Fiona had not expected in a man unacquainted with goats, stopped strolling, and turned his back on Robert. He bent down as if to tie his shoe, and appeared to be studying the ground with great interest. Robert paused and shook his head. It was the first sign of nervousness Fiona had ever seen him exhibit, and she wondered whether this might be a good sign or a bad one.

It was at this moment that a car passed and, for some reason, honked its horn. Robert, momentarily off-guard, paused to look up.

In one swift movement, Pete seized the opportunity. He turned and leapt, flinging himself across the five feet between himself and Robert. Robert froze and then started. Pete landed on Robert's neck, grabbing him by the broken tether. Robert tossed his head and kicked, still holding firmly to the tablecloth, pulling sharply away from the clothesline. Fiona watched, frozen, as the line began to sag. Robert tried to run, and the tether slipped out of Pete's hands, but he caught hold of the tablecloth just as Robert was about to make his escape.

A desperate three-way tug of war ensued between Pete, Robert, and the clothesline, each connected by the fragile threads of Stella's great-grandmama's tablecloth. It was a sight. Pete hanging on to the only vestige of connection to the goat, Robert, determined to finish his meal, the clothesline an innocent and unequal participant, all struggling with arms, hoofs, and napkins flailing.

Suddenly, as if recognizing the futility of combat, the clothesline, it's freshly laundered cargo fluttering a white surrender, collapsed. Startled, Robert shied back and bolted, knocking Pete to the ground, but Pete held fast. Robert headed to the shed, a refuge from this madman and the monstrous rope, dragging Pete and the clothesline behind him. The line and poles acted like an anchor dragging in his wake, slowing Robert's procession through the yard. Realizing that he would make better progress without it, Robert stopped suddenly and indecorously spit out the tablecloth, which was still attached to the line, and then turned and walked mincingly to the shed, head held high. By now the tablecloth—or at least what was left of it—was covered in dirt, grass stains, and what Fiona imagined could only be goat spit.

Fiona gazed at the scene before her. Napkins, cotton blouses, and billowy underpants littered the yard, still attached to the line, but somewhat worse for the experience.

Out of the corner of her eye, she saw Pete standing near the birdhouse. "Which way does Piggy live?" he asked, ever so casually.

"That way." Fiona pointed in the direction of the yellow house, and then gasped as Pete leaned on the pole of the brilliant purple and pink birdhouse, pushing it across the trajectory of the fallen clothesline. With a brief crack it fell scattering intricately carved painted detritus along the ground alongside the already humiliated laundry.

"What are you doing?" Fiona cried.

"Creating a bit of verisimilitude."

She watched in horror as he turned and contemplated the shrubbery and in a lunging movement, trampled a path through young spirea and some hollyhocks and headed off into the woods.

He was gone rather a long time. Fiona regarded the fallen laundry, her mind spinning. There was no way out of this. There would fines, a lawsuit, and possibly a death sentence for Robert—maybe even for herself, she thought. Just as she was reaching the pit of goat despond, Pete reappeared at the edge of the lawn. He looked over to her and motioned for her to come.

"You need to see this," he said, his voice rather low. Dutifully, as if in a daze, she crossed the yard and followed him as he turned back into the wooded part the property. The area was heavy with brush and prickly plants, and the mosquitoes descended promptly to bring her to reality.

"How far are we going?" Fiona asked, waving the bugs away while trying to keep the branches from snapping across her face. It hadn't yet occurred to her that this was someone she had spent barely an hour with. If it hadn't been for the worry about Stella, she would have felt as if they were children embarked upon some summer adventure. Pete stopped about ten yards ahead of her, and she saw him squat down to look at something. He stood up as she approached.

"Is this Stella's property?"

Fiona nodded mutely. He was smiling as he gestured toward a spot with his head.

"Take a look," he said.

Fiona looked closer. Next to a pile of leaves Pete had cleared away, she saw a metal cover, like a sewer cap.

"I stepped on it just now." He was grinning at her.

"What is it?" she asked.

"It's a tank," he said, cheerily. "An underground oil tank."

Fiona looked at him, puzzled.

"So?"

It was at this moment that Fiona heard the distinctive un-muffled sound of Stella's old station wagon coming down the road.

"Oh my God! It's Stella! I hear her car!"

"Quick!" Pete was already leaping through the woods ahead of her and calling out directions. "You pick up the end of the clothesline!" He grabbed the pole and the broken line from where Robert had dropped them, and raced back to Stella's yard. Fiona ran to the other end of the line.

"Pull it taut!" ordered Pete.

"What?"

"Pretend you're the other post! Get to where it was and stand still!"

Fiona grasped the far pole and ran to its original position. Pete placed the other pole into its anchor in the ground, and raced to the spot where the tablecloth had hung.

"Hold tight!" he said. "I'm going to pull on it, and I don't want you to let go."

Fiona could barely stand still, listening with her whole being to the steadily increasing sound of Stella's muffler as it drew nearer. It must be only a minute or two away. She held tightly to the pole as Pete moved in the opposite direction of Fiona's house and Robert. The line, failing again in the onslaught, sagged toward him and fell, scattering the laundry on the ground once again.

"Perfect," he said to himself. He snatched up the tablecloth, ran back into the woods, and returned emptyhanded.

"Ever do any acting?"

Fiona nodded vaguely. "In high school."

"Well you're about to give the performance of your life. Get inside the house and start painting. I'll be back." He seemed to be enjoying himself.

Before she could ask a question, he took her by both elbows and kissed her. "Remember, you've got to believe what you say!"

And he disappeared around the front of the house. Fiona could hear the sound of Stella's truck as it turned the corner and slowed in front of her house.

"Excuse me! Are you the owner of this house?" Through the open windows Fiona heard Pete speaking indignantly above the sound of the car.

Stella's voice rang out in her piercing tones. "Who wants to know?"

"I cannot believe the irresponsibility of some people. How dare you leave a vicious dog loose to attack any passerby. He could have bitten me! He could have bitten a child! That animal is a menace. He is a lawsuit waiting to happen. You should count yourself lucky he didn't bite me; that's all I have to say." Pete paused for a breath and Stella seized her opportunity.

"What are you talking about? I don't have a dog!"

"Don't have a dog? No dog? What am I talking about? He came off your porch and charged me. What do you mean you don't have a dog?"

"I mean," said Stella, comfortably reverting to her normal state of irritability, "that I don't have a dog."

"Then whose dog is it, I'd like to know? And why was he on your porch? He charged me and then ran around into your backyard."

"How should I know? I. Don't. Have. A. Dog," said Stella, her eyes narrowing dangerously. And then, because she couldn't help herself she added,

"What did it look like?"

Fiona held her breath.

"Just about the ugliest dog I've ever seen. Flat face."

There was a pause as Stella digested this information. Fiona realized suddenly that Pete was expecting her to appear. Paintbrush in hand, she slipped out the kitchen door and walked casually toward the front yard. "This," she thought to herself, "could be awkward."

There was Stella, still in her car with the window rolled down, and an expression of angry confusion on her face. Pete stood before her, all righteous fury. Fiona took a deep breath and entered the stage.

"What," asked Fiona, affecting the lofty tone of indignation of one who has been disturbed, "is going on?"

"Tell this man that I don't have a dog," demanded Stella.

Pete turned to look at her, indignation sparking from him.

Fiona looked from one to another, considering her options. She took a deep breath and said nothing. Her eyes met Stella's and locked.

"Tell him!"

"If he's not your dog, why did he run from your porch and into your backyard?" asked Pete, seeming highly incensed. "Do you think I'm stupid?"

"Tell him," said Stella, her teeth clenched.

"You just wait until I call my attorney," continued Pete.

Fiona held Stella's glance for a moment more, then slowly shrugged and turned away.

"Tell him!"

Fiona would not look back.

Something like a growl came from Stella's throat. "Tell him." She took a deep breath. "Please."

Fiona paused in her walk to the house and slowly turned around. She looked first at Stella, and then at Pete. "It's true, you know," she said slowly. "She doesn't have a dog." She could hear Stella exhale from fifteen feet away.

Pete looked at Fiona. Both women looked at Pete, wondering, each in her own way, exactly what would happen now. Stella began to look smug.

Pete frowned. "So then whose dog was on the porch there?" he indicated Stella's house. "It came charging down the steps, and came right for me. I'm convinced if I hadn't had a stick it would have bitten me." Stella and Fiona looked at the stick Pete was gesticulating with and then back at Pete.

"What did he look like?" asked Fiona, pondering the presence of the stick.

"Ugly!" Pete said.

"Piggy!" said Stella, a bit breathlessly. She spoke more to herself than to anyone else. "It must have been Piggy." She scowled, compressed her lips, and nodded to herself. "That dog is a nuisance." She looked up at Pete. "I don't have a dog. I told you." A look of cunning crossed her face. "But I know where it came from. It must belong to the people down the street."

Pete held her gaze, as if unwilling to believe that this was possible. There was another pause, and they all stood looking at one another. Pete spoke first. "Well, in that case, it seems I owe you an apology. I hope you will understand." He extended his hand. "I'm Peter Landry."'

Stella looked stonily at him, her customary manners regnant. Pete turned to Fiona, eyebrows raised.

Fiona felt an inexplicable responsibility for Stella's bad behavior. She put her hand out to take his. "I'm Fiona. I live there," she gestured unnecessarily toward her house.

Pete held her hand a bit longer than required. "Delighted," he said, an ever so faint gleam in his eyes.

Fiona actually blushed as Pete steered the conversation back to the business at hand. "Well, it's quite a mess back there. I chased him back, and he managed to take your clothesline down. Nasty brute."

Fiona began to think he might be overplaying his part.

Stella looked alarmed. "My linens!" she said. And then, as the grim possibilities gathered in her mind: "My tablecloth!"

It occurred to Fiona that nothing Stella could be imagining at this point would be nearly as bad as what had actually happened. Stella sat as if frozen, staring at Pete in horror.

As if taking a cue, Pete cleared his throat. "Ah! Look at the time. Perhaps I'd better let you get on with it," he said. "Ladies." And bowing his head slightly, he smiled politely as if taking his leave from the cotillion, walked to his car with a steady dignity, turned once to wave—no salute this time—and drove away.

Stella and Fiona both watched him go with varying degrees of incredulity. Without another word, Stella pulled the car the rest of the way down the driveway, and jumped out. Fiona stood for a moment as if stunned, then walked dazedly back to the kitchen porch.

A shriek came from Stella's yard as she got her first glimpse of the carnage.

"Oh! No!"

Fiona could see Stella's quick movements as she attempted a fruitless rescue of her linens. Sharp cries of dismay wafted across the yard. Fiona had to resist the natural urge to be helpful. There is nothing I can do in this circumstance, she told herself, that won't make everything worse.

"My tablecloth! My tablecloth! I can't find my tablecloth!"

From the kitchen window Fiona could see Stella look toward the shed. Robert stood, his tether firmly in place, calmly gazing into the distance, an aura of worldly contempt about him.

Stella turned her back and bent down to collect the ruined laundry. It wouldn't be long before it occurred to her to follow the trail into the woods. Fiona comforted herself in thinking that for all of Stella's distress, she, Fiona, was paying for her crime in the wretchedness of lies. "Talk about untruths," she thought to herself. From the yard she could hear Stella's shriek and then smothered choking sobs—she must have found it, thought Fiona—and in spite of herself—in spite of everything—Fiona began to feel a little sorry for her.

At last the wretched job was finished and Stella went up the steps to her kitchen and into the house. Feeling it was safe, Fiona came out to her own porch, sat down on the steps, and put her head on her hands.

The sun was beginning to angle down, those few roses which had escaped Robert's attentions were wafting a soft perfume, and a cardinal was calling from a shrub nearby. Somewhat shell-shocked, and engrossed in her thoughts, Fiona was startled by a familiar snuffling noise, and lifted her head. Having lost his bell in the afternoon's scuffle, Robert had managed to quietly extricate himself and now stood almost sweetly before her, gently nibbling the tips of her paint-covered shoes, a glint of something verging on affection lurking in his yellow eyes.

Chapter Thirty ❖

fter she'd recovered what remained of her wits, Fiona decided she had better try to find some control of the action. For one thing, after yesterday, she needed to look attractive, but not as if she'd tried—and certainly not as if she'd been thinking about how she looked. From now on, even if painting, she'd wash her hair and put on a little mascara.

Thus armed, she sat in her kitchen the next morning drinking coffee. Today was Saturday, which meant, probably, that Champagne Man—Pete, she corrected herself—was still in town. But what was he doing here? For a moment, Fiona toyed with the idea of going to look for him, but she dismissed it quickly. "I'm too old for that," she thought. But he had said he'd be back, and she found herself lingering, hoping to be discovered in some attractive—though disinterested—activity.

She was relieved to see Stella disappear early on. As soon as the sound of Stella's car had faded, Fiona tethered Robert firmly within his fence for an hour or so, during which time she watched him warily from the porch as she drank her coffee, and he chewed absently on a small branch overhanging one corner of the fence.

Fiona was, herself, chewing over her feelings and plans. Along with the looming anxiety about next week's town meet-

ing, she did not want to spend the day waiting for Pete to stop by.
Nor, if he did stop by, did she want to miss him. There were very
few places he could be staying, she knew, but she was not about
to begin inquiries at every motel and cottage on the Island. She
was wrestling with a need to preserve both her dignity and some
minimal control of her own destiny. But she knew, when it came
right down to it, that dignity was expendable.

Irritably, she counseled herself to go ahead with the day as
she had originally intended it. Even so, the prospect of being at
home all day, wondering each moment whether he would appear, would unnerve her in a very short time. She poured herself
another cup of coffee and prowled restlessly around the house.
It was with considerable effort that she convinced herself to sit
down and work on her most recent article. In spite of herself, she
was soon drawn into the flow of writing.

The phone rang and Fiona answered it absentmindedly.

"Hi," said Pete. "It's me."

Fiona was suddenly floating on a warm and gentle wave, all
anxiety forgotten. She smiled into the phone. "I know. I know
your voice."

"Want to walk with me?"

"Yes. Where shall we walk?

"What's good?"

Fiona thought for a moment. It was all good. "I'll meet you
at School House Beach. Do you know where that is?"

"I can find it, probably,'" he said.

"Probably you can. How long?"

"I'll see you there in fifteen minutes. Ok?"

"Ok." She hung up. She saved her document. And with only

a quick glance in the mirror, she grabbed her jacket from the peg and skipped down the porch steps, along the path to her car, singing to herself.

He was waiting for her when she got there, under a stand of cedar trees. They smiled at one another as she approached. He held out his hand and she took it. Without saying anything at all, they made their way to the beach, stumbling on the rocks toward the water.

As it got dark they went back to their cars and Fiona led the way to Nelson's. She introduced him to Eddie, and Pete ordered them both scotch. They ate their spaghetti dinners at the bar, with Fiona introducing Pete to everyone she knew as they came in. He shot pool with Pali and Erik, and bought a celebratory round afterward.

Fiona returned from a visit to the ladies' room to find Pete's seat at the bar empty. She sat back down next to Pali.

"He's in there," Pali said, before she could ask, indicating the dining room with his head. "Erik's making some introductions."

Fiona recalled Pete's popularity at the wedding the night they met and smiled to herself.

"Another round?" asked Eddie, holding his hand over her glass.

"Sure," said Pali. "I'll get this one."

Pete was gone quite some time. When he returned, the guys were all watching baseball on television, and Pete asked Pali something about the game. He was a quick study, Fiona realized, accustomed to blending into unfamiliar settings. No doubt the result of so much travel.

It had occurred to Fiona that he would be leaving tomorrow. She tried to make herself think about the present. He was there now, and she didn't know when—if ever—he'd be back.

At precisely this moment, as he was folding a dollar bill around a quarter and a thumbtack in preparation for flight, Pete leaned over to her.

"I'm planning to stay around for a bit. You don't mind, do you?"

Fiona just looked at him.

"Stay around?"

"I have some time this week. Do you?"

Fiona felt emotion flow through her. She smiled a small smile and looked down. But when she looked back up at him she was grinning. Her smile was the smile of a child at Christmas. "That would be nice."

"Will you have breakfast with me?"

"I would love to."

"So where do people go for breakfast around here?"

Fiona smiled again, a different smile.

"I could tell you, but it will be all over the Island before we get there."

They were sitting the next morning in Fiona's sunny kitchen. Robert had been fed and watered, and now lingered ominously in the barnyard developing his plans for the day. Pete had helped with the Robert chores, and had been honored with some light chatter.

"Aha!" said Robert when Pete came into the barn with Fiona. But he didn't seem to have his usual enthusiasm.

Pete looked at Fiona.

Fiona sighed. "He does that."

"He talks?"

"Uhuh," said Robert.

"Well, yes. I'm afraid he does."

"I'm surprised you hadn't mentioned it. What else does he say?" Pete was studying Robert with interest. Robert seemed considerably less enthralled, turning his back and stamping his feet in his usual way of expressing displeasure.

"BAAAAAAAAAAWB!" said Robert, without warning.

Pete jumped. Fiona regarded him with faint amusement.

"Does he always do that?"

"Fairly regularly."

"I would think it would be in violation of some kind of noise restriction. I've heard jet landings at lower decibels."

"Now you see why Stella hates him."

"And you don't?" Pete gave her the kind of look a stern teacher gives a recalcitrant student.

Fiona looked resigned. "I guess I have come to accept him."

"Have you ever heard of Stockholm Syndrome?"

"It does feel a bit like that," said Fiona ruefully. "Believe me, I have tried to get rid of him, but this whole thing with Stella has made me feel like I have to protect him. It's pretty annoying, actually."

"Hmmm," said Pete.

"BAAAAAAAAAAAWB!" said Robert.

"I would think OSHA regulations would require ear protection."

"I don't think he likes you."

"He'll get used to me. Everyone does. Let's go have breakfast while I can still hear you."

Pete turned out to be a gifted egg scrambler. Fiona made the coffee and toast.

"What would you like to do today?" asked Fiona.

Pete smiled.

The week passed in a blur, and Fiona realized all at once that it was their last day together. Pete had some business in Chicago to take care of, and had to leave the next morning.

"May I come back?" he asked.

"Yes, please," said Fiona.

After a bike ride and an afternoon spent at the sand dunes, Pete and Fiona were meeting Pali and Nika at Nelson's. As they waited for their hosts to arrive, they shot a game of pool in the corner of the bar. Both were quiet as they played, merely relaxing in one another's presence. Years spent hanging out with reporters had stood Fiona in good stead and she was a fierce competitor, but Pete was winning. He paused midshot and looked across the table at her.

"So just remember this." He looked meaningfully at her over the top of his glasses. "Deus ex machina." He took his shot.

Fiona raised an eyebrow.

"Deus ex machina." It was a statement, not a question.

"Right," he said. "It's always my favorite part of Greek drama. I love that for no reason at all a problem can be solved, a love requited, the dead returned from Hades. It's just cheering when things work out well, and it always seems to me that it's a great reflection of reality."

"But," said Fiona, "Deus ex machina is the exact opposite of reality. It's the fake resolution of problems by a lazy writer foisted upon a gullible audience." Distracted, she took a bad shot and watched as the balls bounced randomly around the table. "It's the cheap and easy way."

"Not at all," said Pete, casually shooting the seven into the corner pocket. "It's reality. Life is incredibly predictable in its unpredictability. And generally speaking, the most effective way for good things to happen, is to get someone more influential than you are to pull some strings for you. That's real-life *deus ex machina*. It's how you get interviews, good tables at restaurants, get a chance to make a presentation to a CEO, or convince a beautiful woman that you're safe to go out with. It's life."

Fiona had stopped playing and was absently burrowing a hole in the chalk with her cue. "I hate that view of life," she said vehemently. "I hate the notion that the beautiful people whisper in the right ears so they can sail past the bouncer, while hardworking earnest people never get in the door. It's disgusting. And it's undemocratic. We're not an aristocracy here. We're a meritocracy." Fiona caught herself. She was getting dangerously close to a rant.

Pete looked up at her from over his cue. "I didn't say that string-pulling was the right way, or the only way, or even the best way. I said it's the most effective way. But in any case, if you aren't any good, if you haven't done your preparations, if you don't deserve the access, if you don't have talent, none of it matters anyway. You can get the opportunity, but if you do a lousy job, it won't make any difference. So who says the hardworking and earnest among us don't qualify? And besides," he said, as he prepared his angles, "It doesn't matter whether it suits your philosophy or mine. It's just the way things work. Always has been."

He made a bank shot and sank the last three balls.

The house seemed very empty when Pete had gone. He had left with vague assurances that he would return, but without a set date. Fiona did not press the issue. She knew he would be back.

She threw herself into finishing her article, completed it in record time, and then began another. The town meeting would be in three days. Stella, meanwhile, had been remarkably invisible. Fiona had heard nothing from the house next door, nor had there been any tablecloth stories at the butcher's counter.

Late that morning Fiona received a telephone call.

"It's me," said Elisabeth. "I'm coming to the Island this afternoon. Will you be around?"

Fiona was thinking about the note of excitement in her friend's voice and did not immediately respond.

"Around three," said Elisabeth, not waiting for a response. "See you later!"

And she was gone. Fiona reflected that in the entire conversation she had said nothing more than "Hello."

Promptly at three, Fiona heard steps on the porch, and came around from the kitchen where she had been making lemonade. It took her a moment to realize that the second person standing there with Elisabeth was Roger. She flung open the door.

"Roger! You're back! You're ok!"

To her own astonishment, Fiona's eyes filled with tears and she flung her arms around Roger. He stood awkwardly, not hugging her back until he caught Elisabeth's eye, and then he clumsily put his arms around Fiona and thumped her shoulders. As gracefully as possible, Fiona extricated herself and hurriedly wiped her eyes.

"We have news," said Elisabeth, solemnly.

Fiona looked from one to the other.

Roger stared off into the distance somewhere over Fiona's shoulder as if contemplating some problem in physics.

Elisabeth rolled her eyes at him, smiling. "We're getting married."

Roger returned to the present, and looked at Fiona with bright eyes.

"I brought back a ring."

Fiona was briefly mesmerized by the new experience of direct eye contact with Roger, but quickly turned her attention to Elisabeth's extended hand and the enormous diamond ring she was wearing.

"Wow," said Fiona. She looked up at Roger in some astonishment.

"Nice work, Roger."

Elisabeth was almost giggling with delight. "Isn't it beautiful?"

And then, sounding more like herself, "Are you going to invite us in?"

Sheepishly, Fiona stood back to allow them to enter. "Sorry! Of course! It's just that you took me by surprise. Do you want to sit inside, though? It's beautiful on the porch. Let me get the lemonade. Although..." Fiona stopped and grinned at them. "I think this is more of a champagne kind of occasion, and I just happen to have some. I'll be right back."

When she returned with the champagne and glasses, Elisabeth and Roger were sitting next to one another on the porch swing, holding hands.

"You two!" said Fiona. "Have you set a date?"

"We're planning to open in August," said Roger. "But it's going to be tight."

Fiona looked puzzled. Elisabeth cast a look at Roger and shook her head, smiling.

"We're going to be doing some renovations to Ground Zero. Make it into a combination coffee shop and mini-gallery. And yes," she added, "We have set a date. The sixteenth of September." She smiled at Roger again.

Fiona had been undoing the foil wrap and now expertly opened the bottle with a delicate pop. The champagne fizzed in their glasses as she poured, then handed them around.

"To your happiness," said Fiona, tearing up again. "I am so delighted for you both."

They drank, and Fiona turned again to Roger.

"And to good friends," said Roger, and to Fiona's astonishment he turned to Elisabeth with a dazzling and besotted smile. Birds sang, sunlight drenched the porch, and the scent from the row of ancient peony bushes along the front of the porch wafted over them on the early summer breeze. Elisabeth glowed with happiness.

Just, thought Fiona to herself, pouring another round of champagne, the way a bride should. "So, Roger, where have you been? We've all been pretty worried."

"I was in California. At Barista school."

"Barista school?" Fiona looked as if she thought he was joking. "I didn't even know there was such a thing."

"Yeah, well, I read about it, and thought maybe I'd better learn a bit more about my craft," said Roger, seriously. "I'd been planning to go, but..." he paused, searching for words. "I didn't get a chance to tell anybody."

Fiona's eyes met Elisabeth's, and she raised her eyebrows. "But didn't it occur to you that people would be worried? Didn't you check your e-mail?"

Roger shrugged. "Not really. I lost my phone, and then I thought, 'why do I need it?' I guess I just needed to get away for a while. He looked up at Fiona. "You know. Think things out."

Elisabeth looked at Fiona and grinned. "He was having a nervous breakdown."

Chapter Thirty-One

The community hall was packed and buzzing with voices. It might be June, but the winter heat was still on, and it was hot. The air was thick with the warm moisture of so many human beings, still scented with the flavors of the dinners they'd just cooked and eaten, the cigarettes they'd just smoked, the quick beer they'd tossed back in order to face the ordeal of a public meeting, and occasionally the barn they'd just closed up for the night, all mixed with the aroma of the inevitable coffee urn at the back of the hall.

In the flickering glare of fluorescent lighting, two sections of folding metal chairs, divided by an aisle in the middle and on either side of the room were set up with their backs to the door. At the front were the narrow folding tables that had been used last week for the book sale and the week before for the Girl Scouts' Father-Daughter Banquet. There was an American flag in one corner of the room, and the blue flag of the State of Wisconsin on the other.

In an unprecedented state of affairs, Fiona was so thoroughly distracted that she barely noticed the sign on the door and had no mental space to be annoyed by it. She felt heads turn toward her, saw the eyes, heard the whispers. She found herself reminded of a scene from an ancient Leslie Howard film in which the heroine goes bravely to the guillotine. She felt a kinship with the victim portrayed by some long-dead Hollywood beauty, and tried to emulate her elegant nonchalance. This was difficult, since Fiona's own hands were shaking. The movie heroine, at least, had had a velvet cloak to hide her feelings.

Everyone she knew was there, but Fiona did not want to catch their eyes. She needed to postpone the revelation of their sympathies—if any—and she was not willing to provide any additional sources of entertainment to those who had merely come for the performance. She nodded to them, seated herself near the front along the side of the room, and nervously removed her jacket.

In her apprehensive trance, Fiona's unseeing eyes were focused on the flags at the front of the room. She tried to calm her breathing. She willed herself into the future, when at the end of the evening—no matter the result—she would be able to close her own door on the world and face whatever was to come. In the context of this moment she longed for a lovely trip to the dentist.

Another image, this one of villagers with pitchforks, came unbidden to her mind. How had she ever thought she could win? Here she was, an outsider, pitted against someone whose life had been spent here among these people, someone whose arrogance and sheer malevolence had dominated life on the Island for over forty years. What hope could there be? And who, Fiona wondered, would possibly side with her? The answer was too awful to be contemplated. She looked down at her shoes, and tried to think of happier times.

The meeting was scheduled for 7:00 p.m. She glanced anxiously at the clock. It was a minute after. Trying to appear casual, she scanned the crowd. Where was Stella?

The noise of many conversations did not in any way diminish as the board members walked toward the tables set out in the front of the room. Fiona saw each of them in turn smile and nod, acknowledging some apparently well-known fixture of the community sitting there. Then something barely noticed on the thin edge of consciousness gave her a jolt of adrenaline and she turned her head in the kind of double-take you see in bad movies. There in the front row, leaning back comfortably in his chair, his long legs crossed casually under the clipboard and yellow legal pad on his lap, sat Peter Landry, blithely chatting with Lars Olafsen.

Fiona nearly gasped, and then tried to cover her reaction with an appearance of calm. The room seemed to whirl and twist around her. No explanation was possible for his presence here. None. He had known all about the meeting of course, because she had told him everything. But he had given no indication that he would come. Why would he be here without telling her? And then, how did the board members know him? She wanted to leap up and talk to him, but too much aware of the many eyes that would be on her, she sat back in her metal folding chair while her thoughts buzzed like hornets. She wondered if she were too young for a stroke.

Lars Olafsen, chairman of the Town Board, took his seat and banged his hammer on the long table at the front of the room. The last board members settled into their seats, and conversations around the room dwindled into a low murmur. Fiona forced her attention to the proceedings.

"The meeting will now come to order. We will begin with the Pledge of Allegiance."

The crowd dutifully shuffled to its feet and placed their

hands over their hearts. Fiona took a deep breath. What could Pete possibly be doing here? The familiar words of the pledge filled the hot room and like everyone else, she followed along by rote, her thoughts elsewhere.

Afterward, Chairman Olafsen cleared his throat. "And now for a blessing. Reverend Nilsson, are you here?"

Political correctness was apparently another thing you left when you crossed the tension line, thought Fiona. The Reverend stood from his place in the crowd. It was a small room, but in any case the Reverend was accustomed to speaking in public. His resonant bass voice boomed out.

"Please bow your heads." Everyone did.

"Heavenly Father, we ask that You bless us as we come together in this place, bound by our common interests, our love of this Island, and the compassion and understanding we have for one another as friends and neighbors. Grant our leadership wisdom and tolerance as together we work for our mutual support and well-being in an amicable and prosperous future, so that we may all live in the community of Your Holy Grace. Amen."

Fiona pondered "amicable and prosperous." It was an unusual combination, she thought.

The Reverend sat down and before the murmurings could grow into a roar, Chairman Olafsen banged his gavel again. "We have two items on the agenda, and if we move along, we should all be home in time for *American Idol.*"

There were chuckles in the crowd. He turned to address the town clerk.

"Barbara, does everyone have a copy of the minutes?"

The tedium of the board's regular business had begun. Fiona fidgeted in her agitation. Would they never get to the point? The first order of business was a lengthy discussion of public access to the Island beaches. By long tradition the ends of certain roads—which, on an Island were inevitable—were marked as dead ends, but with gravel access points that could be used as boat launches. The cost of the upkeep—a necessity in the face of natural erosion—had become a point of contention. Tempers were held in check, but this was clearly a topic of import.

The clock stood at 7:46. Fiona was staring at the back of Pete's head, the sound of the discussion having faded to a meaningless drone in the background. He appeared to be thoroughly absorbed in the conversation, sitting nearly motionless and attentive. She had come to the conclusion that he was deliberately avoiding her. But why? Did he think she hadn't seen him? Was he concerned about making her nervous? And how had he known it was tonight? Had she told him of the date? She searched her memory for clues without result.

Meanwhile, she had begun to wonder where on earth Stella could be. The woman was as famously punctual as she was malicious, but unless she had slipped into the room behind her, Fiona was pretty certain that she was not there. This was odd.

At 8:15, it began to appear that the beach access conversation was wrapping up. The question was being kicked upstairs to another level of government. There were bureaucracies of state to deal with here and nothing further could be resolved. The board would bear in mind the input of the residents in making its report to the Department of Natural Resources.

The crowd seemed content with this non-outcome. Chairman Olafsen bestirred himself from his look of stoic tolerance.

He had been reviewing his memories of last week's episode of his favorite show.

"Well, that seems to be all we can do tonight. Let's move ahead to the second item on the agenda."

The small murmurs of the crowd began again.

Having been lulled into complacency by sheer boredom, the pounding of Fiona's heart began anew.

Lars Olafsen scanned the crowd. It was mostly the regulars, and, of course, the new woman with the goat. He was not surprised by what he saw. He pounded the gavel again.

The conversations dwindled away.

"The second item is the matter of a domestic animal being kept in an area zoned for residential use, and related violations of the municipal code." He looked down at a paper on the table before him. He read out the legal description of Fiona's lot. "Better known as the old Goeden place." He paused and looked up at the room. "Town ordinances require that regardless of the disposition of the code violations, we must formally grant permission for the keeping of said animal. The process requires that we must hear from any opposed." He paused meaningfully.

"Is there anyone who would like to speak on this topic?"

The crowd was silent. To Fiona's astonishment, Nancy stood. "I would," she said, her voice carrying to the far corners of the hall.

"The chair recognizes Nancy Iverssen."

"I think we all know what's going on here," Nancy began.

"We have had many instances of animals wandering off. Why just last week I encountered a herd of cows in the road and herded them back with my truck. It's nothing new, and no one ever gets their undies in a bundle about it. But let's face it. Stella DesRoisiers doesn't like Fiona here because she bought the house that Stella wanted for herself, and she just can't forgive her."

The crowd stirred. This was an interesting turn of events. Lars banged the gavel vigorously, but his impassive Swedish face remained blank.

"Please continue," said Lars, politely turning again to Nancy.

"As I was saying," continued Nancy, "There is no reason to persecute someone who has come to live among us as a neighbor. She may be inexperienced in animal husbandry, but the fact that there have been no new incidents since last fall should be an indication that she is learning how to keep the animal under control. Using this circumstance as an excuse to put the animal down is more than unfair. It's inhumane."

Fiona bit her lip nervously and hoped her guilty conscience wouldn't show. Obviously the theater that she and Pete had arranged last week had been successful. And it was odd to hear yourself discussed as if you were a child getting a report card.

"Furthermore," said Nancy, warming to her theme and her voice rising, "I don't know about the rest of you, but I am damn sick and tired of letting one person in this town push everybody else around. Stella DesRoisiers has been a bully for too many years." The crowd murmured. Everyone knew this was true, but no one could deny that it could be highly entertaining.

Fiona studied the faces of the board members. There was one scowl, but the others were unreadable.

"There is no precedent—none—for applying these municipal violations to a goat. It is meant for dogs. And while we're at it, we might want to consider whether there is a dog in town that this ordinance does apply to." Nancy looked around the room.

"That's all I have to say," she said.

There was a smattering of applause as she sat down.

"Thank you, Nancy," said Lars. "Is there anyone else?" he asked, equably.

The audience stirred, but no one stood.

"I don't mean to rush anybody, but I, for one, would like to finish this up." He looked at the expectant faces before him.

"Once we vote on this issue it is closed," he reminded them.

Again there was silence. Fiona shifted nervously in her chair. She was not quite clear about what was happening. She felt a strange but growing apprehension about the well-being of Stella. Could she be locked in a cellar somewhere, or lying on the floor, murdered? If so, Fiona had no doubt who would be the first suspect.

Chairman Olafsen looked along the table at his board.

"I will entertain a motion for a vote to dismiss the municipal citations, and grant a variance in zoning to permit the keeping of a domestic animal at…" he looked down to check the address, and read it into the record. "Better known as the old Goeden place," he added.

"So moved," said Tom Sumner from the far end of the table.

"Second," said Mary Woldt almost instantaneously from the opposite side.

"All in favor?" asked the Chairman.

"AYE!" came a chorus of voices from the board.

"Opposed?" he asked.

There was silence from the board. The crowd was already

beginning to stand and put on their coats as Chairman Lars Olafsen banged down the gavel.

"Motion passed!"

"Move to adjourn!" shouted Tom Sumner above the rising noise of the crowd's dissipation.

"Second!" said Mary Woldt.

"Meeting adjourned!" Lars Olafsen banged his gavel again. His face was grave as he stood to put on his coat and hurry home to watch his favorite show with his wife, but inside, he was feeling uncommonly cheery. "This was a first," he told himself. First time in twenty years. Might be worth celebrating. He thought of the bottle of Tokay he had been saving for a special occasion.

"Now then," he said to one rather wealthy landowner who wanted to discuss the lake access report. "Why don't you call me on Monday so we can give this matter the attention it deserves?" Extricating himself, he skimmed adroitly through his friends and constituents toward the exit.

Pete stood up, gathered his jacket and notepad, and made his way back to where Fiona was standing, trying to take it all in. It was clear that he had known exactly where she had been. He wrapped his arms around her and gave her a bear hug, lifting her feet off the ground.

Fiona couldn't speak. He put her down and stood grinning happily at her.

"Deus ex machina," she whispered, confounded.

"Don't oversell me," he said. "Don't want to set you up for disappointment." He paused and flashed his quick boyish smile.

"Although that would be a damn good name for a sailboat."

Jake and Charlotte came up to them, with Nancy immediately behind. Fiona smiled her gratitude at Nancy. She was still speechless. Nancy punched her cheerfully on the arm.

"I'd say this called for a celebration," said Jake. "My treat! Meet you at Nelson's?"

"Sure," said Pete.

Jake poked Fiona in the ribs and delivered a stage whisper. "I want to hear about this porn business."

"Jake!" said Charlotte, horrified.

Fiona just stared at him, bewildered.

He winked. "Wait until later. We'll see you there."

Pete was looking at her face and grinning. "You have no idea what he's talking about, do you?"

Fiona just looked at him, her eyes round, and shook her head.

"Come on, let's drop off your car. I'll tell you on the way."

Afterward it took him more than half an hour to talk her into coming into Nelson's.

They drove home from Nelson's in silence.

"Shall we have one more drink?" asked Fiona.

"I was afraid you wouldn't ask," said Pete.

"Good. Because you have some explaining to do."

"I thought we might be coming to that." Pete smiled guiltlessly. "What do you want to know?"

"Let's start with this," said Fiona. "What were you talking to Lars Olafsen about? In fact, how did you even know him?"

"We met at Nelson's last week; don't you remember? Erik introduced us, and we had quite a nice little chat."

"And what did you chat about, exactly?"

"I just told him about the oil tanks on Stella's property."

Fiona sat back in her chair, stunned. "The oil tanks?"

"Yes, don't you remember that day with the clothesline? I showed them to you in the woods."

Fiona looked at him blankly. "I don't get it."

"If anyone ever finds out about those oil tanks, which she seems to believe are leaking, by the way—and by anyone I mean the Department of Natural Resources—Stella will be responsible for having them removed and for doing restoration of the soil. It could cost her a fortune. Probably a hundred thousand for soil remediation. At least."

Fiona's face was a study in amazement as Pete went on.

"So all it took was a little word and she realized the error of her ways."

Fiona was stammering. "You…you…*blackmailed* her?"

Pete was unconcerned. "Well, *I* didn't. Exactly. But essentially, yes."

Fiona spoke slowly now as the pieces came together in her mind. "She thinks they're leaking?"

Pete grinned. "She seems to have gotten that idea, yes."

"So that's why she didn't even show up tonight."

"I think so. It was just an easy way for her to take herself out of the picture without seeming to back down in public."

Fiona sat back in her chair for a moment, but her brain was working rapidly.

"Ok, next question."

"Shoot," said Pete. "Wine glasses in here?"

"Yes, on the right. Ok, so I'm trying to get my head around how, just by accident, you wound up on Washington Island."

"Actually, I have a confession to make. It wasn't entirely an accident. In fact, not at all. But if I'd told you I'd come looking for you, I thought you'd be more alarmed than flattered."

"You came looking for me?" Fiona was astounded. "How on earth did you do that?"

Pete sat down across the table.

"After the wedding I called Julia. She told me you and Elisabeth were friends and lived in Ephraim. The rest was pretty simple. Although, I hadn't expected to run into you quite at the moment I did. Parking in front of your house was sheer luck. I just wanted a hamburger."

"Elisabeth?" Fiona seized on the key fact. "How did you know Elisabeth?"

Pete looked sheepish. "Ground Zero, of course."

"Ground Zero? You met at Ground Zero? How? When? What were you doing there? Why didn't she tell me?" Fiona could not contain her astonishment.

Pete looked down for a moment and then looked up, directly into her eyes.

"I told you. I came to find you. Unfortunately, I was foiled by your lovely winter weather."

Fiona looked blank. "What?"

"I came to see you in January but the blizzard closed everything down, and then it was awhile before I could get back."

Fiona was quiet for a moment allowing this to sink in. "You were here? In January?"

"I only got as far as Ephraim. That's when I met Elisabeth."
Fiona returned to her earlier question. "But why didn't she tell me?"

"Because I asked her not to. I wanted to see you myself."

"But we'd hardly said fifty words to each other. What possessed you to come looking for me?"

"I can never resist a woman who knows Noel Coward."

"Noel Coward. You came to find me because I knew Noel Coward."

"Well, yes," he said, looking a little puzzled. "And Shelley. Think how unusual it is to find a beautiful woman who quotes poetry, knows Noel Coward, drinks scotch, and—this was the bonus—lives with a goat, on a remote Island. It's hardly routine. You were irresistible." He got up and went to the counter to open the bottle of wine.

Fiona just looked at him. "You sent the books, didn't you? And the rubies."

"Of course," said Pete.

Fiona paused in her questioning. "It was the most beautiful and amazing gift I have ever received. Thank you."

He looked back at her and smiled. "Happy Valentine's Day."

"But why did it have to arrive at a particular time?"

"Because I wanted to know the precise moment you were opening it."

"I wasn't sure it was from you, though. I couldn't see how it could have been. Deus ex machina," she added, more to herself than to him.

"Well, yes," he agreed. "In pretty much every sense."

Fiona sat at the table absorbing it all.

"You really were irresistible, you know. Besides," he added, looking over his shoulder as he adjusted the corkscrew. "You smelled good."

The next night they went together to a concert at the Performing Arts Center. It was a lush June evening, and the air was filled with the scent of blossoms and newly mown grass. They mingled with the crowd for a bit, many of whom were known to Fiona, and most of whom were casting glances in their direction.

"Not much in the way of anonymity here, is there?" asked Pete as they took their seats.

"Not much."

The lights dimmed and they sat back in their seats. Their arms touched on the shared armrest of the chair.

After a few moments, Pete glanced at her sideways and leaned over to whisper in her ear. "I have never heard this particular version of the '1812 Overture,'" he said.

"It's the lesser-known arrangement for accordion," she told him. They continued in silence, absorbing the concert. When the selection was over, they joined in as the audience applauded enthusiastically. Fiona leaned over to Pete and whispered in his ear. "Wait until you hear 'L'apres-midi d'un faun.'"

After the concert was over, they followed the crowd into the humid night air. Pete put his hand under Fiona's elbow and gently guided her toward his car. With no lights in the parking lot, the stars nearly sang with their nearness. Fiona's mind buzzed with a mixture of emotion and the echoes of Tchaikovsky on accordion. Pete opened her door and tucked her into her seat, carefully adjusting her wrap around her before closing the door and coming around to his side. As he reached for the ignition she stopped his hand, and when he turned to her, Fiona leaned over and kissed him. It was a long, deep kiss, which he returned, and they stayed wrapped in an embrace for a few moments, the newness of passion enveloping them in the thickness of the summer night. Through the open roof came the sound of crickets and katydids, and the hum of the universe as the Northern Lights swirled above their heads.

They sighed, almost in unison, and he kissed her again.

"I think," said Pete, "that I may have to get an accordion."

Fiona was dreaming. She was standing on a hill looking off into the distance. There were dozens of small lakes dotting the landscape surrounded by cedar forests and birch trees. Large birds were flying in great swooping arcs over the valley. At first she thought they were beautiful, and then she saw their tiny red faces and hooked beaks, and realized that they were vultures circling over something dying or dead. She felt a cold chill growing in her heart. Suddenly there were drums in the distance beating out a rough cadence that seemed to grow louder and louder.

Pete and Fiona woke at the same time. There was pounding on the front door, and a man's voice shouting. The room was filled with smoke.

"Fire!" cried Pete.

He sprang out of bed and put his hands on the door. "It's safe. The door is cold. We can go this way." Fiona was pulling on her clothes from the night before. She tossed him a pair of jeans and a T-shirt.

Cautiously he opened the door and called back to her. "I don't think it's the house. But let's get out of here."

They ran down the stairs through the smoke. As they got to the kitchen Fiona gasped. A wall of orange flames thirty feet high filled the scene from the kitchen window.

"It's the barn!" They both said at once. Then "ROBERT!" Fiona screamed and ran from the house. Pete caught up to her and jerked her back.

"Don't be stupid!" he yelled at her.

"Oh my God! Oh my God!" cried Fiona. "No! No! I can't bear it! I can't leave him in there!"

A policeman came running around the side of the house. "Is there anyone else in the house?" he shouted.

"No," said Pete. "Only us."

"My goat!" screamed Fiona. "My goat! He's in the barn!"

They could hear sirens approaching. Pete took her by the arms and shook her hard. "Listen to me! It's too late! The flames are through the roof already. He's dead, Fiona. We need to think about saving the house."

Another police car, four fire engines, and an assortment of SUVs, cars, and trucks began arriving, all the volunteers. Soon men were running from all directions toward the barn with hoses and axes.

Pete did not let go of her. "Come on. Get back. Let's let them do their job."

He pulled her toward the road and held her as huge sobs wracked her body. "I didn't help him! He depended on me and I didn't even help him!" she said it over and over. All she could think of was Robert, of the fear he must have felt and the pain. In a flash she recalled his glittering yellow eyes, the sound of his harsh voice, and a thousand scenes from the past few months flew through her mind. Pete and Fiona stood together by the side of the road for a long time as she wept in his arms.

At last the fire was out, and the ruined barn lay sodden and smoking. The fire chief approached. "It's under control, but we'll stay to make sure it's out." He looked at Fiona. "Someone at Nelson's saw the flames from there and called it in. You're pretty lucky. A spark could easily have set the house on fire." He nodded toward Stella's darkened property. "Or your neighbor's."

They sat together huddled on the steps of the porch watching the firemen wrapping up their work. The air was filled with the smell of smoke and charred things and the sound and smell of the big diesel engines and their radio chatter. The red lights flashed rhythmically over the scene, removing any remaining sense of normality.

Fiona had come to grips with herself and recovered sufficiently to make hot coffee for the men who had saved her house.

Nika and Charlotte were both there with sandwiches and bottles of water for them all. Fiona thanked them tearfully and profusely.

"It's ok, dear," said Charlotte. "It's what we do for each other here."

Dawn was beginning to show through the trees as the last trucks pulled away. Shock had given way to grief, and Fiona felt still and hollow. All was quiet, except for the early stirrings of the birds.

Pete broke the silence.

"I'm sorry," he said. "This is very hard."

Fiona nodded mutely, trying not to cry again.

"There was nothing you could have done. You shouldn't blame yourself."

Fiona nodded again.

Pete took her chin in his hands. "Fiona, it's not your fault."

Fiona looked at him, big tears falling down her cheeks.

"It doesn't matter whose fault it was," she said. "What matters is that he suffered."

"Everyone suffers, Fiona. Every living thing. There's nothing we can do to stop suffering except to be as happy as we can."

"But I want to," said Fiona, now weeping again. "I want to stop the suffering. I don't want anyone to suffer."

"I know, my love. I know." He hugged her to him and held her. "Come on, now, you're shivering," he said at last. "Let's go inside."

Pete put his arm around her, and led her into the house.

The next morning the insurance adjuster arrived before they had even gone to bed. Then began the constant flow of well-wishers. People brought casseroles and cakes, homemade afghans, pies, and bottles of wine. One by one, the men of the Island arrived, driving their pickup trucks and bringing their boxes of tools—many of them the same men who fought the fire—to help to haul away the mess, even as it was still smoking. Pete joined in, and Fiona worked with the women in the kitchen to feed them all.

At the end of the second day, nothing remained but the blackened space surrounded by the old stone foundation, and Pete and Fiona found themselves adjusting to silence around them. Elisabeth and Roger had come, and stayed that evening the way old friends come to sit after a funeral. They sat on the front porch, away from the view of the fire.

Roger, in a rare moment of diplomacy, leaned over to Pete when Fiona had gone inside for a sweater. "Did you find the carcass? Or is it still in there?" His voice, meant to be a whisper, still carried.

"As far as I know, no one found anything," replied Pete quietly.

Roger frowned. "That's not that surprising, I guess, in a fire like that."

Suddenly Fiona appeared. The men looked abashed.

"But here's the thing," she said, obviously having overheard. "We never heard Robert. Normally when he's upset he hollers like crazy. And we never heard a thing. Not a sound."

Pete regarded her soberly. "So you think he got away?"

"Well, it's possible, isn't?" Fiona was trying not to sound desperate.

"It's possible," he said. But she could tell by the way he said it that he didn't believe it.

"I want to know where Stella is," said Elisabeth, trying to change the subject.

Fiona took the hint, and said nothing more about it.

"So, how are the renovations going?" she asked, and the conversation moved on to Roger and Elisabeth's plans for their new venture. But in her own mind Fiona wondered. Robert had never been one to suffer in silence.

On the last Saturday in August Fiona headed over to the mainland for the grand opening of the renovated Ground Zero, and for what she anticipated would be a small reunion with the Ephraim friends. It was a dreary, rainy day, and she was feeling lonely. Pete had departed for places unknown and wouldn't be back until the wedding.

As she drove up, she was astonished to find that there was no place to park. Despite the rain, cars were parked along the road in all directions. Little clusters of people walked along the sides of the road toward the shop.

Inside there was barely a place to stand. A new gas fireplace, which felt good in the damp chill, glowed in the corner, sur-

rounded by a long low sofa and two soft chairs. Original paintings of Door County landscapes hung on the walls on loan from
Elisabeth's gallery, illuminated with halogen lamps. A glass case
was filled with homemade baked goods: cherry almond biscotti,
lemon scones, cherry pie, cardamom coffee cake, and ginger
snaps, and the scent of them all mingled enticingly with the
coffee. Shelves filled with new and used books lined the walls,
soothing, aimless music played in the background, and shoppers
clustered around the long antique table filled with teapots, letterpress stationery, handwoven mittens, and pottery mugs. The
incessant noise of escaping steam filled the air as espressos, cap-
puccinos, and frothed milk were prepared to order. The Angel
Joshua—a name Terry had coined, and which had stuck—stood
in the glow of his manly beauty, and was operating the machine,
along with another assistant, a young woman who was taking
orders and ringing up purchases.

Elisabeth mingled with the crowd, laughing and chatting
with everyone, every inch the hostess.

Mike sat with a mug of coffee at a small table near the fire,
his cherubic face beaming with pleasure at the compliments to
his paintings, his wife making sure that everyone came away
with a gallery brochure. Roger stood behind the counter, having just stepped from the kitchen, wiping his hands on a snowy
white towel and surveying the crowd with something that on
anyone else would have been a grimace, but on Roger registered
satisfaction.

Oblivious to the jostling behind him, Terry stood for a long
time at the register frowning up at the menu overhead, seemingly overwhelmed by the choices before him. Noticing at last

that the delicate cough behind him was a hint, he moved up to the counter, still staring at the sign.

"May I help you, sir?" asked the young blonde barista whose metal stud glittered from her lip.

Terry looked at her, still frowning. She would have been pretty, he thought, if not for the hardware in her face. "Well, now, I'm not completely sure," he said slowly.

The girl leaned forward so she could hear him above the din of the crowd. Terry leaned in, checked to see who was listening, and spoke in an even lower voice. "I'm just wondering. What in the hell is a tisane?"

From out of nowhere Roger stepped in. "A tisane is similar to a tea, but it is made up of various dried fruit, flowers, spices, bark, and berries. It is prepared like tea, and can be sweetened with sugar or honey." He looked solemnly at Terry. "Would you like one?"

"Err…no. I'll have something with coffee. Something different, though." He stopped, as if struck by a strange new thought. "What would you recommend?"

"I think you would like a mochaccino. It's a blend of coffee, chocolate, and steamed milk, slightly sweetened."

"Ah," said Terry. "Ok. I'll try that."

"Cinnamon?" asked Roger.

"Err…sure. Why not?"

"Coming right up," said Roger professionally.

Terry watched mesmerized as Roger prepared his drink, while the bustle of other orders and conversations went on around them. "Here you go," said Roger at last, handing him a cup. "On the house."

"Why, thanks, Roger." Terry took his cup, and was about to move away from the counter when he looked down at his cup. There, drawn delicately in the froth of milk at the top, was a perfectly executed fern leaf.

Chapter Thirty-Two

The day of the wedding dawned crystal clear. The cool summer had given way to an early fall, and the leaves were close to peak color almost a month earlier than usual. Fiona had spent the night at Elisabeth's, and was feeling a little bit hung over after the pre-wedding festivities the night before. The sun was streaming in the windows and creating miniature rainbows on the white bedspread from Elisabeth's grandmother's faceted crystal lamp. Fiona rolled over and peered at the clock. 6:30. She heard the slam of the screen door, and Rocco's deep bark outside. Elisabeth must already be up. Fiona spent a few minutes trying to convince herself to get up and be helpful to the bride. She was interrupted by a tap at her door. "Come in."

Pete walked in, carrying a garment bag and a small duffel, and smelling of fresh air.

"Aw geesh!" Fiona pulled the covers over her head. "You can't see me like this."

"It's too bad you feel that way, because I was just going to put my bags down and get you coffee."

Fiona put the covers back down. "Really?"

"Yes. And is that the best you can do for a greeting?"

"If you come in at 6:30 in the morning you're lucky to get that much."

"I can't actually argue with that." He sat down next to her on the bed and they fell into each other's arms.

"I heard there was coffee," murmured Fiona after a few moments.

"Ok, ok, I'm going." He got up and went to the door.

"And see what you can do about that hair while I'm gone."

Fiona threw a slipper and hit the door.

At precisely three o'clock that afternoon, Elisabeth appeared in the door of the gallery pavilion wearing a dress of cascading ivory lace and looking like a Renaissance painting, her auburn hair falling in waves past her shoulders. Rocco trailed her along the path to the stone arbor and laid down next to Roger, whose hair was lying miraculously flat for the occasion. It was the first time anyone had seen him wearing anything other than jeans. Fiona, in deep purple silk charmeuse that had cost more than she had earned in three months, and silver Italian sandals, rose and stood near Elisabeth. Terry stood with Roger.

In a few brief moments the ceremony was over, and then began the burst of conversation, laughter, and picture-taking that comes after solemnity.

"So where will the honeymoon be?" asked Mike after he had kissed the bride.

"Venice," said Roger. "And then Florence, Siena, and Rome."

"That should be wonderful," said Mike, sincerely.

"Yeah," said Roger. "I got to know Italy when I went over to buy equipment for the shop."

Mike and Terry looked at one another. This was news to them.

"We'll be there for six glorious weeks," said Elisabeth.

"But what about Coffee?" broke in Terry, reverting to the old name in his alarm. He had endured quite long enough without his home base in operation.

"Oh that's all taken care of," said Roger. "Joshua has the day-to-day under control, and I have a coffee consultant coming in to handle the rest."

There was a stunned silence.

"A coffee consultant?" broke in Mike, at last.

"Sure," said Roger, easily. "I got familiar with them while I was at coffee school. They're experts in running coffee shops. Big company. Offices all over the world. They're the ones who found Joshua."

"Well, what do you know about that?" said Terry to no one in particular.

The wedding guests were a mixture of mainland and Washington Island people. Despite knowing nearly everyone, Pete and Fiona were standing off in a corner drinking champagne and looking into each other's eyes, momentarily unaware of their surroundings.

Pali made his way through the crowd, grinning from ear to ear.

"Fiona! Fiona!"

"Pali," said Fiona with real pleasure.

"Hi."

"Fiona, I—sorry to interrupt"—this was to Pete—"but I have something amazing to tell you. I wanted you to be the first to know—after Nika of course."

He could barely contain himself.

Fiona and Pete both looked at him, intrigued.

"It's going to be published. My poem. They took my poem!"

"Oh, Pali!" said Fiona, delightedly. "That's fantastic. Who? Who took it?"

"*Poetry.* Goddamned *Poetry* magazine. Can you believe it?" He was so excited he threw his arms around her and picked her up in a big hug. He squeezed so hard she could hardly breathe, and put her down again, beaming.

"Sorry," he said grinning to Pete. "I couldn't help myself."

"That's ok," said Pete. "Most of the time I can't help myself, either." He reached out to shake Pali's hand. "Congratulations."

"I keep pinching myself. I know it's a cliché, but I can't believe it." Laughing, Pali looked down at Fiona, towering over her. "Ghost poetry," he said. "Who would ever believe it?"

Fiona laughed back at him. "It doesn't matter who believes it. It's published. But if I were you, I'd spend some more time in the pilothouse. You never know when you'll get another visitation."

Pali looked serious. "I have to thank him. I have to tell him."

Fiona nodded solemnly. "Maybe he already knows."

Pali laughed again. "Maybe he does." They shook hands all around, and Pali slipped off to spread his good news.

Fiona watched him go, smiling, then looked at Pete. "I'm feeling a little warm. I'm going to get some ice water and slip outside for a bit."

"I'm going to go talk to Elisabeth," he said. "I'll be there in a moment. Shall I bring you anything?"

She smiled again and shook her head. "I'll be over there somewhere," she said, waving toward the garden, and she drifted off.

Fiona strolled in the autumn night, breathing the fresh air, and after awhile found herself sitting on the bench along the path, listening to the sounds of the party drifting out from the gallery. It was cool here, but it was refreshing after the heat of the rooms. The stars were so thick overhead that they almost resembled clouds. She sipped her water, sighed, and took it all in. She was lost in thought when the crunch of gravel made her aware that she wasn't alone. She looked up to see old Mr. Ingersoll approaching along the path. He stopped, gave her a gracious little bow and lowered his voice.

"Glad to see you've got that drinking problem under control," he said, nodding at the glass of water in her hand. "Terrible thing, drink." And nodding sagely he patted her arm, and wandered past her to find the dessert table.

After the wedding, Pete and Fiona returned to the quiet of the little house on the Island. It was their only night together before he had to go back again.

Outside the open windows came the deep low call of an owl and the slow chirp of a few late crickets. The cool breeze of autumn carried the scent of leaves mingled with wood smoke and the faint perfume of apples from the big ancient trees in the yard. A perfectly detailed thin slice of moon hung near the horizon.

Down the road at the pier, the ferries, empty and still, loomed silently in the darkness. The crews had emptied their last cargo, tied up to the pier, and gone home to their beer or their families. There was no sound of traffic or human voices, but there was no silence. In every garden, field, and wooded path, close beneath the surface of the night, came the roar of the lake from the depths of Death's Door; the rhythmic beat of water moving unceasingly to meet the Island shore.

And then, there was another sound, rising from down the road, not fully discernible from the house, but perhaps another source of Fiona's sense of unease. It was the sound of an ancient station wagon, badly in need of a muffler, making an agonizing start from the lot next to the ferry landing.

Pete and Fiona stood together in the kitchen with their arms around each other. Fiona was quiet. He had said nothing about when he would return.

"Don't worry," Pete said, reading her mind. "I know it's a long way, but now that I've figured out the airport situation here, I'll be able to come much more frequently. You'll see."

"It's not very convenient," she said, trying not to sound as worried as she felt.

Pete looked at her and raised his eyebrows briefly. "Neither are you," he said. "But that hasn't stopped me so far. And don't go adopting any more goats while I'm away." As soon as he said it he regretted it.

Fiona winced. "I didn't adopt the first one," she protested. "And anyway, there would be ice in Hell… Dante notwithstand-ing…" She trailed off. "Poor Robert," she added sadly.

Pete thought a change of subject was in order. "So, will you miss me?"

"Yes," said Fiona. "Yes, I will. But, technically, I still have one more month to go on the dare. And I'll be damned if I give up now."

"That's the spirit," said Pete. And he kissed her.